THE TIMELESS SERIES

BOOK TWO

Only a Matter of Time

Shaelyn Ryan

For the Greatest Friends in the World

Acknowledgements

As with the previous book in The Timeless Series, I owe thanks to many people who have helped me through the writing, editing, and publication processes. Thanks first to my father, who encouraged me to keep writing and helped with editing. Thanks to Mark Leslie Lefebvre, Sharon E. McKay, and Ron Lawruk, authors who took the time to assist me and give me fantastic advice on writing and publishing. Special thanks to the Windsor Public Library and Algonquin College for offering their print services, and the Carleton Place and Beckwith Heritage Museum and Book Gallery for assistance with research. And of course, thanks to all those who read and enjoyed the first book in the series. I couldn't have done it without you.

About the Author

Shaelyn Ryan is a young author who published her first book at the age of fifteen. She currently resides in Carleton Place, Ontario, and enjoys reading, writing, and history.

PROLOGUE

Monday, December 24th, 1900

Tomorrow is Christmas day! I plan to give Matthew this journal tomorrow, but I wanted to make one last entry to fill up the last pages. I simply can't wait to see the look on his face when he opens it! He has grown so much as a person these last few months, I can hardly believe the change. He is no longer the frightened boy he once was with us. He has gained so much confidence and trust, and has really grown on me, and even Grace and Evan, I think! I suppose I shouldn't be writing such things in a book which I plan for him to read, but I'm sure he'll be pleased with my suppositions about his character. He is such a sweet, kind boy, and I am looking forward to having him around as we continue our lives here in 1900. I suppose that's it for me, for I can't think of much else to write, and I shall let Matthew fill in the last pages himself, if he wants. I hope that Matthew will treasure this journal and its insights as much as I do.

A hand slammed shut the journal and tossed it aside. All the pages after that last entry were blank. No more information could be gleaned from them. The owner of the hand glanced up. A large wooden box stood before him, its door open wide. He stood, picking up the journal as he went, and ventured inside, examining the panel of numbered buttons screwed to the inside. He had gone through every scrap of paper in the house, and had learned all he could about the machine in which he now stood. He had done plenty of learning. Now, it was time for action.

CHAPTER ONE

Any Time Now

It's funny the way plans never seem to deliver when one needs them to. It had seemed nearly foolproof at first, but nothing can ever be certain. Grace, her blue eyes downcast and loose strands of brown hair fluttering in the wind, sighed as she remembered how wonderful she and her friends had felt when they had finally come up with the plan. It was a scheme that was meant to allow Grace, Evan, and all the others to return to the life they had been dreaming of with little to no consequence. However, the plan, like so many others before it, had failed, and had left the time travellers with little else to do but regroup.

Grace and Evan were alone together in a large, empty valley, far from the glittering lights of civilisation. A fire crackled in front of them, sparks flying off in all directions. The stars twinkled above, clearly visible away from the light of the towns and cities. Evan stared at Grace, noting the delicate curve of her eyebrows and wrinkles in her forehead. It was clear she was thinking very hard, as she didn't even notice Evan looking at her.

She sat in front of the small fire pit she and Evan had created, silently reminding herself with all her might that one failed plan was not the end. Her dreams would still live on, along with those of the rest of the time travellers. For the last few weeks, all she seemed to be doing was going through the motions, not at all the way she had been when they first arrived in the past. Although, all of this time gave her a chance for self-reflection, and she remembered how she had truly felt back when she first arrived in 1900. She could barely believe it herself, but there she was, in 1900, the era she had long admired from afar, and had finally been able to reach through a lot of hard work and a little bit of luck. She had travelled through time from her present day woes to a new and simpler life in the past. It was unbelievable, but true.

"Grace?" Evan whispered.

"Yes?" Grace replied curtly, retreating from her speech back into her silence.

"How many more days did you say until we get to Norton?"

"Four."

"That many, huh?"

"Yeah."

Evan fell silent; even he was feeling a little depressed. Little more than a day ago, he and Grace had been forced to leave their house in Darcy Lake, where they had once lived with the other time travellers. When they had returned from their native time, Grace and Evan had gone back to the little house and stayed there alone for weeks. Sandra and John had stayed in Connolly Mills upon their return to the past, and Mr. Riddell and Mr. Fitzgerald, along with the children, Eddie, Laura, and Matthew, had gone on to stay in a city called Norton, which was completely new to them.

After a time, and numerous communications between the three groups, it was decided that their plan to stay apart so as to escape attention was fruitless. After what had happened in Darcy Lake, they had to be sure of their safety, but staying apart would get them nowhere. It was a long story that Grace still shuddered to think about. She remembered exactly how she had felt when Clay Kennedy had shown up on their doorstep, armed and ready to end the lives of each and every one of the time travellers. In a way, Grace thought, Clay was really one of the more intelligent and perceptive people they had met in the past. He seemed to sense that there was something amiss about the lot of them; so much so that Grace was constantly expecting him to say something about their time travel.

They had never told anyone in the past about where they had come from, and didn't plan on it. Indeed, Clay was intelligent, but also intolerant, and dangerous. His reason for wanting to kill Grace and the other time travellers, who were more like family to her, was that they had murdered his only daughter, Elizabeth Kennedy. Grace was sure, however, that Clay knew as well as anyone else that his daughter had died of an infection, a fairly common cause for the time. In fact, before her most untimely death, Sandra had tried to save the woman's life with modern day antibiotics, but had carelessly left them with her to be discovered by Elizabeth's best friend and town gossip, Emily Collins. Grace hated to even think about it.

So, to escape the wrath of Clay, the time travellers had fled to the present and come back to the past with the plan of splitting up, which they were now abandoning. Norton, a city five days from both Darcy Lake and Connolly Mills, was their best bet, particularly with five of the time travellers already living there. They seemed, from what Grace had read in their letters, to have a good life there. She was glad that they wouldn't have to uproot again, what with the three children and all. Eddie was Mr. Riddell's son, and the pair were as close as a father and son could ever seem to be. The boy was nine, nearly ten, and Mr. Fitzgerald's daughter Laura was only a couple years younger. Matthew was an entirely different story.

His tale was one that made Grace want to smile and cry all at the same time. He was young, almost sixteen, and his life had changed unimaginably when he had met the time travellers. He had wound up in the past when he and his old friend Trevor were scavenging in Grace's house. Matthew had stumbled upon the time machine and accidentally sent himself back to 1900, far from his old life with Trevor on the streets. At first, he was desperate to escape and return to the present, though he had no family to speak of aside from a drunken and abusive father and a step mother who was no better. The closest thing he had to any sort of family was Trevor, a slightly older boy who had taken Matthew under his wing when he had run away from home. Trevor would stop at seemingly nothing to better his position, and Matthew's, but Matthew was more reluctant to break the rules, not to mention his personal morals.

The boy's life had turned around when he finally accepted the help and love of the time travellers, and he was now remarkably well adjusted for all that he had been through in his short life.

"Grace…? Grace!"

"Hmm… What?"

"Are you cold?"

"No, Evan, I'm fine."

"You sure? You're shivering like—"

"I'm okay, Evan. Can we just be quiet for a while?"

"Grace," said Evan gently, "It's not going to help you to keep it all in, you know. Just tell me what you're thinking about, would ya?"

Grace sighed and stared into the dying flames before her. She *was* cold, but she was more occupied by her own thoughts than how she felt on the outside.

"I'm just… wondering how this is all going to play out, that's all," she said, "It seems like all we've been doing is running ever since we got here, and I just want to know when it's going to stop."

Evan opened his mouth to make a sarcastic remark, but he stopped himself before any words escaped, for he knew that Grace wouldn't appreciate it, even if he was only trying to lighten the mood.

"Listen," he said, after much thought, "We are all going to be fine. We're all going to be together again up in Norton, and we're going to figure all this out. You read the letters, Grace, ol' Fitz and Riddell are living it up in a boarding house with plenty of room for the rest of us at low cost and with a nice landlady… What more could we ask for, Grace?"

"I guess you're right," Grace smiled, waving at a spark that had emerged from the fire, "We're getting another new start."

"Yeah, that's way to look at it! Only a few more days and we'll be starting brand new lives! We's new people, Gracie," Evan said in his best New York accent, "Nuttin' can stop us now!"

Grace smiled and looked up at the stars in the night sky. With no light for miles around besides their own fire, they could see thousands upon thousands of glittering stars.

Grace's spirits were bolstered ever higher at the sight of them all. A few more nights of this wouldn't be so bad, and afterwards they would be in Norton with their family. They would indeed be new people, and together, a new life and a new start were most certainly possible. Perhaps even probable.

■■

Matthew sat impatiently by the door of the boarding house, his foot tapping the wood floor. He squirmed in his seat and adjusted his suspenders. He still found them uncomfortable, even after wearing them for nearly a year. It was simply one of the things about the past he felt he may never get used to.

There was no one else in the front hall besides Matthew. He didn't want to miss when Sandra, John, Evan, and Grace finally arrived. They had sent word about four days ago, and, by Mr. Fitzgerald's calculations, they wouldn't be arriving until tomorrow. However, Matthew chose to believe that they might have left early, or travelled through the night. He wanted so badly to see them again, and the waiting nearly killed him. He would have made himself useful instead of sitting idly by the front door, but everything was finished. The rooms were clean, the beds made, and the food bought. Everything was organized, and all that was left to do was wait.

It was raining heavily outside, and Matthew traced the glistening raindrops on their tracks down the glass of the window at his side. He wondered quietly how Grace, Evan, Sandra, and John were faring out there in the storm. He certainly hoped they weren't getting soaked, but he secretly hoped that maybe the rain would spur them on, and they might arrive more quickly. The ominous clouds rolled across the great city of Norton and lightning struck, bathing the outdoors in a temporary flash of white light. The warmth of summer was drawing to a close, and there was a cold, wet fall ahead.

"Still waiting?"

Matthew turned in his seat, and his foot stopped tapping. For a moment, all that could be heard was the dreary drumming of the rain outside. Matthew smiled shyly at Mrs. Brown, the landlady of the boarding house at which he and the others were staying. She was a kind woman who loved children and stuck firmly to her beliefs. When she was angry, she was a force to be reckoned with. She was a practical woman as well, falling not for the pretty airs and graces put on by others, preferring instead to be honest and frank towards all she met.

Matthew nodded glumly and returned his gaze to the window for a moment. Mrs. Brown sat down in the chair beside him and surveyed the boy with a look of interest and amusement.

"You know, dear," she said gently, as Matthew continued to stare out the window, "Waiting is a difficult thing to do all on your own." Matthew nodded in silent agreement.

"If you'd like," Mrs. Brown continued, "I could use your help with something."

Matthew turned around. "Yeah?"

Mrs. Brown smiled, her snub nose wrinkling and her little brown eyes nearly disappearing. "Well," she began, "I only just remembered that I have some furniture in the cellar, chairs and such, which need to be brought up before the rest of your family arrives. Would you be so kind as to help me bring those up the stairs?"

Matthew smiled; glad he finally had something to occupy him. "Thanks, Mrs. Brown," he answered, "I'll do that."

Mrs. Brown led him to the cellar steps and the two of them made their way down the steep wooden stairs, which creaked disconcertingly underfoot. The cellar was dark and dank, with a wet, musty smell about it. Mrs. Brown lit a lamp and the shadows darted about, constantly shifting position. As Matthew's eyes adjusted, Mrs. Brown led him across the damp cellar to a group of wooden chairs, and a small chest of drawers.

"These need to go upstairs," Mrs. Brown pointed out the furniture, "I would have asked Mr. Riddell or Mr. Fitzgerald, but they haven't returned from the market yet, and I should think they won't be back for a while, what with all this rain.

"It's alright," Matthew reassured her, "I'm sure we can bring them up ourselves."

"That's the spirit," Mrs. Brown smiled, "Now, you go ahead and take those two, and I'll take this one."

With that, the pair made their way up and down the cellar stairs, hauling the furniture to its correct location on the main floor of the house.

"Thank you, dear," Mrs. Brown wheezed when they were finished. Mrs. Brown was, according to most, no spring chicken anymore. She was around the same age as Mr. Riddell, yet had no children of her own. She had had a husband once, an American by the name of Elias Brown, who had grown up in Boston. Mrs. Brown's parents were quite nervous about her marrying a Yankee, but relented when they were told that the couple would be living in Norton.

Mr. Brown was quite well to do, and he and Mrs. Brown had lived in the very house in which Matthew and the other time travellers were now boarding. Mr. Brown would often visit his home in Boston, travelling by ship, until his final visit. He was returning from Boston on the *Daniel Simmons*, and the ship went inexplicably missing. It was never found, and neither was anyone on board. Mrs. Brown was devastated, and was left with no income to speak of. She finally decided to open her home in the form of a boarding house to eke out a living.

Mrs. Brown was very picky about who was to stay in her home, but finally accepted Mr. Fitzgerald, a divorcee, and Mr. Riddell, a widower, and their respective children. She had been reluctant to let in any unmarried men, however many young working men needed a place to stay, for she was afraid they would become rowdy and ignore the rules and curfews. She was paranoid, she knew that, but she was glad to bring in Mr. Riddell, Mr.

Fitzgerald, Matthew, Eddie, and Laura as her first boarders. She figured that with children, these men would be more respectable and respectful.

When Mrs. Brown was informed of Grace, Evan, Sandra, and John's need for a place to stay, she was more than happy to bring them in. Even after spending only a few weeks with her current boarders, Mrs. Brown was convinced that they, and those who were to come, were good people. She enjoyed having the company again, and the financial help.

After helping Mrs. Brown, Matthew returned to his quiet seat by the window, watching the rain and listening to the thunder. A sudden burst of cold air rushed into the room as the door opened. Matthew leapt up to greet the newcomers. They were soaked to the skin, their clothes and hair dripping. Mr. Riddell swung the door shut.

Mr. Fitzgerald removed his hat and hung it on one of the hooks on the wall, then placed Laura on the floor. She was less wet, having been protected by her father, but still the child's nose was beginning to run, and she sneezed more than once. Mr. Riddell took his coat and Eddie's and hung them up. Eddie was faring better than Laura, but he was still drenched, as was his father.

"Welcome back," Matthew laughed, "Did you get a little wet?"

"A *little* is an understatement," Mr. Fitzgerald said.

"I hope the others have found shelter," Mr. Riddell added, "It doesn't look like it'll let up for a while."

"I'm sure they've found somew—" Mr. Fitzgerald was cut off by a series of short raps on the door, and he turned around, brow furrowed in confusion, to open it once more. He shut his eyes against the biting wind and rain as he stepped aside to let in two dark, sopping wet figures. He shut the door behind them and for a moment, all present were quiet. Matthew was the first to speak when he finally saw the faces of the newcomers.

"You're here!"

"Matthew!" Sandra cried, throwing her arms around the boy who was now nearly taller than she, "It's so good to see you again!"

"You too," Matthew smiled, pulling away, "You came early!"

"We couldn't wait any longer," John said, taking it in his turn to embrace Matthew, "The stage coach driver told us he thought it was going to rain, so we hitched a ride with a freighter who was going to be driving through the night to meet a deadline, and here we are!"

The rest of the group greeted each other and they all stood soaking wet in the front hall. Mrs. Brown was soon alerted to the commotion and walked into the front hall.

"You must be Miss Montgomery and Mr. Cooper," she greeted Sandra and John warmly, "Come right this way, dears, and we'll get you all dry and warm again, then we'll have you properly settled in."

The time travellers filed past Mrs. Brown and into the rest of the house.

"Thank you, Mrs. Brown," Mr. Riddell said politely as he passed her.

"You're welcome, dear," she replied with a wide smile.

As soon as the time travellers had changed out of their wet clothes, everyone settled in the parlour in front of a roaring fire in the fireplace.

"Thank you so much for taking us all in," Sandra smiled at Mrs. Brown, who was walking into the room with a laden tea tray.

"It's no trouble, dear," Mrs. Brown replied, placing her tray on top of a wooden chest in the centre of the room, "It was really beginning to get quite lonesome around this big old house with no one to share it with."

Sandra nodded. "I only hope we're not too much," she said, "There are still two more people arriving soon."

"The more the merrier," Mrs. Brown replied. She scooted around the table and collapsed into an armchair. It was quite clear that the poor woman was exhausted, but the smile never left her face. Sandra got the feeling that she was beginning to feel a bit useless before they arrived.

Mrs. Brown was a rather short, stout sort of woman, comparable to the teapot that sat atop the wooden chest. Her stature, however, never stopped her from dong anything she pleased. In the kitchen, she kept a stool which she dragged across the floor to reach all her cupboards and shelves, and she kept as many of her things as she could within reach.

A sudden thought seemed to occur to Mrs. Brown as she sat up and looked eagerly around at her boarders.

"You must be rightly starved!" she cried, addressing Sandra and John, "I'll go and start the supper right away."

"Allow me to help you," Mr. Riddell began, rising from his chair. Mrs. Brown smiled broadly and tilted her head to one side.

"You needn't worry your head about that, dear," Mrs. Brown began, "I'm quite alright, thank you very much."

Mr. Riddell pressed on. "Really, Mrs. Brown," he persisted, "I'd be obliged."

"Well, I suppose if you insist," Mrs. Brown relented, and Mr. Riddell rose and followed her to the kitchen.

"Mrs. Brown seems nice," John said, once they had left the room.

"She's a saint," Mr. Fitzgerald replied, "I can't believe all she's doing for us."

"Just don't get her angry," Matthew shuddered.

"Why, what happened?" John lowered his teacup and held his breath as he waited for an answer. The last thing he wanted was another person angry with them.

"Oh, nothing to do with us," Matthew answered, "Laura, Eddie, and I went to the market with her last weekend, and a man tried to sell her some produce for twice the usual price. She was hoppin' mad! You should have seen her!" Matthew looked around at the others excitedly. "She ended up getting the price *lowered!*"

Laura looked up from her place on the rug and nodded, her blond braids falling behind her shoulders. "She was real angry then! Matthew's right, you shoulda seen her, Sandra!" Laura grinned, revealing numerous gaps in her teeth.

"Now, Laura," Mr. Fitzgerald ruffled his daughter's hair, "Losing your temper is never a good way to solve your problems."

"Well, sure," Laura answered in all sincerity, "But it sure solves 'em for Mrs. Brown!" Mr. Fitzgerald smiled wryly.

"It was actually kinda scary," Eddie added, tracing the lines in the rug. Eddie was not a child accustomed to seeing open anger. His father, Mr. Riddell, was a brooding, silent man, and did not often become particularly furious.

"Aw, don't worry, Eddie," John assured him, "She's just got a short temper sometimes."

"I know," Eddie replied, "I know."

Sandra let out a long yawn and closed her eyes for a few moments. "Sorry," she said, "I haven't slept in…" She shut her eyes again. "I'm not sure how long."

John reached over and tucked a loose strand of hair behind her ear. "I know what you mean," he yawned, "I wouldn't mind going to bed myself."

"It would be rude to go when Mrs. Brown is just fixing supper, though," Sandra decided. John nodded in agreement, yawning all the while.

Laura stood up and walked over to her father. "Daddy," she asked quietly, "Can me and Eddie go upstairs and look through the ster… stereo… stereoscope?"

"If Mrs. Brown says it's alright," Mr. Fitzgerald replied. With that, Laura and Eddie ran off to the kitchen.

"Anyone want to play chess?" Matthew asked those left in the room. It was a new hobby of his ever since they had moved to Norton. Mr. Fitzgerald had taught him to play with an old chess set of Mrs. Brown's, and it helped keep his mind off things. Not only did he miss Evan and Grace, but also his old friends. Living in Connolly Mills, back when he had first arrived in the past, Matthew had made some of the best friends he could ever have hoped for. Rachel, a confident, intelligent girl, who also happened to be the granddaughter of Clay Kennedy, the man who was after the heads of the time travellers, was the first of these friends, and someone who Matthew not only liked, but admired. Alvin was the second, a strong, independent young man with a dream of becoming a farmer. Alice was the last. She was very kind, but also very vulnerable, a fact that some evil stranger had taken advantage of, leaving her afraid and with child. Matthew shuddered to think of it.

"Not just now, Matthew," John replied. Sandra shook her head and smiled. Chess always reminded her of their failed plans, and how she had been one of the people behind them. She and Evan had spent ages placing chess pieces on a map of the county and knocking them down as each idea they thought of showed a sign of failure.

"I'll play with you, Matthew," Mr. Fitzgerald agreed, and the two of them set to putting together the board.

■■

"Is this the one?"

"I think so… It sure looks big enough."

"Yup."

"You gonna knock, Gracie?"

Grace looked over at Evan and shook her head, a nervous smile on her face. The house that faced them was tall and imposing, and sat on what must have been the busiest corner in all of Norton. It was tall and angular, and was painted white with green trim. Grace was certain it was the right house, but she was still reluctant. Her hand shook as she raised it to the door and rapped sharply three times. She took a step back, nearly knocking Evan down the front steps.

The day was bright and sunny, so unlike the storms of the day before, and the air felt cool and clear. Evan's breath twisted and writhed in the air as he spoke, waiting for the door to be answered.

"It looks nice," he said, "Big, and, uh…and…big…"

"Oh, relax, Evan!" Grace snapped, her voice raised, "It's not *that* big, alright. It's a boarding house, for goodness sake!"

Evan threw up his hands in mock surrender. "Listen, Grace, I know you're probably all nervous about this whole thing, but that's no reason to—"

"Grace! Evan!" The door was flung open to reveal Matthew, his face beaming. He turned around and shouted into the depths of the house. "Hey, hey, everybody! Grace and Evan are here!"

Grace crossed the threshold and entered the house. It felt friendly enough; a warm coloured front hall gave the place an atmosphere of home. Evan followed Grace inside, and grinned.

Mrs. Brown entered the hall to greet her new boarders, and was followed by Mr. Riddell. Mr. Fitzgerald approached from the parlour, trailed by Laura and Eddie.

"Very nice to meet you both," Mrs. Brown shook hands with Grace and Evan in turn, "I'm Mrs. Brown, the landlady. I'll place your things upstairs."

"Thank you," Grace replied, and then turned to Mr. Fitzgerald, "Have Sandra and John not arrived yet?"

"They're here," Matthew laughed, "They got here yesterday, only they're still asleep!"

"Asleep?" Evan scoffed, "But it's the middle of the—"

"How did they get here so early?" Grace interrupted, looking to Mr. Fitzgerald for answers.

"They rode through the night," Matthew answered eagerly, "They'll be up later. Come on in! Get comfortable!"

"Don't mind if I do!" Evan sighed wearily, "I'm beat." He peered over at Grace as everyone walked towards the parlour.

"You okay now?" he whispered close to her ear.

Grace nodded. "I'm sorry for snapping at you," she breathed back, "I was just nervous…"

"I understand," Evan smiled, "It's not easy." He stooped down, scooped up Laura and placed her on his shoulders. She shrieked with delight, her laughter echoing throughout the house. The group of boarders took their seats.

"It's pretty cozy in here isn't it?" Evan remarked, scanning the room, taking in the warm coloured walls and furniture. It was a beautiful room, with a large fireplace at one end with an intricately carved mantel above it. On the mantel were a clock, a lamp, and an old photograph of Mrs. Brown's late husband, all meticulously dusted and polished. The furniture was arranged around the fireplace, and consisted of armchairs and a small couch.

"It really gets to feeling like home," Mr. Fitzgerald responded, "Like you've always been here."

Grace opened her mouth to comment, but was interrupted by a sudden flurry of pitter patter steps hurrying down the stairs. Sandra appeared like an apparition from thin air in the doorway.

"I thought I heard…" She paused, her eyes adjusting to the light, "Grace!" Sandra rushed forward to embrace her friend. "I knew I heard you! And Evan!" She turned and hugged him as well. "How was your trip? It's been such a long time, it seems!" Sandra took a seat as John rushed into the room, pulling one of his suspenders over his shoulder.

"Is everything alright? I heard someone running down the stairs…" His face brightened as he noticed the new arrivals. "Evan, Grace!" He greeted each of them in turn and took his seat, rubbing the sleep out of his eyes.

Together at last, the time travellers did much catching up as they sat in the parlour. Before long, the time for supper had come. In most boarding houses, meals were eaten family style, all together at one table, and Mrs. Brown's was no exception.

The meal was one that none of them would soon forget. They ate a large roast beef with gravy and potatoes, the sounds of clinking glasses, utensils, and plates muffled under the gleeful conversation. Mrs. Brown sat at the end of the table, Mr. Riddell and Mr. Fitzgerald flanking her on either side; and she was as much a part of the chatter as anyone else.

"Mrs. Brown, this roast is delicious," Grace complimented her, smiling all the while.

"Thank you, dear," Mrs. Brown replied, "I had excellent help." She smiled at Mr. Riddell meaningfully. Mr. Riddell's face reddened and he mumbled something no one could hear. He had been helping Mrs. Brown cook nearly all the meals since they had arrived, and was quite enjoying himself. He loved the feeling of the heat from the stove, the smells of the herbs and spices, the sight of the steam coiling from the finished meal. He enjoyed the company as well, and teaching Mrs. Brown how to use the various spices was quite rewarding. Before he had begun helping her out, her cooking had been rather bland, lacking any significant flavour, but she had greatly improved since.

Grace smiled at him and took a sip of her drink, then averted her attention to Matthew, who sat across from her, between Evan and John. It was remarkable how the boy had changed since they had first met him. Grace watched him for a moment as he talked animatedly about who-knows-what with John and Evan. The smile that nearly constantly adorned his face nowadays was a rare sight when he had first arrived in the past. If Grace was unhappy at all about the way the rest of their time in the past had been, the one thing she never regretted was taking Matthew in. The good that they had done for him was worth all their trials and failures.

Supper lasted well past eight o'clock, by which time Mrs. Brown decided it was time for her boarders to turn in. Mr. Riddell and Mr. Fitzgerald had work in the morning, and she was sure that the others needed their rest, particularly Evan and Grace after travelling all the way from Darcy Lake. She sent them all upstairs and retired to her private portion of the house.

The time travellers filed up the stairs in pairs of two, which was the most the narrow staircase would allow. The landing opened into a hallway with various doors along its length. Though the house was large, there were not enough rooms for each time travellers to have their own. Sandra and Grace shared with Laura, and Matthew with Eddie. Mr. Fitzgerald and Mr. Riddell split a room, and Evan and John took the last one.

Each room was furnished with two beds, save for Grace, Sandra, and Laura's, which contained three. All the rooms also had a small writing desk, a wardrobe, and a washstand. They were warm coloured, like the rest of the house, and the ceilings were tin, with flowering patterns from one end of the room to the other.

"I meant to ask you," Grace began to address Mr. Fitzgerald once she had reached the landing, "Where are you and Mr. Riddell working?"

"We both work in the Mackay Foundry in Irontown, that's the industrial sector, if you will."

"What do they make there?"

"Stoves, mostly, a couple other things, too."

"How are the hours?"

"Long. Ten hours about. We start at around seven and end at five."

"And the working conditions?"

"Not great. There's already been a few guys who had to quit because of injuries from the machines. If you're careful, though, there shouldn't be any trouble. Problem is, most of these workers are young. Too young."

Grace shook her head. "Not children, I hope."

Mr. Fitzgerald thought for a moment. "I haven't seen anyone younger than sixteen or thereabouts." There was a pause.

"Anyway," Grace let out a long breath she had been holding in, "We should all be going to bed." She turned to address the rest of the group. "Goodnight, everyone."

A chorus of goodnights followed her words, and the group began to break up and disappear slowly into their various rooms, until only Evan and Grace remained. Grace began to follow Sandra into their shared room, but hesitated when she saw Evan still standing in the middle of the hall.

She waited until all the doors had shut, and turned to face him.

Evan walked closer to her, hands in his pockets. "So," he began, "Are you satisfied? Everyone's okay, we're all back together—" he cut himself off, "Wow, that sounds sappy—and nothing bad's happened yet. Can you stop worrying now? Is Grace back on her rocker? Have the marbles returned? The temper ceased its fire?"

Grace crossed her arms. "I never lost my mind, thank you very much," she said stubbornly, "I was worried, that's all."

"Leave all that worrying to Sandra," Evan whispered, "Everything's going to be fine."

"I know," Grace replied, then smiled slightly, "I know."

"Good," Evan answered, "Then goodnight."

"Goodnight, Evan."

With that, the pair retired to their rooms. Grace shut the door behind her and shook her head, though she was smiling. It felt nice to know that she was cared about.

Across the hall, Eddie was settling into bed. He shut his eyes and tried his best to block out the light that shone incessantly from the corner of the room. He lay under his covers for what seemed to him like an eternity before he finally gathered up the courage to speak.

"Hey, Matthew?"

"Uh huh?"

"Could you turn off the lamp, please? It's too bright over here."

Matthew turned around from where he sat facing a small, dark wooden desk, upon which stood a gas lamp, an inkwell, and a solitary piece of paper. A typewriter sat off to the side.

"It'll be out in a minute, Eddie, I promise, I just have to finish this letter."

"Okay," Eddie relented, "Just hurry up, alright?"

Matthew smiled. "Sure."

He turned back to his unfinished letter. It was addressed to Alvin, back in Connolly Mills, who would surely show it to Alice and Rachel. It would be the first letter he had sent them since his return to the past, and it was nerve wracking. How could he explain his sudden disappearance? Where would he say he went? He finally decided to simply focus on his friends and say little about himself. He asked how each of them was faring, beginning with Alvin.

Matthew shivered as he recalled what poor Alvin had gone through to save him and his family from the wrath of Clay Kennedy. He hadn't seen it all happen, but Mr. Riddell could attest to the fact that Alvin had been through a great deal facing down Clay, emotionally and physically. While Rachel and Clay tried to wrest the gun out of each other's grip, it went off, and the bullet skimmed right across Alvin's upper left arm. Matthew wasn't sure how bad the damage was, but he fervently hoped that the wound was merely superficial.

Matthew asked about Alice next. As far as he knew, she was still expecting, seven months to be precise. He hoped she was doing well, for he knew that she had been rather ill for the last few months as a result of her condition.

Rachel was last. Clay was her grandfather, and though she lacked physical injury, Matthew shuddered to think of the mental effect of having an attempted murderer in her immediate family. With both of her parents having passed away, her grandparents, Clay and Penelope Kennedy, were Rachel's guardians and she lived with them in their house.

Lost in thought, Matthew stared absently into the flame of the gas lamp beside his elbow.

"Can you *please* finish that in the morning?"

Matthew shook himself and turned around to see Eddie standing by his shoulder, his little face pinched with frustration.

"Sure," Matthew sighed as he put out the lamp, "Sorry, Eddie."

He shuffled over to his bed, the afterimage of the gas lamp's flame still dancing in his vision. Matthew lay down and closed his eyes, falling asleep almost as soon as he did so. His dreams were contented, for the most part, but every so often, a worry would spring into his mind and he would jolt awake, only to fall asleep again a few moments later.

CHAPTER TWO

Break Time

Matthew awoke the next morning to find he had nothing much to do besides send his letter. Now that all the time travellers were together again, Matthew had no one to sit around and wait for. After breakfast, he finished writing his letter and set out into the streets of Norton towards the post office.

The city felt quite different from the small towns of Darcy Lake and Connolly Mills, and Matthew couldn't quite decide what to think of it. From the smoky district of Irontown to the opulent Kings Park, Norton was home to a vast array of people from every walk of life. It was large and imposing, but Matthew loved walking among the people and imagining what they must be up to. He would hear snippets of conversation as he passed by, and smell the various aromas from each of the shops along the roads. He found that he was beginning to be able to recognize each part of the city by smell alone. He could distinguish the tell tale smell of sawdust in the lumber district from the stifling smog of the industrial sector, along with the myriad other smells in the city. However, Matthew's favourite part of the city was the market. Every turn gave an enticing new aroma, be it the essence of baked goods or the whiff of meat roasting on a spit.

The post office resided on the other side of the market from Mrs. Brown's boarding house, and Matthew was delighted to have an excuse to walk through it. He strode slowly, savouring every sight, sound, and smell that the lively place had to offer. To his disappointment, the day was windy, and so in order to smell anything at all, he had to be very close to the source. Matthew stopped to peer at the fresh bread and eggs for sale, then moved along to a stand of fish which reminded him of the booming industry back in little old Darcy Lake. He tasted some maple syrup, which was still as fresh and sweet as the day it was made, all the way back in the spring. The market was constantly bustling with activity, and Matthew loved every bit of it, from the wagons which clattered along the middle of the road to the children who scampered along the wooden sidewalks.

Matthew would have liked to spend some time with Grace, Evan, Sandra, and John that day; he felt that the already wonderful experience of walking through the market would have been made even better by their presence, particularly after their time apart, but the four of them were not going to waste any time. They had gone out that morning in search of jobs, for they had a life to rebuild.

"Hey, you!"

Matthew turned abruptly and glanced around. He found himself staring into the bloodshot eyes of a red faced merchant.

"Huh?" Matthew managed.

"Are you going to buy anything or just stand there gawkin'?

Matthew tried to avert his eyes from the man's face, but he was standing so close that all he could do was stare at his red visage and smell his fetid breath.

"S-Sorry," Matthew stuttered, and backed away a few steps before turning around and scampering away. He glanced back at the man as he walked, and ran straight into a figure nearly a full head shorter than he. Matthew stumbled and fell, but saw the figure begin to run away, breaking into a sprint.

Matthew picked himself up and dusted himself off, muttering as he did so.

"Must have been some little pickpocket," he mumbled, "Well, I don't have anything to steal so the joke's on..." Matthew paused and reached into both his pockets. Finding nothing, he withdrew his hands and scrutinized them, as though hoping to find what he was looking for buried in the creases of his palms. "Where's... Where's my... my letter? Where's my letter?"

Matthew peered frantically at the ground around him, searching desperately for his missing letter. He dropped to his hands and knees and checked under stalls, carts, and the shoes of passers-by.

"It's got to be around here—unkh!" Matthew rubbed his head where he had hit it against a stationary wagon wheel. "Somewhere," he finished.

Matthew stood again and gazed off in the direction that the pickpocket had fled, and a white envelope caught his eye.

"There you are!" he whispered to himself, making his way towards his lost correspondence. As he marched along, a large covered wagon passed speedily in front of him, carrying his letter away in the spokes of its rear wheel.

Matthew gasped and ran after it, dodging past various obstacles, his eyes never leaving the thin white paper that danced between the spokes of the wagon's wheel.

The wagon turned hastily down a side alley, and Matthew followed behind it as closely as he could. He was catching up, but not before the letter escaped the grip of the wheel and fluttered away on the strong wind once more. Matthew leaned his head back and leaped for it, but it was floating just out of his reach, and flew ever higher as he tried to grab it. Matthew watched helplessly as it soared farther above his head and disappeared over the roof of the building to his right.

"Just great," Matthew grumbled, "Terrific." He kicked the dusty road in frustration. Desperate to get his letter back, Matthew began to search for some way to take to the rooftops and find it once and for all. He jogged around to the back of the building, and was pleased to discover that it was residential, with two balconies protruding from its façade. There were two flights of stairs that led to the uppermost balcony, and Matthew was confident he could climb onto the banister and make his way onto the roof to retrieve his letter. Without wasting a moment, he ran to the staircase and clomped up the steps two at a time. Once he reached the top, some of his nerve seemed to be gone, but he forced himself to scale the banister and balance himself.

Matthew's legs shook as he straightened up and gripped the roof of the balcony. Struggling not to look down, he stood on tiptoe and peeked over the roof. He couldn't see anything, but he was high enough to be able to place his elbows onto the roof. Matthew had to muster all his strength and use them to hoist himself up. He clenched his fists and held his breath, his eyes tight shut as he pushed off the banister with his legs, and pulled with his arms. With great effort, he finally made it, rolling onto the flat roof and catching his breath.

After a moment's rest, Matthew stood and glanced around, wondering if perhaps the search for his letter was by now a lost cause. He walked across the roof slowly, looking for the telltale flash of white. He approached the brick chimney and walked all around it, and when he reached the opposite side, the first thing he saw was his letter, dusty and slightly torn. The second thing he saw was the person holding it. Their eyes met as Matthew's shadow fell across him; eyes Matthew instantly recognized. It was the figure who had run into him earlier, but Matthew recognized him from long before then. He was lost for words, and the boy who held his letter was the first to speak.

"I guess you caught me, Matthew," he said, "But I think it's you who has some explaining to do."

Matthew couldn't believe his eyes. There before him, clear as day, sat his old friend. There he was, all brown eyes and dark, olive skin. His stony features were illuminated by the sun, and his dark hair gleamed in the light.

Trevor squinted up at Matthew. "Shut your mouth, would ya?" he said, "You're freakin' me out." He turned casually back to the letter in his hands, seemingly oblivious to Matthew's utter shock.

"M-me?" Matthew finally found his voice, "Freaking *you* out? *Me*?" His eyes widened and voice rose. "How- wh- how did you get here?" Matthew sat down on the roof, rubbing his eyes.

"What?" Trevor asked incredulously, "You didn't really think I would leave you with your parents, did you? After what you told me about them? After what I saw? 'Course I came back for you! We're like family, you and me! Least we were."

Matthew pinched the bridge of his nose and groaned. "Listen, Trevor," he began, "There are some things I should have told you."

"What, you mean like how those people I saw weren't even your parents? Like how you all left and came to this crazy place?" Trevor shook the letter. "How you almost got killed? I know all that now."

"Trevor, you've gotta understand, I never wanted to keep all this from you, you gotta believe me…"

"Believe you?" Trevor scoffed, "You want me to believe a word you say after you lied to my face?"

"Trevor, I didn't lie to you, I just…" Matthew trailed off, unsure of what to say next.

"Aw, shuddup," Trevor waved his hand dismissively, "I'm willing to forgive you if you tell me everything up front right now."

Matthew told him. He told him about the time machine, about his family, his friends, Connolly Mills, Darcy Lake, Clay Kennedy, everything. If Trevor asked a question, he answered it. By the end of his long tale, Trevor was looking quite amused.

"I guess I understand why you kept it all from me," he said, and Matthew sighed with relief, "But you've got to get me back to my normal place and time and whatever."

"Trevor," Matthew smiled, "I'll do whatever I can."

"Great," Trevor replied, standing up and handing Matthew his much sought after letter, "Where do we start?"

Matthew thought for a moment, then his brow furrowed in confusion. "Wait… wait, wait, wait," he said hurriedly, "I answered all your questions, so I think it's my turn to ask you some."

Trevor shook his head and smiled wryly, then looked up at Matthew. "What do you wanna know?"

"How did you *get* here?"

Trevor chuckled. "It's nothing so exciting," he said, "I went back to that house that we were in and snuck inside. No one was there, so I took a look around. I went upstairs and discovered the time mach—"

"Shh! Not so loud!"

"—ine," Trevor finished, more quietly, "And a bunch of notes, tools, books, and stuff. I read them all, but the one that explained the most- all about *you* and this crazy—" he lowered his voice, "—time travel stuff—was this."

Trevor reached into his jacket and pulled out a small brown notebook, proffering it to Matthew. Matthew's eyes widened as he snatched it up and flipped through the pages.

"This is Sandra's journal! I must have forgotten it when..." he trailed off.

"I read the whole thing," Trevor smiled, "It stops right before Christmas, when she planned on giving it to you."

"Trevor, I know you didn't mean anything by it, but this journal is private. Sandra gave it to me because everyone agreed they could trust me..."

"A little late for that now, isn't it?"

Matthew nodded. "I've got more questions," he said.

"Shoot," Trevor replied.

"What did you do when you got here? How did you get those clothes, and how on earth did you end up here in Norton?"

Trevor looked down as if noticing what he was wearing for the first time. He had on long trousers and a plain, faded beige button down shirt. Even though it was nearing the end of a hot summer, he wore a worsted jacket that looked two sizes too big.

"Well," Trevor began, "I knew when I got here that I couldn't walk around in my regular clothes, so I snuck into the nearest house and took these."

"You stole them?"

"Hey, don't look at me like it's such a crime to steal a few clothes. They had more than enough!"

Matthew shook his head, but let the matter drop. "Then what?"

"I stuck around in Connolly Mills for a couple weeks, and then I saw Sandra and John, those guys who pretended to be your parents last time I saw you. I followed them and sort of spied on them a little. I knew they would recognize me, so after they left for Norton, I got Sam to take me here too."

"Sam?" Matthew wondered, the face of Grace's old pupil flashing into his mind, "Is he here?"

"I dunno, maybe," Trevor answered, "We just got here last night, and then I left. I think he wanted me to stick around, but I had to find you."

"How come you ran off after you bumped into me then?" Matthew wondered aloud.

"I had to make sure it was you," Trevor answered, "You looked so *different* from when we were out on the streets."

"Well, why on earth were you up here?" Matthew gestured below to the roof the pair were still standing on.

"To watch you," Trevor replied simply, "And make sure. It was a stroke of luck when your letter came flying up here. Now I know even more."

"Listen, Trevor, I've gotta know," Matthew began, "Why, if you read Sandra's journal, did you come looking for me?"

"Because," Trevor said, "I have to bring you back."

"*What?*"

"Whadda ya mean, *what?* You don't belong here any more than I do! What kind of life is this?" He paused dramatically. "I've been here almost three weeks, and I haven't seen any indoor plumbing!"

"Trevor, there's indoor plumbing all over the place here, but there's more to life than that! I've got a family here, and friends—"

"I'm your friend! We're a family, we've always been! I've always looked out for you. Haven't I looked out for you?"

"Well, yes, but—"

"But nothing! You can't tell me that you don't ever miss our old life! There's no way you can honestly tell me that you don't miss the freedom we had. We could do anything we wanted, whenever we wanted! What did having a family ever do for you? Huh? Nothin', that's what. They hurt you. Don't you remember that? Wasn't that why you ran away?"

"Yeah... but these people are different Trevor," Matthew countered, "Not all families are like mine was, you know that!"

Trevor swore. "You just don't get it," he implored Matthew, "You've been... I dunno, brainwashed or something! There is no way you can convince me that you're not trapped by your so called *family*, okay, no way. *I* value my freedom."

"Trevor, are you hearing yourself?" Matthew was becoming angry now. Grace, Evan and the other time travellers had turned his life around, and he couldn't stand to hear that fact contested. "I have been happier these last months than ever before in my life! At least ever since my mom died..." He paused, collected himself, and went on. "This family has been the best thing that ever happened to me."

"Aw, whatever," Trevor finished the conversation with a wave of his hand, and then put an arm around Matthew's shoulder, "You just think on that for a while, then you'll see. You're trapped, and I am your key to freedom. But for now, let's just focus on getting back to the present day."

"I'm not going back."

"Whatever. Get *me* back then, if that makes you feel better."

"Sure," Matthew sighed.

"Well, let's get going then!" Trevor insisted, "I've got the time ma—"

"Shh!"

"Sorry," Trevor whispered, "I've got the time machine hidden in the alley. You should probably see it…"

"Wait!" Matthew said, stopping his old friend with a hand on the shoulder, "We burned the time machine… So how did you…?"

"It wasn't burned when I got to that old house," Trevor explained, a bemused look crossing his face.

Matthew could have kicked himself for his ignorance. They had burned the time machine from the 1901 end, not the present day. Evidently, Trevor had taken the time machine into the past again and reopened the portal creating a new time machine in 1901 that was just like the one that Grace had burned. Matthew shook himself, trying to process it all.

"Never mind," he said, "Let's go."

The pair of them clambered down rather unceremoniously from the roof, Trevor having a much easier time of it than Matthew. They clomped back down the stairs together, Matthew clutching his still unsent letter and Sandra's old journal in his hands.

They turned into the alley and Trevor marched ahead, then used his entire body to push some heavy wooden crates aside. Matthew ran to help him, and together, they moved the crates to reveal a light blue sheet with something wrapped up inside. Trevor knelt and unfolded the sheet, then stepped back.

Matthew gasped. "What *happened*?"

He crouched down next to the time machine and ran his fingers over the various pieces.

Trevor scratched the back of his head. "It kinda fell out of the wagon on the way here… and then got trampled by a horse… and another wagon…"

The time machine was in shambles. The wood was split apart, the panel of buttons was twisted and bent, and there must have been at least a million tiny metal parts spilling out in all directions. Among the wreckage was a silver pocket watch that Matthew recognized as belonging to Mr. Riddell, and must have been left behind when they had returned to the past. It was frozen at half past two. Matthew picked it up.

"We," Matthew began, swallowing hard, "Are in so much trouble."

"It's not that bad!" Trevor tried to convince him, "If Sandra knows anything," he gestured towards the journal in Matthew's hand, "Grace'll be able to fix it. I even brought the blueprints!" He dug through the time machine's remains and pulled out a crumpled blue sheet of paper, plans and calculations carefully laid out upon it.

"Yeah... she's not gonna fix it."

"Well, what? Why not?"

"She burned it to the ground when we got here! Don't you think that means she doesn't want it anymore? She's going to be glad it's broken!"

"Well, what about me?" Trevor wondered, "Won't she want to send me back?"

Matthew gave a bitter laugh. "Listen," he said, "I know you've never met her, but from what you read, does she really sound like she would do that? She didn't do it for me, she won't do it for you."

"Just let me talk to her," Trevor said, "I'm sure I can change her mind, and we can both go home."

"I told you, I'm not going back. *This* is my home. And you can't change Grace's mind. And I can't let you talk to her. You can't let any of them know you're here."

"Matthew, that's ridiculous! I have to say something, we can't fix this ourselves!"

"No, you don't get it," Matthew breathed heavily, "They'll think you're a risk, that you'll—" He swallowed. "That you'll give away their secret to everyone in the present. Trust me, if you want to leave, you won't say anything, and you won't be seen."

Trevor nodded slowly, beginning to understand. "Alright," he finally agreed, "I get it."

"Okay," Matthew said, standing up shakily, "Wrap all this up in the sheet." He gestured to the time machine's remnants. "Hide it. The roof will probably be a good place.

Hide it well. Don't lose any of the pieces. Have you got any money?"

"No, why?"

"You'll need a place to stay for the night, that's why. And food, but I guess I can bring you some of that every so often—"

"Matthew," Trevor interrupted, "I thought you knew me better than that. Who needs a place to stay when you've got streets like these? The streets are my friends; they give me everything I need and more." He smiled nonchalantly. Matthew tried to conceal his unease.

"I've gotta go," he said, beginning to back away, "Do what I told you. I'll meet you here tomorrow morning, first thing. Whatever you do, don't get into any trouble, okay?"

Trevor gave a mock salute. "Whatever you say," he replied, "Just think about what I said, alright? About going back."

"Yeah, sure, I'll do that." Matthew began to walk backwards, slowly making his way out of the alley.

"Hey, you know I'm right!"

"Whatever you want to think, Trevor!" With that, Matthew ran out of the alley and out of Trevor's sight.

He let out a shaky breath as he came into the market again. This time he didn't stall, he marched right through and emerged on the other side. He climbed the post office steps with butterflies in his stomach and his head spinning. He couldn't believe what had just happened, who he had just seen. He knew then that the new life he and the time travellers were trying to build was in great jeopardy, and he hadn't a clue what to do.

CHAPTER THREE

Time Passes

Matthew stepped into the post office, his mind reeling. He sent his letter, after buying an envelope and stamp, sealed it, then promptly left. He needed to be alone, to have time to think uninterrupted.

This was a decision that needed to be made with caution. He had already decided he couldn't tell the time travellers what had happened; he already knew from experience what they did when a situation of this kind arose. Matthew smiled nervously as he remembered when the time travellers had found him in the time machine, cowering at their feet in the shadows. They had decided they couldn't send him back, no matter how much he begged, without posing a risk to their own safety, and the safety of the time machine. They had taken him in, and it was the best thing that had ever happened to him. Matthew suspected Trevor would feel differently if they tried to do the same for him. Not only was Trevor determined to return to the present, and bring Matthew with him, he was also much braver than Matthew had been, and much more resourceful. Where Matthew had tried to escape, Trevor would succeed.

Matthew, upon leaving the boarding house, had had the intention of spending the day in town, perhaps finding Laura and Eddie and taking them to see a show, but now Matthew was in no position to be spending time any way he pleased. He had a problem to solve, and a rather big one at that. He decided as he walked through the market once more, this time ignoring anything of interest, that his best bet was to return to the boarding house. Mrs. Brown might be there, but if he retreated to his room she would be forced to give him his privacy. If Eddie happened to be there, Matthew could easily send him away.

Matthew approached the boarding house with a sense of foreboding. In a matter of minutes, everything he knew had changed. Nothing seemed safe any more.

Matthew entered the big house quietly, trying desperately to make as little sound as possible, for fear of being found by Mrs. Brown. He shut the door slowly and silently, and then took off his shoes so that no one would hear him steal across the wood floor towards the stairs. He climbed the stairs swiftly and entered his room, shutting the door carefully behind him.

He was relieved to find that Eddie was not still in the room, and he collapsed onto his bed, tears of frustration stinging his eyes. He buried his face in his hands and pinched the bridge of his nose. His conversation with Trevor flashed through his mind in a whirlwind of angry words and regrettable promises.

"What am I gonna do?" Matthew squeaked from behind his hands, "What am I gonna do?"

Matthew often found that thinking out loud helped him to organize his thoughts, and this instance was no exception, though he had to be sure to speak quietly lest he be found out.

"I have to send Trevor back, no question," Matthew began, standing and starting to pace back and forth beside his bed, "But how? I thought it was going to be easy, but the time machine's broken into a million stupid pieces! I can't fix it, only Grace can, and maybe some of the others, I'm not sure..." He trailed off and continued pacing. "There has to be a way to get it fixed without them knowing, but how? How, how, how?" Matthew let himself fall onto his bed again and continued thinking. "I can't give it to Grace, then I would have to explain why it was here in the first place, and she'd destroy it for sure..." A sudden thought struck him. "Maybe," he said, "I *can* fix it..." He stood once more and rushed to the desk, lighting the lamp as he sat down. He grabbed a sheet of blank paper and began to write down what he was thinking so he wouldn't forget.

Matthew knew he needed to fix the time machine himself, but he couldn't do it without Grace's help. He resolved to somehow obtain her help without her knowing. Matthew added these thoughts to the paper. He could begin by starting a conversation with her, and ask about how the time machine functioned. Matthew continued to scribble on the page before him. He needed her to divulge a sort of step by step plan to rebuilding the time machine. As soon as he had that, he would be able to return Trevor to where he belonged. Matthew smiled, satisfied with his plan, then folded up his paper and placed it in his pocket. If this didn't work, he was afraid nothing would.

Matthew returned to his bed and lay down on his back, staring up at the ceiling, hands folded over his abdomen. He thought over his plan, and the more he thought, the more worried he became. Plans had a certain habit of failing miserably, and this one was already far fetched. However, there was nothing else to do. Matthew could see no other remedy for the situation.

"I'm doomed," he muttered, closing his eyes, "Completely doomed."

Matthew heard the front door open far below him and the sound of muffled voices floated up through the floor. Though he couldn't tell what was being said, Matthew could tell by the tones of their voices that it was Evan and Grace. The sound, normally a comfort, now made him sick to his stomach. He could barely move, so paralyzed by the weight of the situation he found himself in. Any appetite he had had was now gone with the wind, and the idea of going downstairs to greet Evan and Grace became nightmarish rather than appealing.

Then came a sound he dreaded perhaps even more than Evan and Grace at the door. He heard footsteps, coming slowly up the stairs. He had been found out, he just knew it. Someone had seen Trevor and was coming upstairs to tell Matthew to go find him and bring him here, even though Matthew knew he would never come. Thinking quickly, Matthew leapt up as quietly as he could, grabbed his shoes, and scurried soundlessly over to the wardrobe. He opened the doors as slowly as he dared, wincing as they creaked. Then, with an urgency that made his head spin, Matthew stepped into the wardrobe, placed his shoes beside him, and shut the doors.

He stayed there, standing awkwardly, his head and knees bent and leaning away from the doors, hardly daring to breathe. He listened intently as the source of the footsteps reached the landing, and he screwed his eyes shut and held his breath as he heard his bedroom door swing open ever so slowly. Matthew heard the rustling of clothing and a bit of a grunt, perhaps, and then the door closed again. Matthew let out a shaky breath, but he did not emerge from the wardrobe for fear that whoever it was might return. Instead, he contented himself with the comforting darkness and near silence that the wardrobe provided, and sat himself down on its floor. It was a tight fit, and Matthew could feel the hems of his and Eddie's shirts and trousers grazing his head, but he felt safer there than he did out in the open.

Not only did Trevor's presence put the time travellers in jeopardy, but he stirred up long lost memories and feelings in Matthew that he had tried so hard to put out of his mind. He remembered the day he had met Trevor, near the beginning of his time away from home. It wasn't the first time he had tried to run away from home, but it was the last. Trevor had made sure that his cruel father and step mother never found him. He had looked out for him, and the two were good friends. Maybe, as Trevor had suggested, they really were like a family. Matthew shook his head. Though it was true, the complexities of it all were making him feel sick to his stomach.

Matthew sat in that wardrobe for far longer than he should have, by all accounts. He missed the midday meal and his stomach was grumbling by the late afternoon. He knew he would have to emerge before dinner, but he hoped that he might be a little less visibly nervous by that time. His hopes were dashed when he heard Mrs. Brown calling everyone to supper.

Slowly, Matthew opened the doors of the wardrobe, the light from the window burning his eyes. He stood shakily and stepped out, then smoothed out his wrinkled clothes with his hands. He crossed carefully to the wash basin and splashed water over his face and washed his hands.

When Matthew arrived downstairs, he felt guilty. He sat down at the table and watched the time travellers and Mrs. Brown converse happily, not knowing of the danger at their very doorstep. He hated to think that Trevor might ruin their contented lives. They had just gotten back on their feet, and Matthew felt entirely responsible for Trevor's presence.

Matthew remained silent throughout the entire meal. He wanted to say something, in order to avoid any suspicion or unwanted attention, but he couldn't find the words. Even if he had known what to say, he wouldn't have been able to say it. It was like his vocal chords were tied in a knot, along with his stomach. His plate remained virtually untouched.

"Hey, Matthew!" Eddie whispered from beside him, "Can I have your chicken?"

Matthew nodded soundlessly, and Eddie peered around the table to make sure no one was looking as he lifted the meat off of Matthew's plate and onto his own.

"Thanks," he said, then paused, "Can I have your corn too?"

Matthew pushed his plate towards Eddie, indicating that the boy should take whatever he pleased. As Eddie emptied his plate, Matthew was grateful that no one would have to ask him why he wasn't eating.

Matthew went to bed that night with a heavy heart and an even heavier conscience. His dreams were plagued by visions of Trevor sauntering through the streets of Norton in his present day clothing, relieving people of their valuables. Matthew tried to stop him, but it did no good and only incriminated him as well.

He awoke in the middle of the night and couldn't, no matter how hard he tried, go back to sleep. Until Trevor was safely back where he belonged and the time machine destroyed once and for all, Matthew feared he may never sleep or eat again.

CHAPTER FOUR

Hang Time

Matthew got out of bed early the next morning and crept downstairs to meet Grace, who had always been one of the first of the time travellers to wake up each day. He waited in the parlour, and soon enough Grace came sauntering down the stairs.

"Good morning, Matthew," she yawned, upon seeing him, "How come you're up so soon? Normally you're one of the last awake."

"Just felt like getting up early, I guess," Matthew answered casually, though he felt sure that Grace had heard the apprehension in his voice.

Grace nodded absently and sat down across from him, smoothing down her skirts. She glanced at the mantel clock through bleary eyes.

"Well," she said, stretching her arms, "The others'll be up soon." She paused and looked at Matthew. "In the meantime, I haven't gotten to talk to you much since we arrived. How are you liking it here?"

"It's good," Matthew replied, "The city's different from any other place we lived, but I like it."

"Well, it sure seems like you're enjoying yourself," Grace answered, "You were out all day yesterday, we got a little worried when you missed lunch."

"Don't worry, I ate," Matthew lied, "I was out in the market all day."

Grace nodded, and Matthew decided that this was the best time to begin putting his doomed plan into action.

"Grace," he began, glad that his conscience had finally abated enough that he could speak, "I've been reading Sandra's journal, and I just have to know... How did you build the—" He lowered his voice. "Time machine. How did you create it?"

Grace's face became puzzled. "I didn't know you were so curious about it, Matthew," she began, "But it would take me forever to explain. I'm sure you understand it's quite complicated." She laughed musically. "However," she said, "I suppose I can try."

With those words, Grace began to tell Matthew about the process of building the time machine. Her eyes twinkled as she spoke; the topic evidently made her very happy. Yet, as much as she explained it, Matthew found he could not understand. It was as though she was speaking a different language, a language in which Matthew only understood a few words. He realized then that his plan was even more hopeless than he had thought. He was truly doomed.

Grace was interrupted by Mr. Fitzgerald coming down the stairs, and Matthew had to stifle a sigh of relief. He was beginning to feel his anxiety resurface with every word Grace spoke.

"Good morning," Mr. Fitzgerald said. Matthew and Grace replied in kind.

The three of them began to converse, discussing altogether unimportant matters which only served to make Matthew both more relaxed and more anxious all at once. The other time travellers soon awoke to the sound of conversation and came filing down the stairs. Grace turned to Matthew.

"I'll finish explaining later if you'd like," she whispered, smiling. Matthew tried his best to smile back and nodded.

Not long after all the time travellers had awoken, so did Mrs. Brown, and breakfast was served forthwith. Matthew, remembering his promise to Trevor, ate as much as he could as fast as he could, leaving the rest to Eddie, who was delighted to take it.

Matthew left the boarding house as soon as he was finished, telling everyone that he was going to walk in the market again. They all accepted the excuse without a second thought, for they knew of Matthew's love for the place, and had no reason to suspect that anything untoward was going on.

As Matthew walked through the streets, he no longer found any pleasure in the sights, sounds, nor even the smells of the market. Ignoring the assault on his senses, he made his way to the alley where he had promised to meet Trevor. He stood next to a pile of crates marked "machinery" and waited impatiently, hoping against hope that Trevor had managed to stay out of trouble. The town hall bell struck eight o'clock, each ring resounding throughout the city. With every peal of the bell, the city seemed to grow louder. Soon after the town hall bell began its song, so too did the various church bells. Relying on these bells for the time, whistles were blown to summon the workers of the city in to work. By the last chime of the town hall bell, Norton was a chiming, whistling, rumbling cacophony of noise.

Amidst all the noise, Matthew never heard Trevor approaching. He scanned the street ahead of him, oblivious to the creaking of the crates behind him.

"When you said first thing, you really meant it," Trevor laughed, once the noise of the city had abated. Matthew turned abruptly to see Trevor crouching atop the pile of crates, some ways above his head.

"Yeah," Matthew laughed nervously, "What did you do last night?"

"Boy, you really cut to the chase. I did what you told me, if that's what you're worried about." Trevor swung his legs over the side of the crates and hopped down, landing next to Matthew. "But other than that, I just had a little fun."

"Fun?" Matthew's voice and expression betrayed his mistrust.

"Hey, don't worry about it;" Trevor said nonchalantly, "I just hung around town."

"*Where* around town?" Matthew asked, sensing that Trevor was hiding something.

"Here and there," Trevor said, skirting around the subject, then changing it entirely, "So what did you find out? How are we gonna fix this thing so we can go back?"

Matthew decided to ignore Trevor's liberal use of the word "we" and deal with the problem at a later date. Right now, he had bigger fish to fry.

"Listen," Matthew began, "I asked Grace about how she built the... well, you know, and she started to explain it, but I could barely understand a word she said." He sighed heavily and buried his face in his hands.

"Well, what are we gonna do, then?" Trevor asked, "Why don't we just *ask* her to fix it and send us back?"

"I already told you," Matthew said from behind his hands, "That'll never work. When I first got here, I begged them to send me back, but they wouldn't. What makes you think they'll listen to you?"

Trevor put an arm around Matthew shoulder and stared into the bustling streets. "I have powers of persuasion, Matthew, I really do. You remember how I convinced that guy a while back to give us all that food he had back in Connolly Mills?"

Matthew nodded glumly. Though for Trevor it had happened a mere couple of months ago, for Matthew it had been almost over a year. However, he still remembered the occasion vividly.

"You blackmailed him," he said, "That's not convincing."

"Sure it is! So, listen, I'll just go tell Grace or whoever that if she doesn't fix the... the thing... I'll tell everyone around here your secret. She'll have to send us back, and everything will be back to the way it was!"

"Trevor, I can't let you blackmail my family! I—"

"Just shut up for a second and listen! It's not gonna do any harm! She'll fix the thing; we'll go back and leave them alone. It's perfect! Tell me one thing that's wrong with that, huh?"

"Trevor, I could tell you a million things wrong with that plan! It's wrong to begin with! You can't just blackmail someone into doing what you want!"

"Would ya stop with your *morals* for just a minute? This'll work, I know it will! And if it's the only thing that'll get us out of here, then we have to do it!"

He had Matthew stymied. Of course, the plan was *morally* wrong, but *technically* it was the best bet they had. He couldn't admit that to Trevor, but he needed to give him an answer. He decided, after a moment of silent contemplation, to compromise.

"Maybe you're right, but I'm saying maybe. Let me talk to Grace first though."

"Whatever, just hurry up about it, okay?"

"Sure. I've gotta go, stay out of trouble, alright?"

"You got it," Trevor gave a mock salute as Matthew walked out of the alley once more. Trevor had always been so sure of himself, like nothing he did could ever be wrong. He had never told Matthew about his life before he ended up on the streets, but Matthew suspected it wasn't very good. The boy had been brought up without any concept of right and wrong, and would do whatever he pleased to advance his position. Matthew wondered what he did in early twentieth century Norton all day long on his own. He was independent, but he had independently gotten himself into trouble before.

Matthew walked absent-mindedly through the streets, wondering what on earth to say to Grace and the others. He became quite bitter and began to mutter to himself as he walked.

"What am I supposed to say?" he mumbled. Matthew shook his head sourly, angry with the world and with himself. He hung his head and stared at the ground as he walked, not daring to look up and face reality.

"Matthew!"

Matthew's head snapped up and he found himself staring into the dark face of the source of the deep, rich voice he had just heard calling his name.

"Matthew! How good to see you!" Sam took his hand and pumped it up and down. Matthew could only smile. Sam was a man that the time travellers had met in Connolly Mills. When they first encountered him, Grace had discovered that he was illiterate, lacking all but a rudimentary grasp of reading and writing. She had offered to teach him, and he had accepted. Now, after the time Grace had spent teaching him when they lived in Connolly Mills and later Darcy Lake, Sam could read and write just as well as anyone else; perhaps even better.

When Matthew didn't speak, Sam continued. "You know, I was set to come here to look for some permanent work, you know how things are, and I met this young man about your age who wanted to come to Norton with me! It's a long road here, you know, and I couldn't resist the comp'ny. He was a pretty funny boy, though. A little strange, if you ask me. It's funny though, I just saw you talking to him! Can you believe it? It's a small world, eh, Matthew?"

"It sure is," Matthew managed, swallowing nervously, "It sure is." He endeavoured to change the subject. "Have you found any work yet?"

"Nothing steady yet, Matthew, but I will! I freighted a load to Norton for Mr. White on my way here, but I need to find myself a place to settle." Sam replied, his face beaming, his teeth a startling white in contrast to his dark face. Matthew had always liked Sam. He liked his accent, suggesting his African heritage, and he liked his honesty and uplifting optimism, which were always enough to brighten Matthew's day. Always, that is, except for today. Today, Sam's presence only served to make Matthew more worried about his situation with Trevor, especially since Sam served as a second link between Trevor and the rest of the time travellers. Sam, like everyone else in the past, had no idea that his friends were from any other time but this, and the time travellers wanted to keep it that way.

Sam interrupted Matthew's thoughts in that deep, warm voice of his. "Where is everyone?" he asked, "Where are you staying? I should go and see everyone, shouldn't I?"

"No," Matthew squeaked, so softly that Sam couldn't hear.

"I should thank Grace as well," Sam continued, "Come on, you can show me where you're all staying. Do you have a house, like in Darcy Lake?"

Matthew collected himself and found his voice. "No," he said, "We're staying at a boarding house." There was nothing Matthew could do; he had to bring Sam to see everyone. He couldn't lie to him. "I'll take you there," he finished, beginning to walk, "It's this way."

Matthew led the way as Sam talked. The man must have indeed been very happy to see him, for it seemed he would never stop talking. They arrived at the boarding house in no time at all, and Sam and Matthew climbed the steps together, Sam grinning from ear to ear at the prospect of surprising his old teacher.

They knocked, and the door was opened within moments. It was Mrs. Brown who had answered it, and she looked fondly at Matthew, and then noticed Sam standing next to him, hat in his hands. She glanced up at the stranger warily.

"Who's this, Matthew?" she asked, her voice clipped and nervous.

"This is Sam," Matthew replied, "An old friend of ours from Connolly Mills." Sam stepped forward and offered Mrs. Brown his hand.

"Very pleased to make your acquaintance, ma'am," he said politely. Mrs. Brown shook his hand, though Matthew could tell she was still a bit nervous.

"Please," she replied, "Do come in. Miss Perkins and the others are in the parlour."

Matthew walked in, trailed by Sam, who nodded his thanks to Mrs. Brown. She met his gaze with a nervous smile.

Matthew led Sam to the parlour, and as they entered, all eyes in the room turned to them.

"Sam!" Grace exclaimed, standing up and greeting her former pupil, "How are you? It's been such a long time!"

"Very well, thank you Grace," Sam replied, "Very good!" Grace, Sam, and Matthew took their seats, and Sam and the others exchanged greetings. The only other people in the room were Sandra, John, and Evan, who were all, with the exception of Evan, pleased to see their old friend. Evan and Sam had never been on good terms. Neither one had done anything to offend the other; they simply did not seem to like each other. Rather, it was Evan who disliked

Sam, which caused Sam to find himself disliking Evan. From the point of view of the other time travellers, the reason for the tension between the two was obvious, though Evan would never admit it. Evan was jealous of Sam, and of all the attention and affection that Grace showered upon her student. Matthew had always thought that perhaps Evan's jealousy was warranted, for Sam was indeed a very neat, clean, and good looking man with a heart of gold.

"You would never believe it," Sam began, and Matthew felt his stomach drop the floor as he continued, "But I was fixin' to come to Norton an' look for some work, and I met this young man just about Matthew's age. He told me he wanted to go to Norton and, well, I couldn't say no! He was a funny kid, his way of talkin' and all. He never did tell me his name, either. Matthew knows him though, don't you, Matthew? What was his name?"

"Whose name?" Matthew asked, cocking his head to one side in mock confusion.

"That boy you were jes' talkin' to," Sam explained, "Near the market. He's a little shorter than you, skin the colour of bronze, real thick, dark hair—"

"Him?" Matthew interrupted, not wanting Sam to describe Trevor any further lest someone realize who he was, "He was just an old school friend. I was just saying hello."

"But what was his name?" Sam wondered, seemingly desperate to know. Matthew began to feel sick again and his heart was racing. He didn't want to lie, but what choice did he have?

"I- I'm… I'm not sure," Matthew stuttered, "I don't remember, exactly…"

"Come on, Matthew," Grace chided, "You must know his name, you were just talking to him!"

"It was um… Jason," Matthew lowered his voice and averted his eyes, "Yeah. Jason." In fact, Jason was an old school friend of Matthew's from Darcy Lake, but he was certainly not Trevor. Sam nodded, to Matthew's relief, apparently satisfied.

The topic of Matthew's mysterious friend was then dropped, and Matthew remained silent for the rest of Sam's visit. As he sat and listened worriedly to their conversations Matthew noticed Mrs. Brown lingering in the doorway, almost as if she were afraid to come in. As he wasn't truly part of the conversation, Matthew figured it wouldn't go against etiquette for him to get up and cross the room to see Mrs. Brown, and he did so.

"Mrs. Brown?"

Mrs. Brown turned and looked towards the source of Matthew's voice, noticing him standing next to her.

"Yes, Matthew?"

"Why don't you go inside?"

"I'm sure they don't need me interrupting their conversation, dear,"

"They want you to go in," Matthew said, though he really didn't know what the others thought, "Go ahead, take my seat."

"Matthew, dear, I don't think you understand, it's not my place to interrupt on the social gatherings of my boarders..."

Upon hearing Mrs. Brown's voice, Grace turned around and saw her standing in the doorway, Matthew by her side.

"Mrs. Brown!" she exclaimed, "Please, join us."

Only Matthew noticed the frightened look on Mrs. Brown's face, but he led her to his chair anyway, and she sat down, forcing a smile. Matthew got the feeling she had more misgivings than simply intruding upon the social lives of her boarders.

When Mrs. Brown had sat down and seemed comfortable enough, Matthew bid everyone farewell and stepped outside again. Going up to his room would have seemed antisocial, but going out again made it look as though he had something important to do. Matthew decided to simply walk along the streets of Norton, and endeavour to stay as far away from Trevor or anyone else he knew along the way.

Matthew knew the layout of the city from a map that Mrs. Brown had hanging in the upstairs hallway. He had looked it over a number of times, and had familiarized himself with the names of all the different sectors and what they contained. Mrs. Brown's boarding house was located near the centre of the city, in the section that was called St. Edward's.

It could be said that St. Edward's functioned as Norton's downtown, for it housed the town hall, the main post office, and other important municipal buildings, as well as being residential.

To the west of St. Edward's was Irontown, the place of work for many of the city's labourers, including Mr Fitzgerald and Mr. Riddell. A district seemingly always lying beneath a pall of smoke, the people who lived and worked there had a sad history of lung ailments, and many went to an early grave because of it, along with the poor working conditions and a lack of proper safety regulations.

To the north lay Oakton, home of the large lumber yard and mill. Forever noisy and smelling of wood, it attracted many people, if only for the promise of work.

Far to the east, away from the smoke of Irontown and the noise of Oakton, was the King's Park district. This was where the wealthiest inhabitants of the city made their home. It was clean, and boasted the tallest, grandest buildings displaying the latest architectural fashions. It was a place that many in the city, particularly the inhabitants of the Southern Quays, only dreamed of living.

The Southern Quays was the southernmost district, as indicated by its name, and it was also the poorest. The people who lived there often scratched out a meagre existence, and those who didn't fancy helping each other helped themselves to whatever they could lay their hands on, regardless of who it may have belonged to. "Finders Keepers" seemed to be the guiding principle for many who resided in the Quays, and even walking through it was enough to leave one's head spinning and heart sinking.

Matthew, however, was one of the few in the city to genuinely like the Southern Quays. He would never have wanted to live there, but he enjoyed walking through it from time to time. He never felt that he was in any danger from the petty thieves and gangs that claimed their territory there, for he had nothing of value for them to force from him. Matthew simply liked the feeling of the place. It had always felt so much more real than the other districts; the people who lived there so much more human. At the bottom of the social ladder, most in the Quays didn't concern themselves with the shallow etiquette and pretentious rules of society, but rather simply tried to make a life for themselves and their families. Children would run barefoot in the streets without a care in the world, clothes lines ran from building to building far above the heads of the inhabitants below. The houses were packed quite close together, and little sunlight ever seemed to make its way to the cobbles below.

It was towards the south that Matthew decided to go that day, for he was certain that no one would find him there, nor even think to look. Mrs. Brown's boarding house was on the southern end of St. Edward's, and it didn't take long for Matthew to find himself immersed in the eternal gloom that was the Southern Quays. He walked through the cobbled streets slowly, not wanting to attract any attention, and watched as the children played and splashed in the mud by the sides of the road. He noticed unemployed men attempting to fix their crumbling homes, and weary housewives struggling to keep everything in order and everyone's needs met. Members of gangs eyed Matthew as he passed by, many of them no older than him, and some even younger. Scantily clad women on the balconies of houses of ill repute waved down at him, and Matthew found himself blushing and regretting his decision to walk down that particular road.

Nevertheless, Matthew continued on, passing next a run down saloon from which drifted the sounds of drunken laughter and clinking glasses. Some places in the Quays, he knew, ran illegal taverns and bars, as well as gambling houses. Gambling was the way that many in this part of the city attempted to make a living, and it was also the way that many had ended up in such a terrible financial state that they were forced to live in the Southern Quays in the first place.

As Matthew continued to walk on, he passed an old house that looked to be falling apart in every which way. The wooden door was rotting, shingles were falling off the roof, the paint was chipping, and the uppermost front window was smashed in, the tattered curtains blowing in the wind. Ivy was growing from the ground all the way up to the roof and across the façade of the house, giving it the appearance of being strangled by the vines that attached themselves to the bricks and mortar.

Matthew looked upon the house with interest, and saw a figure emerge, burly, middle aged, and angry. The door slammed behind him and he gave the wooden banister that surrounded the veranda a vicious kick, causing it to crack and fall, hanging helplessly into the street. Matthew watched as he stomped down the steps and into the street, and thought it best to stay out of his way. He continued to observe the man from the side of the veranda, ducking behind a piece of the banister the man had knocked loose. He was evidently the loser of some game of chance or another that had just been played inside that house, and appeared to be a poor sport. Matthew heard the door creak open once more and looked up to see the winner, a wad of bills in his hands. His heart nearly stopped.

"Oh, no…"

CHAPTER FIVE

Time is Money

Trevor folded up the wad of bills and stuffed the whole lot into his pocket, his face beaming. After a moment, though, his expression changed. Trevor was very intelligent, Matthew realized as he squinted up at him through the bars of the rotting banister; he didn't want to draw attention to the fact that he had quite a large sum of money, so he kept his expression neutral and hid the bills in his jacket. However, as intelligent as he may have been with regards to his money, he wasn't very skilful at obeying the law. And Matthew, it seemed, wasn't very good at staying out of Trevor's way.

"Matthew!" Trevor exclaimed, upon seeing him crouching behind the banister, "What are you doing here?"

Matthew emerged from where he had been hiding and brushed the decaying wood chips from his sleeves and trousers.

"Nothing," Matthew replied casually, "Just passing through. What are *you* doing here?"

Trevor smiled excitedly and beckoned for Matthew to come closer, then showed him the corners of the bills in his pocket. Matthew feigned surprise.

"Thirty dollars!" Trevor whispered, "I won thirty dollars in there, and hey, I know it doesn't sound like a lot, but I've seen what thirty dollars can get you around here."

"Trevor, I don't think you understand," Matthew began, "This is illegal! You could get into a lot of trouble! Not only are you young, but—"

"Hey, don't talk to me like I'm a little kid, I'm older than you are! And besides, a few games never hurt anybody, and I wasn't cheating or anything. I never did anything *wrong*. Besides it being illegal, name one thing I did wrong. I didn't cheat; I didn't count cards or load the dice or whatever."

Once again, Trevor had Matthew confounded. He couldn't think of anything inherently *wrong* with what

Trevor had done, and if it kept him from stealing and swindling, how could Matthew tell him not to? After all, Trevor was using his own money and his own judgement, so who was he hurting? Matthew decided to leave the subject alone for the time being.

"Just don't get hurt or anything," he said, dismissing the fact that his old friend was completely disregarding him and the law. He turned to leave when Trevor reached out and grabbed him by the shoulder.

"Did you talk to Grace yet?" he asked.

"No," Matthew admitted, "But I will. She's gotta be in the right mood or else you're stuck here forever."

Trevor accepted his answer with a quick nod, and Matthew walked quietly away as the twelve o'clock bell chimed on the town hall far ahead of him. Matthew broke into a run. He hadn't realized how late it was until he heard the bell, and he dreaded missing the midday meal again. He didn't have any money and so couldn't buy his food in the market, and he envied Mr. Riddell and Mr. Fitzgerald their packed lunches, to be eaten at work.

Before long, Matthew arrived back at the boarding house, catching his breath as he climbed the front steps. He sauntered inside unceremoniously, and walked into the dining room to find a very welcome, yet unexpected sight. The time travellers, save for Mr. Riddell and Mr. Fitzgerald, were seated around the table with Mrs. Brown and Sam, and they were laughing! Matthew paused to observe them and smiled, forgetting his troubles for just a moment. Mrs. Brown no longer seemed in the least bit uncomfortable around Sam, and Grace, Evan, Sandra, and John were all enjoying themselves immensely. Grace was the first to notice Matthew standing in the doorway.

"Matthew! Come in and sit down," she said, "We were just finishing. Have you eaten?" Matthew shook his head. Mrs. Brown stood up abruptly.

"I'll fix you something to eat," she said sweetly, "Have a seat, dear."

Mrs. Brown disappeared into the kitchen as Matthew took a seat next to Grace.

"I think she's starting to like you," Grace said, addressing Sam. Sam smiled.

"I hope so," he replied.

"I know so," Sandra chipped in, "She has no reason not to."

"Sandra, when you live in my skin, you see that there doesn't have to be a reason for some folks," Sam answered wisely; "They jes' don't like you." Sandra nodded in understanding. The boarders sat in silence, contemplating Sam's statement sombrely.

Mrs. Brown returned with a flourish and placed a steaming bowl of soup in front of Matthew, who thanked her and began to eat, though his predicament involving Trevor still weighed on his appetite. Matthew became lost in thought as the adults around him chattered animatedly. Every so often, Matthew would look up nervously, thinking that he had heard his name, or worse, Trevor's. He only finished half his soup before he found that he could no longer stomach any more food. He sat in silence, almost motionless, until Mrs. Brown left to go to the market, and Sam announced he had to leave if he was ever going to find a job, and Evan, Grace, and John went with him. Sandra, though John tried to persuade her to accompany them, opted to stay behind with Matthew, Laura, and Eddie. Once Laura and Eddie had left the table and gone to play upstairs, Sandra spoke.

"Matthew," she said, prompting Matthew to look up at her, "Are you feeling alright?"

"I'm fine," Matthew responded quickly, "Why do you ask?"

Sandra smiled wryly. "Don't think I haven't noticed that you haven't eaten much in the last few days. You're going to get sick, you know!"

"Really," Matthew answered, "I'm fine."

"No," Sandra chided, "You're not." She smiled caringly at him, but he couldn't see her, his eyes cast down towards his feet.

"Matthew," Sandra reached across the table, and took his hand, "Look at me." Matthew raised his head and Sandra could see tears glistening in his eyes.

"What's going on?" she asked gently.

"It's nothing," Matthew tried to convince her, blinking the tears away, his voice cracking, "Nothing."

"Evidently," Sandra said matter-of-factly, "It's not nothing." She passed him a clean handkerchief.

"Thanks," Matthew sniffed, "But, really, I'm fine." Sandra gave him a despondent look, and Matthew knew that he had to tell her, right then and there.

"If I tell you," he managed, "You have to promise you won't tell anyone else. Please." He looked at Sandra desperately.

"That depends on what it is, Matthew," Sandra reasoned, "But I'll see what I can do."

"You have to promise. Please. Please."

"Alright," Sandra agreed, "I promise."

"Well," Matthew began, drying his eyes, "I was walking through the- the market one day, and I... I was going to send a- a letter. I ran into someone and lost it, and it flew up to the roof on one of the buildings. I ran to get it, and climbed up and... and..." He paused to collect himself with a long, shaky breath. "Do you remember Trevor?"

Sandra nodded, her stomach sinking as she slowly began to realize what Matthew was insinuating.

"He was on the roof," Matthew admitted, "He's here. He came looking for me, and found the time machine... He came to Norton with Sam, and he's out on the streets right now... and... and... I don't," he paused and sniffled, "I don't know what to do..."

"Oh, Matthew," Sandra lamented, "I wish you'd have told me earlier."

Matthew nodded. "I know," he whispered, "I know. I didn't want anyone to worry, I didn't... I didn't want anything to change. Everything's been so good lately for everyone, and I've ruined it..."

Sandra stood and shuffled around the table, then took both of Matthew's hands in her own. "Matthew," she said, sternly but gently, "You mustn't ever blame yourself. It's not your fault, and it never was. You know that, don't you?" Matthew nodded glumly.

"You still won't tell anyone?"

"I might have to, Matthew, Trevor does pose a big risk to us. His being here is very dangerous."

"And so is his going back," Matthew finished for her, hanging his head, 'That's what he wants to do. He wants Grace to send him back, and he wants me to go too."

"Do you want to go?"

Matthew raised his head, fixing Sandra with an astonished stare. "Of course not!" he nearly shouted, "You, and Grace, and everyone… you're the best thing that's ever happened to me, and I told Trevor that, but he wouldn't listen…"

"Well, he's going to have to, because we're not going to let anything happen to you, do you understand?"

Matthew nodded. "So, can we send him back alone?"

"I don't see why not," Sandra said, "As long as we can be sure he won't reveal our secret to everyone back in the present."

"How can you be sure?"

"We can't. Ultimately, it'll be Grace who decides what to do about him, but the sooner we do *something* and get rid of the time machine again, the better."

"That's the problem," Matthew explained, "Something happened to the time machine."

Sandra fought to remain calm, though inside, she felt like screaming. "What happened?" she asked, hardly daring to breathe.

"It fell off the wagon on the way here, and it's in about a million little pieces."

Sandra's stomach dropped to the floor. "Does he have it?"

Matthew nodded and wiped his eyes. "It's hidden on the roof of the building I told you about. I think it's another boarding house."

"Matthew, listen to me. We need to tell everyone about this, especially Grace."

"Okay, but I have to warn you," Matthew cautioned her, "If she decides, like I think she will, that Trevor is too much of a risk to send back, Trevor is going to threaten to tell everyone about us all."

"You don't know that…"

"He told me," Matthew nodded solemnly, "I know."

"Alright," Sandra attempted to collect herself, "Would you like me to tell Grace, or do you want to?"

Matthew took a deep breath. "I'll tell her," he said, "I don't want to, but I will. It's best that way."

Sandra looked at him fondly. "Okay," she replied, "Whatever you say." She paused as Matthew moved to stand up. "And Matthew?"

"Yes?"

"Try not to worry too much, alright? We'll figure this out."

Matthew could only nod as he left the room, drying his eyes and breathing shakily. It felt good to let someone else share the burden, but it also made him feel sick to his stomach, knowing that he had to tell Grace and the others what had happened, and that if Trevor didn't get his way, he was going to blackmail them into giving him a way back to the present.

Sandra watched him leave, her heart heavy and mind reeling at the revelation. Yet again, they were in danger of being found out, and as much as she had told Matthew not to worry, and assured him that it may be possible to send Trevor back, she knew, deep down, that Grace would say a firm *no*. Once more, their world had been turned upside down, and Sandra sensed that this was only the beginning of their troubles.

Later that day, when the sun was slowing descending, a wobbling sphere on the horizon, the boarders at Mrs. Brown's were just arriving back, Sam in tow. Mrs. Brown welcomed them all inside, and they took their seats in the parlour while Mrs. Brown and Mr. Riddell cooked supper. Matthew arrived in the parlour just in time for Sam's big announcement.

"I've found work!" he proclaimed triumphantly, "I'm going to leave tomorrow morning for Connolly Mills on the train and pack up the rest of my things, and I'll be back very soon! I've already sold my wagon to pay for the trip and lodgings here in Norton!"

Congratulations ensued. The time travellers patted him on the back, shook his hand, told him they were proud. Even Evan wished him well. Matthew was glad he had found work, but also that he would be leaving for a while. It was a long ride to and from Norton, and it would give Matthew enough time to tell Grace about Trevor without implicating the poor man.

Grace invited Sam to stay for supper, and he was delighted to accept. Mrs. Brown was still reluctant, but she couldn't say no when she saw how happy the invitation made him. They ate heartily, without a care in the world, save of course for Sandra and Matthew, neither of whom could quite find room for more than a few bites of the delicious meal. Mrs. Brown looked at them both with disapproval.

"Now, don't you tell me you're not hungry," she scolded, "Mr. Riddell and I prepared this meal special for all of you! Eat up!"

Matthew and Sandra exchanged nervous glances and began to eat once more, taking slow, laboured bites, fighting to finish every last crumb. It was an uphill battle, but they won, even though they felt sicker than ever.

Once Mrs. Brown had dismissed everyone from the table, Sandra hung back as Matthew rose and cleared his plate. When she was certain it was just the two of them left in the kitchen, she spoke.

"How are you feeling?" she asked gently.

"Not so good," Matthew replied, placing a hand over his stomach, "I haven't been able to eat or sleep ever since I found Trevor."

Sandra nodded. "I understand," she said, "But this is a problem we have to face up to, or it'll only get worse."

"I know," Matthew sighed, "I know."

"The sooner you tell Grace the better, and then we can set to fixing things." Sandra certainly sounded worlds more confident than she felt. Matthew nodded in agreement. He looked at Sandra, and found that he was almost just as tall as she was now. He remembered with a pang of nostalgia how short he had been in comparison when they had all first arrived in the past, almost one year ago.

"Could you tell everyone I've gone to bed?" he asked Sandra, "I don't feel much like being around anyone tonight."

"Of course, Matthew," Sandra promised, "I'll see you in the morning."

Matthew thanked her and crossed the house, then climbed up the stairs towards his bedroom. He knew that Eddie would be up in a couple of hours, but he figured that gave him enough time to think about how he was going to tell Grace about Trevor. He was glad Sandra was being so firm about the subject and he didn't have to decide what to do for himself, for if that were the case, Grace may never find out about Trevor until the boy decided he was tired of waiting and put his blackmail plan into action.

Matthew sat down in the desk chair and kicked off his shoes. The world had been so much simpler a few days ago, but now he was left to figure out how on earth he was to inform Grace of Trevor's dangerous presence. Instead of worrying, which seemed to be all Matthew had been doing lately, he decided to try and sleep on the matter, for perhaps, things would, as they say, all seem better in the morning. Matthew doubted it, but thought it might be worth a try, seeing as he had been lacking sleep of late. With that thought in mind, he undressed, washed his face, and went to bed.

Matthew lay down under the covers, but even with his blankets and nightclothes, he felt impossibly cold. He tried to stop thinking about Trevor, and what he knew he had to do in the morning, but it seemed an unattainable feat. No matter how hard he tried—closing his eyes tight shut, counting his heart beats, listening to his own breathing—Matthew simply could not find sleep. It was as though it was hiding, forever running away as he fought to catch it. It was exhausting, yet sleep still would not come, and Matthew began to worry that he might become quite ill if he didn't find some way to finally catch a few winks. In all, Matthew slept for three hours that night, and what sleep he did manage to get was plagued with worried dreams and general discomfort.

Finally, morning arrived, the sun peeking over the grand, imposing buildings of King's park. Matthew lay awake in bed, hands folded under his head, wondering what Trevor was doing at that moment. How much had *he* slept? How much had *he* eaten? Matthew wondered with a wry smile if Trevor had spent his winnings on food, or whether he had stuck to his old habits of pilfering and scavenging for his living.

Today was the day, Matthew was certain. Today was the day he would tell Grace about Trevor, and tonight was the night he would finally get a good night's sleep. As nervous as Matthew was about telling her, he knew that he would feel better once he did, like he had felt when he told Sandra, only on a larger scale. Grace, unlike Sandra, was a born leader, and if *she* didn't know what to do, no one would.

Matthew peered to his left to see Eddie's small form lying under the blankets in the next bed over. If Matthew looked really closely, he could see the rise and fall of Eddie's chest as he breathed, softly and quietly. Matthew smiled, glad that he had quiet little Eddie for a roommate instead of someone who snored, as Laura was rumoured to do on occasion. Not wanting to wake the boy from his peaceful slumber, Matthew decided to remain in bed until he awoke, or at least until the sun came streaming full force through their window.

When Matthew finally allowed himself to emerge from his room that morning, he came into the hallway and found Sandra slipping quietly from her room. She too seemed as though she hadn't slept much, and there were dark circles under her eyes.

"Sleep well?" Matthew asked, his lips twisting into a joking smile. Sandra smiled back bitterly.

"Barely," she replied, "But everything will be fine. Are you going to talk to Grace today?"

Matthew nodded silently and the pair of them headed downstairs to a hearty breakfast. Grace seemed to be in a particularly good mood that morning, which made what Matthew had to do even harder than it already was. After they had all eaten and Mr. Fitzgerald and Mr. Riddell had gone off to work, Matthew stopped Grace on her way up the stairs.

"Grace," he whispered timidly, "Can I talk to you for a minute?"

"Of course, Matthew," she smiled, turning to face him, "I'm listening."

"Well, you see…" Matthew began, fidgeting a couple steps below her, "There's something you should probably kn—"

"Matthew! Could you come here a moment?"

Matthew spun round upon hearing his name. It was Sandra who had called him, and it sounded as though her voice was coming from the kitchen.

"I'll tell you later," Matthew turned back to Grace before dashing down the remaining few steps and racing into the kitchen. He found Sandra standing near the kitchen window, pale as a sheet. Matthew advanced slowly, dreading what Sandra had to say, for he knew it could be nothing good. Her nervous tone had told him all he needed to know.

"There's, uh, someone here to see you," she muttered, stepping aside for Matthew to peer cautiously out the window. Matthew was confronted by the face of Trevor, who was smiling, albeit a bit strangely. It seemed as though he was hiding something.

"Hey, Matthew!" he said brightly, which only made Matthew more suspicious, "Listen, have you talked to Grace yet? You see, the sooner I get outta here the better, you know, and I'm getting kinda tired of waiting, so you better hurry up or I'm gonna hafta take over, okay?"

"Trevor!" Matthew said in a harsh whisper, "What are you doing here? You're just lucky I already told Sandra, or you'd have a whole lot of explaining to do! What did you come here for? I'd have met you in the alley! What's the big rush all of a sudden?"

"Hey, I don't really have time to explain," Trevor complained hurriedly, glancing left and right, "Just tell Grace already and get me outta here!"

"Can't you wait just a little longer? I was about to tell Grace a minute ago!"

"I actually *can't* wait," Trevor endeavoured to explain, "In fact, why don't you just let me in and I'll talk to Grace myself? That'd be a load off your mind, right?"

"No, Trevor, it wouldn't. What has gotten into you?"

"Nothing, just let me in!"

"I can't just let you in! There are people here, people who don't know about you! What's going on?"

"I told you, nothing! Let me in, please!"

"Trevor, I don't know wh—"

Matthew was interrupted by the sound of shouts coming from outside, and it seemed that they were getting closer. Suddenly, Matthew had an inkling as to what was going on.

"Trevor, what did you do?" he hissed in a stage whisper.

"Nothing!" Trevor implored him, "I was just back at that house again when those cops came running in outta nowhere! I ran here, 'cause I knew you'd help me, but they followed me. Now come on, help a brother out?"

Trevor sounded desperate, and Matthew knew that if he was caught by the police, it could spell the end of everything for them. Trevor, unversed in the ways of this past world, would surely be found out. Who knows what they would do with him? Then again, any connection found between Trevor and the time travellers could be a disaster for them as well. There was only one thing to do.

Matthew opened the window further and offered his friend his hand. Trevor reached up to take it, but just as he was about to grab hold and be pulled to safety, his hand jerked back and he let out a cry. Matthew looked up to see two constables, badges gleaming in the morning sunlight, each with a hold on Trevor's arms.

"I know you want to help your friend, son," the one on Trevor's left arm said gruffly, "But there's a place for boys like him. You stay out of his trouble." He tugged Trevor's arm roughly and the pair of them dragged him away, down the street and out of sight.

CHAPTER SIX

Time to Learn

Sandra and Matthew stood motionless, Matthew's hand still stretched out the window, and both of their jaws hanging open. Slowly, Matthew withdrew his hand and let it hang limply by his side.

"We're gonna have to tell Grace about this, aren't we?" he whispered. Sandra could only nod, and the two of them turned on their heels and ran towards the other side of the house and up the stairs. Sandra was the first to Grace's door, and didn't miss a beat as she knocked urgently.

"Grace?" she cried, loudly, yet nervously, "Grace, are you in there? We need to talk to you!"

Grace emerged from the room in a split second, reacting quickly to what she perceived as a crisis.

"What's going on?" she asked, "Is everyone alright? Did something happen?"

Sandra was slow to answer, and Matthew beat her to it. "It's something that I should have told you a long time ago," he panted, still winded from their rush up the stairs, "But that I have to tell you now."

So, Matthew started from the beginning, as he had with Sandra, and how he first met Trevor in the market while chasing his letter, and he continued until the moment that he and Sandra had seen Trevor dragged away just minutes ago. With every word he spoke, Grace's eyes seemed to grow wider and wider, and her mouth gape open evermore. When Matthew had finished, it took her a moment to find her words.

"We need to go down there and get him out," she decided, walking past Matthew and Sandra and starting down the stairs, "Before he says something he shouldn't. Matthew, you come with me to do that. Sandra, go tell Evan and John what's happened and go find the—" Grace stopped at the bottom of the stairs and shut her mouth as Mrs. Brown walked by, smiling up at the three of them.

"Time machine," Grace finished, so quietly that Sandra barely heard her, "Got it?" Sandra nodded and raced away to find Evan and John, while Matthew continued to follow Grace. They reached the front door, and without pausing for even a moment, marched purposefully down the steps and into Norton's bustling streets. The nearest police stationhouse was across the street from the post office, and Grace decided against taking a carriage for such a short distance. It would only hinder them.

They arrived at the stationhouse post haste, and Grace marched straight up to the front desk, behind which sat a bored looking constable.

"Excuse me," she said, "It has been brought to my attention that a young man has just been arrested, and he needs to be let out so I may bring him home."

The constable at the desk removed his wire rimmed glasses and used them to point at Grace.

"You his mother?" he asked, his voice deep and gruff.

"In a manner of speaking, yes," Grace huffed, "So please take me to the boy and let him out of your cells."

The constable narrowed his eyes at Grace, but nevertheless, he stepped down from the desk and led her and Matthew down to the cells, which were located in the basement of the building. They were made for holding people for a short time, before they could be properly tried and convicted, then sent away to prison. Many who stayed there were simply vagrants and drunks, who stayed for a night, were released, and promptly returned to their habitual ways. Matthew glanced at the dark gloomy surroundings and shivered, hoping against hope that he would never end up in such a dismal place. When Matthew and Grace arrived with the constable, Trevor leapt from where he had been seated on the small cot in the corner of the cell and clutched at the bars.

"See?" he cried, addressing the constable, who still maintained his look of boredom, "I told you they'd come for me!" He turned to Grace and Matthew. "You've come to bail me out, right?"

"You could say that," Grace began, her voice holding a certain underlying tone of menace that Trevor did not seem to detect. "Let him out please," Grace continued, "And I assure you, you'll never catch him doing anything untoward again."

"What do I get in return for letting him go?"

Grace's eyes widened. "Are you speaking of bribes, sir?" She contorted her face into a look of shock. "You yourself could be arrested for suggesting such a thing. I certainly hope you don't take bribes for criminals worse than this!"

The constable looked astonished, and nervous that Grace might expose him. He took barely a moment to decide, and since he had never before seen Trevor, decided, just this once, to let him off with a warning. He unlocked the cell and Trevor stepped out, a look of ill-concealed triumph on his face. Grace, thoroughly annoyed, took Trevor by the ear and began to drag him away, her skirts brushing the bars of the cells.

"Hey!" Trevor protested, desperately trying to keep up so that his ear would remain firmly attached to his head, "What are you—ow!"

Grace didn't let go of Trevor's ear until they were safely outside the stationhouse, where she turned to face him.

"I have half a mind," she said, "To give you a good beating! What on earth do you think this is, some kind of game?" She lowered her voice to a menacing whisper. "Just because you're not in your own time doesn't give you license to break the law!" Trevor opened his mouth to protest, but Grace continued on before he had a chance to speak. "And don't play innocent either, I know Matthew warned you and told you not to gamble!" Trevor shut his mouth, lost for words for perhaps the first time in his life.

"Now," Grace decided, straightening up and clapping her hands, "We are going back to the boarding house, you're going to explain yourself, and then we'll decide what to do with you." She began to walk, leading the way through the busy streets, striding so fast that

Trevor and Matthew nearly had to run to keep pace. Matthew couldn't help but feel that Grace blamed him for what was happening. After all, if Matthew hadn't found the time machine in the first place all that time ago, and sent himself back, Trevor never would have found it. Then again, Matthew wondered if this was simply the price he had to pay for being able to live with such a loving and wonderful family. If it was, he maintained it was well worth it.

The trio arrived back at the boarding house within minutes, and there they met Sandra, John, and Evan. Mrs. Brown, luckily, had promised the day before to take Laura and Eddie out to the park with her to feed the ducks, so she was not in the house when they returned. Nevertheless, Grace thought it best to conduct their meeting upstairs in one of the bedrooms, in case she returned early.

John and Sandra lay the time machine, or what was left of it, carefully out on Evan's bed. They sat Trevor down in an armchair and stood in a semi circle in front of him, as though they were conducting an interrogation. Matthew fidgeted where he stood between Evan and Grace. Grace was positioned directly across from Trevor, hands on her hips and her eyes shooting him a mean glare. Evan had much the same look in his eyes, and his arms folded across his chest. John and Sandra, who stood on Grace's other side, met each other's gaze for a fleeting moment, then both fixed their eyes on the floor. Trevor's expression was difficult for Matthew to place. He seemed glad to be out of the dank cells of the police stationhouse, but he also looked quite nervous, an emotion Matthew wasn't sure he had ever seen on his stony features before that day.

"So... are you gonna fix this thing and let me go home?" he asked innocently, nodding towards the broken time machine. Grace bit her tongue. She hadn't come to a decision yet, and wanted to be sure of herself before she did anything that she would regret.

"We'll see," Evan answered for her, "We'll see. Matthew tells me you ended up in those cells because you were *gambling*," Evan continued, spitting out the last word as though it left a bad taste in his mouth, "Is that true?" Matthew glanced up at Evan in confusion. He looked so self-righteous, even though he was himself known for gambling on occasion.

"Well…" Trevor fidgeted in his seat and shot Matthew a desperate look. Matthew gently shook his head. Even accounting for the many scrapes that Trevor had gotten him out of in the past, Trevor deserved to be in this one, and Matthew couldn't help him.

"Well, what?" Evan tapped his foot impatiently.

"Okay, so it's true, what's the big deal?"

"The *big deal* is that now we're all in danger of being found out because of you!" Evan shouted, "Do you have any *idea—"*

"He has an idea, Evan," Grace huffed impatiently, "I've already talked to him. The big question is: Why, Trevor, do you think that I'm going to let you go back? Don't you think that I would have some concerns about letting you return? I mean, it's not like there's anyone there to make sure that you don't tell everyone our secret, is there?"

"I swear I won't," Trevor replied earnestly, "I promise! Really, I won't!"

"Well, Trevor," Grace said, "Since you seem to think yourself so clever, what do you think a reasonable solution would be to assure that you won't tell anyone in the present about the time machine?"

"Look," Trevor began, stretching out his upturned hands in an attempt to get his point across, "I barely even believe all this, and I sure wouldn't if I wasn't actually here, so what makes you think that anyone'll believe me? I'm just some street kid, after all, it's not like I'm the president of the United States or something."

"He has a point," Matthew stated simply, in an attempt to please both parties involved. He only succeeded in pleasing one: Trevor, who smiled weakly up at him with gratitude, yet another emotion rarely seen on Trevor's face.

"See?" Trevor tried to persuade them, "When Matthew and I go, you'll never hear from us or anyone else in the present—er, future... whatever, ever again!"

"*Matthew*," Grace informed him, "Is not going anywhere."

"What? Aw, c'mon, Matthew, I told ya to think about it! You can't seriously want to stay in this stupid place, can you?"

Matthew shrugged. "It's home," he said simply.

"We never had a home before!" Trevor complained, "Why do you need one now? You got family, you got me! We did okay out there, didn't we?"

Matthew nodded. "Sure," he agreed, prompting a smug look of triumph to emerge on Trevor's features, "But I like it here better, and my family," he gestured to the other time travellers, "Is important to me."

"Hey," Trevor countered, "Family can't be that important or I would have one. I'm fine on my own if you don't want to come, but just know that my door is always open if you decide you value your freedom."

"I'll keep that in mind."

Grace, having been thinking while the boys talked, looked up as they fell silent.

"Now that that's settled," she said at last, "I think it's time to make a decision." She looked down the row at the other time travellers, both to her left and her right.

"I think," Grace started to say, "That, though there are risks, we should send Trevor back, if we can." Trevor let out a sigh of relief, and Sandra suppressed a surprised gasp. "It would be more risky to keep him here than to return him to where he came from."

"How long until you fix that thing?" Trevor asked, motioning towards the time machine, "Is it really bad?"

Grace gave the remains of the time machine the once over and ran her hand over some of the strange metal wires and gears. "It's awful," she stated, "But I think I can fix it. Until then," she looked up at Trevor, staring straight into his eyes, which made him flinch ever so slightly, "You're going to stay here."

"*What? Here?*" Trevor cried, gripping the arms of the chair with white knuckled ferocity, "I can't stay here! Won't I be a risk or something? Shouldn't you keep me as far away as possible?"

"Nice try," Evan chimed in, "But we need to keep an eye on you. I don't see what the big deal is though. You get free room and board, free food, *delightful* company..." Evan trailed off with a sly smile as Trevor glared at him.

"Sandra," Grace announced, "I need you to figure out how to tell Mrs. Brown she's got another boarder..." Sandra obeyed and left the room, followed by John, leaving only Evan, Grace, and Matthew in the room with Trevor.

"Are you *ever* in a good mood?" Trevor asked, nodding to Grace with a weak laugh.

"I am," Grace affirmed, "But I won't be until we get this sorted out."

"Until we get the time machine fixed," Evan said, filling the silence that followed, "We'll need to get you up to date, with this time and everything. Isn't that right, Grace?" Grace nodded seriously.

"There's a lot you need to know," she informed him, "And I think for you it's best to start with the laws of today." Grace crossed the room and pulled an old, tattered volume off of Evan's beside table, then handed it to Trevor.

"*Criminal Code,*" Trevor read, and turned the book over in his hands, "Look," he said, in all seriousness, "I've never been really up to date with the laws in my *own* time. Rules aren't really my thing." He tried to hand the book back to Grace, but she wouldn't take it.

Grace was beginning to become even more frustrated with the boy. It had been much easier teaching Matthew, back when they had first arrived in the past. Though Matthew had wanted to return to the present just as much as Trevor did, he was much less outspoken and certainly not as resistant to authority.

"Well," Grace told him in her commanding voice while nudging the book back towards him, "You're going to have to get over that. We'll start with the laws on gambling."

"Oh, oh, I know this one!" Trevor announced sarcastically, "Illegal!"

Grace smiled derisively. "Well, we'll move on then. How about vagrancy? Do you know what the penalty for that is?"

Evan looked at Grace with surprise evident in his features. Normally, that sort of sarcasm and derision was beneath her, but with Trevor, it seemed she had different standards.

Trevor swore and leaned back in his seat. "I might," he answered leisurely, "If you told me what kind of a word *vagrancy* is."

"Vagrancy," Evan answered, taking some of the pressure off of Grace, "Is when a person has no visible means of subsistence, and wanders around, lodging in places like railway cars, deserted buildings, or when someone refuses or neglects to work for a living, etcetera, etcetera."

Trevor leaned forwards in his seat and fixed Evan and Grace with a cold, accusing glare. "You mean me?" he asked, daring them to agree.

Suddenly, Grace felt immensely guilty for her spiteful insinuations. She knew she shouldn't have been so mean, but something about Trevor's attitude towards the world made her want to spite him, to return his complacency right back to him. She knew it was wrong, and vowed to herself that she would be more patient from then on, though it would be difficult. One look at Evan's face told her that he felt the same way. After all, it wasn't Trevor's fault that he had ended up on the streets in the first place.

"I'm sorry, Trevor," Grace quickly apologized, "I never meant to say—"

"No, no, go on," said Trevor, waving his hand for her to continue, "Tell me all the ways I'm breaking your precious laws. I'd love to know them all. I'm sure stealing's in there, and breaking and entering, and a few other things I've probably done."

Grace shot Matthew a distressed look, something entirely uncommon to see on her face. Matthew had to stop himself from laughing at that, for he felt sure that her expression was just the sort of look Matthew had given her on multiple occasions, whenever he felt unsure or lost. Matthew took the hint and stepped up to Trevor's chair.

"We should probably go, Trevor," he said, holding out a hand to help him up, "Have you eaten?"

"I'm not hungry," Trevor replied, swatting Matthew's outstretched hand aside, "I want to hear about what a terrible person I am. Wouldn't you like to stay and listen?"

Matthew was getting tired of this, and resisted the urge to tap his foot impatiently. "You're not a bad person, Trevor," he attempted to assure him, "Now let's go."

Several moments of silence followed, until Trevor rose from his chair and tossed the criminal code to the floor, then marched straight out of the room without speaking a word. Matthew glanced at Grace and Evan, then ran out of the room after his friend.

Matthew caught up with Trevor near the bottom of the stairs and placed a hand on his shoulder. Before he could speak, Trevor turned on him, his face red.

"Just leave me alone, would you?" he shouted, then swore loudly. Matthew flinched as he continued down the remaining stairs and through the hall.

"Trevor, they didn't mean it! You have to understand they just—"

Trevor had reached the front door, opened it swiftly, then slammed it behind him, leaving Matthew with a smarting nose. Without pausing, Matthew threw the door open again and bounced down a few steps, looking this way and that, trying to relocate his old friend. Trevor, however, was nowhere to be seen, having disappeared into the bustling throng of the streets of Norton. Matthew supposed he would be heading towards the market, and the rooftop he seemed so fond of, so he headed off in that direction post haste.

Matthew ran through the market, barging past wagons and pedestrians alike. Soon, he arrived in the alley. He pushed the heavy wooden crates aside and dashed to the end of the alley and up the stairs. He landed on the top balcony, and thought he heard someone shouting at him, but he ignored it and pressed on, scaling the balcony as best he could. Once he had reached the rooftop, Matthew stood and brushed himself down, then continued on, slowly and quietly, towards the chimney, where he felt sure Trevor would be.

Sure enough, Matthew's shadow fell across his friend as he rounded the chimney. Trevor's jaw was set in defiance and Matthew could have sworn he saw the faintest glimmer of tears in his eyes. Matthew sat down beside him.

"Trevor," he began gently, "They didn't mean to upset you…"

Trevor snorted scornfully. "Sure," he said, "Sure they didn't. But who cares? It's true, isn't it?"

"Just because it might be true doesn't make that who *you* are," Matthew replied in a near whisper, searching his friend's face for any sign of forgiveness.

"Yeah, well, I think I know who, and what, I am, okay? So maybe I'm into *vagrancy*, but what's it matter? I'll live the way I want, and no one can tell me how I should make my living. No one!"

"They just want to help you, Trevor, we all do. Haven't you ever wanted a better life? Yeah… You did, once. You used to talk about getting a car and skipping town, and starting a whole new life where no one knows us. Remember? You didn't want to stay on the streets forever. What changed?"

"Nothing," Trevor answered quickly "Nothing changed. You just didn't get it. I don't *care* where I get my stuff from, and it doesn't matter. Sure, I wanted to leave that stupid town, but I didn't want to give up my freedom! We would have been free, Matthew. Family does nothing but hold you back and give you rules and laws to follow. If that's the life you want, Matthew, go ahead and take it, but I'm not going. Even here, I'm not going to give up my life.

Come back and get me when the time machine's fixed, and I'll get out of your way."

"You know I can't do that, Trevor."

"Well, I'm not going back with you."

"C'mon, Trevor! Remember all those times I broke the rules for you? In fact, that's how I ended up here in the first place. Remember how I would look away when you would steal something and pretend I didn't notice? Remember how I would break into places with you and stay the night, even though I was afraid of getting caught? Remember all that? I broke the rules for you, so I'm asking you this one time, just until Grace fixes the time machine, to follow the rules for me. It won't be for long." He paused. "C'mon," he said, quoting Trevor, "Help a brother out?"

Trevor looked up at Matthew somewhat amusedly and snickered. "That is the lamest thing I've heard in my entire life," he began, and Matthew looked worried for a moment, "But I guess I owe you one. But if your *family* keeps on mocking me, I'm out."

Matthew nodded enthusiastically. "Deal," he said, and they shook hands.

Once more, the pair descended from the rooftops and planted their feet on solid ground. Matthew and Trevor walked slowly through the market and talked quietly, avoiding the subjects of family and their inherently different lifestyle choices. They arrived back at Mrs. Brown's boarding house just as Sandra was leaving.

"You two!" she exclaimed, "I was just about to go looking for you! Is everything alright? Grace and Evan tell me there's been a falling out of sorts?" She looked at Trevor meaningfully.

"We're fine," Matthew replied, sensing a certain tension in the air, "It was nothing."

Sandra nodded, yet her expression remained suspicious. "Okay," she said, "Well, come on in, Mrs. Brown will be back soon and then we'll have to ask her if she can spare room for one more boarder."

"What's the plan?" Matthew asked.

"We'll board Trevor in your room and move Eddie in with his father and Mr. Fitzgerald," Sandra replied warmly, "In fact, why don't you two go and get Trevor settled in. I really don't have any doubt that Mrs. Brown will find it in her heart to take him in. Poor woman must have been so lonely before we arrived…" Sandra trailed off and looked between the two boys standing in front of her. "Well, go ahead," she ordered, "We don't have all day!"

Trevor and Matthew hurried upstairs and entered the room, shutting the door behind them.

"See what I mean?" Trevor inquired, "Rules, plans, and commands, that's all you get. I like living with… with an element of surprise!"

"I see," Matthew sighed, if only to please his friend. Trevor sat down in the desk chair, turned it around and put his feet up on Matthew's bed.

"This seems like an okay place," Trevor decided, as though he was sizing up a cold alley or dark tunnel for them to stay the night, as he had once done before Matthew had accidentally stumbled upon the time machine and launched himself into his new life, "What kind of food do you get here?"

"Lots of stuff," Matthew shrugged, "Chicken, soup, roast beef, lots of vegetables, not a lot of fruits…" He trailed off. Trevor had stood up and was looking out the window.

"Nice view," he remarked, squinting to see farther towards the horizon, "What's that place?"

Matthew walked up to the window and let his gaze follow Trevor's pointing finger, and found himself looking at the far off district of King's Park.

"That's part of King's Park," he told Trevor, "It's sort of the rich part of the city I guess. There's lots of nice buildings, but I've heard there's also lots of stuck up people."

Trevor laughed breathily. "Of course there are," he said, "How do you think they got there?"

Matthew chuckled, then heard the front door open, and the chatter of voices: those of Mrs. Brown, Laura, and Eddie.

"Mrs. Brown's back," he said, "Let's hope she says yes."

"Yeah," Trevor replied, "And if not, who cares?"

Matthew fidgeted uncomfortably. He cared. The time travellers cared. He only hoped that Sandra was going to be convincing enough to secure Trevor a place at the boarding house. Otherwise, he didn't know *what* they were going to do.

CHAPTER SEVEN

Long Time No See

Nearly two weeks passed without incident as Trevor stayed on at Mrs. Brown's boarding house. As Sandra had suspected, and Matthew fervently hoped, Mrs. Brown was more than happy to let Trevor board with them, provided they could find the space and pay his rent.

The beginning was difficult for Trevor, as he was still getting used to the rules, and to the time in which he was living. The living conditions as well provided an obstacle for him; for the first week, Trevor could never finish an entire plate of food without feeling sick, as he was not used to the large amounts of food which Mrs. Brown doled out. During the day, Trevor spent as much time as possible outside, but Matthew had to accompany him wherever he went in order to be sure he didn't get into any more trouble.

Matthew had spoken to the other time travellers about Trevor's feelings towards family and rules, and he made sure that they all knew about the condition upon which Trevor would stay. Whenever any of them spoke to him, they chose their words carefully, being sure to avoid anything that might be construed as mockery, for they knew that Trevor would leave at once if the opportunity arose.

And so, almost two weeks after the deal between Matthew and Trevor had been struck, they were walking through the Southern Quays, while Trevor reminisced, as he often did, about his days as a "free man." Matthew listened patiently, trying not to let Trevor's words sink in too deep. There were times that Matthew missed being able to do whatever he pleased whenever he pleased, but he simply reminded himself that he really couldn't do much at all. There were such limitations when it came to living on the streets that it really wasn't freedom. In fact, it had felt more like a prison to Matthew most of the time. He said nothing of the sort to Trevor, for he knew that it would only lead to an argument, but Matthew suspected that he felt the same way sometimes and simply refused to admit it.

"And think about it," Trevor was saying animatedly, "You can go wherever you want, any time, day or night. I'm telling you, I can't wait to get back to my freedom. I'm so tired of staying in one place all the time."

Matthew thought that Trevor was beginning to sound an awful lot like a television commercial, advertising his way of life over and over again, repeating each time with renewed vigour. He noticed that Trevor, as much as he would refute it, was much more lively and animated of recent days. Matthew supposed that it was the result of the good food he was eating, or the company he was keeping, or any number of other things, as Trevor had previously lacked in many of life's necessities. Whatever was causing it, Trevor looked healthier and happier than Matthew had ever seen him. Trevor liked to pretend that he was always waiting restlessly to go home, but his appearance and attitude told another story.

Matthew smiled and nodded to Trevor politely, not wanting to upset him by voicing his own views on the subject.

"Man, I miss sleeping under the stars," Trevor continued wistfully, "Don't you ever miss that, Matthew? No roof above you or walls or anything to block it all out, and—"

Trevor abruptly stopped talking for a second, and disappeared from sight, accompanied by a loud crash. Matthew turned swiftly around and found himself looking at a red faced Trevor who had fallen to the cobblestones. In front of him, partially obscuring him from view, was a tall, trim individual who was leaning over Trevor and an upset crate of various items of food. Broken eggs and spilt milk littered the ground and the figure was scrambling to pick them up, apologizing to Trevor all the while. Trevor was muttering under his breath and brushing himself off, trying to get some egg out of the hem of his trousers. Matthew rushed over and bent to help him up, but stopped cold when he heard the figure speak again.

"Matthew?"

Slowly, painfully slowly, Matthew looked up at the individual.

"Oh, no," he whispered, so faintly that no one could hear, "Why is it always *me*?"

"It is you! It's so good to see you again! Where *have* you been?"

Matthew forced a smile as he stared into his friend's face. The person who had run into Trevor was none other than Alvin Quinn, the boy who had saved his life, and the lives of all the time travellers, when Clay had been after their heads. Alvin was one of Matthew's closest friends, but he had certainly not expected to see him here in Norton, so far away from his home in Connolly Mills. Matthew remained speechless as he straightened up. Though he had missed Alvin, Alice, and Rachel a great deal, with Trevor around, it was not safe for them to be present.

Alvin pulled an envelope out of his pocket and showed it to Matthew. "I received your letter," he said, "But I was just about to leave when it arrived, and you never left a return address."

Matthew nodded and finally found his voice. "It must have slipped my mind," he lied, then paused, and his eyes widened. He had so much to ask Alvin, now that he was here. "How are you?" he inquired, then began spouting off questions as they came to him, "And Alice? How is she? How's the baby? And Rachel, is she alright? How's your arm? What brings you here to Norton?" Matthew stopped talking and shut his mouth, realizing that it wasn't best to begin a conversation now, especially not with Trevor present, but he was so curious, as well as worried for the welfare of his friends.

Alvin's face turned suddenly downcast, and Matthew began to feel sick to his stomach. Alvin didn't say anything for what seemed like a long time.

"What's going on?" Matthew asked nervously, "Is everyone alright? Did someone—" He couldn't finish the sentence but for the dizziness he was starting to feel. He wanted very badly to sit down.

"We're fine," Alvin said quietly, in a most grave tone, "But you should know…"

"Know what?"

"Alice… Alice gave birth to a son the day that Mr. Kennedy went to your house," Alvin replied, his voice taut with emotion, "The child didn't live past that day…"

Matthew nearly staggered back at the revelation. "She… she did?"

Alvin nodded. "Her folks sent her away to Norton to live with her Aunt Jessica after they found out. It was easier than facing everyone back home."

Matthew's expression turned to one of shock. "Where is she now?"

"She's living down this road with her aunt," Alvin replied, "I was just bringing them some things when I ran into your friend here." Alvin laughed half heartedly, trying to lighten the mood. Matthew remembered, with a sudden jolt of guilt, that Trevor was still present.

"Alvin," he introduced them, "This is Trevor. Trevor, this is my friend Alvin, from Connolly Mills."

"Good to meet you," Trevor said, shaking Alvin's hand, trying to keep up with the decorum that the time travellers had taught him.

Alvin nodded. "Likewise," he said, "I'm sorry I ran into you, I couldn't see where I was going with the crate…" He looked down at the broken wooden box and its scattered contents with melancholy in his eyes. Trevor remained silent.

"Where are you staying?" Matthew asked, looking at Alvin.

"With my grandfather," he replied, still gazing at the smashed crate, "He lives in Irontown. My father allowed me to come here after he found out about all that had happened, he thought it would be safer."

Matthew nodded in response. It was said that most of the town of Connolly Mills had relatives who lived in Norton, whether that was where their family originated or that some members of the family had simply moved there looking for work.

"That's where my father works," Matthew replied, causing Trevor's jaw to drop momentarily.

"My grandfather too," Alvin said simply, then set to picking up his dropped food items, or at least those that had remained intact. Matthew bent to help him, and Trevor did his part as well. Finding he could not hold everything in his arms, Alvin untucked his shirt and used it as a pouch to hold it all.

"I should be going," Alvin announced, after everything had been gathered up, "I'll come by to visit whenever I can and we can talk about what happened. Where did you say you were staying?"

"I didn't," Matthew shook his head, "But I'm living in Mrs. Brown's boarding house in St. Edward's on Main Street, by the market."

"I'll come and see you tomorrow, then," Alvin said with a smile, doffing his cap, "Goodbye Matthew, Trevor."

Matthew and Trevor watched Alvin walk away, and when he was out of sight, Trevor turned to Matthew, an incredulous look on his face.

"Your *father*?" he exclaimed, his voice betraying tones of utter disbelief and disappointment, "Your *father*?"

"What?" Matthew cried, "You lie all the time! And besides, Mr. Fitzgerald has been like a father to me ever since I arrived! I even call him that!"

"Last time I checked," Trevor said, "Your father was a gutless drunk." Matthew chose not to dignify his comment with an answer.

Alvin and Alice's presence in Norton worried Matthew even more than Sam's did, and soon all three of them would be in the city at the same time. It was almost too much to handle. Who would have thought that running away to Norton would put them right in the path of not one, but at least three of their old friends? Friends were all well and good, and Matthew would have been delighted had it not been for Trevor. The sooner he could return to the present, the better off everyone would be. Grace was constantly working on the time machine every chance she got, keeping her work well concealed from Mrs. Brown, but she seemed no closer to finishing her repairs than she had been when she started.

Trevor and Matthew arrived back at the boarding house just before supper was due to be served. The pair of them didn't speak to one another throughout the whole meal. In fact, neither of them spoke much at all. Trevor went to bed early that night, leaving Matthew to explain the day's events to the other time travellers after Mrs. Brown had retired for the evening.

"I didn't see that it was him until it was too late," he insisted, "Otherwise I would have taken Trevor and gotten out of there."

"It's alright, Matthew," Grace replied, placing a hand on his shoulder, "It's not a big deal, but it's up to you to make sure that Trevor doesn't say or do *anything* that might give us away."

Matthew nodded in understanding. "Alvin's coming here tomorrow, and I'd like to talk with him," he began, wincing as he prepared to make his request, "And I wondered if someone could occupy Trevor while he visits. It won't be for long, I promise, and—"

"It'll be fine, Matthew," Mr. Fitzgerald assured him, "We've been giving you a lot of responsibility lately when it comes to Trevor, and it's not very fair that it should all fall on you. You take as much time as you need."

Matthew smiled widely and let out a sigh of relief. "Thanks," he replied. "Thank you so much."

The next day, Alvin Quinn arrived as promised, and Trevor was spirited away to the workplace of Mr. Fitzgerald and Mr. Riddell. When Alvin got to the boarding house, Matthew was the only one home, leaving them to situate themselves wherever they pleased. When they had said a proper hello and settled into the parlour, the pair of them set to straightening out the facts.

Alvin told Matthew about the day of the attack from his point of view. He recalled how scared he had been when Matthew remained unresponsive, and how he had thought that he may have accidentally shot him. Matthew laughed at that, but realized full well how brave Alvin and Rachel had been to follow Clay all the way to Darcy Lake from Connolly Mills and try to protect him and his family.

Next, Alvin recounted Alice's harrowing tale. Matthew's eyes grew wider and wider as Alvin described what had taken place, from when they boarded the train right up until he had found her in the upstairs of the doctor's office and she had lost the baby due to the premature birth and lack of proper medical equipment. Matthew wondered if, in the future, the baby might have lived.

"When we returned home after that," Alvin explained, "We knew we weren't safe. Clay would soon return to Connolly Mills and have his revenge on all of us for helping you. Alice was in no condition even to travel, and she had a difficult time of it on the way back from Darcy Lake, I can tell you. I made sure she stayed at her house, where she would be safe, but after she was well enough to travel, her folks sent her here, both because of the baby and Clay." Alvin paused and shivered, though the day was warm, then continued.

"A few days after we arrived back, I was heading upstairs, in my own house, and I heard something against the window. I looked… and Clay was s-standing there with his rifle… I heard a loud shot and I ran upstairs, away from him. My father wasn't home, and I thought he—Clay, I mean—might come through the door, but he never did." Alvin's hand was idly plucking at his sleeve, right above where Clay's bullet had hit his arm the day he had come to save Matthew and his family. "It took me days to convince my father to allow me to leave, and come here, where I could be useful helping Alice and far away from Clay."

"And Rachel?" Matthew wondered, "What about her?" He figured that Rachel, being Clay's granddaughter and living under the same roof as the murderous man, would be the most endangered of all three of his friends.

"Rachel's alright," Alvin told him, "She told me her grandfather won't even look at her after what happened, so I doubt he would hurt her. After all, she is his family."

Matthew nodded distractedly; he was worried about Rachel. "I wish she could stay away from him," he said.

"I've sent word to Mrs. Kennedy," Alvin replied, prompting Matthew to look up in rapt attention, "Asking her to permit Rachel to stay here for a time, but I don't know if she'll agree. All we can do is hope and pray."

Alvin glanced up at the clock and stood up suddenly. "I should be going," he declared with some urgency, "Alice will be expecting me." He paused and thought for a moment before turning back to Matthew. "You know," he said, and Matthew could sense that he was about to ask him something, "Alice hasn't been feeling very well, in her mind, you see, and I wonder if it might help if you came to see her."

"I'd be happy to," Matthew smiled, "I hope she feels better soon."

"So do I, Matthew," Alvin sighed, "So do I."

Alvin and Matthew made for the door, and Matthew was immensely glad that Trevor was otherwise occupied so that he was able to visit Alice. He wondered what on earth he could possibly say to her after she had suffered such a terrible loss.

"When you say that Alice isn't feeling well in her mind," Matthew asked Alvin as they made their way towards the Southern Quays, "What do you mean?"

"She's been feeling very… sad, of sorts," Alvin tried to explain; "She's taken the loss of her child very hard."

"I understand," Matthew began, but stopped when he saw Alvin shaking his head.

"I don't think you do. The loss of a child is something one never full understands until it happens to them," he said wisely.

"No," Matthew agreed, some time later, "I suppose I don't…" Matthew wondered for a moment whether Alice's feelings were similar to his when he had lost his mother, but banished the thought from his mind almost as soon as it had appeared, not wanting to think about his own grief when he was meant to be helping Alice with hers.

They arrived where Alice was staying after spending the rest of their walk in a comfortable silence.

"This is where Alice's Aunt Jessica lives," Alvin stated, looking up at the humble home. Matthew followed his gaze and peered at the house up and down. It was more like a series of small apartments than a house, and like most of the other buildings in the Quays, it needed some extensive repairs. There was a clothesline strung along the uppermost balcony, displaying the worn and faded habiliments of the building's inhabitants.

"She lives in Number Six," Alvin was saying as Matthew stared intently at the house, "Come along."

"Alvin," Matthew whispered as they approached the door to the house where Alice was staying, "What exactly is the... *occupation* of Alice's aunt?"

"You'll see," Alvin replied ominously, and knocked loudly on the door. They waited a few moments, and Matthew thought he could hear shouting and cursing from the inside. Alvin sighed and shook his head, worry in his eyes.

The door was opened by a short, thin woman who wore far too much makeup and curled her hair to the point that it appeared to look something like a mound of thick noodles piled on her head. Her bright red lips formed a smirk and then parted into a grin.

"Ladies!" she called back into the depths of the house, "There's two gentlemen callers at our door!" She giggled and Matthew looked up at Alvin with eyes widened in astonishment. It appeared that Aunt Jessica was running a house of ill repute; a brothel of sorts. Two more ladies appeared at the door, smiling.

"Aren't you two a little young to be comin' around here?" one of them asked.

Matthew's mouth flapped open and shut, unsure of what to say. Alvin stepped forward, hands raised in innocence.

"We're here to see Alice," he said calmly, "If it pleases you..." Alvin trailed off and his face broke into a nervous smile as he noticed, above the heads of the women in front of him, Alice's Aunt Jessica. Jessica's face turned from a polite smile to a frown as she pushed her way through the swarm of women, swatting at them as she tried to get by.

"Would you all mind your manners, or you won't be permitted to use these premises for your work any more, understand?" She smiled again when she approached Alvin. He towered over her by more than a foot, and she had to look up just to see his face. She was certainly a short woman, and thin as a rail. Her hair was a mousy brown, and her features were stony and sharp; her resting face a frown.

"Alvin," she said sweetly, "Alice is expecting you upstairs."

"Thank you," Alvin replied, and led the way to the staircase, Matthew following close behind. As they climbed the stairs, Matthew looked at Alvin's sullen face.

"Who were all those women?" he whispered, though he knew quite well who they must have been, "And what are they doing here?"

"I think it's fairly evident who they are," Alvin answered quietly, "And Alice's aunt, who they all call Miss Jessica, rents them rooms for them to work."

"But why?" Matthew wondered, "And do Alice's parents know?"

Alvin shook his head. "Jessica was down on her luck and she needed some money. Working in a factory would have killed her..." He trailed off, paused, then spoke again. "She had no other way to make money. Alice's mother, Jessica's sister, never knew. Jessica was too ashamed to tell her I expect, but I'm glad she didn't. Otherwise, Alice would have no place to stay."

"Yes, but this?" Matthew continued the conversation in hushed tones, "This is fairly dangerous, is it not?"

"It is," Alvin conceded, "But she couldn't stay in Connolly Mills, and her aunt is a good, strong woman. I help them as much as I can. There's a lock on Alice's door so that the men visiting don't accidentally walk into the wrong room, and her aunt tries to keep her away from them as much as she can. I'm glad of it, but I know she gets lonely."

Matthew nodded absently as they reached the next floor. There was a small landing and two doors. Alvin moved automatically to the one on the right, and knocked, more quietly this time. Matthew bit his lip, afraid of the condition that he might find Alice in. Would she be reclusive? Pale and afraid? Sad? Depressed? He could only guess until he heard the faint "come in" and Alvin slowly opened the door.

The room at first appeared to be devoid of life. There was a tall armchair facing the window, which only afforded the view of the bricks and mortar of the neighbouring building. A bed lay neatly tucked in the corner, and a wooden dresser was on the far right side of the room, on top of which sat a wash basin and two dusty books. Alvin and Matthew stood in the doorway and waited, and within a few moments, Alice's head peeked out from the side of the armchair. Upon seeing the two of them, Alice's downcast face brightened and she stood slowly and carefully, and made her way towards them. Alvin and Matthew stepped forward, meeting her halfway through the room.

"Matthew!" Alice exclaimed, "How lovely to see you!" She embraced him warmly, "Where have you been?" She looked up at Alvin, then back at Matthew. "We've been so worried…"

"I've been here in Norton," Matthew replied softly, "I didn't know you were both here." He smiled at Alice. "How are you?" He paused, wondering whether he should make mention of her terrible loss.

"I'm fine," Alice said, "I take it Alvin has told you what happened…"

"I'm so sorry," Matthew told her sincerely, "So, so sorry."

Tears sprang into Alice's eyes, but she blinked them quickly away. "It's alright," she whispered, her voice thick. Alvin took her by the arm and gently led her back to her armchair and sat her down, then turned it around so that Alice was no longer staring at the dismal, depressing view out the window.

Matthew assumed that this was Alice's bedroom, and he also guessed that she rarely left the place from day to day. Under normal circumstances, Alvin and Matthew would have been strictly forbidden from entering the room. *But then*, Matthew thought, remembering the half dozen women who were loitering downstairs, *the circumstances are far from normal.*

"Would you like to walk outside today, Alice? You haven't left this room in a long while," Alvin asked, crouching next to her armchair and confirming Matthew's suspicions.

"Not today," Alice said, though she looked as if she could use some fresh air, "I would rather stay and talk for a while."

Alvin nodded, not wanting to push her. He knew that she hadn't been feeling well of late, but he also knew that she didn't want to be treated like an invalid, and as soon as she was feeling better, she would be up and about as she had been before the whole terrible thing had ever happened.

On Alice's request, the three of them talked quietly, Alvin sitting on the floor right beside Alice's chair, ready to help her if something should happen. However, nothing occurred out of the ordinary, and Matthew and Alvin left after a few hours, Alvin promising to return the next day. They made their way down the stairs and bid goodbye to Aunt Jessica, shutting the door of Number Six Crookshanks Lane firmly behind them.

"She seems alright," Matthew said, referring to Alice as he and Alvin made their way down the street, "A little ill, but alright."

"She's getting better all the time," Alvin nodded, "She's going to be fine." He smiled, as though the act of saying to Matthew that Alice was going to be alright had finally convinced him of that fact.

They rounded the corner towards St. Edward's and were nearly ploughed over by a couple of rowdy men who were racing top speed down the road. One of them caught Alvin by his left shoulder, and he cried out. Once they had run by, Matthew turned to Alvin, who was rubbing his upper left arm gingerly.

"Your arm," he said, "Hasn't it healed yet?"

"It was nearly healed," Alvin replied, "But when I ran into your friend yesterday and broke the crates, one of the nails must have torn through my shirt and hit my arm right where it was healing. I never noticed until later."

Matthew nodded, and then the two parted ways, Matthew returning to the boarding house, Alvin heading back to his grandfather's.

CHAPTER EIGHT

Until Next Time

"Rachel, dear, would you come here for a moment?"

Rachel stepped into the parlour, curiosity, and a hint of fear, gleaming in her eyes. Connolly Mills, her home, had felt empty of late. With Matthew missing, and Alvin and Alice away in Norton, Rachel felt alone in the world. Her grandfather, Clay Kennedy, was almost always hovering over her, trying to be sure that she didn't get up to anything unusual. He was strict to the extreme, and since the incident in Darcy Lake, he hadn't let his granddaughter out of his sight. However, there were times when he had to leave the house and was unable to take Rachel with him, and in those cases, he left her in the care of his wife, Penelope.

Penelope was a caring, loving grandmother, but she was submissive to Clay's every wish. If he instructed her to not let Rachel leave the house, Penelope obeyed and Rachel stayed indoors. Today was one of those days, and it had been Rachel's grandmother who had called her into the parlour.

"Yes, Grandmother?"

Penelope stood and crossed the room towards Rachel, an envelope in her hand.

"This came for you in today's post," she said, her wrinkled face betraying her apprehension, "There's no return address..."

Rachel tried to keep the surprise out of her features. Ever since Matthew had left her life so suddenly, she hadn't received so much as a note. She wondered whether he was finally trying to contact her once more.

"Now, Rachel," Penelope began gently, "If there is any possibility that this letter might be from that Fitzgerald boy, I can't permit you to open it, you know that, don't you?"

"Of course, Grandmother," Rachel replied as casually as possible, and then took the letter from Penelope's shaking hands. She looked the envelope over, front and back, turning it around and around in her hands as she struggled to come up with some excuse that would allow her to keep the mysterious letter.

"Oh," Rachel began, her face breaking into a false smile, "It's from Mr. Adams. I recognize his handwriting."

Penelope raised an eyebrow. "What does Mr. Adams want with you in the summertime?"

"Oh, nothing at all," Rachel continued her lie, "He would only like to know if I would help in the schoolhouse next year, seeing as I'm too old to go back as a student…"

"Work?" Penelope wondered, taking the letter back from Rachel, "You know that your grandfather would never approve of such a thing. Your place is in the home!"

"But of course," Rachel replied, trying her best not to sound condescending, "I'll write him back right away and tell him I cannot accept his offer." Penelope, satisfied with this answer, let Rachel take the envelope from her and head upstairs to her room. Rachel gripped the letter anxiously, her hands trembling as she opened it in the relative safety of her bedroom. She had known from the moment she had seen the neat handwriting on the envelope who it belonged to. It was not Matthew who was writing to her, but Alvin. Rachel knew, however, that Alvin and Alice were also people with whom she was forbidden to fraternize, due to their involvement in helping her stop Clay from harming Matthew and his family, and Alice's pregnancy.

Rachel pulled a thick piece of paper from the envelope, slowly and carefully, and began to read.

Dear Rachel, she read, *I sent word some time ago to your grandmother, asking her to permit you to come to Norton, for your own safety, but it occurred to me a while after I sent it that she would never allow it. If this letter ever gets to you, just know that Alice and I are safe and sound, and Alice is recovering with each passing day. A few days ago, I quite literally ran into a very pleasant surprise. I was bringing some things to Alice and her aunt, and I met Matthew Fitzgerald in the road, and nearly ran over a friend of his named Trevor. I couldn't believe my eyes, but he was there, and I brought him to see Alice. I assured him that you were safe, but I really couldn't know that, could I? I know that this is a lot to ask of you, and I would understand if you found that it was too dangerous, but Matthew, Alice, and I would love to hear back from you. Until next we meet, Alvin Quinn.*

Rachel grinned. Matthew was in Norton! It seemed too good to be true, but Rachel knew that Alvin would never lie. She was glad that he had had the foresight to not place a return address on the envelope, for if he had, the letter would have gone straight to the trash.

Rachel was incredibly glad that Alvin had managed to contact her, and to find Matthew. Now that she had already given her grandmother an excuse for writing a letter back, all she had to do was write to Alvin and send it off, pretending it was her rejection to Mr. Adams' non existent proposal. Quickly, Rachel wrote her reply, expressing her happiness at Matthew's reappearance and her desire to be in Norton with them. Taking an empty envelope from her desk, Rachel addressed it to the place that Alvin had written on the back of the letter.

Rushing down the stairs, Rachel slowed as she reached the bottom so as not to arouse suspicion from her grandmother.

"I've written to Mr. Adams," Rachel lied, striding slowly into the parlour once more, "May I go to the post office and send it?"

Penelope bit her lip, worried about what Clay might say if she let Rachel go out alone. Within moments, she had formulated a solution.

"I shall accompany you," she said, "I would like to have a talk with Miss Brant at the post office; I haven't seen her in a while." Rachel knew that this was merely an excuse to make sure that she didn't get into any trouble, but she did not protest.

The pair set off, and arrived at the post office without incident. Rachel sent her letter, carefully hiding the address from her grandmother, and she stood quietly and politely as Penelope spoke with Miss Brant. They returned to the house just as Clay was arriving home. The man looked at his wife and granddaughter, one eyebrow raised.

He took off his hat and stepped inside the house, then allowed the rest of his family to pass through. Rachel peered nervously back at him, noting that the scar on the back of his balding skull had faded to almost nothing. She remembered how, after he had accidentally shot Alvin, he had turned to go into the home of Matthew and his family in Darcy Lake, and she remembered the awful metallic thunk as Mr. Riddell had struck the back of his head with a garden shovel. He had fallen unconscious, and for a moment, Rachel had worried that he had died. She shuddered.

"Where have you been?" Clay asked as he hung up his hat on a hook by the door. The question sounded innocent enough, but the wrong answer could be costly.

"Rachel had to go and send a letter to Mr. Adams," Penelope replied, as polite as ever, "He had asked her to work in the schoolhouse this year."

"What did you tell him?" Clay had turned to Rachel.

"I assured him that it was out of the question," Rachel answered confidently, knowing that this was the answer that he wanted to hear.

Clay nodded, but Rachel could tell that he was slightly uncomfortable with the entire matter. She put the thought out of her mind, for it would only serve to worry her.

The small family went about their business for the rest of the day as normal. Rachel helped her grandmother prepare supper, though she hated cooking, and she didn't dare speak unless spoken to as they ate. She felt like a prisoner, locked away inside her house, unable to leave without an escort, unable to even speak. She went to bed early that night and stared at the moon from her bedroom window, wishing that she could be up there, in wide open space, far away from all the hate, lies, and constant apprehension that surrounded her.

■■

Two days later came Sunday, and that morning, as was usual, Matthew and the time travellers were settled in a pew in the St. Edward's community church. It was a small church, but many people attended, leaving only standing room for some. Matthew looked around anxiously just before the service was about to begin, trying to spot his friends, Alvin and Alice. They had promised him that they would be there this week, but they hadn't yet arrived.

The building was constructed from limestone, and there was a beautiful bell tower on top, which rang the hour in deep, joyful tones. The beauty of the church's interior matched the exterior. It was open and airy; high ceilings painted with scenes from the Bible and strung with electric lights along the length. The tall windows set at intervals along the walls let in the sunshine, casting the red cushioned wood pews in golden morning light.

Trevor sat beside Matthew, arms folded across his chest. Sandra had made him a suit for church, but he hated it with a passion. He claimed it was itchy, and looked even more ridiculous than his regular clothes. Trevor was in a foul mood nearly every Sunday, without exception, not only because he hated the suit, but because he didn't like church to begin with. Grace had managed to reason with him on the grounds that going to church was something that people did regularly in this time, and if they didn't, they most likely belonged to another religion, and as much as Trevor didn't like it, it was the way of the world. This news only made Trevor sulk even more about wanting to return to his own time. In reality, the time travellers wouldn't have made him go to church if he hadn't had such a terrible habit of doing things he shouldn't when unsupervised.

"They're probably not coming," Trevor huffed as he looked at Matthew, who was twisting and turning in his seat to get a view of the front door, "So sit down and quit movin' around." He slouched and set his jaw forward angrily. Matthew, not wanting to provoke him, turned to the front and sat quietly, fidgeting all the while.

"Quit it," Trevor barked, and Matthew stopped.

The service began with the organ playing hymns, and the congregation stood and sang along. During the third hymn, the faint creak of the front door could be heard above the singing, and several members of the congregation turned to see what had caused it, including Matthew.

Their curiosity was satisfied when a young couple walked in, a couple who Matthew immediately recognized. Alvin, with Alice's arm hooked through his, led Alice to an unassuming pew near the back of the church. They sat down and picked up a hymnal from the back of the next pew, but they could not begin singing before they heard the whispers. Even with the people singing and the organ playing, Alvin, Alice, and nearly everyone else in the room could hear the hushed conversation going on. The topic, undoubtedly, was Alvin and Alice themselves.

It seemed that even in Norton, Alice's reputation preceded her. People had seen her, rumours had been spread about her, and they were nothing good. People had seen where she was staying, which didn't help the situation in the least. Alice tried her best to ignore it until it died away, but Alvin's face began to turn a bright, angry red. The people in the seat directly in front of them had the audacity to think that they could speak about Alice and not be heard, but Alvin could hear their every word. He heard what they said had happened to put her in *the family way*, and winced as they exchanged their thoughts about Alice's character, and about why exactly she had lost the baby.

Then began the inevitable: the name calling. Alvin's face went from angry to furious in a matter of seconds, and Alice had to place a hand on his arm to remind him of where they were. He let out a shaky breath and turned back to the hymnal as they finished the song.

The sermon, to Alvin's delight, was about judging others, and by the end of it the people in the pew ahead of

Alvin and Alice were looking quite ashamed of themselves. Alvin caught Matthew's eye as everyone was getting up to leave, and Matthew came walking towards them, ducking and dodging between the scurrying churchgoers. He was glad to see that Alvin's expression had returned to a happy one, and Alice was looking to be nearly completely recovered.

"I'm so sorry about what happened when you came in," Matthew began, "I never thought that—"

"It's alright, Matthew," Alice assured him, "It was to be expected."

"You should never have to expect that sort of talk from anyone," Alvin countered, "After all, it wasn't your fault what happened to you."

"Yes, but they don't know that," Alice said gently, "And they've heard rumours, we all have..." She stopped and her face took on a confused look. Matthew and Alvin followed her gaze and found Trevor standing silently behind Matthew.

"Hello, Trevor," Alvin greeted him warmly, "I suppose you've never met Alice, have you?"

"No," Trevor replied, mimicking Alvin's patterns of speech, "I don't believe I have."

"Very pleased to meet you, Trevor," Alice removed her glove and reached out a hand for Trevor to shake. Trevor accepted it.

"Nice to meet you too," he replied, his eyes fixed on Alice's. Alice squirmed under his unfamiliar gaze.

"How do you know Matthew?" she asked, trying to take the attention away from herself.

Matthew and Trevor exchanged glances. They hadn't yet worked out a story for how they had supposedly met. Obviously, the truth was out of the question. Matthew tried desperately to think of an appropriate answer.

"We met when Matthew first came to Norton," Trevor devised, knowing that Matthew had only been there for a short time, "I board in the same house as his family." Even when he was making up a story, Trevor had a hard time referring to Matthew's family without a hint of distrust in his voice. Matthew nodded in agreement, but not without noticing the way Trevor said the word *family*. Trevor still refused to admit that the time travellers were Matthew's family at all unless he had to. Matthew was glad that he at least had the sense to put his personal feelings aside for a time as he spoke to Alvin and Alice.

"Would you both like to come to my grandfather's this afternoon?" Alvin asked, "He'd be delighted to meet you, I'm sure."

Matthew looked at Trevor, who did not return his gaze. He was looking at Alice.

"Are you going?" he asked pointedly, and without much politesse.

Alice nodded, her arm hooked once more through Alvin's as they prepared to leave.

"Sure," Trevor replied, looking to Alvin, "We'll go, right, Matthew?"

Matthew tried to disguise his surprise at Trevor's willingness to attend Alvin's social gathering. He nodded to Alvin, attempting to keep his voice steady and unassuming.

"Of course," he replied, "When should we arrive?"

Alvin pulled a watch from his pocket, the chain dangling from his suit jacket. "Two o'clock?"

"We'll be there," Matthew said, hoping that the time travellers wouldn't object, "See you soon!" Alvin gave them the address, and Matthew waved as Alvin and Alice began to walk towards the door. As Alice turned her back to them, Trevor caught her eye and winked, causing her to turn rigid and face the front. Once they had gone, Matthew turned to Trevor.

"I saw that," he said.

"What?"

"When you winked at Alice. You shouldn't do that. She's been through a lot and the last thing she needs right now is your attention."

"Matthew," Trevor said seriously, looking at his friend, "You can't take away my freedom to wink at girls. I'm not your prisoner."

"I didn't say you were!" Matthew objected, "I only meant that you shouldn't flirt with Alice because of what happened to her, and very recently at that! She's probably kinda nervous when you do that. Not to mention how Alvin would feel about it."

"What? It's not like I'm going to hurt her!"

"I know that! But even if you tell her that, she still needs time to build up her trust again. She can't just take your word for it."

"Whatever," Trevor replied, signalling he wanted to drop the subject, "You're acting like you're a psychologist or something. You don't know what she's thinking."

The pair fell into silence and rejoined the time travellers, who were departing the church. Matthew told Grace about Alvin's invitation, and though she seemed nervous, she thought it best that they keep their promise.

After they stopped back at the boarding house for a couple hours, Matthew and Trevor set off once more for Irontown, where Alvin's grandfather lived. The air became thick and humid, and both Matthew and Trevor began to cough as they approached the industrial district.

Smog hung over Irontown like a warm, fuzzy blanket, and, for those not used to it, presented a foul, coaly smell that could make even the strongest individual stifle a cough. The sky was darkened and the sun blurred as the smokestacks belched out the foul leftovers from the factories. Alvin's grandfather lived in the centre of the district, where the smoke was the thickest and the air the foulest. Matthew and Trevor located the house, which was built similarly to where Alice was staying, and knocked on the soot-covered door.

The door opened within a few moments to reveal Alvin, who invited them in with a smile. Evidently, he was more comfortable in this environment than he was in Alice's aunt's house.

"Welcome," Alvin greeted them, leading them to the small living area, where Alice was sitting in a rocking chair waiting for them. They took their seats and Alvin's grandfather arrived in the room a moment later. Matthew wondered which side of Alvin's family he came from, as he was a short man, standing around five and a half feet, much smaller than his lean and tall grandson. His name, he revealed promptly, was Mr. Jacob Quinn, which told Matthew that he was on the side of Alvin's father. Mr. Quinn brought in a tray of tea and an assortment of foods for the youth to eat, then left them, heading to his room for a much needed nap.

"He works all day, every day," Alvin explained, sipping his tea, "Except Sunday."

"I can't believe he still works," Matthew began, "He's so…" Matthew trailed off, wishing he had kept his mouth shut.

"Old?" Alvin finished with a smile, "He is. He hasn't got enough money saved up to quit, and he's always sayin' that he'll be working in that factory until the day he dies."

Alice shook her head sadly. "The poor man," she said simply. She paused and glanced at Trevor, and her suspicions were confirmed: he was staring at her. She averted her gaze towards Alvin. Matthew noticed and glared at Trevor, who returned his look with an innocent expression that seemed to ask what he had done wrong this time. Matthew shook his head in exasperation.

"Which factory does he—" Matthew was cut off as his teacup toppled to the floor. He groaned, frustrated with himself for being so inept. "I'm sorry" he said, "I'll clean it up, I—"

Alvin interrupted his fretting. "I'll help," he said, ushering Matthew to follow him to the kitchen. Shamefacedly, Matthew shuffled after him to clean up the spill, leaving Trevor and Alice alone in the parlour. At first, all was quiet, with only Alvin and Matthew's voices floating in from the kitchen, and then Trevor leaned forwards and whispered to Alice.

"Hey," he said, "Are you okay? I mean, are you really alright? After what happened to you?"

Alice was taken aback by his boldness, and began to blink furiously; she was speechless.

"How… how do you know? How do you know what happened?"

It was Trevor's turn to be lost for words. He had found out first from Matthew's letter that he had caught, and then from Matthew himself. Not wanting to incriminate his friend, Trevor had to fabricate his story. Remembering what he had seen in church that morning, he made his excuse.

"I heard about it," he said simply, suddenly wishing he hadn't brought up the subject, however curious he was, not to mention how much he wanted to prove that Matthew was wrong about Alice's feelings.

Alice let out a long, shaky breath. "I've been trying to forget about it," she replied, deciding that if he was asking, she may as well tell him, "And I'd rather not talk about it."

"Okay," Trevor said, quickly backing down, "That's alright." Alice nodded, and Trevor thought that he could see a glimmer of tears in her eyes. He began to feel very guilty, and regretted even coming to Alvin's place. He was curious, and wanted Alice to like him, but not to the point that he wanted to hurt her already delicate feelings. He realized with a jolt that Matthew was right, and he should just leave her alone.

Alvin and Matthew returned a moment later and cleaned up the spilt tea, but not before Alvin noticed Alice's change in demeanour.

"Alice?" he asked, "Are you alright?"

"I'm fine," she replied, her voice higher than usual. Alvin wanted to press further, but he let her be, knowing that it would only make her more upset.

The rest of the visit went by rather uneventfully, and Alvin walked Alice back to her aunt's house in the Southern Quays once Matthew and Trevor had left.

"Alice," he said, as they reached the front door, "Did Trevor say something to you when Matthew and I were in the kitchen? Is that why you seemed so upset?"

Alice shook her head and forced a smile. "I'm fine," she answered, "Really, I am."

"You didn't answer my question."

"He just… he just asked if I was alright, after what happened, I mean."

"That was rather forward of him! How did he know?"

"He said he heard it somewhere, but really, he only seemed concerned. He just wanted to know if I was alright, and I am."

"Are you sure?"

"Yes."

"Alright. But you'd tell me if you weren't, wouldn't you?"

"Of course."

"Good. I'm always here to help you, you know that, don't you?"

"Yes, Alvin, I do."

Alvin nodded. "Okay," he said quietly, then kissed her gently on the forehead, "I'll see you tomorrow."

"Goodbye, Alvin," Alice smiled, trying to keep the tears from her eyes. Alvin turned and left, and Alice walked inside and made her way back up to her bedroom. Alvin was always trying to protect her, and she appreciated it more than anything, but there were times when she needed to be alone. She hated worrying him, but sometimes she knew that his anxiety for her was warranted. Her life, after what had happened, would never be the same.

CHAPTER NINE

The Time Has Come

The following morning, Sam returned to Norton. He arrived at Mrs. Brown's boarding house in the afternoon, with a wagon full of his things. Sam didn't have many possessions, and what few he did have fit comfortably in the bed of his wagon. Matthew was envious of Sam's team of horses, a team that reminded him of the time travellers' old horse, Phoebe. Matthew had named her himself, after his mother, who had died when he was only a child. They had brought Phoebe to Norton with them, but had had to sell her and their wagon to pay for their room and board. Matthew missed the wagon rides, and he missed Phoebe, but in a city like Norton, unless you planned to go exceptionally far, a horse and wagon were not needed.

Sam was to stay in a small boarding house in Oakton, where he was to work. Evan and John were also working in the lumber mills in the north of Norton, and the three of them ended up in the same place. They worked for a Mr. Dawson at Dawson's Mill, and were delighted to find that he seemed to be a gracious and understanding employer. Over the next couple of weeks, the time travellers spent quite a bit of time with Sam, and they enjoyed themselves a great deal. They went to see plays, took walks in the park, and spent their last few days of summer in rest and relaxation. Even Trevor seemed to be having fun, though Grace was still resiliently working on fixing their portal to the present.

With the new season of fall upon them, school was fast approaching. Matthew and Trevor were enrolled in Norton's public high school, but Alice and Alvin would not be attending. With the harvest near, Alvin was expecting word from his father at any moment, summoning him back to Connolly Mills to help on the farm, and Alice wasn't returning to school because of her reputation.

Matthew, Alvin, and Alice were gathered in the parlour of Alvin's grandfather's house in Irontown, while

Trevor stayed behind at Mrs Brown's boarding house, trying to help Grace fix the time machine. He had taken quite an interest in it, but was constantly disappointed by the lack of speed with which the project was progressing.

Alvin held an envelope in his hands. He turned it over in his palm and stared at it, then peered up at his friends.

"This letter came in the mail recently," he began, "But I haven't opened it." Matthew and Alice looked confused.

"Why not?" Matthew asked.

"It's from Rachel. I wanted to wait for both of you."

Alice gasped and Matthew leaned forwards. "Are we going to read it?"

Alvin nodded silently and began, slowly, to open the envelope. He read it aloud to Matthew and Alice, and when he was finished, he leant back and let the letter fall into his lap.

"She's been imprisoned!" he exclaimed.

"Now, let's not jump to conclusions," Alice added calmly, placing a hand on the arm of Alvin's chair, "She hasn't been hurt, and that's the important thing."

"I still wish she could be here," Matthew sulked.

"As do I," said Alvin, "But if she can't leave her house, she'll never get here."

"For the moment," Alice sighed, "She's safe."

"I worry she may not be," Alvin countered, standing up and beginning to pace up and down the length of the room, letter held behind his back, "I mean, how could she have sent this letter without Clay finding out what it was? Who it was for?"

"She wrote that she lied, and said it was Mr. Adams she was writing to," Matthew reminded him.

"True," Alvin replied, sitting back down, "Very true. We can only hope he doesn't find out the truth. After all, it wasn't the cleverest lie."

"It was clever enough," Matthew decided, hoping against hope that he was right.

In Connolly Mills, Rachel found herself wondering the same thing. What if Clay saw through her weak excuses? Her poor lies? Rachel sat in her bedroom and pondered these thoughts anxiously as she awaited Clay's return home that evening.

Rachel was close to dozing off when she finally heard the clatter of a wagon approaching the house. She rushed to the window and looked through the gap in between the curtains with one wondering eye. Clay had just dismounted from the wagon and was heading into the house, but just before he left Rachel's field of vision, he noticed her peeking through the curtains and shot her a warning look. Rachel gasped and jumped back from the window.

She heard the door open, and then slam promptly shut. From her place in her bedroom, Rachel could vaguely make out bits and pieces of hushed conversation between her grandparents. Not for the first time, Rachel wished that her parents were still alive. She listened quietly for what seemed like an eternity, and then finally, like the drone of a school bell, she heard her name being called in Clay's deep, sonorous voice. Rachel rose and left the safety of her bedroom, slowly climbing down the stairs, silently praying that her grandfather hadn't found out about her deception. When she reached the bottom, Clay and Penelope were there waiting for her.

"Young lady," Clay began calmly, "I think you may have some explaining to do." He led her to the parlour, where the three of them sat down, the house completely silent but for their movements.

"I saw Mr. Adams today," Clay continued, and Rachel's stomach tied itself into a knot, "And I asked him about his proposal for you to work at the school. Do you know what he said to me?" Rachel shook her head nervously.

"He said," Clay paused for effect, "That he never sent you a letter. He told me that he had never even *thought* of asking you to return to school this year. How do you explain that?"

Rachel felt beads of sweat forming on her forehead. She had known right from the beginning that lying was a bad idea, and that she would eventually be found out. She could have kicked herself for her utter incompetence. Now, it seemed that the only way to disguise her first fib was to tell another.

"I don't know," Rachel answered, trying to keep her voice from quavering, "I only responded to the letter he sent."

"I told you, he never *sent* a letter! Who was it from? Was it from that Matthew boy? Was it?" Clay's voice dropped to a menacing whisper. "You know that I forbid you from corresponding with that boy! The letter was from him, wasn't it? I'll kill him, you know. Don't think I won't find them. You have no business with his kind, do you understand?"

"Yes, sir, but the letter wasn't from M—"

Clay reached back a large, strong hand back and brought it down, connecting it with Rachel's right cheek. She jumped back, startled, her face stinging where he had hit her and tears falling from her eyes. An angry red welt spread across her cheek.

"I want an honest answer!" Clay raised his hand again, but Penelope grabbed his arm.

"Clay, don't hurt the child, she hasn't done anything wrong!"

Clay shrugged her hand away and turned on her. "You stay out of this! This is between me and Rachel! Ever since she arrived here after the death of my daughter, she has disobeyed and dishonoured me!" He turned back to Rachel. "And I would like to know why."

"I never did anything!" Rachel protested, shouting through the tears, "The letter wasn't from Matthew!"

"Then *why* did you lie?"

"I was afraid," Rachel sobbed, sinking into her chair, "I didn't want anything to happen…"

"What? What to happen? Who was the letter from?"

"No one, it was nothing, but I didn't want you to wor— Unkhh!"

Clay had slapped her again across the same cheek, but this time, her head struck the wall beside her. Rachel felt dizzy.

"Who was it?"

"Alvin!" Rachel blurted out, unable to take any more, "It was from Alvin! He just wanted to make sure I was alright, that's all!"

"I warned you never to speak to him! He and that girl, *Alice*, are nothing but trouble! You are to have nothing to do with them, do you hear me?"

Rachel tried to answer, but her words were lost to Penelope's pleas for Clay to have mercy on her granddaughter and Clay's shouts. Rachel's head spun, unable to comprehend what had just occurred. She was scared, perhaps more than she ever had been before in her own home.

Penelope, despite her passive and obedient nature, was trying her best to stop Clay's abuses, but to no avail. Her attempts to stay his hand only served to make him angrier. He picked up a large book from the table and waved it in the air like a madman. Before Rachel could even perceive what was happening, the volume was hurling through the air, straight towards her. Penelope screamed, but Rachel was unable to move in time, and the large text caught her a glancing blow to the left side of her skull, the corner finding its mark just below her eye. Rachel cried out and sank to her knees on the floor, her hand pressed to her face.

Clay was fuming, but the world was fuzzy to Rachel, and she could only gather bits and pieces of everything around her and tried in vain to assemble them inside her head. Her grandmother appeared at her side and grabbed hold of her arm, hoisting her up as best she could. Rachel received the message and rushed up to her room, brushing past Clay as she did so. She heard his voice, loud but unclear, and she continued to run, leaving her grandparents in the parlour. Amid the chaos in Rachel's conscious, she felt a pang of guilt for leaving her tiny grandmother unprotected against the monster that was her husband. It was a strange thing to see the man so unhinged against his own family. Never before in her life had Clay hit Rachel before. Clearly, there was something wrong; something in his mind.

After tripping hastily up the stairs, Rachel reached the door of her bedroom and practically fell into it, slamming the door shut and clumsily locking it behind her. She collapsed in a sobbing heap on the floor, and her tears mingled with blood that had spilled from a gash on her cheek. She felt impossibly angry, but also guilty, and not simply for leaving her grandmother behind. She felt awful for simply putting Penelope and herself into this position in the first place. Clay never would have hit her if she hadn't disobeyed him, and she knew full well the risks that accompanied such behaviour. Rachel could only hope that Alvin, Alice, and Matthew had gotten her letter, and weren't worried about her. She didn't want them to know what had happened; she didn't want them to fear for her, or to be concerned. They had enough problems of their own to deal with.

Rachel stood and wiped the tears from her eyes. Multiple times she stood in front of her mirror as she used water from her wash basin, but not once did she dare look into it at her reflection. She didn't want to know what she looked like. She didn't want to believe that anything had happened. She cleaned and dusted her room as if it were simply a normal day.

As Rachel dusted the top of her dresser, she kept her gaze fixed firmly down, away from the reflective glass that would only serve to remind her of her situation. When Rachel had finished dusting, she sighed, and, in a moment of forgetfulness, looked up, and found herself face to face with someone she barely recognized. The expression of the stranger facing her changed as she continued to stare; it became quite anguished. Rachel raised her hand and gently touched the glass, tracing the angry red line along the reflection of her cheek. She slowly pulled her hand back and touched her own face, fingering the spot just below her eye where the book had hit her. She noticed how it felt; an aching sore that stung whenever she touched it or moved the muscles in her face. She saw the blood that stained her cheeks, and angrily splashed water into her face to clean it away. Her green eyes were swollen and ringed with red, and her light brown hair was a mess. Tears in her eyes, Rachel struggled to make herself look as she had before, combing her hair and washing her face over and over again, but to no avail. She would need time to heal, and she knew as much, but she didn't want to admit it.

Rachel sat down on her bed, listening to Penelope and Clay talking downstairs. They had quieted down considerably, but Rachel could tell by his tone that Clay was still angry. She fell asleep that night as soon as her head hit the pillow, and awoke early the next morning to the sunlight streaming through her window. She felt sore; remembering one by one each time her grandfather had struck her. She felt like crying, but she had no tears left to shed. Now, there could be only action. She had to do something, she wasn't sure what, but Clay had gone too far. Of course, action should have been taken a long time before, but the time had come where Clay was a threat even to his own family. Rachel was afraid, but she was the only one who could, or would, do anything. Penelope, even after what had happened, would continue to kowtow to Clay's every whim.

Rachel, after getting dressed and washing her aching face again, unlocked her door slowly and quietly, and then stepped outside into the hallway. She could hear the clinking of forks and plates coming from the dining room. Creeping down the stairs, she peered over the railing and could just see her grandparents eating their breakfast. They didn't speak to each other, so Rachel continued down the stairs and stood in the doorway. Neither Clay nor Penelope looked up. Rachel cleared her throat, and both her grandparents turned to face her. Penelope had a frightened look in her eye, and she shook her head at Rachel so subtly that Clay didn't notice. Clay stood up, using his imposing stature to intimidate his granddaughter.

"Go to your room," he ordered, his voice betraying no emotion. Rachel prepared to stand her ground.

"Why?" she asked, trying to sound as innocent as she could, "I'm hungry."

"Go," Clay repeated, stepping closer to her.

"Why?"

"You know *why*," Clay fumed, "You disobeyed me. Until you repent of your actions and show me that you'll not try to contact those... those... those *people* again, you will not be permitted to leave your bedroom, except for chores." Clay waited for Rachel to apologize and beg for his forgiveness, but she didn't. She remained silent, then slowly turned around and began climbing the stairs again. She re-entered her room and once again locked the door behind her. Rachel's stomach let out a growl, low and loud.

"You'll have to wait," she told it, "I can't apologize to him. He'll see right through me..." Rachel, not wanting to get hit again, had only one choice. Until Clay had calmed down, she would have to remain out of his sight, and if he wanted her to stay in her room, that was what she would do. Breakfast time came and went, and midday disappeared into the mists of the past before Rachel had anything to eat. Clay had gone out, leaving Penelope to see that Rachel didn't leave her bedroom. Though Clay's wife was exceedingly obedient, she couldn't stand to see her granddaughter suffer so, and knocked lightly on Rachel's door at around three o'clock in the afternoon.

"Rachel," she whispered through the door, "It's me, Grandmother. Don't worry, your grandfather isn't here. Open the door, please."

From the other side of the wall, Rachel stood and tiptoed towards the door, almost as if afraid that Clay would hear her. She unlocked it and opened it just a crack, peeking out to see her little grandmother, a laden tea tray in her arms.

"Are you hungry?" Penelope asked sweetly, "I know your grandfather said that you weren't to leave your room, so I thought that I should bring you something to eat." She paused, waiting for Rachel to answer. She could barely see her through the miniscule crack between door and frame. Rachel opened the door wider and reached out for the tea tray, which Penelope cautiously handed her. She reached up and brushed a stray lock of hair from in front of Rachel's bruised face.

"I'm so sorry," she said, tears clouding her vision, reducing Rachel's face to a blur, "For what he did."

"It wasn't your fault," Rachel insisted, "It was mine. I never should have disobeyed him." Penelope nodded, unable to find fault with her granddaughter's reasoning.

"Still," she said, "He should never have hit you the way he did…"

"Perhaps not," Rachel said, her tone suggesting inner reflection on the topic. She broke a piece of bread off of a slice on her tray and ate it hungrily.

"Won't you just apologize?" Penelope asked, blinking up at Rachel imploringly.

"I can't," Rachel replied, "He would know I didn't mean it."

"I know, dear, but you must try," Penelope counselled.

"No," Rachel decided, shaking her head, "I can't. He'll do it again."

"No, he won't, Rachel! He only lost his temper, he would never—"

"Yes, he would!" Rachel was nearly yelling, "Don't you see what a madman he is? He tried to *kill* people. And you saw what he did yesterday."

"Oh, Rachel, you mustn't dwell on what he did yesterday!"

"I can't help it!" Tears sprang to Rachel's eyes. "Look at me." She stepped forward so her grandmother could see her battered face. Penelope turned her face away.

"Look, grandmother!" Rachel stepped into her line of sight, "Can't you see? How can you ignore this?"

"You'd better drink your tea before it gets cold," Penelope whispered, then turned and marched resolutely down the stairs. Rachel was fuming. She shuffled back into her room with her tea tray, placed it on her bed, and then closed the door as hard as she could. The slam was loud and satisfying, but it did nothing to ease Rachel's pain. It wasn't so much the physical cuts and bruises that hurt her, but more so the emotional wounds. The intention behind Clay's actions. The glint of triumph in his eye. The cool and collected sound of his harsh words. Rachel shivered.

The days passed, but Rachel could not bring herself to speak to Clay for fear of what he might do. She thought it best to remain hidden in her room, where she was relatively safe from his wrath. Penelope brought her food at every opportunity, and tried to encourage her to face Clay, until finally, on the fifth day of her imprisonment, Rachel was ready to speak to her grandfather. Penelope led her downstairs to the parlour once more, and Rachel looked up at Clay, fear in her eyes.

"I'm sorry," she began, her voice thick, "I never should have been corresponding with Alvin. I should have told you the truth."

"So you see now that they aren't worth speaking with? That they are dangerous and immoral people?" Clay asked, one eyebrow raised.

"Yes," Rachel replied, a feeling of guilt for betraying her friends rising quickly inside her, "Yes, I do."

"Don't lie to me," Clay said coldly.

"I'm not," Rachel insisted, "I'll never lie to you again."

"Good," Clay decided, and stepped back, "You may leave your room."

Rachel breathed a sigh of relief and her stomach let out yet another loud groan. After she had been fed and watered, she sat down in the parlour and began to fix a hole in one of her dresses, an activity which she knew that Clay would approve. What she didn't know was that trouble, as much as she tried to avoid it, was about to find her.

"Rachel!" Clay barked from the dining room, "Come in here, this instant!"

Rachel put down her sewing in a hurry and scurried to the dining room, remembering the last time that her grandfather had used that tone.

"Y-yes, Grandfather?"

Clay stepped forward, an envelope in his hand. He waved it in front of Rachel's face and hurled it, in a crumpled ball, straight at her chest. Rachel, fingers trembling, bent to pick it up.

"How do you explain this?"

Rachel opened the envelope and carefully drew out the wrinkled paper inside. It was a letter, from Alvin, Matthew, and Alice. She read it over once, twice, three times, shaking all the while.

"I never asked for them to send a letter," she began to explain, "This is the answer to my reply from weeks ago..."

"How do you explain what's in it?" Clay roared, snatching the letter back from her. He proceeded to read its contents out loud.

"*Dear Rachel*," he read, "*We too wish you could be here with us, but we know your grandfather would never allow it.*" He broke off and looked up at her, his expression livid. "You had the bare faced audacity to wish yourself away? To live with *them?*" Rachel hung her head. Clay opened his clenched fist and slapped her across the face.

"Look at me when I'm speaking to you!" Rachel did as she was told, peering up at her grandfather with a look that, in anyone else, would have induced pity.

"How dare you disrespect me? You have left me no *choice* but to discipline you!" Clay continued, "I will not have you become a shame to our family like that Cosgrove girl."

Rachel was about to protest that Alice did nothing shameful, but she thought better of it.

Clay fumed, frustrated by her lack of response. He shook where he stood, his teeth clenched. He had to make his granddaughter understand, and regret what she had done. It was for her own good. He raised a clenched fist, his knuckles white.

Rachel, sensing what was to come, turned in a flash and began to run up the stairs towards the safety of her bedroom. Clay lunged after her and she felt a sharp pain in her side as the fist found its mark, but she struggled onward, her grandfather close on her heels. Rachel reached the landing at the top of the stairs and hurled herself towards her room. As she fumbled to lock the door behind her, she could hear Clay pounding towards her. Finally, she managed to lock the door just as he began to turn the knob. He began to beat the wooden door, causing the whole lot to rattle and shake so much that Rachel feared it would crumble to bits right before her eyes.

Clay was shouting at her through the walls, and Rachel, tears streaming down her face, made the decision right then and there that she couldn't stay in this vile man's care any longer. Immediately, she began pulling her furniture towards the door, barricading herself in and Clay out. She reached under her mattress and pulled out a pouch of money she had been saving, and then threw it into a carpet bag that she picked up from the floor. She flung open her dresser and stuffed as many items of clothing as she could into the small bag, then closed it firmly and sat it beneath the window.

"Come out of there!" she heard Clay screaming from the hallway, "You will learn, I promise you that!" Rachel could hear her grandmother pleading with him to return downstairs.

Rachel scrambled to straighten out her thoughts. She knew she had to escape, but how? She had no ropes or ladders to go out through the window, and the drop was too far to jump. She rushed to the window and looked out. The grass below seemed to grow ever farther away as she stared at it, the sounds of Clay's shouts and the pounding on the door ringing in her ears. He had to give up soon, but that still left Rachel no alternative escape but the window.

A moment later, inspiration struck. She opened the window all the way and after dropping her carpet bag to the ground, leaned out as far as she could. A mere few feet to her left was a tall maple tree, the leaves full and green. If she could just reach the nearest branch... Rachel leaned and leaned, stretching her arms out towards the tree. Unable to quite grasp the branch, she brought her knees up onto the window sill, and placed her upper body through the window. At last, she managed to reach a branch, and held on to it with all her might. Cautiously, she brought her feet through the window and relied solely on the maple tree for support. The ground seemed to spin beneath her. She began to hyperventilate, the height dizzying.

The branch proved too thin to support her weight and bent at an alarming speed, lowering her roughly to the ground, where she landed with a thump.

After a moment spent checking for any broken bones that may have occurred due to the fall, Rachel scurried away, keeping back from the streets and running full speed until her house was no longer in view. There was only one place to go where she would be safe, and knew she would be welcomed: Norton.

CHAPTER TEN

Time is Precious

Matthew and Trevor spent many a warm, sunny day inside the classroom come time to resume school, and though Matthew enjoyed himself, Trevor was less than amused by the fact that they were kept inside for such long periods of time, not to mention made to sit perfectly still and listen attentively to boring lectures. To Trevor, the teachers always seemed to drone on and on, and he missed the sounds of the outdoors; the whisper of the wind through the tree branches, the buzz of the insects, the songs of the birds, the noise of the people. Indeed, school and Trevor simply weren't a very compatible couple, and he spent every spare moment he had to remind Matthew of that fact.

One such day, Matthew and Trevor were walking through the school hallway after a long day of classes. The school was dimly lit, particularly in the hallways, and the ceilings had similar patterns to Mrs. Brown's. The walls were an off-white, though whether from the paint colour or from years of decay no one knew.

"I've said it once, and I'll say it again: I hate this place," Trevor complained, books held limply at his side.

"Yes," Matthew replied with a sigh, "Yes you have."

"I mean, it's not just that I have to stay in there all day, it's the whole thing. Look around! This place is nasty. The walls and ceiling look like there they're about to fall in or something, and it's always so hot! Would it kill them to put in a fan or two?" Trevor coughed deeply. "And I swear this air is gonna kill me..." Trevor trailed off, his body racked with coughs. It was indeed quite damp inside the school, and the environment was wreaking havoc with Trevor's lungs.

"Yeah, yeah, I know," Matthew smiled, "But, hey, it's the weekend! You don't have to come back until Monday."

"All I can say is the faster Grace and I can finish fixing the you-know-what, the better," Trevor managed between fits of coughing, "I want to go home."

Matthew nodded in silence as they finally crossed the threshold to the outside. Trevor tried in vain to get a deep breath in, but had to settle for being simply able to breathe without rasping terribly. He clattered down the front steps and into the street, elated to finally be out of the building that had ensnared him in its dank, dark depths. Matthew trotted down after him and laughed as Trevor proceeded to try and clear his lungs.

"Let's go back to the boarding house," Matthew grinned, knowing that Trevor would be upset if he called it "home".

"Alright," Trevor agreed, "At least it's a good walk."

The pair began to walk in the direction of Mrs. Brown's boarding house, chatting as they went.

"How'd you do on the math test today?" Matthew asked casually.

"Are you kidding me?" Trevor replied with a bitter laugh, "I barely answered one stupid question! I can't belie—" He was cut off abruptly as he was knocked over by a sprinting pedestrian. He swore loudly.

"Would it kill you to watch where you're going for once?" he shouted once he saw who it was.

"Forgive me," Alvin panted, helping Trevor to his feet, then turning to Matthew, "I'm so glad I found you! You'd better come with me, there's something you must see."

"What's going on?"

"No time... to explain... Come on..." Alvin began to run back the way he had come, checking over his shoulder to be sure that Matthew was following. Matthew hesitated, looking from Alvin to Trevor and back again.

"I'll see you later, alright Trevor?" he said, backing away, "I'll be back soon!" Matthew turned around completely and followed Alvin away at full speed.

"Bye!" Trevor called after him, a smug smile on his face.

Alvin neither slowed down nor spoke until they had reached the edge of St. Edward's and entered the Southern Quays. There, he stopped and knelt to the ground, clutching his left arm.

"Are you... okay?" Matthew panted when he caught up.

"I'm... fine..." Alvin said through gritted teeth, "I've just been having some trouble with my arm... it's alright." He winced in pain.

"So what's going on?" Matthew asked, "Where are we going?"

"You'll see when we get to Alice's," Alvin answered, "But I assure you, it's important." He paused and stood up. "Let's go."

They arrived moments later at the front door of Alice's aunt's house and Alvin walked straight in without knocking, carving a path through the women who stood around, whispering to one another whilst stealing glances at the boys who rushed past them. Alvin led Matthew up the stairs, and then stopped in front of Alice's door.

"I should warn you..." he began, "You may be a bit... shocked..."

"Alright," Matthew responded, tensing as he prepared himself for the worst. Alvin knocked, and the door opened instantly, revealing Alice standing in the doorway.

"Oh, I'm so glad you found him," she said to Alvin, taking his arm and ushering them inside, "And that you came so quickly!"

"Alice, this is ridiculous, I'm fine!"

Matthew jumped at the sound of his old friend's voice.

"Rachel?" he croaked, his voice breaking.

"Matthew?"

Rachel stood up from the armchair in which she had been seated and stepped into the light. Tears sprang to Matthew's eyes. He blinked them away in frustration, only now realizing just how much he had missed her these past months. He grinned broadly and stepped forward, but his face fell as he noticed the angry red marks that adorned her cheeks.

"What happened?"

Rachel looked away. "Nothing," she said quietly, "Nothing, it's... it's fine..."

Matthew took another bold step forward and gazed down at Rachel. "Rachel..."

Rachel hunched her shoulders and turned her head to the side.

"Rachel, come on...what happened? Rachel... Rachel, look at me."

Rachel, reluctantly, peered up at Matthew, revealing the marks on her cheeks and the purple bruise under her eye. Matthew, almost involuntarily, reached up, and his fingers hovered over her face.

"Did Clay do this?" he asked, hardly daring to breathe. Rachel nodded.

"I'm fine," she insisted, "R-really..."

Matthew could see her eyes beginning to water, but she wouldn't let herself cry.

"Aw, Rachel," he whispered, "I'm so sorry. You're sure you're alright?"

Rachel nodded again, and smiled as best she could. "I've missed you all so much," she said, changing the subject, "It's so good to see you again."

"You too," Matthew replied, and opened his arms jovially. Rachel smiled and moved forward to embrace her friend. After a moment, Matthew pulled away and stepped back.

"You should really tell us what happened, you know," he urged, "Trust me, it helps. I know."

Rachel gave him a quizzical look and sat down in the armchair once more, pulling it round to face everyone. She then proceeded to reluctantly tell her friends what had happened and all that Clay had done. She told them about how she had escaped through the window, and how, afterwards, she had used the last of her money to get a train to Norton, and then barely eaten since she boarded because she didn't have enough money left for food. She had arrived in Norton that morning and tracked down Alvin from the address in the letters, which she had committed to memory. He had given her something to eat and drink, and then brought her promptly to see Alice. She wouldn't talk about what had happened to her at first; she remained stoic.

Alice, by the end of Rachel's story, looked close to tears, and Alvin's face mimicked hers. Matthew's reaction, however, was by far the worst. What the others didn't know was that he knew exactly what Rachel had been through. The same thing, and worse, had happened to him. He knew what it felt like. Rachel's story had stirred up long suppressed memories of all the things his father had done to hurt him before he had finally run away from home. Matthew tried to blink away the tears, but his attempts were futile.

"Matthew, don't cry!" Rachel implored, smiling, "It's not so bad..."

"I know, I know," Matthew said, wiping his eyes, "It's okay, really, I'm just so glad you're alright, that you escaped..."

"So am I," Rachel agreed, "So am I."

A moment of silence followed, and Alvin broke it. "We need to find you a place to stay," he said. Rachel nodded in agreement.

"It's going to be difficult," she warned, "I've no money and no family to speak of."

"I'd invite you to stay here, but as you can see," Alice chuckled, "My aunt's got her hands full."

"My grandfather's house is too small to accommodate anyone else," Alvin added.

"And Mrs. Brown's is stuffed to the gills," Matthew attested.

"There must be some place..." Alvin thought out loud, "Any place at all..."

"Wait!" Alice nearly shouted, "Follow me; I think I may have an idea." She stood and scurried to the door, followed closely by Alvin, then Matthew and Rachel. In the hallway, Alice pointed up at the ceiling.

"This place," she informed them, "Has an attic. I've never been up there, but I've seen Aunt Jess go in for things. There may be enough space there for you to stay, if you don't mind being a little cramped." Alice stood on tiptoes and reached up as far as she could, trying to fold her fingers around a small wooden handle in a narrow panel in the ceiling. She felt her fingers brush against the handle, but she wasn't tall enough to grab it. Alvin smiled and raised his hand, easily reaching the handle and opening the attic door. Alice pulled a stepladder from the corner and placed it directly beneath the doorway, then climbed up and looked inside.

"It's a bit dusty," she commented, her voice echoing as she peered around, "But there's plenty of space." She took Alvin's hand and climbed down. "What do you think?"

Rachel looked at each of her friends in turn, painfully aware of how each one noticed the marks on her face all over again, and smiled. "If your aunt will have me," she said, "I'd be delighted to stay here."

After asking Jessica, and Alice putting up a very persuasive argument for her friend, Rachel was allowed to move in. All she had was her carpet bag, so there was no problem fitting her into the attic's limited space.

There was an old spare mattress being stored there, so the four youth took it out and cleaned it, then laid it on the floor to make Rachel's bed. Soon, after reorganizing the boxes and furniture that called the attic home, all that was left to do was send up Rachel's things and let her get settled. Alvin knelt beside the opening in the attic floor and gripped the edges, preparing to lower himself the short distance to the second storey. His feet inches from the ground, a sharp pain in his upper left arm made him cry out and let go of the ledge, sending him sprawling to the ground.

"Alvin!" Alice cried, followed by the others, "Are you alright?" The three of them rushed to the opening in the floor and peered down at their fallen friend.

"I'm fine," Alvin called up to them, "Just fine, it was my arm, that's all."

"Alvin," Rachel began, "It's been some time since your arm was hurt, should it not be healed by now?"

"It was," Alvin protested, "It only started to hurt after I met Trevor on the day I found Matthew. I cut it on a nail from some broken crates." He winced in pain.

"Alright," Rachel said, "Just be careful then!"

"Yes, ma'am," Alvin agreed, smiling through the pain.

After they had gotten Rachel settled in, Alvin and Matthew left, skirting round the ladies who were waiting for their return at the bottom of the stairs. Once they had exited the stifling house, Matthew turned to Alvin.

"I never thought that Clay would be capable of hurting his own granddaughter," he said sadly.

"He doesn't believe he's done anything wrong," Alvin explained, "He only wishes to protect her, but he doesn't know that she only needs protection from him."

Matthew nodded in agreement.

The pair walked back to Mrs. Brown's boarding house, talking very little, each short burst of speech followed by several moments of silence. As Matthew climbed the front steps, Alvin continued on to Irontown.

The night was just beginning, the sun slowly snaking its way to the horizon, and though Matthew knew that he might have missed his supper, he didn't care. All he cared about in that moment was knowing that Rachel was safe and sound at Alice's, far away from her broken grandfather. Matthew stood in front of the boarding house door for a while, watching the comings and goings on the street, feeling contented. He went inside after a time and walked casually to the kitchen, finding Mrs. Brown and Mr. Riddell cooking together and laughing over some joke or another. Matthew stood in the doorway and watched them for a moment. Their backs were both turned to him, but he could imagine the expressions on their faces.

Matthew had to suppress a giggle. The sound of Mr. Riddell laughing was, before moving into Mrs. Brown's, almost unheard on any given occasion. Now, it seemed, he was laughing and smiling more than he ever had before, at least since Matthew had known him. He looked different too; his face seemed less pale and sombre, and the dark smudges that had seemingly always been present below his eyes were gone. His features appeared less sharp and serious, and his outlook on life had done an about face. Where once he was the ever present voice of pessimism, now he was more the voice of reason. Even when the other time travellers had told him about Trevor suddenly appearing in the past, he had been relatively unworried. Matthew wasn't sure what had changed him so drastically, but he knew that he liked this new Mr. Riddell.

"Matthew!" Mrs. Brown turned and saw him out of the corner of her eye, "Where have you been? Trevor arrived back ages ago."

"I was visiting an old friend," Matthew replied, causing Mr. Riddell to raise an eyebrow.

"Well, you've come just in time," Mrs. Brown smiled, "Supper is nearly ready."

"I'll go and wash up," answered Matthew, turning and leaving the room. Mr. Riddell watched him go, a bemused expression on his face. He knew of Alvin and Alice, but so did Mrs. Brown, so why would Matthew have said he was visiting an *old friend*? Why not specify? Was there another *old friend* in town all of a sudden that they didn't know about?

"Are you alright?" Mrs. Brown asked politely, smiling up at Mr. Riddell.

"Yes, it's nothing. I'm only wondering who the old friend was."

"I'm sure you'll find out soon enough. Here, taste this, would you?" Mrs. Brown held up a spoon to Mr. Riddell, who took it and tasted its contents.

"It needs more salt," he decided, handing back the utensil, and the pair of them set to work again.

As Mr. Riddell and Mrs. Brown finished their work in the kitchen, Trevor and Grace were continuing to work on the time machine. They kept it, and all its complex pieces, in Grace, Sandra, and Laura's room, where it would be safe, and they could work on the repairs uninterrupted.

"Would you pass me that?" Grace asked, pointing to a tiny, almost invisible gear that lay on the floor to Trevor's right. Trevor picked it up carefully between his thumb and forefinger, and dropped it into Grace's outstretched palm. She looked quite ingenious, using a magnifying glass to see everything properly, and numerous tools which lay spread all around her. Without the technology of the time in which the time machine was built, Grace had to improvise, using watchmaker's instruments and old, hand powered tools, which made the repairs worlds more difficult.

"I can't believe that all these little pieces can seriously all have a purpose, I mean, some of them you can barely see!"

"Trevor," Grace explained, a note of impatience in her voice, "Everything has a purpose. If even one little thing is missing, it could spell disaster, and you might not be able to get back home."

Trevor shook his head sombrely, but tried not to show his apprehension. He had picked up the time machine rather hastily after it had fallen from the wagon and been trampled, he only hoped he had managed to pick out every little piece from the dusty road. His freedom depended on it.

He heard the door open and spun round, shielding the time machine from view. Matthew smiled from the doorway.

"Supper's nearly ready," he informed them with a laugh, "You'd better come down."

"Sure," Trevor replied, looking back at Grace, his eyes questioning.

"You go ahead," she told him, smiling, "I'll clean up."

"Thanks," Trevor answered, and sprang to his feet, following Matthew out of the room. Once they were out of Grace's earshot, Trevor spoke again.

"So what was going on with Alvin?" he queried curiously, "What was he in such a rush for? What did he want you to see so bad?"

"It was Rachel," Matthew whispered back, "Remember, I told you about her. She's the one whose grandfather tried to kill us."

"Yeah? So what was the matter? I thought she lived in Connolly Mills?"

"She does, or did. She escaped her house and hopped a train to get here."

"Why'd she do that?"

"To get away from her grandfather!"

"I thought you said he wanted to protect her! You told me that psycho would never want to hurt her!"

"I was wrong," said Matthew stiffly.

"What? What did he do?"

"Listen, we can't talk about it right now, can I tell you later?"

"He hit her or something, didn't he? You think he's like your ol' dad, don't you?"

Matthew only nodded. "I'll tell you about it later."

CHAPTER ELEVEN

No Time to Waste

The next morning, Saturday, began like any other. Rachel was safe with Alice, and Matthew and Trevor were heading over to their place so that Trevor might meet Rachel and the five of them could spend the day together. They would discuss what they wanted to do when they arrived, but Trevor already had a few ideas of his own.

"I'm telling you, Matthew, it's fun!"

"Trevor, you promised you'd stay out of trouble! Come on, you should have known I would say no when you asked if we'd like to all go out and drink together, for goodness sake!"

Trevor shook his head. "I'm telling you," he said, "You're missing out."

"Whatever," Matthew replied, "Just don't mention it to the others, *please.* They would be shocked at you, and we just want to fit in."

They arrived at Alice's aunt's house a few minutes later and Matthew knocked politely on the door. It was opened, as usual, by a heavily made-up woman. Matthew had learned long ago to ignore their teasing. The youth were greeted by Aunt Jessica and directed upstairs to Alice's room. Immediately as Matthew entered, he knew that someone was missing.

"Where's Alvin?"

Alice looked up. "I don't know," she replied, a hint of worry in her voice, "He usually arrives quite early."

Matthew shrugged and sat down. Trevor and Rachel were introduced, and conversation began. "What should we do today?" Matthew asked, getting straight to the point in order to avoid Trevor piling in his ludicrous ideas.

"Alvin was talking yesterday about going to see a show," Rachel suggested, "That sounds like it could be fun."

Matthew and Alice nodded in agreement. Trevor opened his mouth, undoubtedly to protest, but Matthew silenced him with a discreet elbow to the ribs. Trevor's jaw slammed shut and he glared at Matthew.

The four youth sat and talked politely for a time, Trevor tapping his foot impatiently all the while. Matthew, becoming severely annoyed, made a suggestion.

"Alvin probably slept in," he surmised, "Why don't we take a walk to his grandfather's house and invite him along. If we don't go soon, we won't make it to the show on time."

"Matthew's right," Rachel agreed, frowning as she noticed Trevor staring at the red marks on her face, "Alvin's most likely only late."

"Well what are we waiting for?" Trevor stood quickly, "Let's go find him!"

Rachel and Alice were confused by Trevor's sudden urgency, but Matthew knew that he was itching to get outside. Trevor was the sort of person who could never stay still for long.

The walk to Irontown was not a particularly short one, and at times Matthew wished that he were riding in a wagon, but no one else seemed to mind. As they approached the smoky district, Trevor's breathing became raspy, and he coughed with every other word he spoke, but he did not once complain, simply glad to be outside, for that was as close to freedom as he could get. Alice wasn't faring well with the smog either, having to clear her throat every few moments.

Matthew was the first to the door of Alvin's temporary home, and he knocked softly. The four youth waited for their friend to open the door, but there was no answer.

"Knock louder," Rachel advised, "Perhaps he's asleep."

Matthew knocked once more, loud enough for it to be heard through the whole house. No answer. He knocked on the doorframe. Still nothing. He resorted to pounding on the door while Alice, Trevor, and Rachel assisted him by calling Alvin's name.

"Maybe he left already," deduced Trevor, "For all we know, he could be pounding on *your* door right now." He looked at Alice, eyebrows raised. Alice shook her head.

"We would have passed him on the road," she said, "He always takes the same way."

"What if he took a shortcut?"

"This *is* the shortcut."

As Alice and Trevor bounced ideas off each other, Rachel pulled Matthew around to the side of the house.

"Something's not right," she decided, whispering to him, "Alvin would never be late. On his father's farm, he wakes up at dawn every morning. Perhaps I'm simply concerned about nothing, but we owe it to Alvin to be sure, don't we?" Matthew nodded vigorously.

"What can we do?"

Rachel's brow furrowed and nose wrinkled as she thought. "It's not at all proper..." she began.

Matthew was silent.

"We could go inside," Rachel finished, "If he's at home, I'm certain he won't mind, after all, his grandfather isn't home today..." She trailed off, frustrated at her own lack of propriety. Matthew closed his eyes tight shut and breathed deeply in and out.

"Alright," he said, "For Alvin."

Rachel and Matthew came back around to the front of the house where Alice and Trevor were still trying to figure out where Alvin could possibly be. They didn't notice Rachel try the door.

"It's locked," she grumbled, "There has to be some other way..."

"What about a window?" Matthew suggested, and then winced, remembering the last time Rachel had climbed through a window.

"Wonderful," Rachel stated, rushing to the other end of the veranda, where a large paneled window was set into the wall. However, upon further inspection, Matthew and Rachel found that the window could not open and the curtains were closed so they could not even see inside.

"Come on," Matthew said, "I saw a window around the side."

The pair of them marched once more around the side of the house and peered up at the second storey window.

"How are we meant to get through there?" Rachel asked, a tone of annoyance in her voice.

Matthew thought for a moment, gauging the distance between the ground and the window.

"I'll lift you up," he proposed impulsively, not taking his eyes off the glassy barrier between indoors and out.

"Matthew, that's hardly—"

"No, no, just listen," Matthew implored, "It's for Alvin. What's the worst that could happen?"

"Matthew, I... What if someone sees? I know I'm not usually worried about propriety, but this—"

"Rachel, I promise you, nothing is going to happen. For Alvin?"

Rachel sighed. "For Alvin," she agreed.

Matthew laced his fingers together and held his hands down near the ground. Rachel stepped up with her right foot, and pushed off the ground with her left. Matthew, trembling with exertion, lifted his hands as high as they would go and Rachel stepped gingerly onto his shoulders, hands pressed against the wall for support. Matthew could scarcely breathe, as the outside of Rachel's skirt was level with his face. He could feel her begin to stand precariously on tiptoe and grip the window sill.

"I can't see in," she called down, "We're still too short!"

"What? Whoa!" Matthew hollered back, losing his balance as he attempted to look up at Rachel. He stumbled back, Rachel keeping her grip on the house even as she screamed in surprise. Matthew felt her feet leave his shoulders and he tumbled roughly to the ground. He opened his eyes just in time to see Rachel's fingers lose their grip.

"Rachel!"

Matthew sprang forward and Rachel came crashing down on top on him. The two youth sat up, dazed.

"Are you alright?" Matthew asked, looking over at Rachel. She nodded absently. Matthew sat up straighter. "Rachel?"

"Shh! Do you hear them?"

"Who?"

"Trevor and Alice!"

Matthew paused and listened. "No."

"Neither do I."

Rachel stood and ran back to the front of the house, Matthew close on her heels.

"They're gone," Matthew commented. Rachel clomped back up the front steps and tried the door again. This time, it swung open.

"Oh, Trevor," Matthew cringed as he remembered his friend's skill at picking locks. Rachel lost no time in entering the house, rushing in and looking around. Matthew followed her and they soon met with Trevor and Alice, who were wandering the main floor, calling Alvin's name.

"Have you seen him?" Rachel asked. Trevor shook his head.

"Let's check upstairs," Matthew said, "He might be up there."

The four of them ran up the stairs, calling after their friend all the while. There were two rooms, and they split into pairs to check each one. Trevor entered the room to the left, Alice directly behind him, and stopped dead in his tracks, swearing almost involuntarily.

"Oh, no," he said, his face losing colour. Alice peered in from behind him.

"What?" she asked, "What do you s—" Alice was thwarted in her attempts at speech by the sight of Alvin, lying motionless on the floor. She pushed desperately past a very ill looking Trevor and knelt beside Alvin.

"Alvin?" she said gently, tears forming in her eyes, "Alvin, can you hear me?" Trevor swore again and clenched his fist against the doorframe, leaning his forehead on it. Matthew, hearing Trevor, felt his stomach drop to the floor. He and Rachel crossed the hallway as quickly as they could and stood behind Trevor, looking into Alvin's bedroom, where he lay on the floor, his head having crashed into his dresser. He looked, by all accounts, dead. There was little to no colour in his face, his eyes were closed, and he was laying face up, arms and legs akimbo. Alice knelt by his head, her back turned to the door, whispering to him. His left sleeve was soaked through by a sticky, watery substance, ringed red with blood, and his left hand was abnormally blue.

Trevor gagged and pushed through Rachel and Matthew, hand over his mouth, back the way he had come, pounding down the stairs two at a time. Rachel and Matthew stood stock still, staring at Alvin. Alice was sobbing, and she turned to look at the two of them.

"Someone please get a doctor," she wept desperately, "Please get a doctor…"

Without a word, Matthew sprang into action, turning and hastening down the stairs, leaving Rachel to comfort Alice as best she could. On his way out of the house, Matthew passed Trevor, who was expelling the contents of his stomach into the bushes. He knew that Alvin's grandfather didn't own a telephone, so it was useless to try and call a doctor from there. The very first thing that entered Matthew's mind was to knock on a neighbour's door and ask them to help him contact a doctor. So, with Trevor still in sight, Matthew hurried up the steps of the closely neighbouring house and pounded urgently on the door. It was opened in an instant by an older woman, who looked as though she had just awoken.

"What is the meaning of this?" she shouted as if offended, "What is your business here boy?"

"My… friend… Alvin Quinn… he needs… a doctor…" Matthew told her, trying to catch his breath, "Please… where's the… nearest one? He needs one… real bad…"

The woman's expression softened as she realized the apparent severity of the situation. "Of course, of course," she clucked, "Do come in, I'll call him for you."

She led Matthew into her house, got on the telephone, and called the nearest doctor. It took a few moments to patch her through, and Matthew stood waiting apprehensively, knowing that every second they wasted was a second that could be used to save Alvin's life. Finally, the doctor was on the line and the woman passed the telephone to Matthew, who desperately tried to explain the dire situation to the man on the other end. The doctor promised that he would be there right away, and hung up. Matthew hurriedly thanked Alvin's neighbour, then tore through her house and back outside. He waited at the front of the house for what seemed like an eternity, watching the streets in all directions for the doctor. Trevor waited with him, but they did not speak.

When finally the doctor appeared at the end of the road, Matthew ran to meet his buggy, telling him as much as he could as they strode purposefully towards the house. The doctor's name was Dr. Camber, and he had a severe, deep look to him, as though he knew that disaster was coming. He appeared to be in his forties or fifties, but he moved with the grace and efficiency of someone half his age. He had his medical bag in his hand as Matthew led him hurriedly up the stairs to where Alvin lay, still unresponsive.

Matthew's nose wrinkled in disgust as he entered Alvin's room once more, a smell reaching his nostrils that could only be described as the stench of death.

"What is that *smell*?" Matthew wheezed.

"Let me take a look," Dr. Camber muttered, ignoring Matthew's questions as he knelt next to Alvin. The doctor unbuttoned Alvin's shirt and carefully manoeuvred it around the boy's left arm, revealing impossibly pale skin around an awful, wet wound that looked as black as the night sky. Matthew knew that it was the exact location where Clay had shot him all that time ago. The foul, rotting smell appeared to be coming from Alvin's arm.

"He has a serious infection," Dr. Camber announced, then turned to the others, "Why was this not reported earlier?"

Alice could only cry, and Matthew was shaking his head. Rachel took it upon herself to answer. "We didn't know, sir."

"This is very serious," the doctor repeated, "Very serious indeed. Based on the rotting flesh and the symptoms you described," he looked up at Matthew, "Your friend has gangrene. His arm became infected, and it has essentially died."

"Will he... will *he* live?" Rachel asked over Alice's anguished sobs.

"We'll try and be sure he does, but I can make no promises. Do you understand?"

Matthew and Rachel nodded. Dr. Camber placed a gentle hand on Alvin's brow. "He's running a high fever," he said, "I need you all to help me, and do exactly as I say if we are going to save this boy's life. Can you do that?"

Matthew and Rachel exchanged glances, then looked down at Alice, who was cradling Alvin's head in her arms. "We can," Matthew confirmed, "But Alice..."

"She's in shock," the doctor told them, "Please move her away from here and give her something to drink." Rachel jumped to obey his orders, leading Alice carefully and gently out of the room.

"Rachel, please!" Alice protested, "I can't leave him there! Rachel!"

Alice's hysterical voice gradually became quieter as Rachel brought her downstairs.

"We're going to have to remove his arm," the doctor decided as he examined Alvin further.

"*What?*" Matthew shouted, "You mean... you mean..." Tears were quick to come to his eyes.

"Amputate," Dr. Camber replied, showing little emotion, "I know it's not what you wanted to hear, but it's the only way to stop the gangrene from spreading."

"Are you sure?" Matthew asked softly, "There's no other way?" The doctor merely shook his head.

"See here, the line of demarcation?" the doctor said pointing to the place where Alvin's healthy skin met his diseased arm in a bright pink line, "This is where the disease has been stopped. If we do not amputate his arm, the gangrene will continue to spread, and he will most certainly die."

"So there's nothing else you can do?"

"Do you want to save his life?"

Matthew looked down at his stricken friend, at his pale face, dark hair, his youth, his promise, the contributions he could make to the world, the value of his young life. Alvin had endangered his life to save Matthew and his family, now it was Matthew's turn to help save his life, even if it meant losing a part of him.

"Yes," he decided, nodding, "Yes, I do."

"Good," Dr. Camber replied, "Let's begin; there's no time to waste."

The doctor ordered Matthew to clear the bed of all its pillows and blankets, of which there were few, until only one thin sheet remained. From there, Matthew helped Dr. Camber lift Alvin off of the floor and onto the bed. Matthew held his breath as they moved him, the stench of rotting flesh made ever stronger. Alvin felt light with his weight distributed between the doctor and Matthew, and Matthew could have sworn he saw him flinch and his eyelids flutter.

Rachel returned to the room just as they were setting Alvin down. She tried not to let the terrible odour bother her as she crossed the room.

"How's Alice?" Matthew asked.

"Distraught," replied Rachel, gazing down at Alvin, "She's with Trevor."

Matthew nodded. He wanted to tell Rachel what they had to do to save Alvin's life, but he thought it best to let the doctor break the news.

"Ah, good," Dr. Camber said upon seeing Rachel, "You're back. I'm afraid, as I've already told your friend, that the only way to save this boy's life is to amputate his arm."

Matthew thought Rachel would cry out or protest, but all she did was take a deep, shaky breath.

"All of it?" she asked quietly. Dr. Camber nodded. Silent tears escaped Rachel's eyes, but she remained calm.

"Where do we start?" she inquired bravely.

Before the doctor could answer, a faint moan was heard from below them. Rachel and Matthew turned to look at Alvin, whose eyes were slowly flitting open. He screwed them shut again in pain and grit his teeth. He opened his eyes again, this time wide. He tried to prop himself up on his elbows, but he was too weak and collapsed back down on the mattress.

"Wh-what's going... on?"

Rachel reached down and took his healthy right hand in her own. "Your arm is badly infected where my grandfather shot you," she explained, her voice thick, "You've got gangrene..."

Alvin's face fell, but he was still confused. "Am I gonna be alright?"

Rachel nodded, trying desperately to keep her tears hidden. "You're going to be just fine," she promised, "Just fine."

Alvin seemed relieved, but in a moment, his expression became worried again. "Where's Alice?" he asked wearily, "Does she know? Is she alright?"

Rachel smiled. Alvin always seemed to be more concerned for others than he was for himself.

"She knows," Matthew said, "She's downstairs."

Alvin nodded weakly and caught sight of the doctor across the room. "Am I gonna be alright, Doc?" he asked, a trace of stoic humour in the question. His voice was weary, but he was slowly becoming more and more alert.

"You'll live," Dr. Camber answered honestly, "But we're going to amputate your arm. If we had time, I would bring you to the hospital, but as it is we nearly lost you, and it wouldn't do to move you at present..."

It took Alvin a moment to comprehend what the doctor had said, and Matthew and Rachel watched his face change from somewhat contented to downright terrified. In a split second, he was wide awake and panicked.

"Oh, you can't do that," he began, trying once again to sit up, but to no avail, "Please, isn't there any other way? I need my arm, doc! I can't do without it… I can't plant or harvest, I'll be all but useless to my father, and I was meant to go home and help him harvest soon… Please don't do this! Anything, anything but this. There's got to be *something* you can do… something… I need my arm… Alice'll never…"

Alvin broke off, tears streaming sideways down his face towards his ears.

"You won't be useful to anyone if you're dead," Dr. Camber replied morbidly, "And if you want to live, you have no choice."

"I can't…" Alvin wept, looking searchingly up at the ceiling, "Dear God, I can't…" He stopped and turned to Rachel and Matthew. "Does Alice know about *this*?"

Matthew and Rachel shook their heads. No one had yet told Alice of what was going to happen to Alvin. They were certain, however, that it would upset her.

"Don't say anything to her," Alvin begged, "If I don't live, I don't want her to—"

"Don't talk like that!" Matthew broke in, "You're going to live!" Rachel nodded in agreement.

"Alice isn't going to think any differently of you," she explained, "Nothing is going to change, Alvin…"

"Rachel, please!" Alvin beseeched her, "Be realistic! An arm is an awfully big thing to lose! It's not as if Alice won't notice it missing…" He trailed off, wincing in pain.

"Notice what missing?"

CHAPTER TWELVE

Just in Time

The three youth and the doctor turned their heads in unison to look at the source of the voice they had just heard. Alice stood in the doorway, looking at Alvin with concern in her eyes. Trevor stood directly behind her, peering into the room over her head. Rachel and Matthew looked at Alvin, questioning expressions on their faces.

"She's going to find out anyway," Matthew whispered to his friend, and Alvin took a shaky breath, staring at the ceiling once more, "You may as well tell her, before she finds out on her own."

Alvin's tears continued to flow freely, and he turned his head back to face Alice. "It's nothing," he began slowly, "It's just... just..." His words were lost as he fought to control his emotion. Alice walked into the room, greatly annoying Dr. Camber, but he said nothing against it. She walked right up to Alvin's bed and knelt beside him, Rachel and Matthew stepping to the side. Without anyone noticing but Trevor, Dr. Camber slipped out of the room.

"What is it, Alvin?" she inquired gently, "What is going to happen? What will be missing?"

"Oh, Alice, I... I can't... They're going... going to... they're gonna get rid of my... my arm, Alice. They say it's the only way to save my... my life..." He turned his gaze back towards the heavens, not wanting to see Alice's expression.

"I know," she said softly, "I heard from downstairs." Tears spilled over her cheeks.

"You did?"

Alice nodded, smiling sadly.

"You're not upset?" Alvin was still staring at the ceiling.

"Of course I am," Alice admitted, squeezing his hand, "But your life is so much more important to me." Alvin turned to look at her, his eyes sparkling with tears.

"But I'll never be able to farm again," he lamented bitterly, "I'll be useless to everyone."

"Alvin, don't say that. You will never be useless, arm or no arm. Nothing could *ever* make me think that about you."

"Alice, you don't understand…" He said, and then muttered something under his breath that she couldn't hear.

"I understand that losing an arm will never change the person you are inside," Alice answered, "And that's the most important thing."

Alvin opened his mouth to protest, but he could not speak. He winced in pain and took a sharp intake of breath.

"Does it hurt very much?" Alice asked, endeavouring to change the topic of conversation.

Alvin nodded. "It's the worst… pain I've… ever felt," he told her from between clenched teeth.

"It'll all be over soon," Alice assured him through her own tears, "You'll be back on your feet in no time at all."

"I hope you're right…" Alvin replied, "I hope you're right."

"Are you afraid?"

Alvin thought for a moment, then shook his head. "No," he said, then sighed, "Not for the… surgery. More for what comes… after." He looked over at his infected arm, the skin around his wound becoming blacker by the minute, it seemed. It smelled terrible, the fetid stench continuing to fill the room. Alvin looked down at his hand, which looked and felt cold and dead.

"Don't be afraid," Alice told him, sensing his fear and looking to Matthew and Rachel for support, "You're going to be just fine." Rachel nodded enthusiastically, and Matthew patted his shoulder.

"You'll be up and around real soon," Matthew assured him, though he felt more like he was trying to convince himself.

Trevor stepped forward, a grim look on his face. "I don't want to scare anybody," he said, "But I think our doctor left."

"What?"

Trevor looked down at Alvin. "He left. Walked out the door. He said something when he passed me but I couldn't hear him."

"Well where does he think he's going?" Matthew replied incredulously, "We need him here!"

As soon as Matthew's voice died away, a carriage could be heard outside. Trevor rushed to the window and looked out, hoping that it might be the doctor returning. His hope was not in vain.

"It's the doctor!" he exclaimed, "He's coming from the neighbour's, and he's got some other guys with him, and they've got loads of stuff with them... I guess he went over there to call them on the phone..."

Before Trevor could say any more, the doctor and his two colleagues entered the house and rushed up the stairs. Dr. Camber introduced the pair of them, surgeons Akers and McDonnell.

The three doctors took it in turns, one at a time, to explain what they were going to do and where everyone should be, as the other two prepared for the surgery.

Dr. Akers, an older doctor with a cracking voice, explained that, instead of using ether to put Alvin to sleep, due to the limited resources, they were going to have to use nitrous oxide, meaning that he would be wide awake, but feel little to no pain during the amputation. Dr. Camber disapproved of this choice, as nitrous oxide was only safe for the shortest of operations, but reconciled himself to it by resolving to work fast.

There was a disagreement between Dr. Camber and Dr. Akers about whether Rachel, Matthew, Alice, and Trevor should be allowed to stay or not. Dr. Akers wanted them to stay and function as nurses, in a way, but only to pass things to them and help keep things in order, not to mention to distract Alvin. Dr. Camber maintained that their emotional attachment to Alvin may cause them to get in the way, or do something rash. Dr. McDonnell remained silent, not voicing his opinion one way or the other.

In the end, to save time, the doctors compromised, allowing one person to stay and sit by Alvin's right side and talk to him while they amputated, as long as they didn't get in the way. Trevor, Alvin, Rachel, and Matthew agreed that Alice was the best candidate. With Trevor's weak stomach, he was ruled out first, and both Rachel and Matthew thought that Alice, having had Alvin at her side as she went through her own ordeal a couple of months previous, would be the best for the job. She was by now calm and collected, and cared very much about Alvin. Alice agreed, though the others could tell that she was apprehensive. The very idea was highly irregular, but then again, so was the situation, and Alvin didn't look like he wanted to be alone.

The others left the room, wishing Alvin luck as they went. Matthew, though he tried not to show it, was frightened. It had all happened so fast, and he shuddered to think what might have happened to Alvin if they hadn't gone looking for him, and hadn't found him in time.

Alice sat on Alvin's right side, remembering when he had come and sat by her bedside after she had had her baby. She felt she owed it to him to do the same in his hour of need. The doctors had said that the amputation would be quick, but afterwards, Alvin would need to be transferred to St. Edward's hospital and remain on bed rest and under observation for some time.

Doctor McDonnell administered the nitrous oxide, or laughing gas, as he preferred to call it, and Alice could see a change in Alvin. He began to smile broadly at her. He looked euphoric; and he was giggling almost uncontrollably.

"Alvin?" Alice laughed, "Are you alright?"

Alvin's head lay facing towards Alice, away from the sight of the doctors who were beginning to operate on his arm.

"I feel wonderful," Alvin replied, his voice lilting, "All the pain is gone! I can't feel a thing!"

"Nothing at all?"

"No, nothing, no pain, anyway." Alvin laughed loudly. "Have they started yet?"

Alice peered up at the doctors, who had just begun to make the first incisions on Alvin's infected arm below a tourniquet that they had tied in place to stop the bleeding..

"Yes," she replied, "But only just now."

Alvin's giggling began to subside, and Dr. McDonnell administered more laughing gas. That was when things began to really change in Alvin. He looked out of sorts, staring at nothing in particular with absolute fascination. He was utterly giddy, and when Dr. McDonnell noticed the change, he stopped administering the gas, and Alvin came quickly back into a lower level of sedation.

"What are they doing now?" Alvin asked, looking up at Alice with twinkling eyes. Alice glanced across Alvin's body and immediately wished she hadn't. Dr. Akers was passing tools to Dr. Camber; scalpels, needles, a bone saw… She could see the doctors begin quickly sawing away at Alvin's arm, right at the socket, and the sight and sound made her sick to her stomach. It was a moment before she spoke again.

"They're… al-almost d-done," she managed, trying in vain to hold back tears. The very thought of what was to come for Alvin was devastating, and Alice kept her eyes fixed firmly on his giddy, contented face, avoiding the sight of his left arm. Alvin noticed the tears streaming down her cheeks and reached up with his good arm, clumsily wiping one away with his thumb.

"Don't worry!" he told her cheerfully, "I can't feel anything. It's like I'm floating on air, Alice, like I can fly…" He burst into laughter. His entire body gave a small jolt as his diseased arm was finally freed from the rest of him, sparing his life. Alice hung her head and sobbed uncontrollably.

"Alice! Alice, stop! Don't cry! I'm alright… al… right…really…"

Alvin's eyes slowly shut and he fell instantly asleep, only to awake again the next moment. The doctors were cleaning the remaining part of his arm with carbolic acid, a technique, they explained, that was introduced by Dr. Joseph Lister to reduce the chances of infection. The affects of the nitrous oxide began to wear off, and Alvin returned to normal.

He squinted his eyes shut, not daring to turn his head and look at where his arm used to be. He clenched his jaw to avoid crying out, for the pain had become almost too much to bear. Dr. McDonnell, having not handled any necrous tissue, carefully closed the wound. The doctors had amputated Alvin's arm using what they called the "flap method", which left flaps of skin from Alvin's shoulder that could be stretched over the now empty socket and sewn together. Dr. Camber dressed his shoulder quickly and efficiently, and then ordered Dr. Akers to run down and prepare the wagon to transport Alvin to the hospital. Alvin opened his eyes and looked desperately up at Alice.

"It's awful, isn't it?" he asked, his eyes flooded with tears, "Tell me the truth."

Alice could barely speak. "No," she managed, her voice soothing and gentle, "No, it's not awful, Alvin. You're going to be alright." She brushed some loose hair from his forehead.

"Alice, please don't lie to me," Alvin pleaded as she continued to hold his right hand, "It's gone, isn't it? They just got rid of my arm. All of it. I can't move it…" He wrested his hand out of her grip and took hold of her wrist, forcing her to look down at him. "This was Clay's fault, wasn't it?"

Alice nodded, her face twisted into a tearful expression. "They say if you hadn't been shot…" she sniffed, "That this never would have happened."

Alvin dropped his hand and stared at the ceiling. "Dear God," he said, his voice choking, "Oh, dear God, what am I gonna do?" He sighed deeply, and then could speak no more, but for the pain that consumed him.

"Alvin, be brave!" Alice implored him, "There is so much more that you can do with your life…" She tried her best to comfort him; she held his hand, kissed his cheeks and forehead, but to no avail. Alvin was devastated. The doctors came and took him carefully out of the room, Alice trailing all the way; keeping hold of Alvin's remaining hand. They loaded him into the carriage and Alice sat beside him all the way to the hospital. Rachel, Trevor, and Matthew were left alone to follow them back to St. Edward's.

Matthew watched the wagon until it rounded a corner and he could no longer see it. The day had started so normally; so unassumingly, yet this was a changing day in Alvin's life, and all their lives. Matthew couldn't help thinking that if he hadn't come to the past, if Clay hadn't thought that the time travellers had murdered his daughter, Alvin would never have been shot and he would still be in possession of his left arm.

Rachel walked alongside him, drying her eyes. She had known Alvin ever since she could remember, and he certainly didn't deserve anything like this. He had never, not once that she knew, done anything unjustifiably wrong.

Trevor hung back, walking a few feet behind Rachel and Matthew. He still felt sick from when he had seen Alvin lying on the floor so motionless. He never told anyone, but he had thought, without a doubt, that Alvin was dead. He had looked so still... Trevor shook his head, banishing the thought from his head, for it only served to remind him of the first times he had seen dead bodies, and those times, they had been undoubtedly lifeless...

Trevor watched as Matthew reached down and took Rachel's hand in an attempt to comfort her. He wondered how Alice was faring, for she, aside from Alvin, had it hardest of all, for it was clear that the two of them were very close. Trevor didn't really understand the nature of their relationship, for they weren't *dating* per se, as young people did in his present day, but they certainly weren't only friends. Trevor tried to content himself with thinking on this matter to distract his mind from the unpleasant present and painful past.

When the three remaining youth arrived at the hospital, it was far past noon, and none of them had eaten since that morning. However, not one of them noticed the lateness of the hour. They approached the hospital, weighed down by care.

St. Edward's hospital was a fairly new establishment; built only seven years earlier to accommodate and care for the city's sick. It was large and imposing, constructed of limestone. There were floral carvings all along the door and window frames, and a large open courtyard with a garden along the outside walls of the hospital. The four youth marched up the wide stone steps, determined to find their friend.

"We'll have to find a way to pay for all of this," Rachel informed them, "Though I'm not sure how…"

"We'll think of something," Matthew assured her, "We'll manage."

Trevor furrowed his brow, confused, but said nothing as they entered the hospital. It felt impossibly clean inside, the walls white and the floors waxed and polished. Young nurses walked by, carrying bundles of clean laundry in their arms, and doctors rushed past distractedly. A kindly nurse directed the trio to the ward where Alvin was staying.

Matthew's eyes widened as they crossed the threshold. The ward, like the rest of the hospital, was a clean white. The floors were vast and sprawling, and lined along the walls on each side were rows of tall beds with metal frames and clean sheets and pillows. Some were empty, ready and waiting for new patients, but most were full.

Though there was very little noise in the room, there were men of all shapes and sizes, and most looked as though they came from the poorest districts of Norton, being the Southern Quays, Oakton, and Irontown. There was a man coughing up blood, a young boy with a broken leg, and an elderly gentleman sleeping fitfully. They were the detritus of the city: beaten down newsboys, factory workers, stable hands, and the like. The nurses tended to them all with love and care, but the majority showed no signs that they would ever recover completely. Among them was Alvin, lying in a bed on the far side of the room, beneath the tall, clear windows that lined the back wall.

Matthew, Rachel, and Trevor skirted past a large desk in the centre of the room, at which sat a nurse who was quietly filling in papers and stacking them off to the side. Matthew glimpsed Alvin's name written on one such paper in a neat, flourished script.

The trio approached Alvin's bed, where he lay, his eyelids drooping, and a small yet unmistakable smile on his face.

"The doctors gave him morphine," Alice explained, looking up at them from where she sat on the edge of his bed, "He's been feeling awfully sleepy, but it seems to have taken his pain away." She looked back down at Alvin, whose eyes had shut completely. He was fast asleep from the pain killing drug, and he looked at peace. Matthew couldn't help but notice Alice holding his right hand, with the other one nowhere to be seen. The blankets were tucked up over Alvin's shoulders, so the wound from the amputation was not visible.

"Has anyone sent word to his father?" Matthew asked, peering down at Alvin's relaxed face. Alice shook her head.

"I wouldn't know what to tell him," she said. She was no longer crying, but the salty tear streaks on her cheeks were still visible in the light from the large windows.

"I'll take care of it," Matthew replied, then instantly wished he hadn't. It was hard enough for him to believe the situation himself, so how would he inform Alvin's own father, whom he barely knew? He supposed that the first step would be to tell his grandfather.

"The nurses say I should leave soon," Alice continued, "To let him rest…"

Rachel nodded calmly. "I think they're right," she attested, "We shouldn't stay long. We can return tomorrow."

"I know…" Alice sighed, "But it's so difficult, knowing what he must be feeling…"

"It is," said Rachel, placing a hand on Alice's shoulder, "But he'll be alright."

Alice nodded. Behind Rachel, Matthew and Trevor said nothing. They didn't know what to say. Everything had happened so quickly, it was like a dream; a terrible nightmare from which they would never awaken.

"Come along," Rachel whispered, noticing that her voice was echoing off of the high ceiling of the ward, "Let's go home." Alice did not protest, and her hand slowly slipped away from Alvin's as she stood and prepared to leave.

"Alice?"

Alvin's voice was hoarse and squeaky, but nonetheless heard over the whispers of the others. Alice turned around and looked at him.

"Where are you going?" he asked, his eyes still half closed.

"Back to my aunt's," Alice replied gently, "I'll be back tomorrow morning before church." She turned around to go once more, finding it difficult to watch Alvin in such a deprived, weakened, and vulnerable state. He had always been so strong, so hearty, and now he seemed to possess neither of those old, familiar qualities. Before Alice could take so much as a step, she felt a set of cold fingers brush her own.

"Don't go yet," Alvin pleaded, "I need to tell you something, some things I should have said a long time ago."

"Alvin, you're very tired, don't you think it can wait?"

"If I wait any more I might never tell you, I dunno if I'll have the nerve again."

"The doctors have you on morphine," Alice explained patiently, "And it could be affecting your mind. I don't want you to say anything you may regret."

"My only regret would be not saying anything," Alvin promised, "Please, just listen a moment, then you can go."

"Alright," Alice said reluctantly, then turned to Rachel, Matthew, and Trevor, "I'll be out in a moment. I'll meet you outside."

Rachel and Matthew continued on their way out, but Trevor stood stock still, staring at nothing. Matthew gently tugged his sleeve and he followed them distractedly away. Alice sat down on the bed once more.

"What is it, Alvin?"

"Listen," he began, drowsiness apparent in his voice, "About my arm..."

"Alvin, I told you, you're going to be alright, I—"

"No, no!" Alvin interrupted, "That's not what I'm talking about. I just... I wanted to tell you... I had so many plans..." He trailed off, peering up at the vaulted ceiling.

"Plans?"

Alvin turned his head to look at Alice again, and his features formed a smile, his eyes shining.

"Yes," Alvin repeated, "Plans. Big plans. For us."

"Us?"

"For us," Alvin affirmed, "I was gonna take some of my father's land he had been saving and build a house on it..." He stopped talking, and yawned deeply, his eyelids fluttering. Alice's eyes filled with tears.

"Go on," she prompted.

"I was gonna build a house, and then take over my father's farm... and I was gonna marry you, Alice."

Alice was taken aback by his admission, but at the same time she had been almost expecting it. The whole world, it seemed, knew of their feelings for each other, and their future had been set for years. However, Alice had had no idea that he had the entire thing planned and ready to be put into action at a moment's notice.

"You were?" Alice whispered.

"I was," answered Alvin, and a note of bitterness began to creep into his voice, "But now it's all over. It was a silly dream anyway..."

"I don't think it was silly."

"Well, it might not have been then, but it is now. I can't build you a house with one arm. I can't farm. You deserve a man who can take care of you. Now I'm just a lousy cripple." He turned his face away.

"Alvin, you are not!" Alice insisted, "I don't need a house, and there are other things you can do besides farming, you know that no matter—"

"Alice, I'm serious. What will folks say if you marry me, huh? A pretty girl like you, they would say, could find a better, more capable man."

"Alvin, the morphine," Alice interjected, "You don't know what you're saying…"

"I know perfectly well what I'm saying!" Alvin nearly yelled, "And I know that once I go back out there into the world, it'll chew me up and spit me back out, 'cause I ain't no use to anyone now. I'm not intelligent enough for anything too scholarly. I can't even work in a factory."

"There are so many things you can still do with your life, Alvin!" Alice insisted, "And you are very intelligent! Please, listen to me, Alvin. Don't give up on your dream…"

Alvin met Alice's eyes. "I don't want to," he admitted, "But you deserve better than me."

"Please stop talking that way."

"It's true, Alice. You know it is."

"It's not."

"It is."

Alice stood up, tears streaming down her cheeks. "I'll be back tomorrow morning," she promised, "We can finish this conversation then, when you're feeling better."

Alvin made no reply as Alice left the ward.

CHAPTER THIRTEEN

His Own Good Time

T he next morning, Matthew awoke with a sense of foreboding. He had promised Alvin that he would inform his father of the amputation of his arm, but first he had to tell Alvin's grandfather. No doubt the man was wondering where his grandson had been all night.

Matthew swung his legs over the side of the bed and sighed shakily. Trevor was still asleep, but Matthew wanted to get up earlier that morning and inform the time travellers of Alvin's plight. He and Trevor had arrived back that afternoon without saying anything about Alvin. They simply weren't sure how to word such a thing, and both were secretly hoping that if they went to sleep and woke up the next morning, they would discover that the whole nasty ordeal had been simply a dream. Alas, this was not the case.

Matthew dressed quietly and crept down the stairs. He wondered whether he should wait for Trevor to get up so they could inform the time travellers together, but he knew that Trevor still didn't trust them and would be reluctant to share any information, even if it wasn't concerning him. Matthew found Grace, Sandra, and Mr. Fitzgerald chatting in the parlour, waiting for Mrs. Brown to awaken so that they could begin preparations for breakfast. Mrs. Brown always insisted that she be in charge of the kitchen and that no one was allowed to take anything from it without her say so. Matthew entered the parlour and noisily cleared his throat.

"Good morning," he said, perhaps more sombrely than he should have for a greeting that was usually meant to be cheery and light.

"Good morning, Matthew," Grace smiled.

"Why the long face?" Sandra asked, concerned.

"It's a bit of a long story…" began Matthew, remembering in vivid detail the events of the previous day.

Mr. Fitzgerald smiled with concern and patted the seat next to him.

"Have a seat," he said, "And you can tell us all about it."

Matthew looked around at all their faces, which were staring up at him expectantly.

"It's about Alvin…" Matthew explained, and by the time he was finished reciting the events of the terrible day, he was feeling quite numb. The experience had been traumatic for everyone involved. During his harrowing tale, the other time travellers had filed into the room and sat quietly, trying to understand the context of what Matthew was saying. The only person in the house, including Mrs. Brown, who hadn't shown their face by the time that Matthew was finished was Trevor.

Matthew explained to everyone how he had promised Alvin that he would inform his father, and how Rachel had mentioned that they would have to pay for Alvin's hospital stay and care.

"Matthew?" Grace piped in, "Don't worry about the money too much. St. Edward's hospital runs mostly on donations, but there will be a small cost, I expect, for the services of the doctors."

Matthew smiled and nodded, too overwhelmed to say anything more. He went about his usual morning business as breakfast was being prepared, and was delighted to be of some help when Evan told him to go upstairs and wake Trevor so they wouldn't be late for church. Matthew ran up the stairs, taking them two at a time, and opened the door to the room he shared with Trevor with a flourish. His brow furrowed when he noticed that Trevor was nowhere to be seen; his bed was empty, the sheets tossed about carelessly, as though he had gotten up in a rush.

"Trevor?" Matthew called into the empty room. Receiving no answer, he walked towards the window, fear in his heart, and looked out, hoping against hope that Trevor hadn't taken that morning to get himself into trouble out on the city streets. Peering straight down, Matthew saw his friend. He was bent over double, his shoulders shaking up and down as though he was crying. Matthew saw him reach up and wipe his mouth on his sleeve.

Concerned, Matthew walked back downstairs and exited the boarding house, then jogged around the corner to where Trevor was still standing. He saw that Trevor had been violently ill, and was recovering as he watched. Matthew stepped forward and placed a hand on his friend's shoulder.

"Yesterday really got to you, huh?"

Trevor twisted his head round to look at Matthew, then let it hang again. "Yeah," he said, "I guess it did."

"You think you can eat?"

Trevor shook his head.

"Do you want me to ask if you can stay back from church today?"

Trevor nodded. Matthew turned to go, but Trevor spoke up before he got too far. "Hey," he called, "Could you... could you make sure they know it's because of yesterday, and not just because I don't want to wear that stupid suit?"

"Sure," Matthew laughed, "No problem."

Matthew ran back into the house and informed the first person he came to, who was John, of Trevor's predicament. John volunteered himself to stay behind and keep an eye on him while the others went to church. With that settled, the remaining time travellers, accompanied by Mrs. Brown, began the walk to church. It was quite close by, situated right in the very heart of Norton, and was only a few doors down from St. Edward's hospital, where Matthew knew Alvin was lying; probably fast asleep, minus one arm.

He entered the church with an air more sombre than in previous days. Yesterday still seemed like a dream, and Matthew prayed more fervently than he had ever prayed before for Alvin's predicament to be merely a solemn memory instead of the harsh reality that it was.

The sermon that Sunday was delivered with what seemed like twice the usual vigour, as though there was someone in particular that the pastor wanted to hear it. Afterwards, Matthew spotted Rachel and Alice, sitting alone in the pew the farthest from the pulpit. He headed over to them, dodging the various members of the congregation without taking his eyes off of his friends.

"I didn't see you earlier," he said breathlessly when he finally arrived where they were standing.

"We've only just arrived," Rachel answered, "Alice had promised to pay Alvin a visit before we came."

"How is he?"

"Stubborn," came Alice's clipped reply. Matthew and Rachel exchanged nervous glances.

"Stubborn?" Matthew ventured, hoping not to upset her.

"Immensely," was her only response. Rachel shot Matthew a look that promised she would explain later.

"I'd like to see him this afternoon," Matthew said cautiously, "Do you suppose I should?"

Alice said nothing, but Rachel nodded. "He's doing much better," she told him, "But his mind..." Matthew cocked his head to one side. Rachel opened her mouth to answer, but Alice spoke before she could.

"If you'll excuse me," she stated, "I'd like to go and speak with the Reverend for a moment." She then strode off, without waiting for approval.

Matthew looked at Rachel, puzzled. "What *did* happen this morning?" he asked.

"Alvin's been quite... depressed," Rachel sighed, "Remember yesterday, when he asked Alice to stay behind a moment?" Matthew nodded. "Alice told me that what he wanted to tell her was... they were his plans for the future. He's given up on them all now, but he wanted to tell her. Nothing Alice says can make him rethink."

"What were his plans?"

Rachel leaned forward conspiratorially. "He said that he was going to inherit his father's land and take over the farm..." Her voice dropped to a whisper. "And he was going to marry Alice."

"And now he thinks she'll never have him because of his arm?"

"Well… he wants her to forget about marrying him and marry someone else. Someone more capable of taking care of her."

"And Alice refuses," Matthew surmised, "I think I understand. May I speak to him alone later? I think I may be able to help."

Rachel glanced over at Alice and watched her for a moment as she spoke with the Reverend, undoubtedly about Alvin. She turned back to Matthew. "That sounds like a wonderful idea," she said, "I'll bring Alice home."

"Alright," Matthew smiled, "I'll see you later." He waved goodbye and began to make his way back towards the time travellers and Mrs. Brown, who were patiently waiting to leave.

"Matthew?"

At the sound of Rachel's voice, Matthew turned around, his expression quizzical.

"Yes?"

"Thank you."

"My pleasure," Matthew grinned.

He explained his situation to Grace when he had made it back through the crowd. She consented, and Matthew was free to walk to the hospital on his own whenever he pleased, as long as he was back at the boarding house for supper. Matthew thanked her and went on his way.

The nurses at the hospital greeted him warmly and allowed him to venture into Alvin's ward on his own. As he walked in, he noticed a new patient being carefully tended to by a team of nurses. He couldn't quite tell what was wrong with the man, but he could hear his moans and groans of pain echoing throughout the vast room. Alvin was situated just two beds down from him.

Matthew approached Alvin with a sense of foreboding, not quite sure how he would react to his presence. Alvin was lying on his back, his eyes open and staring at the blank white ceiling. His one remaining arm was lying across his abdomen.

"Hello," Matthew said breathlessly, waving at Alvin. Alvin merely turned his head, quite slowly, to face him.

"Hello," he replied monotonously. It was clear that he was lethargic, perhaps because of the morphine that he was being given for his pain.

"How are you feeling?" asked Matthew, then thanked a nurse as she brought him a chair to place beside Alvin's bed. He sat down.

Alvin tried to shrug, but found it was quite impossible in his state. Matthew, concerned for his state of mind, not to mention body, attempted to keep the conversation going.

"Has Alice been in to see you today?" Though Matthew already knew the answer, he needed to find a way to bring up the subject without upsetting him.

"Yes," came Alvin's reply.

"She sure does care a lot about you, you know." Matthew bit his lip, wondering if he had already gone too far, even after only being there for a moment or two.

"I know," Alvin answered, looking up at Matthew, "That's what worries me…"

Matthew was certain that he was about to continue, but he was foiled in his attempts at speech by a nurse who came around and asked if Alvin would like to be sitting upright to talk to Matthew.

"I can manage myself, thank you," Alvin replied, his voice clipped and sharp. The nurse shrugged and left to tend to another patient. Alvin lifted his head and propped himself up on one elbow, then reached behind him and pulled the pillow up so he could lean against it.

"Why would it worry you?" Matthew asked, prompting Alvin to continue his earlier train of thought. Alvin hung his head and plucked at the bed sheets with his fingers.

"I can't do anything for her," he said bitterly, motioning with his head towards his lack of a left arm,

"You oughta understand, Matthew. I mean—" He paused and tried to adjust his position. He looked Matthew straight in the eye as he continued.

"If you loved someone," he began, "I mean *really* loved someone, you would want them to be happy, wouldn't you?"

Matthew shrugged. "Sure, I suppose," he replied.

"Well," Alvin continued, "I love Alice, and want her to be happy, and she could never be that with me. Not now…" He moved his gaze back to the bed sheets, where he had plucked out a loose thread and was fiddling with it between his fingers.

"Alvin," Matthew said, his tone very nearly condescending, "You are not your arm. Alice doesn't love you because you had two arms, or because you could farm, or build a house. She loves you because of who you are."

"Well, I was a farmer," Alvin replied angrily, "But my father called this morning. My grandfather's neighbour took it upon herself to tell him about my arm, and my grandfather told my father. He says I'm not to return home until I feel better. And even then, I won't be helping on the farm anymore. As I said, I was a farmer. Now I'm nothing."

"You are *not* nothing," insisted Matthew, "And Alice will never think that."

"She's blind," Alvin said, "Blind to reality. But I can see. It seems like I'm the only one who can. Everyone is telling me that everything's going to be alright, but no one can tell me what I'm supposed to do with my life! I wanted to marry Alice, but I can't if I can't work. I can barely button a shirt…"

"Alvin, there are plenty of things you can do!"

"Name one."

Matthew opened his mouth, but nothing came to his mind. It was a blank slate. He knew that Alvin could never do anything that required both arms, so most physical jobs were out of the question, and he knew how much Alvin hated working inside all day. At school, he had enjoyed himself with learning, but now that he was done, and was supposed to help run his father's farm, he had nowhere to turn. He had often expressed his hatred of jobs that involved working with money, because he loathed the very idea of the stuff, and humanity's constant quest for it. Anything that required him to participate in the consumption of any unnecessary goods would kill him.

"See? You can't," Alvin stated, balling up some of his bed sheet in his fist, "No one can."

"Alvin, I just—"

"I'm very tired, Matthew," Alvin informed him, and Matthew sensed that this was his cue to leave. He got up and left the hospital without a word. He had failed. He brushed past a smartly dressed man who held a large tattered volume in his hands. The individual kept on walking, smiling as he remembered the days of his own youth, always rushing about but never seeming to accomplish anything… He sighed nostalgically. Alvin saw him enter the ward, and their eyes met from across the vast room. He quickly turned his gaze away. The man, a chaplain, strode across the ward with great purpose in his steps, and stopped next to Alvin's bed. He looked down at him kindly, and Alvin squirmed, self conscious of his missing limb.

"Excuse me, young man," the chaplain said, his voice old and deep, "But do you know where I might find a Mr. Percy Whittaker?"

Alvin glanced up, confused. "I think he's just there," he said, pointing to the newly arrived patient, "He arrived a short while ago."

The chaplain followed Alvin's outstretched finger and found himself gazing at a very frightened looking man, who was moaning with pain. The chaplain went to him and began to speak with the man, his voice kind and his words gentle.

Alvin, on more than one occasion in the weeks that had followed, found himself watching the old man and listening to what he said. When he did so, he always pretended to be asleep, for he didn't wish to speak to the chaplain himself. After all, what could he tell him that he hadn't heard already? The chaplain seemed to sense Alvin watching him, though his eyes were barely open, for each time Alvin would stare; he always turned back to look at him. Alvin would quickly roll over and continue to pretend to be asleep. It was the third week of his hospital stay when the chaplain finally stopped by Alvin's bedside. Alvin had just woken from a real sleep, and there was nothing he could do to stop the man from coming to him once he had seen him awake.

"You're finally awake again, unlike him," the chaplain joked, his cheeks trembling as he chuckled, looking towards a dozing Mr. Percy Whittaker. He noticed the empty chair sitting beside Alvin's bed, which had remained there for Alvin's numerous visits from his friends. Alice, Matthew, and Rachel left the hospital each visit even more dismal than when they had arrived, for Alvin remained stubborn and would not turn back on all that he had said to them. The three of them always hoped that one day soon, Alvin would come around, but for the moment, that hope was quickly fading away to nothing.

"Mind if I sit down a while?" the chaplain asked, and Alvin could only shake his head, unsure of what to say to this man. He knew by his dress who he was, but he hadn't the faintest idea what the man's interest in him was. The chaplain stretched out his hand for Alvin to shake, and Alvin took it.

"You're lucky," he said, nodding at Alvin's right hand, "You can still shake hands. I'm Reverend Charles Bakker, very pleased to make your acquaintance. You may call me Charles, if you like."

"Alvin Quinn," Alvin replied, "Pleased to meet you as well."

"Well, Alvin," the reverend asked good naturedly, "What brings you to a fine establishment like this?"

"Gangrene," Alvin replied sourly.

"I see," Charles smiled, "And the doctors had no choice but to amputate, did they?"

"No, sir."

"You're lucky," Charles said for a second time, "It could have been much worse. I've seen gangrene kill a man twice your size."

"I suppose so."

"Don't feel so bitter! Providence has spared your life!"

Alvin was beginning to wonder when the annoying cheeriness of this man would come to an end. He didn't want to be rude, but words came gushing forth and he was powerless to stop them.

"So they tell me," he said, his voice resentful, "But what kind of a life will it be? That's all I'm left with is my life! All my plans have been foiled; all my hard work is for nothing. What kind of a life is that?"

The Reverend Bakker simply kept on smiling in his gentle way. "A divine one, Alvin, a life filled with new possibilities."

"You can't truly believe that. What use is a farmer with one arm? I had plans, so much that I wanted to do…"

Charles looked at Alvin's face and detected the eager curiosity beneath his bitter exterior. He wasn't simply being sarcastic; he was truly daring the chaplain to find a new purpose for his life. And while Charles could not give him that, for it was something he would have to find on his own, he could give him a bit of guidance and wisdom, and the Reverend sensed that that was all the boy truly needed. He opened his tattered and torn Bible and turned the musty pages until he came to the one he was looking for.

"Let me read you something," he said, "From Proverbs six verse nineteen. *A man's heart deviseth his way: but the Lord directeth his steps.* You see? The plans you made were not what God has in store for you. Everything that happens is for a reason, and we may not understand it, but it is what it is. Take Jeremiah twenty-nine verse eleven. *For I know the thoughts that I think toward you, saith the Lord, thoughts of peace, and not of evil, to give you an expected end.* He has plans for you, even without your arm. It is important that you understand that this was not His doing."

"I know," Alvin whispered, letting his head hang, "But I wish I knew what to do. I'd like to be married, and have a family, but if I can't work, then what will I do? I can't support a family like this." He made an attempt to shrug what remained of his left shoulder.

"Alvin," the Reverend explained gently, "Physical work is not the only means of supporting a wife and family. You seem to be a very intelligent young man, and very thoughtful. You'll learn what God has in store for you in His own good time."

Alvin nodded slowly, and, sensing that he was beginning to understand, Charles stood.

"I'm afraid I can't stay," he lamented, "But you may ask for me whenever you please. I am never far away. Good day, Alvin Quinn."

"Good day, Reverend."

With that, the chaplain left the ward, abandoning Alvin to his thoughts. Alvin knew that it would be a long time before he was discharged from the hospital, and that gave him a sort of peace of mind in knowing that he would have time to think on all that the reverend had said. Alvin began to reflect upon the way he had spoken to his friends, Matthew and Rachel, and, even more regrettably, on the way he had treated Alice. He had divulged all his plans and dreams for the pair of them and then told her that none of them would ever come true. He felt unbearably guilty, but he was still bitter about the loss of his arm, and the inevitable loss of his dream of farming.

Over the next few days, Alvin would visit Charles in his office, and he slowly began to realize that the plans he had made could be modified, and he wanted Alice to be included in them. Vaguely aware of the morphine still coursing through his veins, he made a plan to apologize profusely the next time she came to visit, and to make things right. If, Alvin realized with a sudden jolt, she ever wanted to come back...

CHAPTER FOURTEEN

Time Heals All Wounds

It was the first of October, and the leaves were beginning their slow changes—from greens to oranges, yellows, and reds. Yet, with all the change in the landscape of the city of Norton, there seemed still to be no change in Alvin. Rachel, Matthew, Alice, and Trevor had not seen him in nearly a week. The last time they had spoken to him, they had remained disappointed with his emotional progress. His arm was almost entirely healed, but his heart remained broken. Dr. Camber had said that it was a part of the process for him to be so upset for so long. He maintained that the loss of a limb was something that one grieves over, like the death of a departed loved one. Matthew found this concept difficult to grasp, but he and the others all tried their best to be patient with their friend.

Out of all of them, Alice was finding this the most difficult. She would stay away from the hospital for days at a time, because to visit Alvin in such a state was like torture. Matthew and Rachel tried to convince her to visit more often, for if anyone could coax him out of his anguish, it would be her, but she would have none of it. If he didn't want to see her, and it didn't seem as though he did, she wouldn't force him to. It was only because of how much she missed him that Matthew and Rachel were able to convince her to accompany them to see Alvin on that crisp Tuesday afternoon.

The three youth climbed the stone steps with a sombre air about them, not speaking, each one silently praying that this would be the day that Alvin finally showed some improvement. They entered the building and made their way through the busy halls towards Alvin's ward, their faces downcast. Rachel reached out and took Alice's hand.

As they approached the door to the ward, a warm, muffled sound escaped from within. Upon opening the door, they could sense a change within the entire ward. It seemed brighter, livelier, less depressing. The sound began again, this time more distinctly, and it was clear that it was coming from the far side of the room.

"He's laughing," Alice breathed, a smile forming on her face. The trio continued into the ward, watching as Alvin and his grandfather, who sat on the chair next to his bed, shared a joke with a passing nurse. Alvin was nearly doubled over with laughter. He was dressed and sitting on the edge of his bed, his back to the door. Mr. Quinn spotted Rachel, Alice, and Matthew from his seat, and lightly tapped Alvin on the knee, pointing to them with his other hand. Alvin twisted around to look at them, and his smile faltered for a moment.

"Alice," he said, more quietly than he had been speaking before, "Matthew. Rachel... I..." He stood to face them, steadying himself by placing his hand on the bed post. He opened his mouth again, but no words came. Instead of speaking, he walked to them, his gait slightly lopsided.

"We're so glad you're feeling better, Alvin," Matthew said, grinning, "Welcome back." Rachel nodded in agreement.

"Thank you. I hope you can all forgive me for these past weeks. I wasn't myself."

Rachel and Matthew smiled. "We wouldn't hold it against you, Alvin," Matthew replied.

"Alice?" Alvin said, searching her face for any sign of forgiveness, "I really am sorry. I shouldn't have told you all those things I did—about my plans, I mean—and I shouldn't have gone back on them. Consider it all as good as my word now."

Alice remained silent.

"Alice," Alvin continued, "I may not have two arms, but I'm going to build you that house, and I'm gonna run my father's farm. We'll have a nice big family with lots of children..." He paused. "We'll be so happy, Alice, so happy... I promise."

Alice smiled, knowing full well that what he was saying was next to impossible without help and money, but she didn't want to discourage him, not after all that he had been through. It was not the time to talk of harsh realities. She looked up and saw a tall, elderly chaplain standing in the opposite corner of the ward, and he was smiling at her. Alice grinned back. Everything was going to be alright.

The four youth returned to Alvin's bed and sat on its edge. They laughed and joked the entire afternoon until it was nearly supper, and they had to leave. Only Alice stayed through the dinner hour, and until dusk. The pair made up for lost time, and continued dreaming of the future, which seemed closer and more real than it ever had before.

■■■

Matthew took it upon himself that afternoon to walk Rachel back to where she was staying at Alice's aunt Jessica's house. They spoke together the entire way. Most of the conversation was about Alvin, but eventually it turned, through no fault of her own, to Rachel.

"How are you feeling?" Matthew asked her, "You've been through nothing but trouble lately. When was the last time you had a proper day of rest?"

Rachel laughed wearily. "I'm not rightly sure," she replied, "There was what happened with my grandfather…" She trailed off, trying to show Matthew that she didn't want to pursue the subject. "And then I came here, and that was when Alvin got sick…" She laughed out loud, turning her twinkling eyes to Matthew. "Perhaps I'm some sort of curse," she devised, "Trouble follows me wherever I go! I've only been in Norton for a few weeks and already nothing good has come of it!"

Matthew smiled. It was good to see Rachel laughing again.

"You could never be a curse," he said, and immediately wished he hadn't, for it only made Rachel laugh all the harder.

"Perhaps not," she said, "Perhaps not!"

"You know," Matthew began, changing the subject back to Rachel's ordeal with Clay, "You can't see the marks where he hit you anymore."

Rachel's hand shot self consciously to her face, but she said nothing.

"There's been something I've really been meaning to tell you," Matthew continued, "About my family—"

Rachel stopped him mid-sentence with a hand on his arm as they approached Aunt Jessica's house. She was staring, eyes narrowed, at a man who was emerging from her home. He was short, bulky, and wore tattered clothing. His smile was crooked, revealing a row of decaying teeth.

"I feel as though I've seen him somewhere before," Rachel said, squinting at him. They stood behind the neighbouring house, where they were close enough to see the details of the man, but far enough away that he couldn't hear them speaking about him. Rachel looked at Matthew, her face puzzled.

"Don't you feel like you know him?"

Matthew shook his head. "I can't say I do," he replied, "But I'll take your word for it."

"Anyhow," Rachel finished quickly, "I should be going. Goodbye, Matthew!" With those words still hanging in the air, she ran off and disappeared into the house, leaving Matthew to walk the rest of the way to Mrs. Brown's on his own, his story burning on his lips. He had desperately, in that impulsive moment, wanted to tell Rachel about what his father—his birth father—had done to him. He wanted to be able to empathize with her, and he didn't want to keep it all a secret from her any longer.

Matthew arrived back at the boarding house just after supper was over, and was preparing himself for the scolding that he felt he would inevitably receive from Grace, who had given him the condition of arriving back before dinner was served. However, all Matthew got was a warm supper and some kind words. Evidently, the other time travellers knew of the stress he had been under lately.

After Matthew had eaten, he was ready for a good night's sleep, and he arrived in his room to find Trevor lying awake in bed, hands folded behind his head.

"Feeling any better?" Matthew asked him as he kicked off his shoes. Trevor had been ill for weeks. He barely ate, and slept most days. The doctor had been by, but could find nothing physically wrong with him.

"Not really," Trevor sighed, "Still pretty bad."

"This can't be just from seeing Alvin that day," Matthew laughed, "I didn't know you had a weak stomach!"

"Cause I don't!" Trevor insisted, rolling over to face the wall, "You wouldn't get it."

"Hey, try me!"

"Naw," Trevor decided, "I'm too tired. I'll tell you some other time."

"You know what?" Matthew said as he pulled on his nightshirt.

"No, what?"

"I came—" He paused as he struggled to fit his arm through one of the sleeves. "I came *this* close to telling Rachel about my father."

"Yeah?"

"Yeah, I did."

"Well maybe you shouldn't."

Matthew turned around to face Trevor, who still had his back turned to him. "Why not?" he asked sincerely.

"I dunno, she probably won't get it, or it'll make things weird. Trust me, you don't want to say anything."

"But, I do," Matthew insisted.

"Just think about it, okay? Goodnight."

"Goodnight."

■■■

"Thank you," Sandra said as John poured her a cup of tea. They were seated alone in the parlour, a tea tray having been left out for them by Mrs. Brown. Sandra couldn't sleep, and she hoped that perhaps some sort of tea in Mrs. Brown's vast collection could help her to do so. John was staying up with her out of courtesy, for Sandra could tell that he was itching to get some well deserved sleep. He had been helping Trevor through his queasiness lately, and, though he was weary, he wanted to stay up with Sandra until she felt that she could sleep.

Sandra took a long, deep drink and placed the teacup gently down on the tray. "I'm worried about Matthew," she admitted. John poured himself some tea as well.

"How come?" he asked, "The boy's doing fine. He's got all his limbs, and he—"

"John!" Sandra exclaimed, "Don't be so morbid! You sound like Evan!"

John chuckled. "Sorry," he apologized, "It's been a long day."

"I'm worried about him because of everything that's going on around him," Sandra explained, "Alvin's arm, Trevor..." She paused and looked at John inquiringly. John said nothing.

"How is Trevor finding things, anyway?" she continued, genuinely curious, "I do hope he's not still holding the same attitude he was when he first arrived."

"He's quieted down some," John reflected, "But he swears like a sailor!" Neither John nor Sandra could contain their laughter.

"I'm almost surprised he hasn't tried to escape yet," Sandra pointed out. John shook his head.

"Not me," he said, "He needs us to send him back. Plus, I think he likes being part of a family more than he lets on. Have you noticed how well he gets along with Laura and Eddie?"

"I have," Sandra affirmed, "It's remarkable."

"Yeah, he's certainly one of a kind. I'd forgotten what it was like to be that age. There's so much stress and worry over nothing."

"Some of them never grow out of it," Sandra remarked wisely.

"That's for sure," John replied, and put down his cup of tea. They continued talking quietly into the night, and it was quite late when they finally decided to retire.

■■■

The following Wednesday, Trevor had to return to the school that he dreaded so much. He tried to insist that he was still feeling ill, but the time travellers would have none of it, and they sent him off with Matthew as usual.

"I *hate* this place," Trevor said as they climbed the steps.

"Fifty two," came Matthew's cryptic reply.

"What?"

"Fifty two. How many times you've said those exact words."

"You've been *counting*?"

Matthew shot him an exasperated look, and the school bell rang just as they were entering the dank building. They had separate classes that morning, so Matthew was forced to shout down the hallways so that Trevor could hear him as they went their different ways.

"Do you want to visit Alvin after school today?"

"Sure," Trevor shouted back, "I'll meet you in front!"

Matthew looked around warily. Shouting in the halls was an offense in this school, and the last thing he wanted was to get in trouble with anyone. Trevor often got into trouble for talking out of turn in class and using profane language, and Matthew wondered how long it had actually been since he had been to school in his present day.

Today was the day that Alvin would be discharged from the hospital. Rachel, Matthew, Trevor, and Alice stood by his side after school that day as Alvin took his final steps outside of the hospital, shielding his eyes against the sun. Each and every one of them hoped he would never have to return.

Alvin took a long, deep breath of fresh air, filling his lungs and clearing his head. The staff at the hospital had taken him off of the morphine in the last week, and he was still adjusting to the absence of the once ever-present wonder drug.

"It's such a beautiful day," he remarked, looking around at the stunning fall colours as the leaves of oak and maple trees fell around the youth while they walked down the cobbled streets. Their first stop that glowing Wednesday afternoon was Alvin's grandfather's house to help Alvin settle back in. His father had been unable to save enough money to venture to Norton to see his son, but he sent word often, and Alvin replied, assuring him that he was doing well.

Seeing as Alvin had lost his arm the first time his father had let him stay away from home for a long period of time, Mr. Quinn understandably wanted his son to return at his soonest convenience, but the matter was left entirely up to Alvin and how he was feeling. Truth be told, though he was well enough to travel, Alvin was not ready to return to Connolly Mills just yet, for he didn't wish to see the fields he could no longer plough, and was still apprehensive about Clay Kennedy. He had tried, over the course of his hospital stay, to forgive the man responsible for the loss of his arm, but he still could not find it in his heart, and he didn't want to go home until he could.

Matthew was still getting used to the way Alvin's shirt sleeve hung uselessly empty on his left side, as were the citizens of Norton. When Alvin passed, they would stare at him, wondering innocently what had happened to such a young man that he should lose a limb. Alvin's face flushed bright red under their penetrating gaze.

"Don't pay them any mind," Alice whispered to him, her arm held in the crook of his, "They're simply curious." Alvin nodded bravely and they walked on. Alvin himself was still adjusting to the lack of weight in his body. The doctors had told him that an arm was approximately five percent of his total body weight, and it felt strange to be rid of that five percent. His balance was off, and he noticed that he began to lean more heavily on his right leg due to the lack of weight on his left. He felt odd and out of place among the people of Norton, but he tried not to let the feeling bring his spirits down. He was happy that Alice was walking alongside him, and it made him feel very proud that she was still willing to be seen with him and be stared at right along with him.

"Shall we take in a show?" Rachel suggested, "Just as we planned to do all that time ago?" Alvin suppressed a nervous laugh. Alice peered up at him.

"What do you say?" she asked, "Shall we complete what we planned to do before this happened?"

Alvin took a deep breath and nodded. It would be his first step back into the realm of normalcy. Over the course of his hospital stay, Alvin's moods had been up and down, but he had refused to give up on his dreams again. This fact worried Alice nearly as much as his lethargic, depressed self had, for at any moment he may try to do something that he was simply not capable of. Alvin's courage was admirable, but he seemed to be quite in denial about the reality of his condition. He knew, to be sure, that people would always look at him strangely, and think him different, but he had resolved that, even if this bothered him, he would not let it hinder the achievement of his dreams.

The five youth saw a lovely production of Shakespeare's *As You Like It,* and enjoyed themselves immensely, the comedy helping them to forget their present troubles and immerse themselves in escapades of the wonderful cast of characters. Matthew, however, couldn't manage to keep his eyes off of Alvin's perpetually empty left sleeve. He began to wonder what sort of advancements were being made in prosthetics, and whether Alvin would be a good candidate for an artificial arm. He shook his head and tried to concentrate on the play, but he couldn't help realizing that it may not be very likely that Alvin could get a new arm, for he would never be able to afford it, and even if he could, he would never be able to use it properly, like a real arm. The thought depressed Matthew, so he turned back to the play, sobered by his dismal conclusions.

By the time they left the theatre and stepped back into the streets, the sky was darkening with every passing moment, and the sun was disappearing on the horizon. There was something disconcerting to Matthew, Alice, Alvin, and Rachel about the streets of Norton at night, but Trevor was right at ease among the sly and sneaky characters that roamed the cobbles in the shadows. He barely even seemed to notice them, but the others grew quite uncomfortable, watching each step they took and keeping their gaze to the ground.

"I hope we don't miss curfew..." Matthew shuddered, "Mrs. Brown would have a fit."

"We won't," Trevor assured him, "And if we do, I can get us in so she'll never even know."

Matthew didn't want to answer Trevor for fear it might seem as though he approved of his statement. Even with Matthew's worries, they decided to walk Alice and Rachel home with Alvin before they ventured back to the boarding house.

A few minutes later, they arrived at the home of Miss Jessica to see her standing at the door, shouting up at an individual only slightly taller than she. He was the same man Rachel had seen the day that Matthew had nearly told Rachel about his own painful past. That same squat man with the rotten smile was standing before the house, being beaten off by Aunt Jessica, her hands flapping in the air as though swatting at a fly.

"There he is again!" Rachel exclaimed, "Alvin, haven't you seen him before?"

Alvin squinted at the man, the gears in his mind turning as he racked his memory for any appearance of such an individual. His search yielded nothing.

"Can't say as I have," he replied, and then looked down at his companion, "Alice?"

Alice, without taking her eyes off of the victim of Aunt Jessica's scolding, shook her head quickly.

"Alice, are you alright?" Alvin pondered, peering down at her ashen face.

"Hmm?"

"Are you alright? You seem rather pale."

Alice shook herself and smiled amiably. "Oh, it's nothing," she said dismissively, "It must be the cold weather…"

The youth approached the warring adults with caution, and it became clear that the man in question had done something unacceptable and would no longer be allowed to employ the services of any women who stayed in Miss Jessica's house. Alice's aunt was desperately trying to drive him away, but to no avail. All her efforts were met solely with jeers and taunts; the man would not be moved. After a time, she gave up, and received Rachel and Alice into the house, slamming the door behind her with all her might. Alvin, Matthew, and Trevor turned around to leave, but before they could be on their way, the man shouted to them. The three boys looked back at him quizzically. What business could he possibly have with them?

"Don't I know you from somewhere's?" he said, addressing Alvin, "Where're you from?"

"That's no business of yours," Alvin replied coolly, "And I think it's best if you be on your way now."

"I don't like your *sass*," the man replied, his mouth twisting into a rotten grin, "I'll do what I like."

Alvin opened his mouth to answer, but Matthew and Trevor pulled him back and led him calmly away, knowing that it was not a good time for a confrontation.

CHAPTER FIFTEEN

Confession Time

As the days went on, Alvin adjusted to his lack of a left arm, and the others helped him along as best they could. They spent much of their time together, though Matthew and Trevor kept on going to school, wishing away the doleful hours until they could once again return to the wondrous outside where their friends were always waiting. Matthew worked hard at his studies, but Trevor was less engaged. Neither Matthew nor the time travellers could blame him, though, for they knew of his free spirit, and as much as they wished to dampen it and have him settle for what he was given, they knew that such a feat was impossible.

On the Friday afternoon following Alvin's discharge from the hospital, Rachel and Matthew were walking through St. Edward's after school let out. Rachel had taken to waiting at the bottom of the steps leading up to the school for Matthew to come out each day. The first day, she had asked Trevor to join them for a stroll through town, but the boy was off like a shot as soon as he came out the doors. Matthew was apprehensive about what he did when he was in the city by himself, but he had to dismiss his worries, for Rachel would surely know that something was wrong if he was anxious. Matthew tried as hard as he could to remain calm and casual.

"Where are Alvin and Alice today?" he asked as they strode through the St. Edward's market, enjoying the sounds and smells.

"Alice wasn't feeling well, so Alvin stayed with her at her Aunt's."

Matthew's brow furrowed. "Is she alright?"

"I believe so," Rachel sighed, and looked up at Matthew, "She seems upset or perhaps afraid…" She shook her head. "I'm really not sure. It's been nearly a year now since what happened to her, you know…"

Matthew nodded, and tugged her gently aside as a large wagon rolled past.

"I remember," he remarked sadly, shaking his head, "I hope she's alright." After a moment of silence, he turned to look for the source of a particularly fragrant smell that was wafting through the air, and found himself staring at a man who was standing by the side of the street selling a wonderfully aromatic pastry. Matthew and Rachel exchanged glances and smiled. Matthew gave Rachel his arm and they carefully crossed the street towards the delightful scent. Halfway across, they were stopped by the very same man that they had seen outside of Miss Jessica's house a few days earlier. Rachel was beginning to tire of his endless presence.

"You!" she exclaimed, then blushed as she remembered, too late, to hold her tongue.

"*You!*" the man retorted, "You're awful saucy, ain't you?" He reached up and clamped his hand around Rachel's jaw, "If you don't learn to control that mouth of yours," he warned, "You're gonna run into some trouble."

Rachel's eyes widened and she tried to pull away, finding that his grip on her jaw was too strong for her to escape. He wouldn't let go, and with his other hand he grabbed her wrist. Matthew felt Rachel's arm tense in his own.

"Let her go!" Matthew demanded, placing a hand on the man's arm, shaking as he did so. The man didn't reply, pushing Matthew roughly to the side and drawing his face in closer to Rachel's, his stagnant breath assaulting her nostrils. She tried once more to pull away, but her efforts were in vain.

"You'll keep your mouth shut next time, won't ya?"

Rachel did her best to nod, and she was let go. Matthew rushed her across the street and away, putting as much distance between them and that awful man as possible. Once he felt they were far enough, he stopped and turned to face Rachel.

"Are you alright?" he panted, searching her face for any sign of injury, physical or otherwise.

Rachel nodded slowly and rubbed her jaw. "I think so," she replied, "But I know from where I recognize him."

Matthew raised his eyebrows. "Where?"

"He lived in Connolly Mills for a very short time, and left sometime after you did."

"Do you know who he is?"

Rachel set her jaw forward and glanced mistrustfully back the way they had come. "I believe his name is Sidney Beagle," she decided, "And I think I know why he left."

■■

"How are you feeling?" Alvin asked benevolently as he handed Alice a glass of cool water.

Alice swallowed it down to the last drop and let out a shaky breath, relaxing slightly. Her hair, contrary to etiquette, was loose around her shoulders as she had not left the house all day. She was positively sick to her stomach, and the cold water did nothing to relieve the awful feeling.

"Better," she admitted, "But I still have this awful feeling in my stomach that won't go away..."

"Would you like something to eat?"

"Oh no," Alice said firmly, "I couldn't eat."

The pair were seated in Alice's room, Alice on her bed, Alvin in the chair. He felt good to be on the giving end of concern and pity instead of the receiving, but he worried for Alice. Ever since the awful occurrence almost one year ago, she had been a different person. Alvin cleared his throat and leaned forward in his chair.

"I know something's bothering you," he insisted, "Please tell me."

"It's nothing, Alvin," she promised, "Really."

Alvin looked at her patronizingly.

"Alvin please!" Alice said, smiling at his expression, "Don't look at me like that!"

"Alice, it can't be helped!" Alvin replied, "I know something's wrong!"

Alice's smile dropped from her features to be replaced by a tired, frustrated expression, which greatly startled Alvin.

"Alvin, please," she repeated, "I mean it. It's nothing. Please let me alone."

Alvin's eyes became filled with hurt and he stood, his expression dark.

"Shall I return tomorrow?"

Alice shrugged without looking at him. Alvin slowly backed away and turned from her, gently opening the door and stepping silently outside. Tears spilled over Alice's flushed cheeks the moment the door closed behind him.

Alvin tried to keep the sorrow and hurt from his face as he marched down the stairs and through the house. His fingers closed around the doorknob, but before he could so much as turn it, the door swung open, just grazing his nose. He stumbled back and tried to reach out his left arm to stop himself from falling, remembering too late that it was no longer there to save him.

"Alvin!"

Alvin felt a hand grasp his own and pull him to his feet a moment after he hit the floor. Looking up, he saw Matthew's kind and worried face looking into his. Rachel was standing behind him, peering down at Alvin, a puzzled look adorning her features.

"Where's Alice?" she asked.

A glance from Alvin towards the stairs was all Rachel needed, and she rushed past the half dozen ladies who were standing and whispering, casting their gazes towards the youth every few moments. Alvin and Matthew watched as Rachel pounded up the stairs, and listened as she flung open Alice's door without knocking.

"What is going on with everyone?" Alvin wondered, a hint of anger and frustration in his voice, "Something's wrong, I can *feel* it! I may have lost my arm, but I haven't lost my mind!"

"It's not that..." Matthew took one look at the whispering ladies, and grabbed hold of Alvin's arm.

"Not here," he said, and dragged Alvin outside and shut the door.

"Alright," Alvin said, once they were in the street, "*What* is the matter?"

Matthew was wringing his hands, and he hesitated a moment, knowing it would be unwise to tell Alvin about Rachel's suspicions.

"I dunno…" Matthew lied, avoiding Alvin's intense gaze, "Rachel was just—"

Alvin reached up in a blind panic and gripped Matthew's shirt collar with his right hand, and if he hadn't stopped himself, he would have lifted Matthew clean off his feet.

"What is happening? Is Alice alright?" he demanded, still keeping a tight hold on the front of Matthew's shirt. Matthew grabbed his wrist, and spoke with as much composure as he could possibly muster.

"Alvin," explained Matthew, "Everything is fine. Alice is fine. Rachel only needs to speak with her a moment."

"Don't play me for a fool, Matthew," Alvin responded wearily, letting go of his collar, "I *know* when something wrong has happened." He peered up at the façade of the house. "Please tell me what they're talking about."

Matthew sighed and promised himself that he would apologize to Rachel later. She had told him explicitly *not* to tell Alvin about her theory, for it would only upset him, but Matthew couldn't stand the manic look in Alvin's eyes. After all he had been through, Matthew just wanted to keep him happy, and by not telling him, he was only causing him more suffering.

"Alice asked me to leave," Alvin admitted, before Matthew could say anything, "Just now. She told me to let her alone. Tell me what's wrong with her. I know that you know."

"Alright, alright, I'll tell you. But, you must promise not to overreact."

"To *what*?"

Matthew, realizing that perhaps the word *overreact* was not yet in use, quickly changed the subject.

"Never mind. Rachel and I were walking in the market, and we saw that man again."

"Which man?"

"The man that was being scolded by Miss Jessica," Matthew explained, "The one Rachel thought she recognized."

Alvin's face went slowly from puzzled to enlightened, and he nodded, signalling Matthew to continue.

"Well, we ran into him, and he wouldn't let us pass, and he went right up close to Rachel's face—"

"Is she alright?"

Matthew nodded. "She says she remembers where she knows him from."

"Where?"

"He lived in Connolly Mills and left just after my family did."

"And?"

"And… she thinks… she thinks that he might be the one who attacked Alice."

Matthew looked up at Alvin, cringing, waiting for his reaction, which he felt sure would be one of distress and deep anger.

Alvin's face turned red and he shook with rage, the fingers on the end of his hand trembling violently. He took deep breaths, and clenched his fist. Through gritted teeth, he spoke.

"It can't be..."

■■

Mr. Riddell and Mr. Fitzgerald, unaware of the turmoil currently enveloping the lives of their young friends, were tidying the room they shared. Over the course of their stay there, they had never thought to spend much time keeping it in order. Neither man was a particularly untidy person, but any room can become messy when its inhabitants are constantly strapped for time. They had just gotten off work at five o'clock and were chatting as they cleaned.

"How has Mrs. Brown been lately?" Mr. Fitzgerald asked, "I only see her at meals nowadays, we're so busy with work and all, but she seems... distant, lately."

Mr. Riddell sighed in his melancholy way. "You've noticed too?" he wondered.

"She just... doesn't seem to be herself lately."

"I think it's about her husband. He's only been gone a short time, and there's just over a month to the anniversary of his death."

"Oh dear..."

Mr. Riddell nodded, nervously taking a spider from the floor and walking to the window.

"She sure makes him sound like a great—" Mr. Riddell paused to open the window and put his hand through, vigorously shaking off the spider, "Man," he finished.

"I'm sure he was," Mr. Fitzgerald replied absently, smoothing out the blankets on his bed.

"Well, all I can say is that she sure deserved a man like him. Well to do, handsome, intelligent..." Mr. Riddell trailed off and sat still for a moment.

Mr. Fitzgerald paused and glanced at his friend, registering the defeated look on his face and the sorrow in his eyes.

"She reminds you of Sophie, doesn't she?" he ventured, knowing full well that this was the case. Mr. Riddell's wife, who had died in childbirth, was often uppermost in the man's thoughts.

"Yeah. Yeah, she does. She even looks a little like her. And Eddie... Eddie loves her. She's been like a mother to him these past weeks. Every time I look at her I can't help seeing Sophie... I must be going crazy..."

Mr. Fitzgerald smiled wryly and walked over to his friend, then sat down beside him. "Listen to me," he said kindly, a hand on Mr. Riddell's shoulder, "You are not going crazy, alright? It's a natural reaction. Anyone else in your shoes would be thinking the same thing."

"I mean it, though," Mr. Riddell persisted, "It's scaring me. I have these dreams where she talks to me and when I'm awake every time I turn my head I have to look back because I think I've seen her face. It's the same way I felt when she first died… Like she wasn't really gone at all, just hiding in the shadows…"

Mr. Riddell's talk was beginning to take on a more sinister air; his mind was certainly in turmoil.

"I don't know what to do anymore…" He trailed off and shut his eyes.

Mr. Fitzgerald was at a loss. He couldn't quite picture how his friend was feeling, though he felt he had some vague idea. He had no clue, however, what could be done about it.

"You'll be alright," he assured him weakly, "Everything passes."

Mr. Riddell, his face buried in his hands, nodded, and Mr. Fitzgerald rose and left. He felt that what his friend needed the most at that moment was to be left alone.

■■

The life that Sam had been leading ever since arriving in Norton was, needless to say, much less eventful than his old life in Connolly Mills. He missed his home there, but there was no man in town willing to hire him after he was let go when the blacksmith he worked for shut his doors. Perhaps he couldn't find employment because people were afraid of him. He wasn't an intimidating sort of man by any means, but his association with Grace, Evan, and the other time travellers left him in a bad position. The people of Connolly Mills were still afraid, regardless of whether or not they had heard the real story. Clay Kennedy, however strange and broken he may have become, was still a powerful man, and what he said was taken by many of the town's inhabitants as the gospel truth. Because of this influence, Sam had to move elsewhere to find a way to make a living, and Norton was like the Promised Land to a man like him.

Sam had finally found work in the district of Oakton, where he had worked in one of the saw mills along the northern river that passed by Norton on its way south. At the beginning, he was working side by side with Evan and John, but after a few weeks, work began to slow down, and Sam was one of the employees they laid off in order to save money. Now, he worked longer, harder hours and wasn't paid nearly what he deserved, but he was happy. He had had to leave the boarding house he lived in for a small set of rooms in much poorer condition than he had previously been accustomed to. He rarely saw the time travellers any more—his work made sure of that—but he did often see one person in particular who had grown quite fond of him, unbeknownst to anyone else.

"Hey, Sam!" Trevor hollered out to him over the whirring machinery, as he did nearly every weekday.

Sam waved back at his young friend. For a long time, Sam had seen neither hide nor hair of the young man with whom he had travelled to Norton, but in recent days, Trevor had found him at his workplace and attempted to rekindle their old friendship. Trevor found that he liked the atmosphere of Sam's workplace, all the noise and movement, and he enjoyed watching the goings on.

Trevor approached Sam and waited patiently as he pushed a large slab of wood towards the spinning saw blade and split it perfectly in two. Trevor kept his distance from the saw, which glinted menacingly in the sun. He cringed as Sam's dark fingers came closer and closer to it as he pushed the wood through, until he stopped and pushed the rest of it through with a long pole. Unlike any table saw Trevor had ever see before, this one had no guard. There was nothing to keep Sam's hands from being sliced just as easily as the lumber with which he worked, and Trevor hated it.

"I wish they would put a guard on that!" he shouted over the noise, nodding at the saw.

"What?" Sam yelled back, cupping a hand over his ear. Trevor only shook his head, realizing that he shouldn't speak of things that may not exist yet. He had been getting better lately at watching what he said, but he still had the occasional slip-up every now and then.

Sam shut down the whirring blade and sat down on a pile of lumber behind him.

"How are you, Trevor?" he asked jovially, brushing the sawdust off of his shirt.

"Good," Trevor replied, as he always did, though most days he felt far from it. The time machine that he and Grace were working to rebuild was nearly finished, and every moment it remained in disrepair contributed to Trevor's overall anxiety. He had wanted to return to the present day ever since he had arrived in the past, but after the amputation of Alvin's arm, he felt he couldn't wait any longer. Even watching Sam depressed him sometimes. He liked being around him, and he liked to watch him work, but the life Sam led as a general rule left Trevor feeling quite dispirited. The other workers would talk about him behind his back, when they thought he couldn't hear. They would make rude jokes and speak using words that even Trevor had never heard before. In a show of silent solidarity, Trevor stood by Sam as he was tormented.

"I'm glad," Sam replied, waking Trevor from his reveries, "How was school?"

"Fine," answered Trevor, "It was fine. Boring, though."

"You always say that!" Sam insisted, "You must be learning something! It may be boring, Trevor, but you must appreciate it. I never got to go to school, you know. I didn't even know how to read until Grace taught me."

Trevor looked up and his brow furrowed. "You didn't?"

"'Course not!" Sam laughed, "You think they'd let me?"

"Well, why not?"

Sam's face turned thoughtful and he reached out his hand "You got your books with you?" Trevor nodded. "Show me your geography book."

Reluctantly, yet with a great deal of curiosity, Trevor pulled out his geography textbook and handed the volume over to Sam, who opened it and began to leaf through it. He stopped on a page near the middle of the book.

"Look here," he said, showing the page to Trevor, "Look what it says here under this drawing of the African man." Trevor peered at the page and followed Sam's finger as he trailed it above the words he wished for Trevor to read.

Trevor glanced at it and read, his brow furrowing and nose wrinkling with every word. "Sam," he said, "I can't even read that out loud! That's terrible! Why would people…"

Sam took back the book and closed it. "That is what they teach in your schools. Do you understand? They could never have someone like me there."

"Sam," Trevor protested, "I had no idea…"

"I know you didn't, Trevor, but that is the way the world is." Sam shrugged and made ready to continue his work.

"Sam, you should know, it's not fair for you to be treated like this."

"I know that! Maybe one day it'll change. In fact, I think it will. You just wait and see."

"Oh, it will," Trevor commented absently, staring at the dusty ground, "I know it will…Maybe not completely, but it'll be better than this."

"I'm glad you think so, Trevor!"

"Huh?" Trevor looked up.

"You know, Trevor," Sam said, a faraway look in his eyes, "I always wondered what it might be like to visit the future. Haven't you?"

Trevor peered down at his feet, tracing a line in the dust with his shoe. "Well, sure Sam, of course. But, it's impossible."

"Perhaps it is now, Trevor. But one day in the future, it will be possible. I know it will."

"How can you be so sure?"

"I don't know. I just am." Sam paused. "You know, I read a book recently about a time machine."

Trevor's palms began to sweat, and he began to tap his foot and bite his lip. "You did?"

Sam nodded excitedly. "It was called *The Time Machine*. A man named H.G. Wells wrote it. A man travels into the future, and you would not believe what he sees, Trevor, he—"

"I can't stay long today," Trevor interrupted, "Maybe you can tell me about some other time. I'll see you later!" With that, he ran off, waving as he went.

CHAPTER SIXTEEN

Time to Apologize

"Now, Alvin," Matthew attempted to calm his friend, "Don't get too upset, now…"

Alvin was trembling from head to foot and his face was redder than Matthew had ever seen it before.

"Upset? Matthew, I'm more than upset. What he did to her…" Alvin trailed off and breathed in deeply.

"Alvin, listen, you're always telling people to have mercy—"

"This isn't about mercy, Matthew! Do you think that he showed mercy to anyone a day in his life? He sure didn't show it to Alice, and she never did anything to offend him! She was in the wrong place, at the wrong time, with the wrong man in town! He'd be hanged if they caught him, Matthew! Do you understand? Even if he did nothing else wrong in his entire life, what he did to Alice was enough. I bet he doesn't even regret it! I should have known it was him with the way he looked at her… She's not safe, and neither is Rachel, for that matter, until he's locked up! I won't let him do any more harm!"

"It's not your place, Alvin, let the police deal with him. Rachel even told me that Alice didn't want retribution—"

"It's not about retribution either!" Alvin shouted, then continued more quietly, "It's not about that, as much as I'd like to take revenge on him, it's about keeping them safe. Keeping Alice safe. A man like that shouldn't be allowed to walk the streets, and I can't let him."

"What are you going to do?"

Alvin looked up at the façade of Number Six Crookshanks Lane and let out a long, deep breath that he had been holding in.

"First," he said, "I'm going to talk to Alice."

"Are you sure that's wise?" Matthew wondered.

"Whether something is wise or not, sometimes it must be done," Alvin stated, and with those words, he marched back towards the door and knocked. It was opened by Rachel, who stepped aside to let him in as she left the house. Alvin nodded his thanks and disappeared inside.

Matthew walked slowly over to Rachel. "Well?" he wondered. Rachel nodded.

"Alice knew it was him from the very first time we saw him. She didn't want to say anything, but it simply plagued her. She thought that Alvin would want to go and get revenge on the man, so to protect him—Alvin, I mean—she remained silent all that time." Rachel glanced back at the door. "You told him, didn't you?"

Matthew looked at the ground. "He seemed so tortured," he explained, "I had to tell him."

"What did he say?" Rachel asked.

"He was angry. Really, really angry. But he says he doesn't want revenge. He does want to at least put the man behind bars, though, to protect Alice. Do you think we'll ever see that man again, though?"

Rachel nodded. "I do," she said sincerely, "He used to come around here a lot, according to Aunt Jessica, and every time he comes, she tries to make him leave for good, but he always returns." Rachel shivered. "I can hardly stand it."

"Neither can I," Matthew agreed, "Neither can I."

■■■

"Alice?"

Alice wanted to ignore the gentle knocks at her door and the concerned voice behind them, but she couldn't. Instead, she wiped her eyes and smoothed out her dress. She stood up and faced the door of her bedroom, and in a hoarse and crackling voice, she spoke.

"Come in," she said feebly.

Alice watched as the door swung slowly open and Alvin entered the room. His expression was softer than before, and his tone of voice quieter and gentler. He let his hand, which was clutching the doorknob, fall to his side.

"Alice," he began, still standing in the doorway, "I'm sorry. I'm so sorry. I didn't know… I didn't know that that man… I didn't mean to upset you when I asked why you were feeling so low, I was only concerned…" Alvin's voice had dropped to a whisper and his gaze was downcast. He could only imagine the bottled up pain and fear that Alice must have felt when she first saw that man. The sudden realization that she *had* seen him after all when she was attacked—and that his face had been a suppressed memory—must have been horrific. Alvin felt sure that if it had been him with those awful memories, it would have been too much to bear. Yet Alice hid her feelings for so long, and he wished that she would pour them out to him, for he was certain that it would make her feel just a little bit better if she would simply let it out.

"I'm sorry," he repeated, trying to keep his voice level, "I'm so sorry, Alice…"

Alice watched as he raised his head to look at her, and her lower lip began to tremble. She hated to cry, and yet ever since the terrible events of earlier that year, it seemed that she had been doing an awful lot of it. Alvin's presence only served to bring her own feelings to the forefront, but somehow, that seemed to be just what she needed.

"Don't be sorry, Alvin," she managed, "It's… it's not your fault…" Alice broke off, tears streaming down her cheeks, her breathing shaky, "It's been a difficult time for all of us…" She tried to speak more and further her point, but found it nearly impossible. Her throat was constricted and all she could manage were heavy choking sobs. Her hand flew up to her mouth and hid it as she cried, muffling the sounds of her sorrow.

"Alice, it's alright!" Alvin assured her gently, taking a step forward, "It's alright…"

Alice nodded, but did not meet his gaze. Alvin stepped forward again and Alice finally let herself go and began to cry into his shirt.

"Shh," he whispered, running his fingers through her hair, "It's okay. You're safe now. You're safe. I won't let anything happen to you…"

The pair of them stood there for a good while longer, Alvin whispering reassurances as Alice allowed her tears to flow freely. Truth be told, Alvin was having a difficult time trying to keep himself composed. The boy was a born empath, and so his feelings were a mixture of sadness for Alice, and deep, intense rage against the man who had attacked her and continued to invade upon her sensibilities to this day. He was even angry with himself; that losing his arm had caused her so much pain.

Alice could feel Alvin's heart racing a mile a minute, and she was still afraid that he would want to exact his revenge against the man. In all honesty, she would not have minded to see him go behind bars, but Alice was concerned that Alvin would put himself in harm's way in order to avenge her, and that was the last thing she wanted.

"Alvin," she breathed, once her sobs had subsided.

"Yes?" he answered, close to her ear.

"Promise me… Promise me you won't get yourself hurt because of me. Don't try and fight him. Please. Please don't try and take revenge."

"Alice," he said, speaking in the softest tone he possessed, as though he was afraid of hurting her ears, "You deserve to feel safe, and to *be* safe. With him around here so much… I fear for you, Alice."

"Please, Alvin. Please just promise you won't get hurt."

Alvin sighed and breathed in deeply, resting his cheek against her hair. "I promise," he reluctantly agreed at last, "I promise."

■■■

Much time had passed since Rachel had run away from Connolly Mills, and ever since, her grandfather had been trying desperately to find her. His first thought was that she had run away to be with Matthew and his family, but as the days passed, a new thought began to formulate itself in his mind. Perhaps, he thought, he may have been too hard on her. Perhaps she really was telling the truth. He put this new thought into words for his wife, and she fully assented to the notion. Both she and Clay then set out to look for their precious granddaughter, checking all the nearby farms and asking everyone they knew, and many people they didn't. However, no one seemed to have seen her.

Dejected and angry, Clay was slumped in his armchair in the parlour. He couldn't bear to think of what may happen to Rachel out there, all alone in the world. However, the thought occurred to him that Rachel wouldn't truly be alone. He was fairly certain that she had run away, and Clay knew that the first place she would run to was wherever Matthew, Alvin, or Alice was. The problem was, he didn't know where any of them were. For the remainder of the day, until the dead of night, Clay sat. Penelope was busy cleaning upstairs, and so he was utterly alone, and he felt like sitting in the dark. He stood, put out all the lamps, and sat back down again, with only the silvery light of the moon for company.

"Where did you go?" Clay wondered to himself, staring into the blackness that surrounded him, "Why did you leave?" He paused and screwed up his face, gripping the arms of his chair so his knuckles turned a ghostly white.

"That's a ridiculous question," he continued, addressing himself, "You know why she left. You hit her. You know that, you idiot!" Clay stopped talking again and stood abruptly, his breathing heavy and fists clenched. After a moment, he slowly sat down again and sighed.

"You're insane, you know," he said darkly, "Every minute you're feeling different. Penelope's always telling you to stop worrying. Stop believing yourself to be persecuted. But you can't do it. You never could. Everyone's your enemy. Especially the people who killed your daughter…"

Having reminded himself of his daughter's untimely demise, and the reason he believed to be behind it, Clay stood again. He paced back and forth, hands hovering around his grief stricken head.

"They killed her in cold blood," he whispered, his pacing becoming frantic, "She was ill and couldn't defend herself, so they killed her. But, why? Why, Clay, *why*? I don't know! She was weak... They're murderers! And they're more than that..." Clay trailed off and stopped in his tracks, an image of Alice Cosgrove flashing into his mind. He could never decide if he believed that she was attacked or if it was Alvin who had caused her pregnancy. Either way, he hated Alvin. The boy had stood in his way when he tried to finally bring his daughter's killers to justice, and he would never forgive him for that. He could never forgive him for preventing his doing the one thing that might bring him peace.

"If he hadn't gotten in the way..." Clay groaned, resuming his trek back and forth across the parlour, "If he had just let me do it... Rachel would still be here..."

"Clay?"

The man in question spun round to face the door at the sound of his name, unsure of whether it was truly being called or if it was merely another figment of his distraught mind. It had seemed, in recent days, that people were constantly calling him. He often heard Rachel's voice calling out to her grandfather, but Penelope's, his wife's, was most common of all.

"Yes?" he ventured.

Penelope stepped into the doorway, a lit lamp in her hand. "I think I've found something," she said.

Clay walked slowly towards her, his eyes adjusting to the light. She held a thin sheet of paper in her feeble little hands, which Clay gently lifted from her, holding it near the light. Reading it carefully through, he discovered it to be a letter, from none other than Alvin Quinn. With trembling hands, Clay turned the paper over in his hands and found, written in small script near the bottom, a return address. He read each letter and number over and over until he had committed it to memory.

"Does this mean that Rachel's gone to..."

Clay nodded solemnly and straightened up to his full height, letting the letter fall to his side.

"Norton."

■■■

Night had fallen upon the city of Norton, yet not all of its inhabitants were sleeping. Aunt Jessica's house was abuzz, men scurrying in and out at all hours of the night, knocking discreetly on the door; business as usual. Alice and Rachel had long ago grown used to the constant hum of activity and slept as peacefully as was possible most nights.

Alvin had left just before nightfall, having kept Alice company most of the afternoon. However, even with all his reassurances and comforting words and gestures, Alice found that sleep still eluded her, as it had for days on end. She contented her nervous mind instead with listening to the various noises of the night, the chatter downstairs, the clatter of the wagons outside. It was very nearly midnight when Alice's eyelids finally began to droop and her exhaustion overcame her. She had slept for no more than a few hours when she heard a sound that would have woken her from the deepest slumber.

"Hey!"

Alice sat up abruptly, her eyes wide open, and listened carefully to every sound, her senses running at full capacity, adrenaline rushing through her veins and making her heart pound furiously.

"Hey!" the voice came again, and Alice lifted the sheets away and peeled slowly out of bed. The source of the voice appeared to be from outside, so she tiptoed towards the window. Far below, standing between Aunt Jess' house and the neighbour's, was a short, stout figure. In the darkness, it was difficult to see who exactly it was, but Alice knew. She jumped back from the window upon her first glance and felt the impulse to scream, but no sound came. She stood in silence, her back to the door of the room, and after a moment, the voice continued.

"You gonna come down, doll?"

It sounded wicked and sharp, each syllable delivering a stabbing pain to Alice's stomach. Alice found herself shaking her head uncontrollably, trembling from head to toe. The taunts continued from below, growing closer together with each one, as though the man was warming to the subject. Soon, Alice could not hear the words, only the drone of the voice, which would not cease in her ears. She turned around and pulled desperately on the doorknob, seeking an escape from this waking nightmare, but the door had been locked to prevent anyone from entering the room, and Alice was too distraught to remember the key. She simply continued to pound on the door and tug uselessly on the knob, twisting and turning it until her fingers grew numb. It was only then that her body would finally let her speak. And she yelled for help with the force of anyone twice her size, waking any in the house who had been sleeping.

Multiple ladies of the night came rushing to Alice's door until the hall was a crowded mess of women, all of them wanting to help but none quite sure of what to do. Many tried to open the door, but the lock held. A loud muttering began, each woman trying to tell the others what to do, but no one being able to discern any proper action.

Rachel, who had always been a heavy sleeper, was one of the last in the house to hear Alice's screams. However, when she did, she did not waste a moment. Springing out of bed, she opened the attic door to reveal the swarm in the hall beneath. Desperate, she did the only thing she could do.

"Look out!" she shouted, and promptly dropped to the floor. She felt no pain from the fall; she only stood up once more and pushed her way through the masses towards Alice's door.

"Alice?" she yelled, "Alice!"

Receiving no response, Rachel pounded on the door and attempted with all her strength to turn the knob. It jolted violently, having been loosened by the pounding and hitting of Alice and the numerous worried ladies. One of the more resourceful of the bunch came rushing up the stairs with a butter knife in her tiny hands and handed it off to Rachel, who jammed it into the lock mechanism. Finally, the lock gave Rachel flung open the door and tossed the knife to the side. By this time, Alice's screams had subsided and Rachel could only hear faint muttering and quick breathing.

Rachel scurried inside, followed closely by the other inhabitants of the house. They found Alice crouched in the far corner of the room, her chair pulled in front of her like a shield.

"Alice, what happened?" Rachel asked gently, seeing the distress in her friend's eyes. Alice did not answer. She did not even look up. Her gaze remained fixed firmly forward, staring at something only she could see. Rachel reached out and touched her arm, then quickly withdrew as Alice flinched violently and withdrew further into the corner.

"Where's Aunt Jessica?" Rachel interrogated one of the women standing behind her, "Where did she go?"

The woman shook her head. "I don't know," she replied, then repeated herself, "I don't know. The last time I saw her, she left the house with Janet, she looked fairly upset..."

Rachel stood up and gathered her wits. She considered going to find Alvin, for she knew he would be able to bring Alice back to her senses, but he lived too far away. The next person who sprang to Rachel's mind was Matthew. He wouldn't likely be of any help, but the adults of his family might possess knowledge enough to know what was happening. Ushering everyone out of the room, Rachel began to put her plan into action.

"Listen," she began, attempting to spell out instructions to the house's many inhabitants, "I want one of you to go to the address..."

Rachel couldn't finish her sentence but for the incessant chattering among the terrified ladies.

She sighed, "I'll go." With that, she turned to the nearest woman and ordered her to keep the noise at a minimum and everyone out of Alice's room.

Mrs. Brown's boarding house was not far, and the distance was made all the shorter by Rachel's speed. Rachel ran through the streets and climbed the steps to Mrs.

Brown's two at a time. The door was answered after Rachel's third spurt of knocks by a dishevelled looking Sandra, followed shortly after by Mrs. Brown, then Grace and Matthew.

"What in heaven's name is going on?" Mrs. Brown wondered, her eyes blazing.

"It's… it's Alice…" Rachel began, trying to catch her breath, "She's… I don't know… she's afraid… She's gone into hysterics…"

Sandra stepped in front of Mrs. Brown and placed a hand on Rachel's shoulder.

"Slow down," she advised, "Catch your breath, now. That's it. Now what happened to Alice?"

"I—I'm not sure… She was sleeping, I assume, and then all of a sudden I heard these awful screams. Her door was locked and we got in, but Miss Jessica wasn't home, and I didn't know what to do. I found her sitting in the corner… She was talking very quietly and when I got near her she tried to hit me…"

Grace's brow furrowed. "This wouldn't have anything to do with what happened to her…?" She let her sentence finish itself.

Rachel shook her head. "I don't know, I don't know. Perhaps."

"Why ever didn't you call someone?" Mrs. Brown asked incredulously, "I know we're not far away, but even so…"

"I never thought of that," Rachel admitted, "I just… I just knew I needed *someone.*"

"I understand, dear, it's difficult to think straight in such circumstances," Sandra comforted her, wrapping a shawl around her shoulders, "You did the right thing."

Rachel swallowed and nodded.

"Let's go," Grace stepped outside and started down the steps, purpose in her stride. Rachel turned quickly and followed suit, scampering into the street, still in her nightgown. After a moment of silence and stillness, Mrs. Brown hurried after them, her skirts flapping in the night wind.

Matthew and Sandra exchanged glances.

"Do you think she's okay?" he whispered, his eyes betraying his inner worry to Sandra.

"I think she'll be alright," Sandra replied, beginning to take her first steps into the chilly autumn night, "But we haven't seen her yet."

Matthew, his self consciousness having gotten the better of him, had quickly put on a pair of trousers before leaving his room when he heard the knocks at the door. He felt rather vain upon noticing that the others were all still in their nightclothes, for they had sensed the emergency and put it ahead of themselves.

He followed Sandra into the night and after walking briskly through St. Edward's, they crossed the vague border that lay between their district and the Southern Quays. The difference in atmosphere was amazing. Sleepy St. Edward's could not hold a candle to the night-time activities that occurred in the poorer section of the city. There were men that loitered around buildings, smoking and whispering, and women in little clusters of two or three who were laughing and smiling, long, thin cigarette holders poised in their hands. The wisps of smoke coiled in the night air with a strangely artful quality, the particles scattering as Matthew and the others sped through.

When the five of them arrived at Miss Jessica's house, they found Alice's door still crowded by the worried inhabitants of the house. They all liked Alice very much, and didn't wish for anything to happen to her.

"Excuse us," Sandra said, touching the shoulder of the nearest girl as she fought her way through, Matthew close on her heels. The pair caught up with Mrs. Brown, Grace, and Rachel in Alice's room. It felt different to Matthew at night, as though the entire house had taken on a new personality, like it had some hidden dark heart deep within it. Goosebumps arose on Matthew's arms when he saw Alice cowering in the corner, visibly trembling.

Sandra crouched awkwardly beside her, peering around the chair. Alice did not respond to her presence, keeping her gaze unfocused and forward facing.

"Alice?"

Alice's head turned, ever so slowly, until her gaze met Sandra's.

"Do you want to tell me what happened?" Sandra's tone was soft and caring, her motherly spirit helping Alice to feel more comfortable.

Alice looked down at her lap and nodded slightly.

"I heard his voice..." she began, her voice tiny, leaving Matthew and the others straining to hear.

"Whose voice, dear?"

Alice squirmed and drew her knees up closer to her chin. "You know..." she started to say, willing Sandra to understand.

"It's alright, honey, he's not here," she said, her voice lilting, "It was only a bad dream."

"Umm—" Matthew stepped forward, hand poised to tap Sandra's shoulder. Grace reached out a hand and grabbed his wrist.

"Don't interrupt," she hissed.

"But it's important—"

"Shh!"

Alice glanced up at Matthew, her eyes filled with fear.

"There's something you should know..." Rachel said, and Mrs. Brown looked, eyes narrowed, between Matthew, Rachel, and Alice.

"What exactly is going on?" she asked, perceiving that there was something the three youth knew that she didn't.

Grace turned to Matthew, eyes wide. "You mean that you know who... And he's here?" she hissed.

"I'd been meaning to tell you," Matthew admitted, scratching the back of his head.

"*Who* is here, Grace?" Mrs. Brown's curiosity was overcoming her.

"I'll explain later," Grace promised, and then turned back to Matthew and Rachel. "Are you certain?"

The pair nodded in unison. Grace let out a long breath and leaned against the wall, hand against her forehead as Sandra continued to comfort Alice.

CHAPTER SEVENTEEN

Hard Times

"So *now* she remembers who did it?" Evan asked incredulously. He, along with the rest of the time travellers and Mrs. Brown, was in the parlour at the boarding house the morning after Alice's frightening episode.

"Rachel thinks it must have come back to her when she saw his face," Matthew replied from his perch on the windowsill beside Trevor.

"So why didn't she say anything when you first saw him?" John wondered, "How come she kept it a secret?"

"She was afraid, John," Sandra reminded him, a hand on his arm, "And probably doubting herself."

"Doubting or not, something must be done!" said Grace, gripping the back of Evan's chair, "If he's around that house as much as they say he is, it isn't safe for either of those girls to be staying there until he's caught and turned in."

"Agreed," Mr. Fitzgerald assented, nodding, "After what happened in Connolly Mills..." His voice faded away to nothing.

Mrs. Brown bobbed her head in concurrence with his unfinished statement. Grace had filled her in the previous night on the details of Alice's unfortunate circumstances.

"Until the situation is sorted," she said confidently, "They are both more than welcome to stay here as long as need be." She bent and picked up Eddie, who had been loitering about below her.

"Are you sure, S—Mrs. Brown?" Mr. Riddell looked up at their landlady, his face growing pink as he hoped she wouldn't notice his little slip of the tongue.

"Quite certain," came the reply, "There's plenty room enough in my part of the house. Granted, it is highly irregular, but exceptions can always be made for those in need."

"Alvin's not gonna like this, is he?" Trevor whispered to Matthew as the rest of the group discussed living arrangements.

"What, Alice staying here?"

"No, about the guy. Does he know?"

"He knows that he's in the city, but not about last night."

"I'll bet he wants to kill the guy…"

"No, he would never do—or even think—that, I don't think. I'm sure he'll be mad though, when he does find out."

"Who's gonna tell him?"

"No one. Alice begged Rachel and me not to say anything, she's afraid he'll go and get himself hurt."

"So, how's he going to find out if no one tells him?"

"Oh, he'll find out," Matthew said absently, peering through the window, "He always does."

∎∎

The train station, which stood some way out from the main roads of Connolly Mills, was bustling. The soft morning sun shone above; the sky was cloudless. Clay Kennedy, the letter with Alvin's address written on it nestled safely in his pocket, was waiting behind a posh and stylish young couple to speak with the ticket vendor. The couple were arguing about the price of the tickets with the vendor, and each one of them had raised their voices, struggling to be heard over the other.

Finally, after a long and drawn out battle which the young couple lost, Clay was able to move forward and speak his piece. Penelope was not with him, having opted to remain at home in case Rachel was indeed hiding somewhere in town and decided to return home. Clay was going to be travelling alone to the city of Norton with the aim of finding his runaway granddaughter. Before he boarded the train, however, he wanted to talk to the ticket vendor and ask if he had seen Rachel.

"Hello," he began, trying desperately to remain polite, "I'm looking for my granddaughter, Rachel Reid. I believe she boarded a train here some time ago, headed for Norton. She's about sixteen years old, brown hair, green eyes. Probably no more than five feet and five inches. She's—"

The ticket vendor stopped him with a wave of his hand. "Look, sir, we have many young ladies of that description boarding trains here all the time. If you think I'm gonna remember one specific, you're mistaken."

"I have a photograph," Clay offered, reaching into his jacket and pulling out a small card. Penelope had found the picture in Rachel's bedroom, tucked away in one of her books. It was a rather foolish portrait depicting Rachel in what looked to Clay like Darcy Lake, standing with Alvin, Alice, and Matthew. Their faces all bore the most peculiar smiles, and they looked quite silly. Clay hated the picture, mostly for the presence of Matthew, Alvin, and Alice in it, but it was the only one he had of Rachel, and he figured that people remembered best when they had a visual aid. He showed the picture to the ticket vendor and pointed to his granddaughter.

"That's her there," he said, "Did she ever board a train here?"

"I told you, I don't remember specifics!" the man nearly shouted, "I've seen hundreds of people!"

"Come on, think man, it's important! She's missing!" Clay shoved the picture forward once more, forcing the man to take a closer look. Rolling his eyes, he peered at the photograph in exasperation, but then his brow furrowed and his eyes widened.

"I don't know the girl, but I know this one!" He was pointing excitedly at Matthew, "He was here last year, on Christmas!"

"Christmas?" Clay wondered, then shook his head, "Listen, I'm not looking for him, I'm looking for her, and if you're done thinking I'll take one ticket to Norton on the next train out."

The vendor shrugged and let Clay buy the ticket. The ride to Norton was a long one, and there would be many stops in between, but the sooner Clay knew where Rachel was, the happier he would be.

■■■

"You're moving out?" Alvin asked incredulously. He was standing in the threshold to Alice's room, having just arrived to check in on her. Alice nodded absently and set to folding up her clothes on the bed.

"Why?" Alvin continued, stepping inside, "Did something happen?"

"No," Alice lied, "All I know is that Aunt Jessica needs Rachel and me to stay away for a while."

"Well, how come?"

"I told you, I don't know." Alice placed the remainder of her things in her bag and lifted it from the bed.

"Let me," Alvin offered, and took the bag from her, lifting it in his one hand while trying desperately not to lose his balance.

"Mrs. Brown invited us to stay with her at the boarding house until my aunt can take us back."

Alice followed Alvin down the stairs and through the house to the front door.

"I'll take it from here," she said, reprising her luggage, "Would you mind staying here and helping Rachel with her things? She should be back from the boarding house soon, and I told her she could expect to see you here."

"Are you sure you don't want me to walk with you?"

"I'll be fine. It's only a short distance and Mrs. Brown is meeting me on the way."

Alvin looked sceptical, but he obeyed her wishes and stayed behind, watching nervously as she rounded the street corner and vanished from sight. He turned and shut the door behind him with a creaking sigh.

The house was fairly empty that particular afternoon, with only a couple of its residents dozing in the parlour. Alvin, feeling restless, plucked a volume at random from a small shelf near the back of the house and sat down in an armchair to read it. Luckily, the spine was broken so the book could rest comfortably in his lap without the need for an extra arm to hold it aloft. He took to drumming his fingers on the arm of the chair as he read, letting the muted tapping sounds fill the otherwise noiseless room.

All at once he heard a crinkling, crackling noise, and for a moment he peered curiously at his busy fingers, wondering how on earth they had made such a sound. Then it came again, louder this time, and Alvin placed the book aside and stood, following the noise as best he could. It led him to the front door once more, and he opened it cautiously and stepped out. The street appeared normal, the levels of traffic consistent with what they had always been. The sound came to Alvin's ears a third time, and he walked around to the side of the house, entering the narrow alley between Jessica's home and the neighbour's. There, he stopped cold.

"What are you doing?" he asked, his voice tremulous. He was addressing the man standing beneath Alice's window, tossing pebbles up towards the glass. He knew the moment he laid eyes on him who he was. The rotting smile, the foulness of his entire being; it was obvious that this man was Sidney Beagle, the one who had attacked Alice. The man to whom he was supposed to be merciful.

"What's it look like, I'm tryina get someone's attention!" the man retorted. Alvin glared at him and his fist clenched.

"Whose?"

The man turned to him again and snorted. "That's my business." He paused, eyes narrowed. "Hey," he continued, "Ain't you the one I saw with the girl that lives up there?" He gestured towards the window, far above his head. "She's a catch, ain't she?"

Alvin's face reddened. "You leave her alone."

"Why should I?"

"I know what you did to her."

The man froze and fixed Alvin with an icy stare. "I didn't do nothin'," he stated, "I dunno what you heard, boy..."

Alvin was ready to haul off and strike him, but he restrained, remembering his promise to Alice. He remained silent, looking into Beagle's eyes for any sign of remorse or regret. He found none.

"I said, I don't know what you heard, but I didn't do nothing, alright?" The man was getting closer and closer to Alvin, until he could smell his fetid breath as he reached up and took hold of Alvin's collar. "Y'understand?"

Alvin reached up and gripped the man's wrist. "Let me go," he said, as calmly as the situation would allow, "Let me go."

"Not until y'admit you didn't hear nothin'!" He shook Alvin by the collar. Alvin tried to pull away, but the man's grip was too strong. Apart from his heavy breathing, neither sounds nor words escaped Alvin's lips.

"I said, you didn't hear nothin'!" He pushed Alvin roughly against the wall and held him there. "I gave her what she was askin' for, that's all."

Alvin, forgetting his promise, could no longer take this man's evil words. Gritting his teeth, he let go of Beagle's wrist and balled his hand into a fist, connecting it with the left side of his jaw. Stunned, he let go of Alvin's shirt and staggered back, his hands shooting to his face.

"She never asked for anything from you!" Alvin shouted, his face twisted into a grimace, "You... you... you're— Augh!"

As Alvin was speaking, Sidney Beagle had regained his bearings and began to fight back, throwing Alvin to the dusty ground and pinning his arm to the cobbles.

"I'm what?" he challenged, "What am I, boy, huh?"

He threw a punch at Alvin's face, drawing blood from his nose, and another which was sure to produce a black eye.

"What am I?"

"Evil," Alvin choked, coughing, "You're evil…"
He tried desperately to kick the man, but to no avail, and trying to free his arm was an exercise in futility.

"Evil, huh? Well, think what you want, but you didn't hear nothing, y'understand now?" The man twisted Alvin's arm up behind his back, prompting him to cry out in pain, and tears to spring to his eyes. "Y'understand?"

Alvin, blood and tears blurring his vision, nodded as best he could.

"Good," he heard, "This never happened."

Alvin felt the man roughly let go of his arm and stand up, kicking him viciously before turning on his heels and running out of the alley and away, leaving Alvin on the ground, bruised and bloodied. He lay there for some time, trusting the shadows of the alleyway to mask his presence from passersby as he wept in pain.

His physical pain was nothing next to the pain he felt emotionally. He had broken his promise to Alice and gotten himself hurt fighting her attacker. Though he had not instigated the battle, he had thrown the first punch, and he felt a world of guilt that settled in the pit of his stomach and would not go away. Not only that, but he was disappointed in himself that he had not put up a better fight.

Remembering with a jolt that Rachel would soon arrive, Alvin mustered all his courage and strength to sit up. His shoulder felt as though it was on fire, his eye throbbed where it had been hit, and there was blood still pouring from his nose. Biting his lip, Alvin leant on his arm and stood up at last, then staggered awkwardly down the alley, his legs shaking. There was a horse trough across the road just a few feet to the left of the alleyway, and if he could just get there unnoticed, he could wash away the blood and pretend that he had sustained the black eye from a fall or other such accident.

He rounded the corner of Miss Jessica's house cautiously and was nearly knocked head over heels.

"There you are, Alvin, I've been looking for you!" Matthew exclaimed, steadying his friend, "Rachel is busy getting settled, so I came here to collect the last of her…

What *happened*? Are you okay?" Matthew stepped back and took in the sight before him. "Alvin, what did you do?"

"Matthew," Alvin began, swaying where he stood, his hand on Matthew's shoulder to steady him, "I can explain, but you can't tell Alice, I mean it. It's all my fault…" Tears mingled with the blood on Alvin's face and he hung his head.

"Come inside," Matthew said, ushering his friend towards the door, "We've got to get you cleaned up."

Matthew led Alvin carefully inside and up the stairs, finding a wash basin left in Alice's old room. He sat Alvin down in the armchair and soaked a cloth in the water.

"Now," he said, trying to hide his worry, "What on earth did you do?"

"It was all my fault," Alvin repeated, "I heard a noise outside and I went to look, and I found him."

"Who?" asked Matthew, though he felt he already knew the answer.

"The man, if you can call him that, who attacked Alice. He was… he was throwin' rocks at her window, hopin' she was up there… I asked him what he was doing—ah!"

"Sorry," Matthew apologized, removing the cloth from near Alvin's black eye, "Go on."

"He said he was trying to get her attention. Told me she was a *catch*. And worse. He said she asked for what he did to her. Said she was askin' for it… That was… that was when I hit him. I know I shouldn't have but he was making me so *angry*. I should have known he would hit back."

"Everyone makes mistakes," Matthew assured him, "As long as you're alright."

"I'll live. I just… I promised Alice I wouldn't do it. Fight him, I mean. She's gonna be so mad at me…"

"I'm sure she won't, it wasn't your fault."

"But it was! If I had done the right thing and left well enough alone, I wouldn't have confronted him. If I hadn't lost my temper, I'd never have been hit."

"Alvin, you can't blame yourself for this!"

"It's too late, I already have." Alvin smiled wryly at his own joke. "Bad luck seems to follow me wherever I go, doesn't it?"

"I'm afraid I can't disagree with you there," Matthew laughed, "But it will soon pass, and everything, one day, will be as it was." He smiled to himself, thinking how much he must have sounded like Sandra.

"I sure hope you're right."

"I know I'm right," Matthew stated, now reminding himself of Evan, "You just wait and see."

Alvin smiled, but his face quickly fell. "What am I going to tell her?" he wondered, his voice laced with desperation, "I don't want her to know I broke my promise…"

Matthew opened his mouth to answer, but no words came. His conscience wanted him to tell Alvin to be honest and speak only the truth, but he knew that saying such a thing would be hypocritical, for if there was one thing he hadn't been to his friends, it was honest. However, he couldn't tell Alvin to lie to Alice's face; that would be even worse.

"You do what you think is right, Alvin," he replied, turning the question back on his friend, "But I'm sure Alice will forgive you either way."

Alvin nodded slowly, his brow furrowing. "Wait a minute," he began, raising his hand for Matthew to stop what he was doing, "Alice hasn't been entirely truthful with me, has she?"

Matthew felt the colour drain from his face. "W-what do you mean?"

"About leaving here," Alvin explained patiently, "She told me that she doesn't know why she and Rachel have to leave. It's because of him, isn't it?" Alvin cocked his head toward the window, which was covered in dusty pockmarks from the stones that had been tossed from below.

"You're not angry, are you?"

"No, not angry. She didn't want me to get into trouble, that's all, and neither did the rest of you. He was here last night too, wasn't he?"

Matthew nodded, cleaning the last of the blood from his friend's hand. "You shouldn't mention it to her," he said, "It's best if you pretend you don't know."

"Alright," Alvin agreed wearily, "Let's go to your boarding house and help them get settled. I want to forget this whole thing."

"Won't she notice?"

"Notice what?"

"Your bruises, and your eye! You said you didn't want to tell her, but she'll find out just from looking at you!"

Alvin stood and brushed some dust from his shirt. "I know. I owe her the truth though, it is my fault, after all."

Matthew grinned. "I wish I was as honest and upstanding as you," he said. Alvin scoffed.

"Don't be so hard on yourself, Matthew, you've proven yourself a very trustworthy friend to us all."

"Thanks," Matthew smiled nervously, wishing that what Alvin had said was true.

The pair then went on their way, walking swiftly through Norton's busy streets. Neither said much, and Alvin walked with his head down, trying to hide his face from the city's many inhabitants. Before long, they arrived at Mrs. Brown's boarding house, Matthew carrying Rachel's small bag. They were greeted at the door by Rachel, who had been passing by on her way to the parlour.

"Oh good, you're here," she exclaimed, "Do come in, both of you, Mrs. Brown has been ever so hospitab—" Rachel stopped mid sentence and gasped at the sight of Alvin's battered face. She was about to speak again when Matthew reached up and held a finger to his lips.

"Shh," he whispered, "I'll explain everything later. Where's Alice?"

"She's in there," Rachel replied, pointing to the door to Mrs. Brown personal chambers, "Sleeping." She looked up at Alvin nervously.

"I know he was there last night," Alvin told her, "I imagine she didn't get much sleep."

Rachel turned to Matthew, eyes wide and mouth clamped tight shut, her expression scolding him for telling Alvin what Alice had made them promise not to.

"He figured it out," Matthew said defensively, "I didn't say a word, honest!"

Rachel relaxed and let Matthew lead her into the parlour, where the time travellers and Mrs. Brown were waiting. Alvin had elected to leave and return later to speak to Alice when she woke up in order to avoid making a scene amongst the adults.

Matthew and Rachel sat down on the couch, a piece of furniture much different than that of the same name in the time travellers' present day. It was raised at one end and covered in intricate patterns, and situated quite low to the ground.

"Thank you again for taking us in, Mrs. Brown," Rachel said, "I don't know what we would have done without your hospitality."

"Nonsense, dear, think nothing of it," Mrs. Brown replied humbly, "It's been so nice having this old house full of life again."

"How's Alice?" Sandra asked, nodding to Rachel.

"She's gone off to sleep," Rachel answered, "I hope she's feeling better soon."

"I don't think that'll ever happen until the man who attacked her is off the streets," Evan commented.

"I'm afraid there might not be much we can do about that," Matthew added sadly. Trevor, who had been seated on the windowsill, gave a quiet snort. Matthew's head snapped towards him and he watched as Trevor stood abruptly and made for the stairs, his face stormy. As Trevor began to pound up to the next floor, all eyes were on him. Matthew turned to face the others.

"Excuse me a moment," he said nervously, and quickly arose and followed Trevor.

Upon entering the room they shared, Matthew found his friend seated on his bed, his back to the door.

"What got into you back there?" Matthew asked, a hint of frustration in his voice.

Trevor sighed, and, keeping his back to Matthew, stood and crossed the room, hefting his geography text book from where it sat on the desk. He turned to Matthew and opened the book to the same page that Sam had shown him the day before.

"Read that," he said listlessly, pointing to the offending paragraph.

"Trevor, what does this have to do with Al—?"

"Just read it."

Matthew obeyed and read through the passage carefully.

"Oh, Trevor, this is about Sam, isn't it? Listen, this is just the way things are right now, it gets better, you've seen. There's nothing we can do right now."

"That's the problem!" Trevor shouted, snatching the book back from Matthew, "You always say that! You just let everything go, like it's not really a problem!"

"I can't make people change, Trevor! What do you want me to do, stand up and order everyone to change their ways?"

"You don't get it, Matthew! It's not just about Sam. It's what you said about Alice. You said there was nothing we could do, but there is! If you'd just stop accepting everything and start wanting to change it, we'd both be better off right now!"

"What are you talking about?"

"I'm talking about when we were living on the streets. You just accepted everything! You never tried to help me build a better life!"

"I just didn't want to steal things like you did! There are other ways to get what you need!"

"I didn't hear *you* suggest anything! And how about now, huh? You haven't helped me and Grace rebuild the time machine—"

"Shh!"

"You never even seemed to care when I was coughing up a lung at that stupid school, you never try to change anything!"

"There are some things that just can't be helped, Trevor! I know you're upset about Sam, and Alice, and I know you're mad at me, and I promise I'll try and help with the you-know-what, but there's nothing I can do sometimes! I'm not magic, okay?"

"It's not just you, okay, it's everything. It's living here and waiting to be sent back to a place where I still can't help myself. I thought when I took you in that together we might have a chance at a normal life. That we could make a little money and start to rebuild our lives, you know? But you were too scared and helpless! All the time you were whining about stealing and your dead mother and I didn't know what to do! You just followed me around like a lost dog!"

"Hey, it was hard for me too, you know! How would you feel if you knew your father was looking for you and that if he ever got you back you might not ever see the light of day again? And you knew that your friend was putting himself in danger to keep you safe and all you could seem to do to repay him was tell him he was wrong?" Matthew felt tears of frustration spring to his eyes. "And you knew that if your mother hadn't died you wouldn't be in the situation you were in?"

Trevor swore and tossed the geography textbook to the floor. "You think I don't know how it feels? Do you have any idea what I went through before I ended up on the streets? Do you have *any* idea?"

"I *asked* you, but you never said anything! Maybe I might find it easier to sympathize with you if you told me what on earth happened!" Matthew began to feel guilt rising up in his chest, constricting his throat. He hated to argue with Trevor, especially after all he had done for him, but it was nearly impossible to keep his temper in check with all he had been through, both recently and long ago.

"You wanna know what happened? Fine. I was eleven years old. My parents had been having some…issues, both of them. No one ever told me exactly what it was. All I knew was that I came home one day and they were both gone."

"Gone?" Matthew's tone had softened considerably.

Trevor nodded and wiped his eyes discreetly. "Yeah. Our living room was a crime scene. I guess they did some bad stuff, and the police came to arrest them. One of them, they never told me which, pulled a gun, and the police killed them both. They did it on purpose, so they wouldn't have to go to jail, I guess. I always thought it was my fault. I got so mad, I hated myself so much. My sister and me were going to live with my aunt, but she couldn't take us in so we got stuck in foster care for a couple years, until I started acting up and they kicked me out when I was thirteen. They put me in a group home, but they kept my little sister. Two years later, I ran away. I was done with being told what to do and people were starting to talk about me like I was some kind of case for them to solve. I was the kid whose parents were crazy."

"Trevor, I'm sorry, I had no idea…"

"Of course you didn't, I never told you! I didn't even want to think about it! I felt so guilty, and I never saw my sister after I got kicked out of that stupid foster home. I didn't want to leave her all alone there, but they wouldn't let me see her. So I figured I'd take you in, and maybe that—maybe that would make me feel like a better person. Like I hadn't abandoned her."

"You didn't abandon her, Trevor, I'm sure she's doing fine where she is…"

"This is what I'm talking about! You want me to just forget about her! To just accept the whole mess!"

"I didn't say that!"

"She hated it there, Matthew! She wouldn't let go of my hand when they came to get me to take me to the group home. She wanted to come with me. Once I finally got away from the home, I went back and looked for her at their house, but she wasn't living there anymore. She could be anywhere. I can't just let that go, and everything that's going on only reminds me of what I didn't do!"

"Trevor…"

"Just shut up, Matthew, okay? I don't want to talk about it. I'm getting out of here."

"But the time machine isn't ready yet!" Matthew had dropped his voice to a whisper.

Trevor rolled his eyes. "That's not what I meant. I'm going to stay with Sam a little while until all this with Alice and everything blows over. I can't take it anymore."

"Grace is gonna be mad…"

"I don't care. I need to get away. Come and find me when you're ready to stop accepting everything for what it is."

With that, Trevor stormed out of the room and down the stairs, carrying with him nothing but his pride.

CHAPTER EIGHTEEN

A Long Time

Clay arrived in Norton on a sunny Saturday afternoon, the train pulling into Norton's station at half past two. As quickly as he could manage, he disembarked and immersed himself in the great city of Norton. The scene that confronted him as he entered the city made him uncomfortable. For a man used to the quiet and calm of a small, country town, Norton was monstrous.

Disoriented and tired, Clay supposed that the best thing to do first would be to find a place to stay while he searched for his missing granddaughter. There were numerous hotels in Norton, all outside his budget. The boarding houses were better suited to him and his financial constraints, so he set to looking for one straight away, daring not waste any time.

Like most of his neighbours in Connolly Mills, Clay knew the names and reputations of the city's various districts, and as a result of this knowledge, he avoided the Southern Quays as best he could. His search began in St Edward's, the heart of Norton. Carrying his bag alongside him, Clay made his way from boarding house to boarding house, and having been turned away from three and been unable to pay for two by the time the town hall bell chimed five, he was beginning to despair. Ten minutes after five, he found himself climbing the steps of a large, white house with green trim. It was located on what must have been the busiest corner of Norton, very close to the invisible border between St. Edward's and the Southern Quays.

The door was opened in a few moments by a portly matron with a snub nose and small eyes. Her face was severe, but not without a certain motherly component, and her expression was kind.

"What can I do for you sir?" she asked, smiling up at Clay.

"I'm looking for a place to stay for a while," he replied, removing his hat in respect, "Is there any chance you have room to spare for me? It won't be for long, I hope."

Mrs. Brown's face turned sorrowful. "I'm sorry," she apologized, "It's so full here I'm afraid I'm all full. I've already got twelve boarders as it is, and that's really too many for anyone's comfort."

"Are you certain there's no room at all? As I said, it would only be for a short time."

Mrs. Brown shook her head. "I'm sorry. I really am. I wish you luck finding someplace else to stay."

Clay nodded. "Thank you ma'am, I'm sorry to have bothered you."

"It's no bother," Mrs. Brown replied cheerfully, then paused in thought. Clay had turned and was beginning to saunter down the steps when Mrs. Brown called out to him.

"Wait just a moment!"

Clay looked over his shoulder, his eyes questioning.

"You may consider Mrs. Thompson's rooming house," she suggested, "It's just up the road near Thompson's butchery, that's her son's business, you see. The rent is fair, and she's very kind."

"Much obliged, ma'am." Clay faced forward once more and finished making his way down the front steps.

"Good luck," Mrs. Brown said, waving, then turning around and stepping back inside.

The afternoon quickly faded away and darkness had nearly completed its descent upon the city. Mrs. Brown hoped that the kind stranger would soon find someplace to stay, for the streets of Norton were dangerous by night. The rowdy emerged to celebrate the coming of the shadows and the obscurity it cast upon them; illicit activities of all kinds took place at all hours. Somehow, Mrs. Brown's visitor didn't seem to her the type of man to engage in such things.

The house was relatively quiet when Mrs. Brown returned inside. Grace was reading in the parlour; Sandra sat near her, scribbling in a journal. Mr. Riddell and Mr. Fitzgerald were due to arrive back from work soon, as were Evan and John. Grace itched to get into the workforce in whatever small way she could, but had yet to find a suitable job.

Matthew and Rachel were also in the parlour, settled on the floor, engaged in a quiet game of chess. The atmosphere of the entire house seemed eerie and unfamiliar to Mrs. Brown. She wondered where Laura and Eddie had gone off to, for without the lively pair, Mrs. Brown's world seemed empty. She had never had any children of her own, and always regretted it.

"Who's winning?" she asked, taking a seat near Matthew and Rachel.

"Tough to say," Matthew smiled, moving forward a pawn, a look of concentration settled on his face.

"We're starting our second game," Rachel answered, then looked up at Mrs. Brown and grinned, "I won the last one."

"I see," Mrs. Brown sat up straighter and glanced around the room, "Where's Alice? It'll be supper soon."

"Oh, I meant to tell you," Rachel said distractedly, "She went to Alvin's for a while, but she promises to be back before curfew."

"I'm sure she will, dear. I'll let you two return to your game. Supper will be served at the usual time."

"Thank you, Mrs. Brown," the pair replied in unison, smiling up at her.

Mrs. Brown left and began to prepare the evening meal, and before long, Mr. Riddell and Mr. Fitzgerald had returned, Eddie and Laura had reappeared, and Evan and John arrived just in time to eat.

The meal passed uneventfully, the food good, but not excellent, and Mrs. Brown and her boarders retired to bed early, their minds and bodies tricked by the early setting of the sun. Alice had returned by this time, having been escorted through the city by Alvin. Matthew, before he was allowed to retreat from the day, was subjected to answering the same question over and over again. *Where,* everyone seemed to wonder, *was Trevor?* Matthew patiently explained to each one of his friends and family where he was, and why they shouldn't worry, and what exactly he was going to do to convince Trevor to return.

The next morning was as sunny and bright as the previous day, and the brilliant sunlight streamed through Matthew's window, sweetly awakening him. Sundays, Matthew observed, always seemed to have a cheery quality to them, even if the weather chanced to be unfavourable. His stomach gave an unpleasant lurch as he remembered that Trevor was gone, and that he was responsible for convincing him to return to the boarding house, for he was the only person to whom Trevor was close enough to be able to do so.

The morning whisked by, the minutes fading into hours, until Mrs. Brown and her boarders were ready for church. They walked through St. Edward's at a leisurely pace, chatting contentedly as they went. The sun warmed the chilly air, but did little to rid them of the cold feeling that had begun to settle in the very marrow of their bones. Winter was approaching, and they were painfully aware of it.

"Do you suppose Trevor will be at church this morning?" Rachel asked, peering at Matthew.

"I don't think so," he replied, "He always hated it, and I don't think Sam will force him."

"No?"

"No. You haven't known Trevor as long as I have. Believe me, he's stubborn."

"You can't have known him *so* long," Rachel pointed out, "You met him when you moved here, and that wasn't very long before I arrived. Nor Alice and Alvin, for that matter."

Matthew felt the colour drain from his face. It seemed he was always walking on eggshells with his friends. Even something as seemingly insignificant as when he had met Trevor could come back and destroy him; giving away the secret of the time travellers. With as much grief as Trevor caused him at times, Matthew still felt more relaxed with the way he spoke to him. Speaking with Rachel, Alvin, Alice, and others who truly belonged in 1901 was nerve wracking at the best of times. However, Matthew found that his relationships with them were rewarding, and he never wanted to be deprived of them, however dangerous they might be.

"Trust me," he stuttered, smiling nervously, "I know."

"If you say so," Rachel shrugged.

"I do," Matthew insisted playfully, "I fully and unequivocally do."

"Unequivocally? They're certainly improving your vocabulary in that school of yours!"

Maybe they are, maybe they are..." Matthew turned to Rachel, a curious look crossing his features. "Do you miss it?" he asked, "School, I mean. I know you were often bored, but it wasn't all bad, was it?"

Rachel laughed loudly, throwing back her head. "I must admit, I do miss it sometimes, but then I think of old Mr. Adams and I stop being so foolish!"

"But, what about... Well, what about a... a higher education? University, college...?"

"I don't know," Rachel replied thoughtfully, "When I was a girl, I wanted to be a doctor, like Dr. Cooke. He would visit our house when my mother was with child, and when my younger brother Leroy was ill. I admired him so much; I wanted to be just like him, at least until Leroy was taken by the consumption. Silly, isn't it?" Rachel smirked. "Me, wanting to be a doctor!"

"Well, why would it be silly?" Matthew wondered, his eyes wide.

"Oh, Matthew, don't patronize me!"

"I'm not, I promise!"

Halfway up the front steps of the church, Evan turned around and fixed Matthew with a suspicious stare.

"Matthew," he scolded sarcastically, "What are you doing now?"

"Nothing!" Matthew blushed furiously, "Nothing!"

Evan narrowed his eyes and mouthed, "I'm watching you," prompting a giggle from Rachel.

The time travellers, Mrs. Brown, Rachel, and Alice all took their seats once they entered the church, and waited for the service to start.

"I'm not too late, am I?" Alvin smiled, appearing at Alice's side.

"Not at all," she replied with a light hearted laugh, "You're just in time."

As the congregation got settled, Matthew became restless. He wondered if Trevor would come with Sam. He doubted it. He was almost *certain* he wouldn't. Nevertheless, he fidgeted and worried, imagining various conversations in his head.

"Something bothering you, Matthew?" Sandra tilted her head to one side.

"It's just this whole thing with Trevor," he whispered, "I'm worried he's going to get himself into trouble, or that I won't be able to convince him to come back, or... I dunno."

"Hey," Sandra replied, placing a reassuring hand on his shoulder, "It'll be okay. We've been through worse, haven't we?"

"Yes, but—"

"It's going to be fine, Matthew! Trevor may be reckless, but he's smart. Trust me, it'll be fine. Why don't I go with you this afternoon to Sam's, just to check on him?"

"No, no, we shouldn't do that. Thank you, though. I just think he'll probably be even more angry at everyone else than he is at me."

"I understand. Just don't worry for now, hmm? Not until we have something to worry about."

Matthew forced a smile. "Okay," he said, "I'll try."

"That's the spirit!"

The service commenced as usual, with no sign of Trevor. Matthew could detect apprehension in the faces of the others, particularly Grace. The time machine was close to being finished, but without Trevor to take it back to the future, it remained dangerously idle.

All enjoyment which may have been gleaned from the sweetly sung hymns and the pastor's profound words was denied to Matthew. Trevor was uppermost in his thoughts. The walk back to the boarding house was equally fraught with anxiety.

"I wish you'd say something, Matthew," Rachel insisted, "You've been so quiet!"

"I'm sorry," he began to apologize, "I'm just so *worried* it's making me sick..." Raising his head to look at Rachel, Matthew caught sight of a familiar figure out of the corner of his eye.

"Trevor!" he hollered, waving at his old friend, who was walking with Sam in the opposite direction, "Trevor!" Matthew dashed across the road and stopped in front of the pair, breathless.

"Trevor, I'm sorry. I really am. What you said... You were right. I'll try to change. I will. Really." Matthew dared to meet Trevor's eyes, only to discover them smiling. Trevor was laughing heartily, and even Sam was grinning.

"It's okay, Matthew," he said, placing a hand on Matthew's shoulder, "I was... I was wrong to be so mad."

Matthew's eyes widened and he had to clamp his mouth shut tight to keep his jaw from dropping in surprise.

"Are you—Are you serious?"

"Yeah," Trevor looked down and kicked at the dusty ground, "I talked to Sam about the whole thing, and I should have been more..." He sighed in frustration. "I should have been more *understanding.* Just don't rub it in, alright? 'Cause I did have a point!"

"I know you did, I know, believe me. Please, let me make it up to you somehow. Why don't we do something fun this afternoon? Just forget about everything. What do you say?"

"What *exactly* did you have in mind?" Trevor asked, scepticism laced in his voice.

"I dunno... Anything you want, I guess." Matthew leaned in and spoke in Trevor's ear so that Sam couldn't hear. "As long," he said, "As it's legal!"

Trevor snorted. "What does that leave?" he said sarcastically.

"Well... Plenty! Just ask Sam, or Rachel. Or anyone. Give me a chance, please!"

"Alright, alright!" Trevor smiled, "I'll meet you at the boarding house at two, so you'd better have something by then!"

"Got it! Thanks! See you later!" Matthew turned and darted back across the road.

"Have you solved your problem with Trevor?" Rachel asked upon his return. Matthew nodded, catching his breath.

"Tell me," he said, "What would you suggest to do for fun on a Sunday afternoon?"

CHAPTER NINETEEN

Play Time

Matthew gripped the handlebars of his borrowed bicycle, terror in his heart. Rachel's suggestion for a Sunday afternoon activity, though it seemed to please Trevor for reasons unfathomable, was one about which Matthew was apprehensive.

Rachel had wanted to ride bicycles through the city and stop outside of King's Park and have a picnic near the river. Matthew, however, was unsure that such a mundane activity would satisfy Trevor's reckless heart. Even so, to please Rachel, he proposed the notion to Trevor, who seemed quite content with the plan. Not wanting him to change his mind, Matthew never asked him why.

The decision left Matthew between a rock and a hard place. He didn't have a bicycle for himself, much less any for the fourteen other people (all the inhabitants of the boarding house plus Sam and Alvin) who were to join him for their day in the city. He took his dilemma to the boarding house, and Mrs. Brown immediately ventured into the cellar, calling for Mr. Riddell to follow her. Moments later, they emerged with a large tandem bicycle, built with two seats, one in front of the other. According to Mrs. Brown, a friend of her husband's had given it to them years ago. Mrs. Brown had never liked it, believing it to be unladylike to ride, but her husband had thought the thing ingenious, and so she had kept it, even after his death, to please him.

Matthew had thanked Mrs. Brown profusely, and he and Rachel set off to locate more "freedom machines." Rachel insisted on calling them this, saying that bicycles have been a tool for suffragists in their quest for women's rights.

By the end of their search, they succeeded in procuring three bicycles, in addition to Mrs. Brown's. Sam had one for travelling to and from work, and lent it to Trevor for the day, and Matthew and Rachel borrowed two more from some of Matthew and Trevor's classmates. By half past two that afternoon, everyone was at the boarding house, ready to leave. The privilege of riding the borrowed cycles went to Matthew, Rachel, Alvin, Alice, and Trevor. Grace assured Matthew that the adults, as well as Eddie and Laura, would get on fine without ten additional bicycles, which would take ages to collect. It was a blessing already that the ones they had were free of charge.

Finally packed and ready to leave, Matthew stood outside the boarding house, furiously clutching the handlebars of his bicycle.

"What are you waiting for, Matthew?" Rachel asked as she waited by his side, seated upon her own freedom machine.

"Oh, nothing..." Matthew began, biting his lip, "I'm just..."

Rachel glanced at him sceptically. "Have you ever ridden before, Matthew?"

Glad that he hadn't had to admit the fact himself, Matthew shook his head. "No one ever taught me," he divulged, "I never had a bicycle..."

"Alvin taught me," Rachel said, "On his bicycle, when we were younger. He taught Alice too. It's really not very difficult. Here, just stand like this. That's it! And put one foot on the pedal, like so." Rachel showed him on her own bike. "And you push off... this way." She launched herself forward and circled round, stopping again by Matthew's side. "Now you try!"

Mimicking her movements, Matthew went cautiously forward, his heartbeat pounding in his ears. He wobbled slightly, and had to stop himself from falling numerous times, but after a few tries, he felt comfortable enough to continue forward.

"There, you've got it!" Rachel called out, following him down the road, "Just don't be nervous, you'll be fine! Look straight ahead, now."

Though the advice was sound, Matthew found it entirely impossible to follow. He tried hard to relax, but the fear of falling held a tight grip on his heart. He contented himself with trailing behind Rachel, the pair of them chatting as they rode. The time travellers, Mrs. Brown, and Sam were walking some distance behind the cyclists, talking merrily. Laura rode on her father's shoulders, and Eddie walked between Evan and Grace, who each had a hold on one of his hands and would swing him in the air every few steps, much to the boy's delight. Mr. Riddell and Mrs. Brown both carried baskets filled with sandwiches, biscuits, and other such treats to be consumed upon their arrival at the desired destination just outside of King's Park. Sandra and John strolled with Sam, discussing the events of the day, and, more importantly, how Trevor was getting along without them.

Sam assured them that Trevor was fine, and that, as far as he knew, the boy wasn't getting into any trouble. The explanation he had given Sam for leaving the boarding house was that he and Matthew had had an argument, and he needed to spend some time away to clear his head. Needless to say, Sandra and John were relieved to hear that nothing untoward was happening with regards to the runaway.

At that moment, the aforementioned runaway was quite enjoying himself. He whooped with delight as he sped down a dip in the road, quickly leaving St. Edward's behind in favour of the opulent King's Park. Trevor had never been fond of King's Park, if only for what it symbolized: the power and influence that the wealthy held over the poor. However, he loved it for its emptier streets, where he could swerve and turn and speed without worry of running into anything.

He had left Alvin and Alice behind a few moments ago, unable to resist the call of the open road. The pair went at a leisurely pace, perched upon Mrs. Brown's tandem bike. Alice sat in the front and steered, for having two hands upon the handlebars made the pair feel safer than Alvin's one. They talked and they laughed, reminiscing about their childhood when Alice would sit on the handlebars of Alvin's bicycle and they would ride through the streets of Connolly Mills, not caring who saw them.

Alice's mother had once scolded her for such unladylike behaviour after hearing about her exploits from Rachel's decorous mother Elizabeth, so Alvin had taken her instead into the country, where they enjoyed the hills and wildflowers, and remained unseen by the town's more demure residents.

Mrs. Brown pursed her lips at the quickly vanishing cyclists, her own demure spirit showing through in her expression. Mr. Riddell, who walked alongside her, was quick to notice the change in her countenance.

"Is there something wrong?" Mr. Riddell asked, his voice low and sweet. Mrs. Brown shook her head.

"No, no," she said, "Nothing at all. It's only…"

Mr. Riddell waited patiently, knowing that speaking would only serve to make Mrs. Brown retire further into her own thoughts. True to his theory, his silence paid off, as Mrs. Brown began to explain herself.

"It's just the speed of the world these days. When I was young, I would have been scolded for riding such a contraption; flying about on my own, skirts flying everywhere. It was simply indecorous, you understand."

"Quite, quite," Mr. Riddell muttered, wishing to acknowledge her words without interrupting.

"The world has changed," Mrs. Brown said with a bitter little laugh, "And there's nothing anyone can do about it. Before you know it, women will have the vote. And then what, hmm? I suppose next we'll all be driving around in those blasted motorcars I've seen around, eh?"

Mr. Riddell's brow furrowed. He had barely heard Mrs. Brown's last sentence but for his surprise at her penultimate phrase.

"You don't believe women to be deserving of the vote?" he asked, his curiosity genuine.

Mrs. Brown sighed. "It's more complicated than that, I suppose," she admitted, "When Elias was alive, we made all political decisions together, and he voted for us. He was the one who did things; who accomplished the things we worked on together. He was the leader, and I the follower. I thought that it was the way any respectable couple should be. However, seeing the way that you and your family behave…" She paused, searching for the right words. "It has changed me, I think, perhaps for the better. I'm evolving right along with the world. Of course, there are some things in which I shall remain forever steadfast."

"And so you should," Mr. Riddell advised, "Sometimes there are changes that are simply unacceptable."

"That there are," Mrs. Brown agreed, "That there are."

Mr. Riddell could only nod. He wanted to tell Mrs. Brown the reason that he and the other time travellers had come to the past, and to assure her that he too found the world to be moving much too quickly, but he couldn't. He could do nothing but stand and nod dumbly, for he couldn't risk Mrs. Brown finding out their secret.

Far ahead of them, Trevor had stopped cycling at the base of a short hill. He had found the perfect picnic spot in a vast open field on the banks of the river. The grass was long and yellow, and little golden wildflowers sprouted freely in all directions. Leaning Sam's bicycle up against a gnarled oak tree, Trevor stood still and closed his eyes, greedily taking in as much fresh air as his lungs could hold. The open space was freeing, and Trevor felt so much more alive away from the stifling hustle and bustle of the city. Looking out across the river, the sky seemed to stretch on forever. Fluffy white clouds scudded across the great blue expanse, geese soaring beneath them in their clever v-formations, honking and squawking all the while. Trevor stared over the river at all the open space, daring not turn around to face the crowded city's filthy skyline. If he tried hard enough, he could imagine that he was back in the future, and that behind him, skyscrapers reached up into the clouds and planes flew across the sky, leaving long, misty trails in their wake.

Alvin and Alice soon appeared, speeding down the hill to meet him, shouting with delight. The pair came to a juddering halt by Trevor's side, laughing loudly.

"I'd forgotten how much fun that was!" Alice commented, smiling back at Alvin.

"So had I," Alvin replied, red faced and struggling to catch his breath.

"How far away do you think the others are?" Trevor broke in, still not looking at the city. Alvin dismounted the bicycle and marched up to the top of the hill, raising his hand to his brow and peering back the way they had come, scouring the landscape for any sign of their friends.

"I don't see anyone…" he began, calling down to Trevor and Alice, "They're probably still back in—Oh, wait! Here come Rachel and Matthew! The others can't be far behind." Trevor nodded absently as Alvin came shuffling back down the hill.

Rachel and Matthew were indeed on their way over, but one last obstacle remained in their way.

"Ready?" Rachel asked, a gleeful smile adorning her features.

Matthew gulped and blinked furiously. "Uh huh," he replied, "Ready as I'll ever be…"

"Then here we go!" Rachel pushed off and raced down the steep little hill, Alvin, Alice, and Trevor cheering from the bottom. Matthew, not wishing to appear a coward in front of his friends, particularly Trevor, who would surely never let him forget it, followed suit. Cautiously, he lifted his foot from the ground and let the bike propel him forward. The terrain was difficult to manoeuvre, especially for a first time cyclist, as it was strewn with rocks, logs, and other forms of debris. Matthew fought to keep his balance, but his efforts were in vain. With a cry, he toppled sideways into the grass, losing his grip on the bicycle and rolling off down the hill before finally stopping at the bottom, where he found himself lying face up among the wildflowers.

Matthew sat up in a daze and placed a hand to his head while he waited for the world to stop spinning.

"Matthew!" Rachel cried with a laugh, kneeling in the grass beside him, "Are you alright? Why'd you let go?"

Slowly, Rachel's grinning face came into focus and Matthew smiled weakly. "I dunno," he admitted sarcastically, "I thought it might be fun." With those words, he let himself fall back into the soft grass and let out a tremendous laugh. Rachel lay down beside him, and soon all five youth were lying on their backs in the sprawling meadow, making up a sort of five pointed star. The sun shone down on their upturned faces and caused them all to squint.

"You know," Rachel began, "This reminds me of our day at the fair all that time ago. Remember?" She immediately regretted her words. Matthew grinned, remembering the picture they had taken together by Darcy Lake. He hadn't known that it was considered foolish to smile in a photograph, and had mistakenly told everyone to "say cheese", an expression which had both baffled and amused his friends. However, the amusement of the day had been short lived, as the news of Alice's condition had come to light, and the afternoon had ended shrouded in misery and guilt.

Alvin's eye throbbed at the memory of his confrontation with Alice's attacker. It was healing well, but it was still dark and painful, and the mention of the day at the Darcy Lake fair had reminded him of it. He remembered the day so perfectly. The weather was beautiful, much like it was now, and it formed a part of the picture that had stayed in his mind ever since. He recollected the event in third person, as though he was watching his own actions from afar. He saw himself tremble and cry out as Rachel told him and Matthew that Alice was with child. He could hear his own cracking voice as he demanded to know why Alice had done such a foolish and hurtful thing. He could see his own reactions as Alice begged him to believe that it was not her fault. He shut his eyes and shook his head, dispelling the memory from his thoughts. He still felt guilty about the way he had treated Alice in those few moments. He took her hand in the grass and squeezed it warmly.

The youth all fell silent at the memories Rachel had inadvertently stirred up, and Alice bit her lip. She hated when she was reminded of those awful months. The memories would never truly go away, but as hard as she tried to ignore them and move on, things always seemed to get in the way. She shuddered as she recalled Sidney Beagle standing below her window and calling to her at Aunt Jessica's house.

Trevor frowned. He hadn't the faintest idea what Rachel was talking about, but, sensing the tension that had descended upon his friends, made no comment.

"What are you all doing down there?" came Laura's little voice as she marched over to where Matthew was lying and put her hands on her hips.

"Oh, not much," Matthew said, grateful for the distraction, "Just lying around..." With one swift movement, he sat up and swept Laura off her feet, placing her haphazardly on his shoulders. Laura squealed with laughter and held on tight, clamping her little hands over Matthew's eyes.

"Hey!" Matthew cried out in mock horror, "I can't see!" Arms outstretched, he lumbered in circles, much to Laura's amusement.

"Go straight," she giggled, and Matthew obeyed her command, walking slap bang into Mr. Fitzgerald, who turned and smiled upon his children.

"What on earth are you up to?' he asked, "Playing Blind Man's Bluff?"

"What?" Matthew heard Laura reply from his shoulders.

"Blind Man's Bluff," Mr. Fitzgerald repeated, "It's a game, like tag. Someone is blindfolded and has to try and catch the other players without looking."

"We used to play it when we were small," came Rachel's voice from behind Matthew, making him jump. He hadn't heard her approaching, even in the tall, rustling grass.

"That we did," Alvin chimed in from Matthew's right, "And Rachel was a dab hand at it! She nearly always won."

Though Matthew couldn't see her, he could tell that Rachel was smiling.

"I haven't played that game in years," Alice said, her voice coming from somewhere just beyond Alvin, "We used to have so much fun…"

"Can we play it?" Laura asked sweetly, leaning her chin on Matthew's head.

Though the game was childish, Rachel, Alvin, and Alice held no objections. Even Trevor seemed to like the idea. After all that had befallen the youth lately, it would feel good to return to childhood, even if only for a time.

"I daresay we can," Rachel grinned, delicately lifting Laura from Matthew's shoulders, giving him back his sight. The world swam slightly before him, and he had to blink furiously to dispel the blur that had settled in his vision.

"Here," Mr. Fitzgerald said, handing Matthew his tie, "Have a blindfold."

"Thanks," Matthew replied, taking the broad navy tie from him, and then turning to his friends. "Who'll go first?"

"Matthew!" Laura announced, "I want you to go first!" She hopped up and tagged him on the arm, grinning from ear to ear.

"Oh you do, do you?" Matthew said with mock severity, "Well I suppose if Miss High and Mighty Laura Fitzgerald says it, it must be so, hmm?"

Laura nodded, trying to keep the glee out of her face.

"Alright," Matthew proclaimed, "So it shall be!" He closed his eyes, bent on one knee and held out Mr. Fitzgerald's tie. "Blind me, your highness!"

Threatening to collapse into a fit of laughter at any moment, Laura took the tie and wound it around Matthew's head, fumbling to make the knot at the back tight enough so that it didn't slip down over his nose. Rachel knelt and helped to tighten the knot and then the pair of them stood up.

"What should I count to?" Matthew asked, straightening his makeshift blindfold, "Ten?"

"Twenty!" Laura ordered, "And don't peek!"

"As you wish!" Matthew replied, saluting in her general direction and beginning to count out loud.

The others scattered in various directions, Laura running to invite Eddie to play. Alvin and Alice scampered over the hill and sat down at the top, peering down at Matthew as he finished counting and stood shakily, arms outstretched. Rachel stood stock still, the tall grass rustling around her.

Trevor, Eddie, and Laura had ducked behind the big oak tree, peeking out from their hiding place while desperately trying to stifle their laughter.

Matthew, quite literally blind to what was unfolding around him, stumbled onward, listening for any sign of his prey. Having never played the game before, he wasn't entirely sure what to expect. Would his friends hide the entire time and make themselves difficult to locate by remaining silent? Or would they come out and taunt him, make him chase them? So far, the reality appeared to be the former.

Suddenly, a long, low whistle could be heard over the voices of the adults, who were setting up the picnic by the river. Matthew turned towards the sound abruptly and continued forwards, struggling to find his footing as he ascended the steep hill. The whistling continued, the monotonous note becoming a fully fledged tune.

Alice, listening to Alvin's melody, fought a losing battle against her own mirth, laughing out loud. She and Alvin watched as Matthew sauntered towards them, jumping to their feet and scrambling past him, down the hill and towards the river.

The game continued for a time, the title of "it" being passed on through nearly everyone playing, until the weariness of boredom began to set in. The players took a break for lunch, sitting by the river as they ate the sandwiches that had been packed for them. Alvin in particular ate his sandwich happily, for it was one of the few foods he could eat without needing someone to cut it for him. He never invited anyone for supper anymore, embarrassed by the fact that his grandfather had to dismember all his meals for him as though he were a small child. Alice had come over the other day, but they had not had a meal together; Alvin was far too proud.

The afternoon was slowly waning away, and the air was becoming ever cooler. Laura sat by the river next to Trevor as the others packed up the picnic and prepared to leave for home. She shivered slightly, wrapping her arms around her knees. Trevor's brow furrowed.

"Are you cold?" he asked, peering down at her as he reclined nonchalantly, listening to the rush of the river and the rustle of the grass.

Laura nodded. "A little," she said, and then looked up at him, "Are you?"

"No," Trevor replied, "No, not really." He paused, thoughtful, then straightened up and removed his jacket, putting it around her little shoulders. "Here," he said, "That better?"

Laura smiled. "Thanks," she said, pulling the light coat tighter around her. Trevor grinned back, only to see Laura's head turned away from him, looking back up over the hill. He followed her gaze and found himself staring at the faint figure of a man, standing almost totally still, staring down at their gathering.

"Who's that?" Trevor asked.

"I don't know," Laura answered, her nose wrinkled and eyes squinted, "But it looks like…" She turned pale and her eyes widened. Her voice dropped to a whisper. "It looks like Mr. Kennedy."

Trevor felt his heart speed up. "I'm sure it's not," he said, "You're just imagining things. What does he look like, anyway?"

"Like that!" Laura hissed, pointing up the hill. Trevor pulled back her hand.

"I'm sure that's not him," he repeated, "He's far away from here, isn't he?"

Laura pursed her lips. "I guess so…"

"Well I *know* so," Trevor insisted, "So don't worry about it."

CHAPTER TWENTY

Supper Time

Clay stood over the grassy, rocky hill, near the opulent district of King's Park, looking down upon a large gathering that was spread out by the river. He didn't move. He *couldn't* move. He had finally found her. He had gone to the address from Alvin's letter earlier that day, but had found it empty. Now, he had found Rachel.

Even from so far away that she was only a figure in the distance, he knew that the person at whom he was looking was indeed his granddaughter. She held herself the same way her mother had, standing tall and confident. He recognized too the cut of her dress, the familiar style of her hair. There was no doubt in his mind that it was Rachel, and he knew who she was with. Matthew Fitzgerald, standing only slightly taller than his granddaughter, was positioned next to her. And what was this? Was that his hand on her arm that Clay detected? A deep anger rose in his chest. He had thought that Rachel had fled to Norton to escape his wrath. That she knew Alvin, Alice, and of course, Matthew, were there, and they would help her. Now, he was unsure. He kept watching them from above. Why wouldn't Matthew let go of her arm?

"Let her go, you blasted boy!" he growled under his breath, "Let her go!"

The wheels in his mind began to turn, a nervous train of thought taking off at full speed. She had come to Norton because she was afraid of her own grandfather, only to walk into an ever-more dangerous trap. They had pulled her in, beguiled her into their way of thinking. Only now, Clay perceived, she couldn't leave. She wanted to, but couldn't. She was trapped. Kidnapped. Held against her will. That was why the boy wouldn't let go of her. He was afraid that she might run away and return home to the safety of her own family. That must be it. It *must* be. He had to rescue her. He was her only hope. She needed her grandfather more than ever now. Why, oh, why had he not been rid of Elizabeth's murderers sooner? Why had he not done it when he had the chance? Now they had Rachel in their clutches. Clay paused. He knew he had to save Rachel and bring her home, but he would have to be smarter about it this time. No more spontaneous attacks. He would have to be more calculated, more cunning. This time, he knew, *this time,* he wouldn't fail. He had a plan.

▪▪▪

Mrs. Brown, on the way back into the city after their excursion, invited all present to return to the boarding house and have Sunday dinner.

"There'll be plenty of food," she said, "And I'd be happy to have you. All of you."

"That's very gracious of you, Mrs. Brown," Sam accepted her invitation with a wide smile, "Thank you very much."

"Alvin, dear, you'll come too, won't you?" Mrs. Brown smiled, turning to him.

"I dunno," Alvin replied, becoming increasingly conscious of his missing arm, "My grandfather... he'll be expecting me..."

"He can join us," Mrs. Brown said generously, "He's quite welcome."

"It's a very generous offer, Mrs. Brown," Alvin said nervously, stopping at the steps of the boarding house, "But I really couldn't ask you to—"

"Really, I insist. I'll call Mrs. Tenny, she's his neighbour, and she'll run over and put him on the telephone." With that, Mrs. Brown climbed the steps of the boarding house and disappeared inside. Alvin bit his lip, but said nothing as the others headed into the boarding house.

"Aren't you coming?" Alice asked. She was standing at the top of the stairs, looking down at him. Alvin nodded solemnly, resigning himself to the fact that he was going to have to face up to his inabilities. Slowly, he followed Alice inside.

The door swung quietly shut as Clay looked on, his brow furrowed. He had been skulking in the shadows for some time, following the group all the way back to here: the very boarding house in which he had nearly stayed. A few of them, Rachel included, had been riding bicycles. Only now did he understand how full the boarding house truly was. With the family he hunted stayed numerous other people. Alice Cosgrove, that Sam fellow from Connolly Mills, a boy he didn't recognize, Alvin Quinn... Clay blinked. Alvin Quinn, he noticed, was missing an arm. His left sleeve hung by his side, empty. Clay smiled smugly. The boy deserved his fate.

So this was it. This was where they were keeping Rachel hostage. He'd save her alright. It was only a matter of time.

■■

Mrs. Brown poked her head into the parlour, where her guests and boarders were engaged in polite conversation. "Supper's ready," she said, smiling, "Wash up and have a seat."

Alvin's grandfather, Jacob Quinn, had arrived shortly before dinner, a wide smile on his face. He was glad to have been invited out, for it wasn't a luxury in which he often partook. He had been cooking for himself every day since his wife had passed away some years earlier.

Standing to obey Mrs. Brown's orders, everyone in the parlour filed out to wash their hands and sit down. The last to stand, Alvin shuffled after them reluctantly, casting a pleading glance towards his grandfather, which went unnoticed.

"Hey, Matthew!" Trevor called, rushing past Alvin, who was on his way out through the parlour door, "Matthew?"

"Yeah?" Matthew turned around to face Trevor as the others walked past.

"Hey, I just... I just wanted to thank you," he said, "For today. It was nice to get out. Away from the city."

Matthew smiled. "It was Rachel's idea," he admitted, "And to be honest, I wasn't really sure you'd like it. It seemed too…"

"Legal?"

Matthew nodded. "Sorry," he said.

"Don't be," Trevor smiled, "It was a good day. It reminded me of my old life, you know. It was almost like I was back…" He dropped his voice. "You know."

"I know. And I'm glad you enjoyed yourself."

"Thanks. Now let's go eat, I'm starving."

At last, everyone was seated, steaming plates at each place. Mrs. Brown presided at the head of the table, overseeing the equal distribution of each dish. On the other end, Mr. Jacob Quinn sat, all smiles. Alvin was on his right, and Alice was next to him. Beyond them were Rachel, Trevor, Matthew, Eddie, and Laura. The rest of the adults were seated along the other side of the table. Mrs. Brown said grace, and the company tucked in, compliments following the first few bites. Alvin, however, could only stare nervously at his plate.

"Mrs. Brown, this is wonderful," Mr. Quinn said, projecting his voice to the opposite end of the table, "Thank you so much for—Oh…" He trailed off, noticing how his grandson's plate remained untouched. He pushed his plate aside and pulled Alvin's toward him. "Sorry, Alvin," he said jovially, "I almost forgot. It'll just be a moment, now."

He began to cut Alvin's food, and Alvin hung his head, his face reddening as he felt all eyes on him. Matthew winced. He hadn't realized the true limitations that Alvin faced because of his missing limb. Having to have someone cut his food for him must have really hurt his pride, for Alvin was indeed a proud young man. He didn't fear showing grief in front of others, but to be treated like a child in front of all his friends, in front of Alice… Matthew understood his pain. He thought he heard a sniffle rise from Alvin's end of the table.

Mr. Quinn continued to saw away at Alvin's food until he had cut half of his meat into bite size pieces.

"There you go," he smiled, "I'll finish the other half when you're done."

"Thank you," Alvin said weakly as his grandfather pushed back his plate. Swallowing his pride, Alvin took up his fork and began to eat quietly. Soon, conversation resumed, and Alvin's plight was pushed into the background. It remained however, in the back of Grace's mind, as she attempted to engineer a solution to his problem.

It wasn't long before Alvin finished what he could of his supper, but his pride stood in the way of asking his grandfather for further help. He twisted a loose thread from his trousers around his fingers under the table. Alice, noticing his idle silence, reached out and stayed his hand. Startled, Alvin glanced up at her, and then, ashamed, back down at his lap. Without saying a word, Alice let go of his hand and reached over him, picking up his fork and knife. She began, slowly, carefully, and ever-so-discreetly, to cut the rest of his meat. Alvin looked on helplessly, tears welling up in his eyes, which he blinked angrily away. If he married Alice, she'd be cutting his food for him the rest of his life. Was that the kind of life she deserved?

"Alice," he whispered, his voice thick, "Alice, it's... it's okay. I'm not hungry anymore." In all honesty, Alvin didn't feel like he'd ever be hungry again.

"It's alright," Alice whispered, her voice gentle, "I promise."

Alvin, unable to take it any longer, raised his head. "May I be excused?" he asked, looking in Mrs. Brown's direction. His hostess nodded, her face betraying her concern. Rising, Alvin pushed back his chair and left the room.

Alice bit her lip. She wanted to follow, but knew it would never be allowed so soon after Alvin had gotten up. She remained silent, waiting for him to return or for supper to run its course, whichever came first. Alvin's grandfather seemed oblivious to his grandson's embarrassment, and continued to laugh, joke, and make merry until the meal was done.

Matthew, a few minutes after Alvin had left, looked around the table nervously. He was worried for his friend. He knew it would be inappropriate for Alice to have followed him, but he could see the anguish in her face. Rachel too could sense this, for she placed a hand on Matthew's arm and nodded towards the door through which Alvin had disappeared. Message received, Matthew asked to leave the table and made his way out of the room, placing a reassuring hand on Alice's shoulder as he passed.

He emerged from the dining room and glanced around. The door to the parlour stood open, but the room itself was empty and still, and he knew that Alvin wouldn't dare venture upstairs. It simply wasn't proper. The only other place besides Mrs. Brown's personal rooms was outside, so Matthew stepped across the hall and gently pulled open the heavy wooden door. Sure enough, there was Alvin, sitting on the top step, head in his hand. His elbow leaned against his knee, giving him a troubled and weary look. Silently, Matthew pulled the door shut behind him as he stepped out onto the landing. The wooden planks gave a slight creak beneath his weight, but if Alvin heard this, he did not react.

"You alright?" Matthew asked, taking a seat beside him. Alvin looked up, his bruised eye giving him a dark and ominous mien in the light of the setting sun.

"Yeah. I'm just… thinking…" Alvin let his gaze fall again and examined a crack in the length of the stair below him.

"Thinking?"

"Yeah. Thinking."

"May I ask what about?"

Alvin squirmed, then sat up straighter. "Everything," he said, "Everything."

Matthew, tiring of his friend's angst, tried in vain to stifle a smile. "Can you be a little more specific?"

"My entire life!" Alvin cried, "Nothing is the same anymore. I have to rethink the rest of my life. I thought I'd done all my thinking, but tonight's made me start again…"

"Alvin, listen." Matthew bent to look at his face. "I know it's been difficult. I know that you don't think you can achieve all the things you wanted to. But that doesn't mean you can give up on everything else."

Alvin looked up, his brow furrowed. "Who says I'm giving up?"

"No one," Matthew assured him, "I just... Alice is worried about you."

"I know," Alvin sighed, "I know she is. And I'm worried about her. I can't give her any kind of future. Not now..."

"Hey, hey, hold on a minute! You've got plenty of time to think about the future. Right now, she needs you to be there for her. She needs to stop worrying about you. You can give her that, can't you?"

"Yeah." Alvin took a deep breath. "I'm... I'm sorry, Matthew. It's just the food, and the attention, and the inability to do things for myself..."

"I understand."

"I feel so... trapped! It's like I can't escape it. And it's never coming back." He nodded towards his missing arm. "I wish this feeling would go away."

"It will, in time. I know it will. It's just all that's been happening recently, that's all. You haven't had time to get used to it yet. Between getting shot, then losing your arm, Sidney Beagle coming back, your fight with him, Alice having to leave her Aunt's place... It's been a lot. Give yourself some time."

"I know. Thank you. You've been through quite a bit yourself, you know."

Matthew smirked. Alvin was clearly tired of talking about himself, and was trying to divert the attention to Matthew. Matthew, happy his friend was at least willing to talk, followed the direction of the suggested conversation.

"We all have," he admitted, "Every one of us." A picture of Rachel upon her arrival in Norton flashed into his mind, and he cringed.

A moment of silence ensued, before Alvin broke it, standing up awkwardly, nearly falling as he tried to use his missing left arm to push himself up. "Let's go inside," he suggested, "I can't stand the thought of Alice worrying over nothing."

Matthew smiled as he stood and followed Alvin inside. Hopefully, today would mark an end to their constant suffering.

■■

In the shadows of the dying day, Clay was hidden from view. He had been lurking in the darkness outside of Mrs. Brown's boarding house for hours. The light was fading in the west, but he would not—no, could not—leave when he knew that his Rachel was trapped inside. Just as he was about to finally force himself to abandon his post, the door of the boarding house slid open, and out stepped Alvin Quinn, his empty sleeve swinging wildly at his side. Clay watched him sit sluggishly down on the top step and place his head in his hand. He looked... anguished. Clay smiled gleefully at the thought. Watching the boy as a hawk watches its prey, he waited patiently for something, anything, to happen. Right on cue, some time later, Matthew Fitzgerald emerged from the building and sat down next to Alvin. Clay listened intently as the pair began to converse, but from where he stood, concealed from view, he could only make out certain words.

"...doesn't mean you have to give up on everything..." Clay heard Matthew exclaim as Alvin sat, head in hand. Clay edged forward, straining to hear more of what was being said.

"Who says I'm giving up?" he heard Alvin reply angrily, looking up. Silence followed, as Clay was unable to make out what Matthew was saying. After a moment, his ears caught another of Alvin's sorrowful phrases.

"I'm worried about her..." More silence. Clay watched Matthew sit up straighter.

"Hey, hey, hold on a minute!" Matthew's voice floated down, then became hushed once more. Clay thought he could make out the words "stop worrying" as Matthew continued to speak. As Clay continued to strain to hear, more phrases became clear, but Clay's addled mind could only truly make sense of a few words.

"Trapped... escape... fight with... him? No... her," Clay muttered under his breath, repeating words as he heard them, "Worrying over nothing..." Suddenly, it all became clear. Clay's blood began to boil. There was no longer any trace of doubt in his mind. He had the whole story worked out in his head.

Rachel had gone to Norton not to escape her grandfather, no, but to please him! She went to confront the people who killed her mother, and was using Alvin to track them down. Then, they had found her before she had found them, and they had kidnapped her in order to keep her from talking. Yes, that was it! Alvin had been brainwashed, and was having doubts about what they were doing to poor Rachel. The words Clay had heard: trapped, escape, fight with her; all referred unquestionably to Rachel. She was trying to escape their evil clutches and return home.

Evidently, Alvin's apparent anguish had been his conscience, but that loathsome Matthew boy had come out and talked him right back into their trap. He convinced Alvin that he was worried about nothing. He used Alvin's pride against him, accusing him of giving up! This was it. This was, beyond any doubt in Clay's mind, what was happening. They were holding his Rachel hostage to keep her quiet about her mother's murder. And he was going to get her back, at the same time ensuring the downfall of the family he hated so much. Indeed, they would all be gone before the first snowfall, if Clay Kennedy had anything to do with it, and Alvin with them. It was time to put his plan into action.

■■

A low, warm light enveloped the parlour. It emanated from a tall, slim gas lamp near the fireplace, casting its glow over Sandra, who was seated in a chair, listening to the crackle of the firewood which had long ago ceased to emit any measurable amount of light or warmth. She stared lazily at the mantelpiece, her eyes wandering between the decorations. A yawn escaped her, and she shivered slightly.

"I didn't know you were still up."

Sandra turned abruptly to find John standing at the base of the stairs in his nightclothes, a puzzled look on his face.

"Sorry," Sandra replied, "Did I wake you?"

"No, no, not at all. I just came down for a glass of water."

"Oh. You're not feeling sick, are you?"

"No. Just thirsty, is all. What are you still doing up?"

Sandra sighed. "I was just writing in my journal. I didn't want to keep Grace up with the light, so I came down here, and, well, I suppose I was just too lazy to go back upstairs."

John chuckled and took a seat across from her. "I didn't see Trevor tonight," he said, "After dinner, I mean."

Sandra nodded. "He went home with Sam. He's been having a rough time of it. The sooner he can go back home, the happier he'll be."

"How long do you think it'll be until we really can send him home?"

"I don't know," Sandra said, shrugging and sitting back in her chair, "But it shouldn't be long now, with the way Grace has been talking."

"No?"

Sandra smiled, the lamplight glinting in her eyes. "It should be ready any day now, she's been saying. I wasn't sure I'd ever say this, but I think I'll miss Trevor when he's gone."

John smirked. "I thought you might," he said, "And I guess I will too. It'll get a little boring around here without him, I think."

"Oh, don't say it like that! Boring is what we want! Boring is safe. Boring is nothing awful happening. No one getting hurt, or losing an arm, or getting in fights... Boring is a good thing."

"I most wholeheartedly agree." John paused. "Do you think Trevor will tell anyone about us when he gets back?"

"What, about our time machine?" Sandra whispered, her voice barely audible as she leaned forwards. John nodded. Leaning back, Sandra wrinkled her nose.

"You know," she said, "It's odd, but I don't think he'd say anything. I think he understands the danger now, and in a strange way, I trust him. He's very intelligent, more so than we give him credit for. He's survived on his own for so long, he's become almost wise, in a sense."

Slowly, John nodded. "I know what you mean. I hate to think of sending him back to be all alone again though. I mean, look at all the good we've done Matthew. He's a new person. Couldn't Trevor be the same?"

"I'd like to think so," Sandra sighed, "But I think this time we have to trust him. He's not like Matthew, he never was."

"What do you mean?"

"Matthew has a strong sense of his own morals and values. He knew very well right from wrong, even before he came to us. Trevor is more ruthless. He knows what he wants and he'll stop at nothing to get it. Matthew has boundaries. Trevor doesn't."

John attempted, in vain, to stifle a laugh.

"What?" Sandra asked, a little louder than she meant to, "What on earth is so funny about a boy with no morals?"

"Oh, it's not that," John explained, "It's just that I expected you say something about his eyes. Trevor's, I mean. The way you used to talk about Matthew. You used to talk about how sad and lonely his eyes were. Do you remember?"

"Of course, though I'm surprised you do!"

"Well," John pressed, "What of Trevor's eyes?"

Sandra laughed and sat back in her chair, a twinkle in her own eyes. "They're... dark?" She paused, straining to remember Trevor's chiselled and pointed features. "His whole face is sort of gaunt. The poor boy has gone through much more than he's letting on, I know it. His utter disregard for authority at times is nothing short of a bad upbringing. You can see that in his eyes too. There's this sort of spark of rebellion in them, but behind all that is a troubled, lost soul."

"You're so eloquent."

"Thank you." Sandra yawned deeply. "I think it's about time to hit the hay though, wouldn't you say?"

"I'd say it's past that by now."

"Goodnight, John," Sandra laughed, rising from her seat and heading towards the stairs.

"Goodnight, Sandra," John called after her as she disappeared from view into the dark recesses of the narrow staircase. Seizing the gas lamp, John followed her up, bid her goodnight once more, and blew out the tiny, sputtering flame, plunging the hall into warm, comforting darkness.

CHAPTER TWENTY-ONE

Time Wasted

"**I**'d like to report a kidnapping."

Clay's gruff voice was barely audible over the hustle and bustle of the thronging police station. It was late afternoon, and there was much going on in the St. Edward's stationhouse. Clay stood before a tall desk, addressing a policeman in full uniform on the other side, who was smoking a thick cigar nonchalantly. The officer looked him up and down, his misgivings showing in his eyes. To him, the angry-faced man before him looked more like the kidnapper than the concerned citizen. Nevertheless, the man was reporting someone missing—kidnapped no less— and as an officer of the law, it was his duty to collect all the details before making a judgement.

"Who's been kidnapped?" he asked of Clay, leaning forward, as he found it difficult to hear over the din of the stationhouse.

"My grand—"

Abruptly, Clay was cut off by a noisy commotion near the front doors. Turning to look, he found himself staring at a large group of constables, all uniformed and helmeted, who were struggling to arrest a young lady. Normally, Clay presumed, this would not have been a difficult task for half a dozen able-bodied policemen, but this woman was putting up a fight. She had a wild look in her eyes, and her hair hung loose about her shoulders as she beat back the men with clenched fists.

"Who is she?" Clay wondered aloud.

"Anna Hastings," the policeman replied, "She's been in and out for weeks. Her father died some time ago, and she's been caught trying to rob his grave three or four times since. She insists that he's not truly dead—excuse me a moment." Putting out his cigar, the officer to whom Clay was speaking hurried towards the group of fighting constables to help. Norton, Clay thought, was full of the strangest characters.

Patiently, Clay waited for the officer to return to the desk. He could wait a few moments. He wanted to save Rachel desperately, but in order for his plan to work, he would need patience in no small quantities. This time, instead of going after his daughter's murderers—now Rachel's kidnappers—on his own, he was going to bring them to justice through the law. They had escaped him, but they would not escape their fate at the hands of the police and the criminal justice system. They would surely, Clay knew, be hanged for their crimes—namely Elizabeth's murder. As for him, he would relish every moment. He could imagine the fear on their faces as the fatal sentence would be handed down; the imploring looks in their eyes, that begging for mercy he knew so well. Mercy, however, would have no bearing on their fates once handed over to the law. No, they would be tried, found guilty, and hanged, nothing merciful about it. Justice would finally be served.

Clay's patience was stretched quite thin that day, as there seemed to have been some grisly murder at one of the rougher mills up in Oakton, and many officers, though it was not truly their jurisdiction, were sent off to help interview suspects and witnesses. Other constables were busy with their work; hauling in tramps from the streets, talking to witnesses, locking up offenders, dragging in troublesome children by their ears. All was daily work for these men, and they had a reputation for being rough with their suspects, even those who, in the end, were not guilty of the crimes of which they had been accused.

Having been almost studiously ignored for a great many minutes, Clay was beginning to feel the effects of his bottled anxiety and impatience. His foot began to tap restlessly on the wooden floorboards, and his fingers drummed noisily on the desk. He was soon confronted by a constable, in a uniform identical to the one that the cigar smoking officer had been wearing.

"What're you doin' standin' there?" he asked. He was young, Clay noticed. His hair was cropped short and he had a pleasant fresh faced quality about him, though his attitude clearly did not match his squeaky clean appearance. Most likely, Clay thought, he was new to the job.

"I'd like to report a kidnapping," Clay repeated himself through gritted teeth. The young constable edged back, evidently intimidated, though he tried, in vain, not to let it show through his words.

"Well, I'll help you out if you quit all that tappin'," he said, nodding at Clay's still fidgeting fingers and foot, "It's drivin' me mad."

Irritated, but willing to swallow his pride if it meant rescuing Rachel, Clay fell still. The officer, taking a seat behind the desk, began to ask questions. Who was kidnapped? What did she look like? When did he last see her? Does he know of anyone who might want to take her? Clay answered all these questions and more with a precision and calmness that made the constable trust him, and immediately, officers were deployed to search the city. Most of them, however, were sent to one place in particular: a large, elegant white boarding house with green trim which stood on the busiest corner in all of Norton. Clay suppressed a grin as he watched the policemen rush out to find his granddaughter and arrest her kidnappers. The first part of his plan complete, he had but to wait for them to arrive back with the family he so loathed, and watch them dig themselves six feet under.

■■■

The tall, wooden grandfather clock in the front hall of Mrs. Brown's boarding house struck the hour. Its sound was deep and echoing, and it could be heard all through the house. Matthew, upon hearing it, looked up from the game of chess he was playing with Rachel.

"It's five," he remarked, pushing forward a pawn, "The others should be getting back soon."

Rachel nodded, her forehead wrinkled in concentration as she surveyed the board. She was winning, it seemed, but with one wrong move, Matthew could turn the tables.

They were the only ones home besides Mrs. Brown, Laura, Eddie, and Alice. Matthew had come home from school some time earlier, and, as usual, Rachel had waited at the foot of the school steps. Some of the other schoolboys, as it was mostly boys who attended, teased Matthew about it, but he assured her that he didn't mind. Laura and Eddie walked home from their school on their own; something Matthew knew would most likely have been deemed unacceptable in the future. Sandra still held something of the protective anxiety that seemed to seize the parents of the future, and was originally reluctant to let Laura and Eddie travel through the city without someone to guide them, but was forced to stand down due to the fact that she would never be available to perform the duty herself. She had recently secured a job, along with Grace, as a telephone operator, and the extra money was helping a great deal in paying for the rent.

Alice looked up, bleary eyed, from the book she was reading on the couch nearby. After the events of the previous night, Alvin needed some time to himself, and though Alice worried for him, she understood that he needed space. Often, she knew, emotional healing took longer than physical.

"Who's winning?" she asked, struggling to clearly see the pieces on Rachel and Matthew's chess board. When she read, her eyes often had trouble readjusting to seeing things farther away, even so much as a foot or two.

Rachel moved her bishop piece forward as far as she dared and sat back contentedly. "Check mate!" she announced, leaving Matthew staring, bewildered, at his surrounded king.

"Rachel, apparently," he responded glumly, "I never saw it coming!" He looked up, glancing from Alice to Rachel and back again. Alice blinked furiously, trying to make her friends' faces appear less fuzzy.

After Rachel, Alice, and Matthew had cleaned up the game and located Laura and Eddie, the rest of the time travellers arrived home. Supper, Mrs. Brown informed them, would be ready in about half an hour, and no one was to be late.

To Matthew, half an hour was a wretchedly inadequate amount of time in which to do anything worthwhile, so when Laura asked for help with her arithmetic homework, he was happy to oblige, as it gave him something useful to do that could hopefully be achieved in such a short time. The pair of them sat on the couch and Laura explained her trouble with fractions, a hopelessly self-important branch of mathematics in Matthew's eyes. They worked studiously, Laura angrily hushing any interruptions.

Alice had returned to her book, and the working residents of the boarding house had decided to get some much needed rest. This left Rachel to her own devices, and she wandered into the kitchen for want of something to do. Within the brightly lit, quaint little room, Rachel found Mrs. Brown and Mr. Riddell hard at work preparing a small roast for supper. Eddie trailed at their heels, and Rachel winced as he got constantly in the way, expecting Mrs. Brown to scold him for getting underfoot. Though she had a reputation for having a quick temper, Mrs. Brown's patience was endless when it came to Laura and Eddie. She was naturally motherly, and having no children of her own, she treated them, along with Matthew, Rachel, Alice, and even Trevor, whose reputation she well knew, like precious gifts. She would laugh at their jokes, no matter how ill-conceived they were, she insisted they all give her a kiss goodnight, and she would smile in this matronly way she had every time she saw them. It was this smile which greeted Rachel as she walked into the room and took a seat at the small, round kitchen table, where Mrs. Brown was peeling potatoes.

"Hello, dear," she said as Rachel sat down, "How are you?"

"Very well, thank you," Rachel replied, "And you?"

"Quite well, quite well," Mrs. Brown smiled, "Though I'm dreading the winter. It promises to be quite cold this year, and I can already feel it."

"I've always rather liked the winter myself," Rachel said, getting a faraway look in her eyes, "Watching the snow fall has a way of warming my heart. It's just so pretty."

"Well it certainly does nothing to melt the chill in my bones," Mrs. Brown complained, "I for one can't wait until it's come and gone."

Rachel smiled. Mrs. Brown looked up from her potato peeling, mock severity in her eyes. "Well don't just sit there smiling," she ordered, rolling a brown potato across the table, "Get to peeling! We may need a few more from the cellar once you're done with those."

■■

"It's so close," Grace breathed, "So, so close!"

Sandra, John, and Evan stood before her, holding their breaths. Evan was smirking, Sandra biting her lip to keep from shouting in excitement, and John's eyes were wide open, as though he was worried that if he blinked too often he might miss something important.

They watched eagerly as Grace stood inside the time machine, screwing the panel of numbered buttons back into place. It was the final step before the time machine could officially be deemed to be fit for use once more. Trevor, they all knew, would be elated.

After finishing her final task and checking to be sure that everything was properly stuck in place just where it should be, Grace emerged from the machine and stood with her friends and beheld the fixed time machine. It didn't look exactly how it had before it had been broken, making it quite a sight to behold. Much of the external wood had been changed, leaving it with a mismatched combination of both dark and light lumber. Some internal parts had also been replaced, which proved to be no easy task, considering the difference in technology between the era in which it had first been built and the time in which it had been reconstructed. The panel that Grace had only just finished putting back into place was badly dented in places after Trevor's accident, but otherwise unharmed. When beheld from a distance, the machine had something of a crooked appearance, and the door hung at an angle just off centre. However, for all its minute faults, in the grand scheme of things, Grace judged it ready for use. Tomorrow, they would locate Trevor and send him home.

"It's... different," Evan said, squinting at the machine and turning his head at various angles to attempt to straighten the whole affair.

"Yes, but it'll work!" Grace exclaimed, her voice hushed in veneration for what she had wrought, "I know it will."

"Trevor is going to be so happy to finally go home," remarked Sandra, and only John could detect the hint of sadness in her voice.

"Yes, I'm sure he will," Grace replied, not taking her eyes off of her creation, "We'll get him over here first thing in the morning!"

The others nodded. Sending him away in the spur of the moment would be too conspicuous; they would have to wait, however impatiently, until morning, when they could send him off when he stopped by to walk with Matthew to school. In the meantime, the other time travellers should know of their plans.

"Well, what now?" Evan piped in, as the others stood staring in rapt fascination at the time machine, "It looks a little flimsy to be collapsing it the way we used to."

"That it does," John agreed, and Sandra and Grace nodded their assent.

"So what do we do with it?" Evan wondered, "'Cause I'll shoot someone if it breaks again." Grace glared at him, indicating that his snark had not been well received.

Grace gazed at the machine thoughtfully. "Here," she said at last, beginning to push it towards the back wall, "Now it can't be seen from the window."

"What with our being on the second floor and all," Evan mused, tapping his chin, "Wouldn't you say that just maybe—just maybe—it might be more likely to be seen from the *door*?"

"Real cute," Grace retorted, "I was getting to that."

Promptly, she moved a tall room divider into place in front of the time machine, obscuring it almost completely from view.

"That good enough for you?" Grace smirked.

"Hmm?" came Evan's reply, for he had been momentarily distracted by the tasteful aroma arising from the kitchen below.

"Good enough?"

Evan cast a fleeting glance at the time machine's hiding place and nodded. "Sure," he said, "Sure. Let's head downstairs now though, I'm starving."

■■

"Not hungry?"

Trevor stared at his bowl of stew without the faintest hint of an appetite. He knew he had lost it somewhere during school, but he couldn't quite pinpoint exactly where.

"No," Trevor sighed, pushing away the bowl and slumping back in his chair, "Not really."

"Is something the matter?" Sam sat down next to him at the table. It was a poorly constructed piece of furniture, so that if one was to place a marble at one end of it, it would roll immediately to the other.

Trevor looked around. He had been living with Sam for so short a time, but he could tell already that his conditions were unfavourable, particularly for the upcoming winter. The walls seemed to do little to protect from the chill of late autumn, and there was only a small stove for heat. Sam scratched out a meagre existence, making a fraction of the money he had been earning before the lay offs at the mill where he had worked alongside Evan and John, but he was happy.

Sam laid claim to two rooms. One was his bedroom, a name which aptly suited it, as the only thing that fit inside it was a small bed. Everything else was in the second room.

He had a wooden tub for bathing, a bowl for washing the few dishes he had, and the lopsided table. Trevor hated the place for how small it was, but, after discovering that this was where Sam lived, he had chosen to remain there with him as an act of silent solidarity. The small space made him feel stifled, so he ventured out often, but he liked Sam's company more than he disliked his home.

"Do you ever wish," Trevor ventured, tracing the length of the table with his finger, "That you lived someplace else? Somewhere you could be accepted?"

Sam gave a wry smile. "I wish that people would change, Trevor," he answered simply, "Of course I do. But that is not the reality right now. One day, after my lifetime, things will be different."

A sudden thought entered Trevor's mind. "How old are you?" he asked abruptly.

Sam could only laugh. How funny this boy was! He remembered the time he had spent with Trevor on their way to Norton from Connolly Mills. He had thought him strange then as well, but his abject weirdness had subsided to a dull yet notable aura of difference. Trevor, like him, often felt he didn't belong. Sam found his quirks endearing, and had become quite attached to the boy. However, in recent days, his demeanour had changed from simply strange to something far more sinister, as though he was hiding something.

"I'm thirty five," he said, grinning, "Why do you ask?"

Trevor's mind set to work. He wanted so badly for Sam to see the change that would occur in the world. He wanted Sam to be able to live long enough to see Martin Luther King Junior deliver his "I Have a Dream" speech. He wanted him to see the famous and beloved African-American movie stars, and experience a world where he wouldn't be the first to be laid off from a job even though he was one of the best workers. A world where he could be treated as an equal. The numbers spun in Trevor's head. If Sam lived to be eighty, which may have been stretching it a little, he would die in 1946. As far as Trevor was concerned, that wasn't long enough.

"No reason," Trevor lied, "Just curious."

"Why do you always ask me if I wished I lived somewhere else?" Sam pressed, "This must be the hundredth time."

Trevor froze. Was he giving himself away somehow? Did Sam suspect that he didn't belong to this time? He should have known, after their conversation about time travel and H.G. Wells, that it was not wise to make so many insinuations about where he came from.

"No reason," he repeated, "Just curious."

"Trevor, I know something's wrong, and I know it has something to do with me. Now, what is it?"

"Nothing. Why do you keep asking me that?" Trevor couldn't meet Sam's eyes. He suspected him! Somehow, he had given himself away. He had said the wrong thing one too many times, and if he didn't think fast, they would all pay for it.

"You jes' seem upset, that's all," Sam said, noticing Trevor's strange behaviour, "After what I showed you in your geography book, and after I told you about *The Time Machine*, you've been acting even stranger than usual."

"Than usual?" Trevor felt as though he might explode at any moment. Sam thought him strange, and had thought him strange from the very beginning. It was only a matter of time before he figured the whole thing out.

"I'm sorry," replied Sam, feeling guilty for letting it slip that he thought Trevor an odd individual, "I didn't mean it that way. You've jes' been acting out of the ordinary. Is there something you need to tell me?"

"No," Trevor said, standing hastily, his chair screeching across the floorboards, "I just need some fresh air. I'll see you later." With those words ringing in the air, Trevor beat a swift retreat, the guilt that he could not tell Sam that things would most certainly get better weighing heavily on his mind.

■ ■

"How are the potatoes coming, dear?" Mrs. Brown asked, calling across the kitchen to Rachel from where she was standing, tasting some of the vegetables that she and Mr. Riddell had been preparing.

"They're nearly finished," Rachel replied, "This is the last one." She held up a half peeled potato in her hands so Mrs. Brown could see.

"Very good," Mrs. Brown smiled, inspecting the finished spuds that lay glistening on the table, "I think we may need two more, though. Would you mind going down to the cellar to get them when you're finished?

"I'll go right now," Rachel smiled, placing the last potato with the others. She was glad to be of some help to Mrs. Brown. The woman had given her so much; it was the least she could do to help with the cooking.

The stairs to the cellar were located in the front hall, blocked by a heavy wooden door. Rachel pulled it open and was relieved to find a lamp hanging just inside the door, as the cellar, being underground, had no windows, and no other source of light. Lighting the lamp, Rachel carefully began to make her way down the steps, the door swinging ominously shut behind her. The stairs creaked under her feet, but felt solid enough.

When at last she reached the bottom, the atmosphere had changed dramatically. The air felt cold and damp and the lamp Rachel held in her trembling fingers didn't seem to give off enough light to reach the darkest corners. Rachel heard a faint scuttling noise some ways to her left, and her head jerked towards the sound. As a rule, she was not a nervous person, and things like mice and spiders had never bothered her, but in this damp new environment, an unfamiliar feeling of apprehension held her in its clutches.

"You're being silly," she told herself, forcing a smile, "Just get the potatoes and go back upstairs."

The only problem was that Rachel, having only lived in Mrs. Brown's boarding house for a short while, did not know the layout of the dark, eerie cellar. She had no idea where Mrs. Brown might keep her potatoes. She took a few tentative steps forward. A strange, tickling feeling crept across the back of her neck, and she spun round, only to find herself entangled in cobwebs, which she angrily brushed away.

"Potatoes, potatoes, potatoes," Rachel repeated to herself, her voice echoing around the cellar. It was filled with a great variety of things. Old furniture lay in clusters around the corners, boxes filled with dusty china were piled high. Mr. Brown had had many hobbies it seemed, for the cellar was filled with their remnants. Fishing equipment lay propped against walls and scattered across the floor, golf clubs lounged on an old couch, and numerous hunting rifles could be seen, of all shapes and sizes. It occurred to Rachel that quite a profit could be made from Mr. Brown's equipment, but Mrs. Brown was far too emotionally attached to them to ever be rid of her husband's things. Looking around, it was as though Elias Brown was still living; as though he might march down the stairs at any moment and take up one of his old pastimes.

Suddenly, as though it had only just appeared, Rachel caught sight of a large wooden box in the far corner of the cellar. It had a hinged lid, and the word "Potatoes" was painted across the front in large, curling blue letters. Heading towards it, Rachel had to push aside numerous boxes and articles of furniture, as well as many of Mr. Brown's forgotten sporting paraphernalia. For a woman who kept the rest of her home in a condition of constant organisation and cleanliness, Mrs. Brown had sorely neglected her cellar.

Halfway to the potato bin, Rachel froze. Directly above her, heavy footfalls echoed from the main floor. Dust and dirt fell from the ceiling, sprinkling Rachel's shoulders and hair. Someone had just come in the front door, and, now listening intently, Rachel thought she could hear multiple pairs of feet, most likely clad in heavy, cumbersome boots. She shivered. They were most unlike the familiar sounds of her friends' walks. Alice made close to no noise at all when she walked through the house, or even the streets. After years of creeping around her own home, trying not to wake her younger siblings, Alice had mastered the art of stealth. It could have been Alvin at the door, but Rachel knew too well his confident yet light gait. Mr. Fitzgerald and Mr. Riddell were already inside, but one of them could have slipped out without her noticing and was only now returning. Rachel shook herself. All these crazy suppositions were getting her no closer to the potatoes she needed. Shaking her head in annoyance with herself, Rachel continued on.

She couldn't help but notice, however, that the commotion above her head was growing. The front hall seemed to be filled with people, and Rachel couldn't shake the feeling that something awful had happened. It wouldn't be the first terrible thing to happen, to be sure. Tragedy had seemed to follow her so closely in recent days that Rachel now nearly expected it wherever she went.

Taking the last step towards the all-important spuds, Rachel let out a little cry of horror. Something had taken hold of her leg, and wouldn't let go. She spun round to confront the beast. After a mere moment, Rachel's abject terror dissolved into annoyance once more. She had merely stepped into the path of a fishing net that had been stretched taut between two broken dining room chairs, and it had encircled her hapless limb as fishing nets were apt to do to those who tread on them. Cursing her foolishness, Rachel knelt and began to untangle herself, little by little.

"Rachel Reid?"

Rachel stood in a flash, nearly tripping, as her leg was still entangled. She peered back towards the staircase, from whence the voice had come. It was an altogether unfamiliar voice, deep, sonorous, and with an air of menace.

"Who's there?" she called, trying in vain to keep the fear from her voice.

A pair of boots could then be heard tramping down the cellar steps, almost frantically. Rachel recoiled, leaning up against the potato bin and clutching its edges tightly. Then, into the lamplight emerged a figure in full police uniform. Rachel didn't move, but her body relaxed tremendously. After all, what would a policeman do to her? They were meant to be the guardians of all that was good and just in the world, and Rachel had no reason to believe they were anything but.

The man who approached her was surprisingly young, his face open and clean, his close cropped hair of the lightest blond just visible from beneath his helmet. He couldn't have been long out of high school.

"Rachel Reid?" he repeated, his voice seeming too large for his small frame.

"I am she," Rachel replied, trying to keep her entangled ankle out of his sight. With a sigh of relief, the officer stepped forward and grasped her arm, his grip gentle but firm.

"Good," he said, "We've come to free you and return you to your grandfather. He's waiting at the station." He stepped forward, attempting to drag Rachel back above ground. Rachel, however, wouldn't budge. Her mouth had gone suddenly dry and she lacked the power to speak. Her grandfather? Here in Norton? It was impossible, a mere trick of the mind. She must simply have misheard the officer. And yet, for all she tried to persuade herself that such a reality couldn't be true, Rachel knew that she had not misheard. She knew, deep down, that her freedom simply could not last. Her grandfather would catch up with her sooner or later. It had simply happened, and at a moment in which she had borne no thought of the man. What could she do? There was nothing left to do but protest, but Rachel's mind was muddled and her voice impaired.

"No!" she cried, for it was all she could muster, "No!"

"Hmm? Oh!" The kind, ignorant officer had caught sight of her entangled ankle. "How could I have been such a fool? I should have realized they'd have had you tied up, else you would have escaped!" He knelt down and began to untie the stubborn knots. Before he was finished, Rachel found her words.

"You can't take me back there," she said insistently, "My grandfather, he's not in his right mind. What did he tell you? What has he said about the people upstairs?"

"Well he said you've been kidnapped, but I s'pose you'd know that, wouldn't you? He's asked us to find you and rescue you, and here we are. You're free!"

"No, no. You don't understand. I was free here! My grandfather, he's the one who was keeping me prisoner! Please, you must believe me, nothing he says is true!"

"Now, now, I expect you've been down here for a long time, so you're not thinking right." The officer's voice became suddenly lilting, as though he were speaking to a small child, or even some domestic animal. Its very sound began to frustrate Rachel, and his continued ignorance even more so.

"He's mad!" she continued to insist, "Completely mad! Please don't let him take me!"

For a fleeting moment, the officer's young face seemed to show him to be deep in thought. He shook his head and smiled. "I admire your enthusiasm," he said, "But you're safe now; you needn't worry about them upstairs hearing you." He tilted his head and glanced up at the ceiling. "Your grandfather seemed perfectly sane to me, only he was worried! Come now, and we'll put an end to his fears."

"You're wrong," Rachel said, trying to remain calm, "You're wrong. Why won't you believe me? I'm telling you, I am here of my own accord. I haven't been kidnapped, I ran away from home."

"I cannot refuse the evidence I've seen with my own eyes!" The young constable's eyes flashed. "You were tied up just now!"

Rachel rolled her eyes, fighting back tears of frustration. "I wasn't tied up. I came down to get some potatoes for Mrs. Brown, and my foot was caught in a fishing net."

"Alright, alright. Supposing you weren't kidnapped, I still must take you to the station. I cannot simply let you go when your poor old granddad is looking for you, and there have been some mighty accusations against Mrs. Brown's boarders."

Rachel sighed. It was hopeless. What else could she do but submit? If she had nothing to hide, and if Matthew and his family were truly innocent, which she was certain they were, both for the murder of her mother and her own alleged kidnapping, then the justice system would surely let them go free and convict her grandfather. His actions had been very real, and Rachel was certain there must be evidence against him somewhere or another.

Rachel stepped forward, taking care to avoid the fishing net, and allowed the constable to take her by the arm and direct her upstairs, utterly helpless and ashamedly potatoless. When they arrived on the main floor, Rachel saw the last of Mrs. Brown's boarders being taken outside, hands behind their backs. How humiliated they must have felt! She cleared her throat, for a great lump had risen there and refused to be swallowed down. Matthew, the last of the accused, was just being led out the door, and turned his head back at the sound. Before the constable guiding him could force him to face forward again, Rachel met his gaze. His eyes were wide with raw, blind fear, but behind his terrified façade there lay a brief message of hope. Rachel swallowed hard.

CHAPTER TWENTY-TWO

Doing Time

The dark police wagon bucked and jolted as it sped down the streets of Norton, headed for the stationhouse. Inside, the time travellers sat, sullen faced and frightened, in the darkness. Shafts of light escaped through the metal bars that were stretched vertically over the three small windows. Matthew looked up from where he sat on one of the two wooden benches that spanned the sides of the wagon. The light was fading, though he could still see the worry in the faces of those around him. None of them had expected it. It had been Mrs. Brown who answered the door, letting enter half a dozen police constables, truncheons in hand. Their leader, or at least most forceful and superior member, had barked at Mrs. Brown to tell them where they might find Rachel Reid. Mrs. Brown, to her credit, kept a cool head and told them that Rachel was in the cellar, fetching some potatoes for supper.

By this time, Matthew and the other boarders had rushed into the front hall to see what all the commotion was about. One of the constables, a young blond, strode off through the door of the cellar, letting it swing shut behind him as he clomped down the stairs. Once he had gone, the real trouble began. The leader, who was a rough, burly man with a heavy black moustache, began to bark accusations at those gathered in the hall, and informed them that they were needed at the station immediately. They could comply, or be arrested on the spot. They chose the former.

Matthew glanced around once more. He could feel the tension in the air. Mrs. Brown, who was quicker to anger than to fear, had gone pale, and sat in the far corner, eyeing the others warily. Matthew felt sorry for her. It was not, however, a mere twinge of empathy or feeling of sorrow, but a dull, persistent ache in his chest. Mrs. Brown had opened her home to them all, and look at where it had gotten her. Who could she trust? The accusations were severe, and Mrs. Brown, aside from a few short months knowledge of their characters, didn't know what to believe. Matthew let out an audible sigh, and leaned back against the wooden wall of the wagon. He was certain that Clay Kennedy was behind the whole thing. Who else would have sent police to find them, with allegations of murder and kidnapping on their lips? No-one but Clay.

"Are you alright, Matthew?"

The boy in question looked up, finding himself gazing into the kindly face of his adoptive father. Mr. Fitzgerald seemed oddly calm, given their current situation. His expression was one of compassion, but not of worry. Matthew was comforted by his presence.

"I'm okay," he nodded, speaking in a whisper, "Just a little scared, that's all."

"Don't be afraid," his father assured him, "We've done nothing wrong. Clay may not see it that way, but the police won't arrest us for something we didn't do. Rachel will tell them what really happened. We'll probably be home before it gets too late."

Matthew nodded, his mind already far away. Rachel had not looked hopeful in the short glance he had caught of her. She didn't seem afraid, at least not like he was, but there was an uneasiness in her face that Matthew couldn't get out of his head. He just hoped, for all their sakes, that this would end well, but the relentless feeling that it would not continued to gnaw away at his insides.

Sandra glanced up and caught Matthew's eye, trying her best to smile broadly in the face of her evident fear. Matthew returned the gesture.

Laura and Eddie weren't with them, and Matthew was glad of it. He had told Laura to stay put with her books while he went to the front door to see what all the commotion was about, and she had obeyed him. Even now, she and Eddie were probably sitting in the house, wondering where they had all gone. The situation was nightmarish, and Matthew feverishly hoped that the pair of them would be smart enough to stay inside and find themselves something to eat. He couldn't bear the thought of the pair of them, whom he saw as his brother and sister, all alone. Matthew shook himself, banishing the thought from his mind. It would do them no good to dwell on the subject.

The wagon juddered to a halt, and another half-dozen constables arrived to open the door and lead them out, escorting the lot of them straight into the police stationhouse. It was chaotic, with policemen and criminals, victims and reporters littering the premises. Barely able to keep his eyes focused on one thing, Matthew took in the scene. There was a tall, wooden desk off to the left of the front doors, and ahead there were doors leading into various offices and interview rooms. The Chief Constable, a surly man with wispy white hair peeking out from beneath his hat, approached the group that had just arrived.

"These the kidnappers?" he asked of his constables, his voice flat and monotone. Matthew couldn't see, but he was sure that one of the officers behind him had nodded.

"Very well," the Chief Constable said, the wrinkles in his face standing out in the fading light, "Place them in the cells until I call for them!"

"The cells?" blurted Evan, louder than he meant to. Grace elbowed him in the ribs.

"Yes, the cells," the Chief Constable repeated, and then looked around, "As you can see, we have a lot on our hands today, so you'll just have to wait. Unless you're anxious to be done with the matter and would like to sign a confession, of course." Evan opened his mouth to speak, but no words came.

"I thought not. The cells, gentlemen." With that, the wispy haired policeman turned and left their presence to deal with a more pressing matter and the constables obeyed his orders, escorting the accused to the cells, which were located in the basement of the building.

Head hanging, Matthew began to follow the others down the steps, a policeman following close behind him. He glanced up one last time, and, just to his left, through the door of the Chief Constable's office, he saw a sight that made his blood run cold. Clay Kennedy was standing, bold as brass, in front of the low wooden desk, speaking to the officer who sat behind it. Rachel stood beside him, silent. It was not the Chief Constable to whom he was speaking, but another officer of perhaps the same age. Matthew walked on, reflecting on how much older Clay looked than when he had last seen him.

The holding cells were a miserable part of the building that housed the police station. Dark, damp, and dismal, they were, with only two barred windows to provide any light apart from the few oil lamps which hung on hooks at the ends of the narrow hall. On either side of the hall stood cold iron bars, behind which reposed all manner of criminals. There were drunks snoring on the low cots, thieves running their swift fingers along the bars, among numerous others who rested in different positions all throughout the cells. There were four in total; one held women, three held men.

Unceremoniously, two constables unlocked the first male cell and shoved John, Evan, and Matthew inside, whilst two others pushed Mr. Fitzgerald and Mr. Riddell into the second. Grace, Sandra, Alice, and Mrs. Brown were placed in the female cell, opposite Matthew, Evan, and John.

Looking around warily, Matthew found that they had been placed in a cell with two other men. One was old and grizzled, his eyelids drooping as he sat on the cot; the other was middle-aged, his own eyes shifty, glancing round at the newcomers with a kind of disdain that Matthew found most alarming.

The others didn't fare much better in their own cells. The other male cell, into which Messrs Riddell and Fitzgerald had been placed, also held three men, one of which dozed on their cot while the other two stood in the corner, whispering to one another between furtive glances at the officers who stood on guard.

The women shared their cell with one other; a young lady with a round, flushed face and bright, flashing eyes, whose hair hung loose about her shoulders. She had been seated on the cot when they arrived, but when they had been locked up once more, she stood and strode forwards to greet the newcomers. Matthew watched, fear plain in his face, as the woman approached Grace with a wide smile.

"Anna," she introduced herself, sticking out her hand for Grace to shake, then doing the same to the others.

"Grace," Grace replied, looking down at the girl. She can't have been a day over twenty, as far as Grace was concerned, and she wondered what she had done to be taken down to the holding cells.

"You're probably wondering why I'm here," Anna said, grinning up at Grace, who was taken aback by the girl's astuteness. She nodded in silence.

"I suppose you could say it was quite a *grave* matter," Anna laughed, inducing nervous giggles in the other women. Grace wasn't sure she'd heard anyone from the past ever make a pun. It was considered folly. Anna, however, did not seem to care. She was a pretty thing, with round face and eager eyes, and evidently a sharp tongue full of clever witticisms. Grace and Sandra began to feel more comfortable around this lady, for she seemed not only harmless, but friendly. On the other hand, Mrs. Brown had retired to the far corner of the cell, not speaking to anyone, nor even meeting their eyes, and Alice was listening quietly to Anna, her hands gripping the iron bars behind her with a fierce tenacity. Matthew spied this and leaned forward, nearly reaching his head through his own bars. His cheeks were chilled on either side by the cold metal.

"Alice?" he said in a stage whisper, causing the girl in question to turn around and look at him. "Are you alright?"

Alice nodded uncertainly and gave a weak smile without ever letting go of the bars. "I only wish they would hurry so we could leave soon."

Matthew nodded in understanding. "Me too," he said, and then added, "I'm sure they will."

Darkness soon fell, and Matthew was unsure of how long they had been waiting in the damp cells, but he felt it must have been at least a few hours. Mrs. Brown now lay on the cot with her back to the hall; though it was clear she was not sleeping. At home she had always had a light snore that Matthew could hear from upstairs, for her room was directly beneath his own, and at present the reassuring sound was absent. As the night wore on, the basement of the police station fell silent, save for the heavy breathing and muttering of some of the inmates. Anna was awake, but out of respect for the others, whom she had called "friends" numerous times that night, she was silent. Every so often it became apparent that she was stifling a giggle, most likely from some clever pun she had come up with but was polite enough not to say.

Matthew did not sleep, though Evan and John had succumbed to their weariness some time earlier. He was too nervous, and the thought of Rachel upstairs with Clay, if they were indeed still in the building at all, upset him. Hunger gnawed away at his stomach, for supper had been left uneaten at the boarding house. His thoughts wandered restlessly; from Rachel and Clay, to Laura and Eddie, to Alvin, to Mrs. Brown, to Anna, to Trevor and Sam, and back again.

By the time the cells were lit once more by the early morning sun, Matthew had not slept so much as a wink, and there were heavy, dark circles under his eyes. He was light headed; his thoughts jumbled together like pieces of an unsolved puzzle.

"When do you think they'll come for us?" he whispered to Evan, who sat next to him, rubbing the sleep out of his bleary eyes.

Evan yawned and stretched theatrically. "I dunno, Matthew, but it'd better be soon. I'm starving." His stomach gurgled, as if on cue. "See?"

Matthew bit his lip and screwed his eyes tight shut. The pain in his own stomach was growing unbearable, and it was now coupled with a pounding in his ears that grew stronger with every passing moment.

"Are you alright, Matthew?"

The boy opened his eyes and furrowed his brow. The voice that had spoken to him was warm and lilting, and unlike any he was familiar with. His vision cleared and he found himself looking into the face of Anna, her features half hidden by the two sets of iron bars that separated them.

"How'd you know my name?" Matthew asked.

"It wasn't difficult to figure out," she replied, grinning, "I heard people speaking to you." She paused, tilted her head to one side, and went on. "Are you alright?"

Matthew nodded slowly. "Just tired," he managed to reply, "And hungry."

"Nervous, too."

"Huh?"

"You're nervous. I think you're innocent, you know. I would be too if I had been accused of a crime I never committed." Anna smiled.

"How do you know I'm nervous?" Matthew wondered, suddenly becoming defensive and sitting up straighter, "Have you been eavesdropping?" Matthew shut his eyes again. His voice no longer sounded like his own, and the words he spoke seemed twisted and bent out of shape in his mind. He reminded himself of a small child.

"No! No, nothing of the sort. You're biting your lip. It's a mannerism of yours which makes it easy to tell how you're feeling. Don't worry, Matthew. They'll come for you and your family soon and you'll be set free."

"Thank you," said Matthew, still slightly confused, "Thank you."

"Does anyone have the time?" came Grace's voice from behind Anna. Mr. Riddell pulled out his silver pocket watch— which he had had fixed since it had been returned to him— and looked at it, squinting in order to read its small numbers.

"It's nearly eight," he said, and gasps could be heard all around as the prisoners reacted to the time. Mrs. Brown and her boarders had been incarcerated for over twelve hours.

"Excuse me!" Anna called out, now standing with her hands clutching the bars. A constable who was standing guard glanced at her, signalling his acknowledgement.

"When are you going to let us out of here?" she asked him sweetly, "We've been waiting for quite a long time, you know."

"We'll get to you when we're ready," the guard snapped, his helmet quivering on his head.

"Now, there's no need to be so—" Anna was cut off by the sound of heavy boots tramping down the stairs. A moment later, in walked the Chief Constable, flanked by his Detective and two other constables. All four of them had the appearance of not having gotten enough sleep, but their misery was clearly nothing compared to the hungry, weary prisoners they kept.

"Perkins," the Chief Constable read unenthusiastically, "Grace Perkins?"

Grace turned abruptly, her skirts swishing. "Yes?" she asked, eyebrows raised. The Chief Constable said nothing, merely nodding in her direction. An officer sauntered up to the door of the cell and unlocked it, took Grace by the arm and led her out. Unable to even glance back, Grace was forced up the stairs and disappeared from the view of the others.

"Evan Wells," the Chief Constable continued, "And Nicholas Riddell."

The remaining constable and Detective unlocked the other cells and pulled out the required inmates, then locked them once more. Before leaving, the Chief Constable walked around to each cell and pulled hard on the door to be sure it was properly secured. After a moment, the holding cells were in silence once more, aside from the calls of encouragement that Anna offered up to the departing accused.

Matthew's blood ran cold. What was going to happen to them? Would they be questioned? Tortured? Who would be next? He backed away from the cell door towards John, who laid a reassuring hand on his shoulder. Mr. Fitzgerald, reading the distress in his face, reached through the bars and ruffled his hair. Matthew felt like crying. Not because he was upset, though he was, but because his mind was so addled from hunger and lack of sleep that even these small comforting gestures were enough to make him want to bawl like an infant and bury himself in his father's arms. He did no such thing, however, for he knew it would do no good to become visibly upset, and he must pull himself together if he was going to help prove them innocent. Blinking away his tears, Matthew took long, deep breaths, and waited to be called upstairs.

CHAPTER TWENTY-THREE

Interrogation Time

The morning air felt chilly against Alvin's exposed skin, which was comprised solely of his face and his ears. The rest of him, from head to foot, was clad in the garments of near winter; a light fall jacket and a glove borrowed from his grandfather kept the biting wind and cold from seeping too far into his bones. He was trekking across the city with the intention of taking Alice out to see a show and then have lunch; a meal wherein he wasn't obligated to eat with a fork and knife.

Finally, he arrived at Mrs. Brown's boarding house, climbing the steps and raising his gloved hand to knock. For many moments, no one answered, and he knocked again. Still nothing. Beginning to become frustrated, he pulled off his glove with his teeth and rapped a third time on the large door. At last, he heard the scurry of feet, and the door, with a considerable amount of effort from the person on the other side, slowly opened.

Alvin's brow furrowed, as he found himself staring at no one until he peered down, finding little Laura Fitzgerald standing before him.

"Hullo, Laura," he said cheerfully, then looked past her. "Where's Mrs. Brown?"

"I don't know," Laura answered earnestly, "She's not here."

Alvin crouched down and looked the little girl in the eye. "Very well," he said, and smiled, "Is Alice in?" Laura shook her head. Alvin's face became more and more confused with every response he heard.

"Where is everyone?" he asked, "Have they all gone somewhere?"

"They left last night," Laura informed him, stepping back to let Alvin come inside, then shutting the door behind him. Alvin stopped cold.

"And they haven't been back?"

"Nope. They went with some police last night, and they didn't come back yet. Eddie and me are going to school in a few minutes. I don't want to go until they come back, but Eddie says we should."

Alvin couldn't believe what he was hearing. Police? Never came back? The whole story—as much of it as he had heard—was chilling. Something bad had happened, he knew that much for sure. He just didn't know what.

"Laura," he began, crouching once more and gripping her by the shoulder, "Did you hear what the police said? Did they say why they were leaving?"

Laura shook her blonde head. "No, but Eddie did. He said they said something about kidnapping, but that's all he heard."

"Where's Eddie?"

"He's in the kitchen, making breakfast."

As though by some fatherly instinct, Alvin scooped Laura up in his arm and rushed into the kitchen, where he found Eddie, smearing butter haphazardly over a slice of bread. He placed Laura on the counter.

"Eddie," he said urgently, "What's happened? Where is everyone?"

"I heard Laura tell you everything I know," the boy replied, not taking his eyes off of the bread he was accidentally stabbing holes in, "The police took them all away and they haven't come back yet." He paused and looked up. "Can you help me with this?" Eddie held up the slice of bread and the knife, then, remembering Alvin's missing left arm, put them down again. "Sorry," he said, "I forgot."

In his fear that something terrible was happening to Alice and the others, Alvin only nodded. He had no time to think of his own losses right then; only of the present situation. In a tremendous rush, he brought Laura down off the counter and took her hand, then looked Eddie straight in the eyes.

"We're going to go find them," he announced, "Come along; let's go to the St. Edward's stationhouse, perhaps that's where they took them."

"Are you sure we won't get in trouble?" Eddie wondered.

"I'm certain," Alvin replied, and nodded towards the door, "Let's go."

Reluctantly, Eddie climbed down from the chair on which he had been standing and followed Alvin and Laura to the door, two slices of bread held firmly in his hands. The pair, unbeknownst to Alvin, had not eaten since lunch the day before, and Eddie was starving. Laura felt the same, and the look in her eyes when he handed her the slice of bread was one of full and unutterable gratitude.

Alvin held Laura's hand the entire way, and Eddie walked on his other side, so the trio seemed to be huddled together against the wind. As they went, various scenes played themselves through Alvin's mind. He imagined Mrs. Brown and her boarders being taken away and bundled into a police wagon, with Laura and Eddie looking fearfully on. He imagined them in the police station, confronted with the accusation of kidnapping. Whom they had supposedly kidnapped, Alvin could not know for certain. He could only hope that they would soon be found innocent and set free.

They arrived at the police station just as the clocks were striking eight, and the three of them climbed the steps in a flurry. Alvin's urgent manner had made Eddie and Laura more worried than before, and they began to understand that something very serious was at play.

Letting go of Laura's hand, Alvin pushed open the door and strode inside, looking around for any sign of his friends. He approached the first officer he saw.

"Excuse me, constable," he said, taking up Laura's little hand once more, "Is there a Mrs. Brown here with her boarders? They left the house last night with police and haven't been seen since."

The constable, a blond man with a fresh, open face, raised his eyebrows. "And who might *you* be?" he asked, looking Alvin up and down, his eyes lingering on the empty left coat sleeve for a moment before returning to the youth's face.

"Alvin Quinn," came the instinctual response, and the officer nodded slowly.

"Wait here a moment," he said, and, without taking his eyes off of Alvin for more than a few seconds, walked towards a man with wispy white hair who wore the uniform of a Chief Constable. Alvin and the children watched as the men whispered, and the white-haired man produced a folded piece of paper from his pocket. Simultaneously, the pair glanced up at Alvin from the paper, and the Chief Constable nodded. He folded the page back up, and before he could so much as place it back in his pocket, Alvin felt a tight grip on his arm, much too strong to be Eddie or Laura. Alvin looked behind him and saw the blond officer with one hand around his arm, the other brandishing a truncheon.

"Right this way, Alvin Quinn," he said, "We've been looking for you."

"Looking for me?" Alvin asked incredulously as he was led roughly away, "Whatever for? What's happening? Have I done something wrong?" The constable didn't answer him, and he became aware that he no longer had a hold of Laura's hand. "Laura? Eddie! Don't go anywhere, alright? Just stay there, I'll be back soon!" He tried to turn and look back at the pair of them, but the constable pushed him forward. Unceremoniously, he was bundled down a flight of stairs into the basement of the building, nearly losing his footing several times. He would have fallen straight down had it not been for the officer's grip on his arm.

"Please, tell me why I'm h—Alice!" Stunned, Alvin was locked into the second male cell with Mr. Riddell. Once it had been locked, he flung himself towards the bars and grabbed hold of one, and wedging his feet between them.

"Alice!" he called across the hall diagonally to where Alice was standing, gripping the bars of her own cell, "What's happening? Why are we here?"

"We've been accused of kidnapping Rachel," she replied, her voice thick, "The whole lot of us. It was Clay who did it, and he has Rachel now. They've just taken Miss Perkins, Mr. Riddell, and Mr. Wells upstairs, we believe to be questioned."

Alvin's face fell. "And you've been here all night?" Alice could only nod. Alvin opened his mouth to speak, but no words came, only a pained and pitying sigh.

"Alvin," Matthew whispered leaning against the bars that stood between his cell and Alvin's. Alvin turned to look at him, and Matthew knew that he must have looked as bad as he felt, for Alvin's expression was one of utter astonishment. Alvin approached the bars and leaned in to better hear what his friend was about to say.

"Alvin, how did you find us?" He paused in the middle of his speech and his eyes went wide, his countenance betraying his inner turmoil. "Did you see Rachel upstairs? Is she alright?"

Alvin shook his head. "I didn't see Rachel," he replied, in a whisper of a volume that matched Matthew's own, "But I was going to take Alice out this morning, and I found Mrs. Brown's nearly empty, save for Laura and Eddie. They told me what little they knew."

Matthew seemed taken aback for a moment, remembering how worried he had been for Laura and Eddie when they had been left alone all night. They had entirely escaped his mind; in his sleep deprived state, he could recall only one thing at a time.

"Are they here?" he asked urgently, "Have they eaten?"

"Yes," Alvin nodded, "They had some buttered bread on the way here; I don't know if they'd eaten before I arrived."

Mr. Fitzgerald approached Alvin from behind and laid a hand on his shoulder. "You've seen Laura?" he asked, his voice husky and low, "And Eddie?"

"I'm sorry, sir," Alvin said, letting his head hang, "I lost them upstairs when a constable dragged me down here." Instinctively, Mr. Fitzgerald peered up at the ceiling, as though he could perhaps see his daughter through it. Matthew's stomach churned as he realized that though he was responsible for only himself, his father was burdened with care not only for himself, but for his children as well.

"Don't worry, Alvin," Mr. Fitzgerald reassured the youth, "It wasn't your fault. They'll be safe with the police, I'm sure. We'll be out soon. Grace and the others up there will tell the officers all they need to know, and we'll be set free."

■■■

"Your name, please."

"Grace Perkins," Grace replied, her arms folded across her chest. She was seated in an uncomfortable wooden chair before a wide table, behind which sat her interrogator, who was furiously scribbling her name down on a piece of paper. They were in an interview room, and it was much smaller than Grace had expected. The room was lit electrically, casting soft yellow light over the pair. The walls were papered a dull mahogany, and the single door was set into the wall farthest from Grace, presumably to prevent the escape of the interviewees.

The man in front of her straightened his wire rimmed glasses. "Alright, Miss Perkins," he said, peering up from his page for a moment to look her up and down, "You understand that you've been accused, along with your entire family, your landlady, and her other boarders, of kidnapping a Miss Rachel Reid..." He looked up again and narrowed his eyes at her as though waiting for a response. He glanced back down at the page for a moment, before returning his magnified eyes to meet Grace's. "Is this true?"

"Absolutely not," Grace snapped, and the man seemed to shrink at her words. Evidently, it had not previously been his job to deal with the interrogation of suspects.

"My name is Detective Urwin," he said, trying a new approach. If his suspect was going to be difficult, and it looked as though she was, he hoped she might be more cooperative if he acted more like a friend than an interrogator. "I'm an Acting Detective, really," he continued, "Jones is down with consumption, so they appointed me until we can find a suitable replacement."

Grace was beginning to become impatient. First, she had been left to rot in the holding cells overnight with no food, and now she was being forced to participate in small talk with the station's Acting Detective. She took a deep breath and collected her thoughts as best she could, though she was worn out from lack of food and sleep.

"I'm sure you're doing a wonderful job," she replied through gritted teeth.

Urwin's face broke into a smile. "Why, thank you," he said, "But to business, now. How did Rachel Reid come to be living at Mrs. Brown's boarding house?"

"She had been living with Alice Cosgrove's aunt," Grace explained, her impatience with the man subsiding, "And when it became unsafe for them to continue living there, Mrs. Brown invited both Alice and Rachel to stay at the boarding house until more permanent arrangements could be made."

Urwin scribbled down all she had said onto his paper. "Unsafe, you say?" he wondered, "Where does this aunt live? What is her name?"

"Jessica," Grace faltered, "I... I don't know her surname. I believe her address is Number Six, Crookshanks Lane, in the Southern Quays."

Urwin flinched when Grace uttered the address, hoping against hope that Grace didn't notice. "They were..." he paused and cleared his throat, "They were living in a house of ill-repute?"

"How did you know what it was?" Grace asked, her brow furrowed.

Urwin's mouth flapped open and shut for a moment before he could collect himself and find his words. "I've made arrests there," he said defensively, "It is well known among all the constables."

"So you can see why it had become unsafe?" Grace said, attempting to avoid bringing up any talk of Alice's attacker. Urwin nodded and cleared his throat again.

"Now," said Urwin, changing the subject, "You said *permanent* arrangements. Are you indeed aware that Rachel Reid is under the custody of her grandfather in Connolly Mills, and therefore had no need for any permanent living arrangements? But of course, you must be. You sought to keep her in your own custody, to keep her from revealing you and your family as the murderers of her mother, Elizabeth Kennedy. You wanted to keep her quiet, and the only way you could do that was to steal her away from Connolly Mills and keep her imprisoned until you figured out what to do with her!" Urwin's voice had risen to a near shout, but Grace was not intimidated.

"We did no such thing," she said coolly, "Rachel came to stay with us at Mrs. Brown's because Jessica's "house of ill-repute" as you call it, became unsafe. Rachel left Connolly Mills of her own accord, ask her yourself. And her mother died of an infection, not murder."

Urwin seemed flustered. He hadn't been the one to interview Rachel, nor had he heard reports on what she had said. His face was beginning to turn red when another line of argument scooted into his head. Standing up, he crashed his fists into the table and his chair was nearly upended. He began to pace back and forth alongside the table as he spoke.

"What was she doing in the cellar, then?" he stormed, turning back to face Grace and stabbing a finger into the table in order to make his point, "I have it on good reports that she was found in the cellar of Mrs. Brown's boarding house, tied around the ankles with a fishing net so that she couldn't escape! What do you say to that?"

It was Grace's turn to be flustered. She hadn't the faintest idea of what he meant by spouting these obvious lies in her face. All she could hope to do was deny it.

"That is completely untrue!" she said, losing her composure at the last moment, "Rachel was never in the cellar, and she certainly wasn't tied with any fishing net! The last I saw her, she was greeting me at the door when I returned from work yesterday!"

"Lies!" Urwin screeched, "All lies!" He turned towards the door and began to shout to two constables who were standing outside. "Take her away! I'm done here."

Grace could barely breathe. What had she done? Had she somehow incriminated herself? She was so angry, she could feel her face turning red. However, she remained calm as the officers led her roughly out of the interview room.

After she had gone, Urwin slumped back into his chair, blowing out a long breath. That had been his first interrogation, and he was sure it had gone well. He let out another long breath, winded as he was from all the raving and shouting he had done. He wasn't sure if he would be able to muster that kind of emotion again, though he knew he had at least one other suspect to interrogate. It was very difficult for him to become so angry, though Grace's utter lack of reaction had aided him in becoming suitably frustrated with her. He only hoped that his next suspect would do the same.

Urwin pulled his watch out of his pocket by the chain and glanced at it. The evidence was not favourable for a conviction, and he personally did not believe that the people he was questioning were in any way responsible for the apparent "kidnapping" of Rachel Reid. He shuddered as he thought of Clay Kennedy. The man, with his sinister lined face and angry scowl, intimidated him, and gave rise to a feeling of intense uneasiness whenever he saw him.

■■■

"Mr. Wells," the Chief Constable began, pacing back and forth before his suspect, "Will you please recount to me how Rachel Reid came to be under your care?"

Evan sat back in his chair, an unintentional air of nonchalance surrounding him. He had to stop himself from folding his hands behind his head, for fear of appearing disrespectful both towards the officer and the situation.

"She was never under *my* care, you understand," Evan began to explain, "She was under the care, really, of Mrs. Brown, the landlady."

"Immaterial!" the interrogator stormed, "Tell me how she came to be at your boarding house!" He turned to face Evan in a flash and slammed his hands down on the table. Evan was startled. This once weary, wrinkled looking, white-haired old man had transformed before his eyes into someone filled with an untamed rage. He had fire in his once tired eyes.

Chief Constable Bentley, unbeknownst to Evan, was known in the stationhouse as a brutal man in a state of either constant infuriation or constant weariness. Evan sat up straighter and raised his hands in front of him calmly.

"Now, now," he said, in a voice that seemed almost patronizing, "Calm down." Bentley's face turned an angry shade of red, and Evan put his hands down, resigning from his condescension. "She and Alice Cosgrove came to us because a man who had attacked Alice almost a year ago was harassing her, and we thought it safer to bring them both to live with us."

"And what right did you have to steal Miss Reid away from her home in Connolly Mills and bring her to a faraway city?" Bentley continued to storm, "What gave you the right to do that?"

"No, no," Evan insisted, shaking his head, "That's not at all what happened! She ran away from home and was living with Alice's aunt Jessica when the man who hurt Alice found them there. Then, and only then, did we *invite* them to live with us."

"Was it so that you could shut her up?"

"What?"

"Did you take Rachel and lock her in the cellar of Mrs. Brown's boarding house to keep her from revealing the truth about how you murdered her mother?"

"Not *that* again!" Evan blurted out, realizing too late the weight his words would carry.

"So you are aware that these accusations have been standing for some time?"

"Yes..."

"Do you deny them?"

"Of course!"

"Then why did you kidnap Rachel Reid?"

"We never kidnapped her, alright? She came of her own free will!"

Bentley thrust forward his hand and gave Evan a shocking blow to the side of the head. Dazed, but not terribly hurt, Evan squinted up at his interrogator as though expecting him to strike again.

"That's not what Miss Reid told us," Bentley informed him, "So you'd do well to confess now and spare yourself the trouble."

"I can't confess to a crime I never committed."

After another open handed blow from Chief Constable Bentley, Evan's interrogation was over.

▪▪▪

Inspector Tillman, Mr. Riddell was certain, had been interrogating people from the moment he could talk. The man appeared as though he was born to ask questions; to play with the mind of the one he was interviewing. Mr. Riddell, though he knew that the man was playing cruel mind games, fretted over every word he spoke.

Tillman was a calm sort, his emotions never showing through on his face, at least from what Mr. Riddell could see. He was cool and collected, with not a dark, thinning hair out of place. He held a notebook open in his hands and a fountain pen rested behind his ear. He and Mr. Riddell were around the same age.

"You say Mrs. Brown was the one who invited Rachel and Alice to stay at the boarding house?" Tillman glanced up at his suspect, his eyes gleaming. No menace leaked through his voice or his words, but his presence was enough to make Mr. Riddell's palms begin to sweat.

Mr. Riddell nodded nervously, hardly daring to look up. Tillman mimicked his gesture, scribbling in his notepad. His handwriting was spidery and thin. If Sandra had seen it, Mr. Riddell knew, she would say that it was indicative of his personality, like a tiny, invisible spider, ready to strike at any hapless creature who happens across his path.

"And why did she feel she had to invite them to stay with all of you?" Tillman continued.

"She—she was worried about them…" Mr. Riddell tried desperately to explain in the clearest possible manner, so as to appear as though he had nothing to hide, "They were staying in the Southern Quays, with Alice's aunt—a Miss Jessica, I believe—and the house soon became unsafe for two young ladies from the countryside. I'm… I'm sure you understand why Mrs. Brown felt the need to take them in." Mr. Riddell was reluctant to mention the exact *occupation* of Miss Jessica, and as a result, he knew that he sounded suspicious. However, he wished not to get anyone else into trouble, even though it might cost him.

Tillman continued the interrogation. "Can you explain how Rachel Reid came to be in the cellar of Mrs. Brown's boarding house?"

Mr. Riddell was stymied. He and Mrs. Brown had been cooking supper together when the police had arrived, and Rachel hadn't been in the kitchen with them at that time. He remembered her being there, and then, all of a sudden, while he was talking with Eddie, she had disappeared. He hadn't bothered to ask Mrs. Brown where she had gone, but now he wished he had.

"I don't know," came the only truthful response, "She was in the kitchen the last I saw her… I suppose Mrs. Brown sent her to get something." A lengthy pause ensued.

"Mrs. Brown… I spoke with her a few moments ago," Tillman lied, "She did seem a very kind, compassionate woman. Wouldn't you agree?" Tillman looked up at Mr. Riddell through narrowed eyes.

"She is," Mr. Riddell agreed, nodding slowly, "She certainly is."

"And what are your feelings towards her?" Tillman asked, writing in his notebook even as he spoke. Mr. Riddell was taken aback. What could his feelings for Mrs. Brown possibly have to do with the matter at hand? He felt sure that this must be some trick of the mind, designed to catch him off guard, but an aversion to answer the question would translate into disobliging behaviour, something that would only incriminate him further.

"She's… she's a lovely woman. Kind, generous. Bit of a temper." He paused and looked up at Inspector Tillman, who nodded, urging him to continue. "She… she… Mrs. Brown…" Mr. Riddell stammered uncontrollably. In truth, Mrs. Brown reminded him of his deceased wife, and over the months he had known her, he had grown to care a great deal for her. It was not a physical or passionate love, but more of an esteem in which Mr. Riddell held her. He thought her entirely the most generous, kind hearted, no-nonsense person he had ever met, and aside from his son, there was no one alive he thought he would rather spend time with. He looked up at Tillman again, who was still waiting for him to go on.

"She's wonderful. She has become a very close friend of mine."

Satisfied, Tillman sat back. "If she is as kind and caring a woman as you have just described her," he began, a shifty look settling in his small, unscrupulous eyes, "Then why did she tie Rachel in the cellar with a fishing net?"

"She did no such thing! She was with me the whole time, in the kitchen!" Mr. Riddell seemed fit to faint, his face growing paler by the moment.

"Then who did?" Inspector Tillman cried, "Who was it?"

Flustered, Mr. Riddell did his best to respond. "No one!" he insisted, "She was never tied up in the cellar, I give you my word! The last time I saw her was in the kitchen just before we were arrested! I don't know how she got into the cellar!"

"So she was in the cellar, then?" Tillman was as calm as a still pond as he interrupted his suspect, his body betraying no sign of the discomfort or emotion he was so mercilessly stirring up in Mr. Riddell.

"No! I don't know!"

"Think man! Who would have put her there?"

"No one! Please, no one! I can't think of anyone who would do such a thing!"

"Do you consider yourself a sane man, Mr. Riddell?"

"What?" Mr. Riddell was startled at the sudden change of topic.

"Are you sane? Are you certain you are? I mean, how can Rachel have been both in the cellar and in the kitchen at the same time? Has your mind been tricking you? Have you hidden the memory away so deep within your mind that you believe it wasn't you who placed her in that cellar? How can you trust yourself?"

"I... I..." Mr. Riddell stammered, sweat breaking out on his forehead, "I am perfectly sane, perfectly. What makes you think that I could be insane?"

"Where was Rachel, the cellar or the kitchen?"

Mr. Riddell attempted to collect himself. "First the kitchen, then the cellar."

"You admit, then, that she was in the cellar?"

"If you say she was, what choice have I but to believe you?"

"If you were truly innocent, you would continue to protest."

CHAPTER TWENTY-FOUR

Wrong Place, Wrong Time

T he cells were slowly emptying of the time travellers. Once they were taken out for questioning, it didn't appear they would be returned, most likely so that they could not converse with those who had yet to be interviewed. The situation was making Matthew, who was now alone in his cell with a solitary drunk, increasingly nervous.

John had just been taken away, and Sandra was also gone. The door which swung open and closed at the top of the stairs was like a portal to a long-forgotten world through which one's comrades continued to disappear. Anna was still waiting patiently to be called upon, her good nature pleasing to Matthew, but unsettling to Mrs. Brown, who, apart from Alice, was the last of the accused in the cell with the punster.

Mr. Fitzgerald was calmly observing, as though trying to distance himself from the situation. He watched the other criminals, listened to what they said, trying to make sense of them. From Anna's constant stream of witticisms, he gathered that she had been caught in the act of grave-robbing, a common enough offense among the poorer population, though the longer he listened, the more Mr. Fitzgerald believed that Anna had not dug up a grave for the purpose of stealing from it. He believed that she was a woman in mourning, for a fiancé, perhaps, or a close friend. Maybe even a parent. From what he could tell, in a momentary lapse from sanity, Anna had rushed into the cemetery in broad daylight and begun to dig. In fact, if one looked closely enough when she stood in the light, they would be able to see streaks of dirt on her dress and face, and tearstains on her cheeks. It appeared that she too was trying to distance herself from her situation, continuing to keep up a contented façade.

Alice and Mrs. Brown listened quietly to Anna's speeches, neither one of them paying much attention. Mrs.

Brown's mind was filled with misgivings that she couldn't ignore, and being stuck in a small holding cell without anyone she knew she could trust was weighing on her heavily.

Alice too was plagued by niggling doubts and uncertainties. She sat in the corner of the cell nearest the door, and Alvin mirrored her position from his side of the corridor. Every so often they would glance up at one another and smile weakly, but before long each was lost in their own world again, too tired and anxious to bother one another with their thoughts.

With a heavy sadness filling him, Matthew observed all of this, almost unable to stand the eerie silence which filled the cells, and the haunted looks on the faces of his companions. He began to long for the opening of the door far above; for an officer to come down and take him upstairs, simply for want of an escape from the damp, weighty atmosphere he faced in the holding cells. He wanted to see Evan and John again. He wanted to see Grace and Sandra. He wanted to see Rachel. It felt like aeons since he had so much as looked at them. He took to staring at the door at the top of the stairs, familiarising himself with its texture and colour as best he could from so far away. He would believe he saw it opening, only to discover, upon a single movement of his head, that it was only wishful thinking. He closed his eyes, but was unable to sleep.

After what seemed like days spent between the actions of staring at the unmoving door and gazing at the ever changing patterns inside his eyelids, Matthew finally saw the door move, and this time, it was not his imagination. It swung quickly open, and there came three figures bumbling down. Matthew blinked repeatedly, trying desperately to make out the faces of the vague, dark shadows that he knew must be policemen. When they reached the bottom of the stairs, he had to blink ever more furiously to convince himself that who he saw was not simply another trick of his sleep deprived, poorly fed mind. There were indeed two officers, that much was clear, but the third figure was of a man who had momentarily escaped the minds of all those still residing in the cells. As the officers dragged the man forward, Matthew met his gaze, and received a cruel wink. He shuddered. It was none other than Sidney Beagle, the man who was the reason behind Rachel and Alice's move to the boarding house.

Matthew's breathing became quick. In which cell would he be placed? Not his own, he hoped, but changed his mind as soon as he had made it up. It would be far better for the man to be placed in a cell with him than with Alvin, who would surely pick a fight. The latter had obviously noticed the newcomer, for his face was an angry red, and his brow furrowed. His jaw was set forward in silent defiance, and his knuckles, which gripped the bar in front of him, were a ghostly white. He stood as Beagle was shoved into his cell, but he did not face him. His blazing eyes met no one's gaze as he stared indignantly at the floor beneath his feet. The officers locked the cell once more and headed back up the stairs, and though Matthew longed for a peek at the outside world through the swinging door, he could not tear his eyes away from his friend.

Alvin didn't move, and Matthew watched in dumb fascination as Beagle approached Alvin from behind and addressed him.

"Hey, you!" he said, nearly shouting, "Ain't you that cripple I pounded a while ago?" No answer. "Well, ain't you?" Alvin still would not so much as look up. Beagle was beginning to get frustrated, and Matthew could see Mr. Fitzgerald's eyes on the man as he took a step towards Alvin. It was clear that he was not going to have to face Beagle alone.

On a sudden impulse, Beagle launched himself forward, fist raised. Before Mr. Fitzgerald could stop him, he had brought down a heavy blow on Alvin's shoulder, knocking the boy into the wall. Alice, from across the hall, cried out and clung to her bars, wishing that she could do something to help her dearest friend.

Alvin stood, dizzy from his head hitting the bars. Finally, he faced his assailant. He looked back and forth between him and Alice, his hand pressed against the wall for support. Mr. Fitzgerald had taken hold of Sidney Beagle's arm, and had him in an iron grip. Matthew looked upon his father in admiration and awe, his jaw hanging slightly open. How would this end? There was no way that he could keep Beagle from his revenge for very long, and Alvin was in no condition, mental or physical, to fight back. Matthew noticed Alice from across the hall. He could see the fear in her eyes, but could tell that it was no longer fear of the man who had attacked her, but of the mutual hatred that was held between him and Alvin. It would be impossible for Alvin to subdue the man—he may have been shorter, but he was much stronger and heavier, not to mention he had the advantage of having two arms. Alice was visibly shaking.

"Listen," Alvin finally said, holding his hand up in surrender, "I'm sorry. I am. I didn't want to fight you, and I—" Alvin paused, noticing that Beagle's eyes were no longer on him. He followed the man's gaze, finding it cast upon Alice, who was staring back at the pair of them, still trembling. Beagle's face was lit up with recognition, and he shook himself out of Mr. Fitzgerald's grip much more easily than Matthew had hoped possible.

"Look who's in there!" Beagle exclaimed, glancing patronizingly back at Alvin, and then turning back to face Alice from across the two sets of bars, "What got you in here? You been *working*? I knew you was stayin' at that Jessica's place for a reason! Too bad you been caught, doll!"

Alice gritted her teeth, not wishing to give him the satisfaction. No longer was she afraid, at least not with her assailant behind bars. Her only worry was for Alvin, whom she knew would never allow Beagle to insult her with impunity. She was right, but after being hit, Alvin's mind was spinning. He couldn't think straight, and though he knew that Beagle was asking for it, he couldn't bring himself to even say a word. He felt like crying, but he held it all inside in dumb silence, his breathing quick and shallow.

Taking it upon himself to protect Alvin, Mr. Fitzgerald took hold of Sidney Beagle's shoulder from behind and spun him around. Matthew's heart pounded at this sudden turn of events.

"What?" Beagle spat, staring up at Mr. Fitzgerald, fire in his eyes.

"Leave her alone," came the reply, "She doesn't need to listen to you."

"What if I don't?"

Beagle tried once more to wrest himself out of the grip of the bigger man, but this time, he was unable to escape. Matthew bit his lip. Would Fitzgerald hit the man? He looked angry enough.

"You'll face me," he finally replied, his voice filled with a calm menace that made Matthew's hair stand on end. Beagle was silent for a moment, staring up at Mr. Fitzgerald in defiance. After what seemed like an eternity, he rolled his eyes.

"Alright, just lemme go."

Mr. Fitzgerald complied. Upon being let go, Beagle retreated in the far corner of the cell, and Mr. Fitzgerald approached Alvin, laying a hand on his shoulder.

"Are you alright, son?"

Alvin nodded, still looking through the bars at Alice, who smiled at him. Weakly, he returned the gesture and sank to his knees, his arm limp, leaning his forehead on a cold iron bar. Matthew could have cried just to look at him, for he was a picture of weariness, his shoulders slumped and head down. He looked for all the world like a suffering saint.

There was silence once more, until, moments later, the door at the top of the stairs swung open once more. Matthew turned and stared, peering up into the sliver of light that slowly shrank as the door shut once more. Two officers pounded down again, as they had done on so many occasions during Matthew's stay in their holding cells, and stood at the foot of the stairs. Matthew's eyes widened as he watched them open up a clean white sheet of paper and read from it; hoping that finally he would be called up into the world again.

Chief Constable Bentley cleared his throat and read off the names. "Alice Cosgrove..." he paused and coughed gruffly, "And Alvin Quinn."

Matthew's face fell as he realized once again that this would not be his turn to leave the cells, but he was glad to be able to see Alvin and Alice leave. Alvin hadn't been there for very long, but he had suffered equally to—if not more than—the rest of the inmates.

Alice looked up as Inspector Tillman unlocked the door of her cell, and was making to stand when he took hold of her arm and pulled her roughly to her feet. The same thing was happening to Alvin, in a nearly perfect mirror image. Matthew had to blink in order to convince himself that it wasn't a trick. Both officers held the arms of their suspects as they locked the cells once more, and turned around to face one another. The officers nodded to each other, as though confirming that these were indeed the accused who were listed on the sheet of crisp white paper.

In the short moment in which they nodded to one another, a silent conversation passed between Alvin and Alice. Their eyes were wide with fear, but there was an understanding between them that this too would pass. Everything did. They had learned that lesson time and again, and though it was a comfort to both of them, they were beginning to doubt its truth. Things weren't passing as quickly as they should, it seemed. Their silent reassurances to each other lasted but a moment, until the pair of them were dragged away, Matthew watching their backs as they disappeared into the world he longed to return to.

■■

"Justice is inescapable, young man," Bentley stated, leaning nonchalantly against the desk, "That's what I always say."

Alvin stared up at him in angry defiance. "There is no justice in losing an arm for something you never did," he countered. No matter how much he seemed to insist that he hadn't deserved what Clay had caused, Bentley wouldn't believe him. He maintained that he had gotten what he deserved when he lost his arm. He believed in poetic justice. Alvin was less confident that such a thing could exist.

"Do you deny that you arrived at the house with a gun?"

"No, but I was only trying to save innocent people from harm! Mr. Kennedy would have killed them if not for me and Rachel!"

"You and Rachel?" Bentley began to pace back and forth, hands folded behind his back, "We have it on good authority that Rachel was not with you at the time of this... this... this attack. How do you explain that?"

"I can't. She was with me. Ask anyone. Anyone but Mr. Kennedy will tell you that she was with me. Have you spoken to her?"

"You're lying!" Bentley accused, "She told us that she was at home! In Connolly Mills!"

"That's a lie! She was—unkh!"

Alvin looked up, Bentley's face swimming in his vision. He had received a blow to the side of the head, and a sudden flash of blinding fear shot through his mind. He hadn't a left arm anymore—what would happen to his mind if these constant assaults continued? He knew, deep inside, that the fear was irrational, but he had seen his fair share of injuries to the brain. He had seen people in Norton wandering the streets, whispering under their breath; shouting. They could no longer work because of some incident that had left them unable to read, write, speak clearly... A loss of his arm was one thing, but for Alvin to lose the one thing he had left—his mind—was quite another. Bentley raised his arm, preparing to strike his suspect again.

"Stop!" Alvin's arm was up in a feeble attempt to block the next blow, "I'm telling the truth, you must believe me!" Another blow. Alvin could feel the blood rushing to his head. He felt dizzy.

"Please," he begged tearfully, wishing he could fold his hands before him, "Please, I can only tell you the truth. I can only say what I know!" This time, the strike came to the right side of his head.

"Alright! Alright!" Alvin could barely see; his vision blurred so that all he could register was a dull light, "What do you want me to say? What must I confess? What lies can I possibly tell to make you happy?"

"No lies!" the Chief Constable yelled, cuffing Alvin round the head, "Tell me the truth!"

"The truth about what?"

"About Rachel! Tell me how she came to be locked in the cellar at Mrs. Brown's boarding house!"

"The cellar? She was in the cell—?"

Bentley cut him off again, his fist sending a wave of pain through Alvin's chest. Between blows, which now came in a constant stream, Alvin could see the man looking back at the door to the interrogation room, a quizzical look on his face. Each time he glanced back, he nodded towards the door and delivered another strike. Alvin was knocked out of his chair. As he scuttled towards the corner of the room, trying to shield himself from the officer's assaults, he could have sworn he heard crying. And then screaming. In a moment of panic, he thought it was Alice. Were they doing the same thing to her as they were to him? Alvin tried to stand, reaching for the edge of the table as best he could, only for Bentley to knock him down again. He was trapped, his back pressed against the corner of the wall opposite the door.

Breathing heavily, Alvin could just make out the figure of Alice in the doorway, her arm held by Inspector Tillman. She had seen the whole thing; been forced to watch as a confession was beaten out of Alvin. She was crying, that much was clear, and she soon began to spout a whole string of lies. She told them that they had kidnapped Rachel, and tied her in the cellar. She admitted to helping poison Rachel's mother the previous year, resulting in her death. She told the officers everything they wanted to hear, and Alvin was powerless to stop her. Soon, after they had heard everything they felt they needed to hear, the beatings stopped. Alice tugged her arm out of the grip of Inspector Tillman, who made no move to stop her from rushing into the room, and dropped to her knees next to Alvin. The officers left the room, locking the door behind them.

"You shouldn't have said all those things, you know," Alvin wheezed as Alice helped him up and led him to the chair from which he had been knocked.

"I know, I know," Alice sobbed, "It was all I could do to stop them. They could have killed you! I'm sorry…"

"Don't be sorry, Alice," Alvin said, rubbing his right temple, "You were only trying to help me. I only hope we can help Rachel…"

■■■

"You shouldn't do that again," Urwin said emphatically, "It was too much."

Detective Urwin, Chief Constable Bentley, and Inspector Tillman were walking through the stationhouse, towards the Inspector's office. Bentley was still puffing from his assault on Alvin, and repeated every few steps that he was becoming too old to continue with such brutal tactics.

"I agree with you, to some extent," Tillman replied, taking a swig from the bottle he was holding, "But we did secure a confession."

"A false one," Urwin countered, adjusting his glasses and then pausing outside of the Inspector's office door, "We can't continue with this. It isn't right."

"Who are you to say that the girl's confession was false?" Bentley huffed, "She seemed truthful enough to me!"

"You know as well as I do that to make her watch you strike that boy was enough to make her say anything we wished her to!" The policemen opened the door to the office and stepped in.

"So what have we got?" Tillman asked, leaning against the doorframe.

"We've a confession from Miss Cosgrove," Bentley began, "And I'm sure with a little more persuasion—"

"We've nothing but a false confession, a man who believes he's insane, and a boy who's liable to press charges against us," Urwin interrupted. "Perhaps we should end the investigation," he suggested cautiously, "We've no evidence, and if we're caught taking bribes…"

"Shh!" Bentley hissed, "Not so loud! We can't end the investigation now, we've still the girl to worry about!"

Tillman folded his arms across his chest. "You're right," he admitted, "She did say that she had been kidnapped…"

"And locked in the cellar," Urwin finished uncertainly, "But her grandfather was with her when she gave her testimony. Perhaps it would be wise to interview her alone…"

"Have we spoken to Mrs. Brown?" Tillman asked, ignoring Urwin's suggestions, "She's the owner of the boarding house; perhaps it was her. The others may not have known."

"Then why would they try and hide it by fabricating a story of danger in the Southern Quays and an invitation to live with them?" Bentley stormed, "This investigation is getting nowhere! What about Rachel's mother? Have we any proof that they killed her?"

"None," Urwin answered, "We've spoken to some of her friends in Connolly Mills, and by all accounts, she died of an infection. Well, all accounts save for one. An Emily Collins insists that she was murdered, but the constables we sent to speak with her have all denounced her as insane."

Bentley brought his fist down on the desk, setting the objects upon it clattering in a disorganized symphony. "We must have something besides Mr. Kennedy's accusations and Miss Reid's testimony! Send for Emily Collins! And send some constables to the house on Crookshanks Lane, but be sure they don't get into any trouble!" he boomed. Pausing, he looked up at his comrades. "Bring up Mrs. Brown, Mr. Fitzgerald, and the Matthew boy. Perhaps the guilt lies within them."

■■■

Finally, Matthew was free of the damp, dark holdings cells and had returned to the world as he knew it. It had taken his eyes a moment to adjust to the new light, but he was glad to finally be able to return above ground. He had been taken out of the cells along with Mrs. Brown and Mr. Fitzgerald, but as soon as they reached the top of the stairs, he had been separated from them and not seen them since. He hadn't seen anyone else he knew either, and was now in an interrogation room that set his hair standing on end. There were splotches of blood on the table before him, and all along the floor leading to the corner opposite the door. He wondered, as he waited to be interrogated, who it belonged to.

The door creaked open, and Matthew sat in rapt attention. Chief Constable Bentley strode in and took a seat across from him, folding his hands above the table. Seeing him in better light than in the cells, Matthew was struck by how much the man looked like his birth father. He had the same empty expression, the same hairline, even. He could smell alcohol on the man's breath. Matthew suddenly felt sick. However, it was not a lack of food that caused his stomach to twist and turn the way it did, but the presence of a man who reminded him of all the memories he had buried so deep within his mind as to nearly forget them.

"Matthew Fitzgerald?" Bentley asked, peering up at the boy with an accusing gaze.

Matthew nodded. "Yes sir," he replied, his voice quiet.

"How old are you, Matthew?"

"Sixteen, sir."

"Sixteen... And how long have you known Rachel Reid?"

"About a year, now."

"Has she ever expressed to you a want to leave her grandfather? To run away?" Bentley's eyes narrowed.

Matthew's own eyes widened. Could they be investigating Clay instead of them? Rachel must have said something. Of course she had told them the truth! What excuse would she have to lie? What motive? Matthew relaxed slightly, relieved. He should have known all along that the police knew they were innocent! There was no evidence against them, for how could there be? Matthew tried to stifle a smile. The others were probably back at the boarding house, getting something to eat and recounting their adventure to Laura and Eddie. There could be no other explanation as to why they had not been returned to the cells after having been taken away for interrogation.

"Yes sir, she did," Matthew replied, leaning forward a bit, "Many times. I'm sure she told you what he did to her."

The Chief Constable peered up, his eyes flashing. "She told us nothing of the sort! You're telling lies."

Matthew tensed, fear filling him once more. How could Rachel not have told them about Clay's abuse? He struggled to find the right words to respond to the officer.

"What did she tell you?" he asked, unable to think of any other response.

"Frankly, she told us that she had been kidnapped, but all of you are saying that she ran away! Now, who do you think we are more likely to believe?"

"R-Rachel, sir, but—"

"But nothing! Did you lock her in the cellar because she tried to run away from you? Were you trying to keep her from telling the truth about what happened to her mother? What happened in Darcy Lake when Mr. Kennedy arrived to seek justice? How did you succeed in taking Rachel from her home in Connolly Mills?"

Matthew's jaw hung open, his mind trying to make sense of all the questions that had been spouted at him.

"She wasn't locked in the cellar!" Matthew began insistently, "I never did anything like that! And we did nothing to her mother, either! She died of an infection! Rachel ran away from home; we never took her. I haven't been back to Connolly Mills in months!"

Having spoken his piece, Matthew sat back, his face glum. Tears of frustration welled in his eyes. He felt betrayed; betrayed by this policeman he didn't even know. He had believed that the man would help him, but it appeared he was only interested in accusing him.

"And in Darcy Lake?" Bentley asked, his eyes softening slightly as he tried to make Matthew feel more comfortable. He sensed that he would gain nothing in making the boy feel accused.

"Darcy Lake? I haven't been there in a while either... Oh, you mean what happened there?" Matthew looked up, his face betraying his mistrust. "You wouldn't believe me."

"The truth always comes out, Matthew," said the Chief Constable, addressing him by name in hope of making him feel more at ease, "And I'd like to hear your side."

Matthew hesitated. He felt that something wasn't quite right, but he couldn't tell what. He dismissed the feeling as best he could, blaming it on his lack of sleep. What could possibly go wrong in telling the truth? The story of what happened in Darcy Lake would not compromise the secret of the time travellers, and it might persuade the police to believe them. In any case, it was worth a shot.

"Alright," Matthew agreed, "I'll tell you." He paused and swallowed, the mere thought of bringing the events back into his mind stirring up much unwanted emotion. "It all began in Connolly Mills..."

CHAPTER TWENTY-FIVE

At the Same Time

"I tried," Matthew sobbed, "I tried, really, I did. I... I... I told them everything I could, but he still didn't believe me!"

"It's alright, Matthew, I know you tried your best. Something just isn't right about all this. It's not your fault. You did your best." Mr. Fitzgerald was embracing his son, trying to comfort him. The interview had not gone at all well, if Matthew's judgement was to be trusted. Along with the others, he had been returned to the cells after everyone had been questioned, and was now placed in the same cell as his father. Sidney Beagle was still there, but Alvin had been moved into the other male cell, away from his aggressor. Of all those who had been interrogated by Chief Constable Bentley, Alvin was, by far, in the worst condition for his ordeal. While Matthew had come away with a black eye and bruised ribs, and Evan and John were virtually unscathed, Alvin was left with a bleeding lip, a sore head, and a battered arm.

Matthew and Mr. Fitzgerald were the only source of noise in the cells, their voices echoing off of the walls. The others—even Sidney Beagle—were silent, lost in their own thoughts and worries. Alvin was propped up against the corner of his cell, his eyes shut, a trail of dried blood standing out against his chin. No one could tell whether he was sleeping, but he was not responding to the voices around him. Alice had tearstains streaking her cheeks, and she sat as close to Alvin as she could from across the hall between the male and female holding cells. Evan was pacing back and forth through the cell, John watching him impatiently. His footfalls made not a sound. Grace and Sandra were in much the same position, and Mrs. Brown sat in the back corner of her cell. She seemed calm, given the circumstances, and the others found it a sort of comfort to see her seated on the cot, sitting regally upright, a neutral expression adorning her features.

Matthew looked up at his father, his eyes filled with tears. He had failed. He had failed his father, he had failed his family. He had failed his friends. Far worst of all, he had failed Rachel. He had tried so hard to tell the whole story, without leaving out any important details while at the same time not incriminating himself, or his family and friends.

And yet, somehow the story had become twisted under the wrathful gaze of his interrogator. His words, which he had thought out so carefully, became jumbled as soon as they escaped his lips. A story of Alvin's heroism and Rachel's bravery became a tale of betrayal when the Chief Constable began to ask questions which Matthew could not possibly answer. Lies were shouted at him, making him question his own memory, and his mind became so mixed up that he no longer knew the truth from a falsehood.

Once Matthew had returned to the cells, however, and seen his father, everything came flooding back, and he wished he could have a chance to do the whole thing over and fix his previous mistakes. Now, he could only feel the guilt of having sealed the fate of his entire family; the people who had cared enough to take him in and make him feel loved and wanted such as he had not felt in a number of years before he met them. And yet, Mr. Fitzgerald made it clear that they forgave him, and it was this that caused him to feel the greatest guilt of all.

"It's alright, son," Mr. Fitzgerald assured him, smoothing out his son's ruffled hair, "We know you tried your best. We all did." He let out a sigh such as Matthew had never heard escape him before. It was filled with hidden melancholy that the man, a normally optimistic person, rarely displayed. It only made Matthew feel more ashamed.

"I never thought that this would happen," Matthew sniffed, "I can't believe it…"

"I know," Mr. Fitzgerald replied, "It all seems like some kind of nightmare, doesn't it?" Matthew could only nod in agreement. He glanced up at the tiny, barred window near the back corner of their cell. Daylight was streaming through. He wondered how long it would be until they could walk in that daylight without worry. He wondered where Rachel was in all of this, and why on earth she would have told them so many lies. Then again, if they had treated her anything like they had treated him, it was no surprise that she would have become confused.

"Don't worry," Mr. Fitzgerald assured his son, "It'll all be over soon. There's nothing to worry about. We've done nothing wrong, you just remember that."

Unable to respond but for the lump that had risen in his throat, Matthew bobbed his head up and down and clung to his father's shirt, waiting for the end of this awful ordeal to finally arrive.

■■

Trevor tapped his finger against his desk impatiently. It was early afternoon, about an hour after the school's scheduled lunch time, and Matthew was nowhere to be seen. Trevor had been looking around the school for him at every free moment, and had spent his entire lunch time wandering the halls and peering into classrooms. He had even gotten a warning from one of the teachers that he wasn't to be loitering about.

Exasperated, Trevor was now seated in his least favourite class, Mathematics, stealing glances at Matthew's empty seat every few moments. It was unlike him to miss school, and if Trevor had known that he was going to be absent, he never would have bothered to walk all the way from Sam's home in Oakton to the chilly school in St. Edward's. He had even waited for Matthew outside the boarding house, and when he didn't show up to walk to school, he had assumed that he had gone on ahead, for Trevor himself often arrived at the boarding house late.

"Mr. Anthony! If you would please face the front and stop fidgeting, perhaps the rest of the class could accomplish something."

Trevor turned abruptly, finding the Mathematics teacher, Mr. Barnes, staring at him sternly. He stifled a sigh.

"Yes, Mr. Barnes," he replied, taking up his pencil and feigning rapt attention, "I'm sorry." Trevor watched as Mr. Barnes turned around again and began to write out more problems on the blackboard. He set his jaw forward and leaned his head on his fist. He would be paying Matthew a visit this afternoon, and he sensed that it wouldn't be pleasant.

When finally the school day came to an end, Trevor gathered his things and sprinted for the door, knocking several students out of his way as he went. He could hear them yelling after him, but it was better to continue on his way than to face the horde of angry schoolboys. Books and still full lunch bag in hand, Trevor made for Mrs. Brown's boarding house, bitterness filling his heart. How dare Matthew leave him alone at school without telling him first? How dare he let him suffer through the day by himself? Vague accusations ran through his mind, but the lack of a serious reason for his anger only served to make him more bitter. He arrived at the boarding house, his stomach growling for his uneaten lunch. Trevor knocked loudly. No answer. He knocked again, more insistently this time. Still nothing.

"Come on," he muttered under his breath through gritted teeth, "Where are you? Open up already!"

"You lookin' fer Mrs. Brown?" A voice floated up to Trevor from the street, causing him to turn from his rapping at the door. He faced a short, round faced man in a top hat and suit, who was squinting up at him, a permanently confused expression adorning his face.

"Yeah," Trevor answered warily, "You know where they all are?"

"Sure," the man replied, moving a hand to point down the road in the direction Trevor had come, "The police came yesterday and took her and all her boarders down to the station."

"What for?"

"I dunno what fer, but they should still be down there, I 'spect."

"Thank you," Trevor said, dropping his things on the top step and rushing back down into the street, "Thank you very much!"

Running through the streets of the city of Norton was an exhilarating experience, the constant dodging of carriages and pedestrians sending a thrill through Trevor that he remembered feeling when he would speed down the highways of the future in "borrowed" cars. This, coupled with the fear that Matthew and the other time travellers were in trouble, was enough to make Trevor feel sick to his stomach.

He sprinted up the steps of the St. Edward's police stationhouse two at a time and burst through the doors, gleaning strange looks from the officers inside. He peered around frantically before rushing up to the front desk.

"Excuse me, have you seen—?"

Trevor paused, recognizing the officer at the desk as one who had taken him in for gambling. He didn't have to wonder long whether the officer had remembered him as well.

"Hey!" The officer climbed down off his stool and came around to the front of the desk, taking hold of Trevor's arm, "I remember you! You was brought in for gambling! What kinda trouble're you in now, huh?"

"Nothing, nothing, no trouble," Trevor protested, pulling free his arm, "I was just wondering if you'd seen—" He paused again, his gaze falling across the room on Rachel, who stood by the side of a man with a widow's peak and a gruff, commanding voice.

"Rachel!" he called out to her, "Rachel! What's going—?"

"That's quite enough," came a voice from behind him, and Trevor turned to see a surly man with wispy white hair place a large, dry hand down on his shoulder.

"What's happening?" Trevor asked, slightly intimidated by the way he was held firmly in place by this stone faced officer.

"It's nothing of your concern," came the reply, "Unless you can tell us anything about the kidnapping of Rachel Reid."

Trevor paled. He hadn't the faintest clue what the man meant in saying such a thing, and decided it would be best to remain ignorant and find another way to contact Matthew and the others.

"No," he shook his head, his voice sounding hollow and distant, "No, I don't know anything about anything like that."

Chief Constable Bentley looked the youth up and down, trying to find any signs of guilt in the way he held himself. However, he could find no such thing. He knew Rachel, that much was certain, but the look in his eyes was enough to tell Bentley that the boy knew nothing of any kidnapping. He paused a moment in his thoughts, not letting go of Trevor's shoulder.

"How do you know Rachel Reid?" he asked, wondering if he could establish any connection between this boy and the individuals he had locked up in the cells.

Trevor glanced up at the policeman as best he could, craning his neck to try and get a better look at the man's face. His mind worked frantically to come up with a plausible excuse for knowing Rachel, for he sensed that it would be best if he didn't link himself to the time travellers, as he knew that they were most certainly in some kind of trouble. He evoked his skilful excuse making from his days on the streets of Connolly Mills and spoke in his most serious tones.

"I met her in the market a while back," he said, his voice still missing some crucial element that gave it any depth of sound, "We became acquaintances."

"When did you see her last?" the Chief Constable demanded to know, his own voice full and booming.

"Not long ago," Trevor answered vaguely, "I can't remember the exact day."

"If you remember anything at all," the Chief Constable said, "You come right back here and tell me. Do you understand?"

Trevor nodded and shrugged his shoulders exaggeratedly in order to free himself of the grip of the overbearing officer. In a flash, he was outside once again, wondering what to do next.

■■■

As the day wore on, Matthew grew more and more anxious. He had heard the school bell ring some time ago, and wished that he was there, completing math equations and perfecting his grammar. Anything would be better than being stuck in these cells, breathing the dank, stagnant air. Trevor would be angry with him when he finally got out, that much was certain. However, the idea of Trevor's wrath only served to make him want to escape even more than he already did. He *wanted* Trevor to be angry with him. He wanted to be able to make his excuse and be forgiven, and to tell Trevor all that had happened since the day before. He began to play the scene through his mind; a picture of Trevor yelling at him in the way he did, his arms gesturing in the air to further his point. He saw Trevor's face falling when he would explain what happened. He could almost hear his voice...

"Matthew!"

Matthew's body gave a jolt. He couldn't have been imagining it that time. He spun round, facing the wall. His eyes met those of his father, who smiled weakly at him. He saw Sidney Beagle dozing in the corner.

"Matthew!"

He spun round again, unable to tell from where the voice was coming. Anna met his gaze and waved at him. Matthew ignored her. He heard the voice swear in a harsh whisper.

"I'm at the window, you idiot!"

Matthew turned once more and looked up at the barred window. There was no glass, allowing both the elements and Trevor's voice free entry.

"Trevor!"

Hopping up onto the cot, narrowly avoiding the toes of a man who was lying on it, Matthew stood on tiptoe to meet Trevor's height. The others in the cells were only vaguely aware of what was happening; their eyes and ears lazily waiting for sleep to embrace them. Even Mr. Fitzgerald, who had seen Matthew bound across the cell, was not in any way conscious of Trevor's presence.

"What's going on?" Trevor hissed, hating the look of crazed hope in Matthew's eyes, "What are you doing here?"

"I knew you'd find us," Matthew whispered excitedly, "I knew you'd come! I can't tell you how good it is t—"

"Answer the question! How'd you end up here?"

"They think we kidnapped Rachel!" Matthew answered, the old fear returning to his eyes, "Clay's here. He's done it this time. We're done for, now."

"Oh, you've got to be kidding me," Trevor sighed, "Alright, alright. Now shut up about all that "done for" stuff. We'll figure this out."

"Okay, okay," Matthew agreed breathlessly, "We'll figure it out."

"Alright. Calm down. I'll go and get Sam, and I'll be back soon. In fact, I'll be back tonight."

"Tonight?"

"Yeah. I'm busting you outta here."

Matthew gasped, nearly falling off of the cot. "Trevor, you can't do that! There's people, and the police, and... and..." Matthew was at a loss for words. He should have known that Trevor's plans would be drastic. He should have known that in looking to Trevor for help he would be stepping to the wrong side of the law. It was his way.

"We'll get caught. I know we will. We'll be in so much trouble, Trevor, you can't be serious!"

"Shut up already! You're *already* in trouble! People try and break out of prison all the time, it's normal. If you get caught, the worst they'll do is put you back in."

Trevor's thighs began to hurt from crouching near the ground for so long, and the pain made him ever more annoyed with Matthew.

"That's not the worst they'll do, Trevor, you haven't seen it. I mean look at m— Trevor! Trevor!"

Tired of Matthew's endless struggle with his morals, Trevor had stood and begun to leave. Matthew watched him go, desperation in his voice as he shouted after his friend.

"Trevor! Trevor! Trevor, please come back! Trevor! Trevor!" Tears sprang into his eyes again, and he held the bars in the window, trying desperately to shake them free, though he knew it was impossible.

"Matthew!" In an instant, Mr. Fitzgerald's hands were gripping his left arm and the man's face was close to his own. Almost uncontrollably, Matthew was yelling after Trevor. With a wild, crazed look in his eyes, he trembled and wept, knowing in his heart that this was not going to end well.

■ ■

Angrily, Trevor headed back towards Oakton. Sam would probably be done work by the time he returned, and they could talk out the situation, so Trevor reserved his walk back for silent, impatient brooding. In his mind, he was the victim of this entire ordeal. After all, none of what was happening was his fault. He had not been the one whom the police suspected had kidnapped Rachel. He was not the one with whom this Clay fellow had a bone to pick. He was the victim, for he could never be sent back to the future without the time travellers, and the longer they were stuck in jail, the longer he would be stuck in the past. Trevor kicked up dust and dirt as he continued on his way, not stopping to apologize as he brushed against passersby.

Finally, he arrived in Oakton, passing by the mill at which Sam worked. It was still running, but he suspected that Sam had already left. Either way, Trevor did not dwell on the matter, too busy with his own worries to care.

"Sam!" Trevor shouted as he burst through the door, glancing left and right for any sign of his friend, "Sam! Sam, I— Where are you?"

Standing in the doorway, Trevor could see both of Sam's rooms, along with all his meagre belongings, and Sam was not among them.

"He must not be back yet..." Trevor muttered, pacing back and forth. He debated whether he should try and meet Sam on his way home from work, but decided against it. Sam was an adventurous sort of man, and would often experiment with new routes home, and Trevor had no idea which way he would be taking. Crashing down into one of Sam's two dining chairs, Trevor held his head in his hands, elbows leaned on the table. His head spun with ideas; half-baked schemes and plans to break Matthew and the others out of the police stationhouse. They skipped through his mind like grasshoppers, flitting and flying first one way, and then the next.

In a sudden flurry of emotion, Trevor leaned back and slammed his fist down on the table, shaking it disconcertingly. He swore loudly, not caring who heard. His heart pounded and his legs shook with fury. He was nervous; anxious, but he would never admit it, not even to himself. He found it far easier to mask his feelings of unease with anger and bitterness than to face up to his uncertainty.

"Trevor!" Sam's voice floated from the doorway, his tone gently chiding, "You're going to let in mice!"

"What?" Trevor replied, lifting his head, genuinely unsure of what Sam had meant by his statement.

"You left the door open," Sam explained, closing it behind him as he walked into the room, "You're going to let mice inside!"

Trevor's face remained confused for a moment, his eyes squinted and mouth hanging slightly open. Sam's own face lost its friendly smile as he approached his young friend.

"Are you alright, Trevor?"

"What? No!" Trevor leapt up, his thoughts gathering themselves in an instant, "No! It's Matthew, and Grace, and everyone! The police came to Mrs. Brown's and took them away... They were... Clay Kennedy..." Trevor struggled once more to collect himself. His first thought upon receiving Matthew's news was to find Sam and request his help, but now that he was finally talking to him he was at a loss for words, his anxiety showing through his sullenness. This only served to further annoy him, which made him more anxious. It was a vicious circle.

"Calm down, Trevor," Sam insisted, leading the boy back into the dining chair, "What happened? Where's Grace? Where is everyone?"

Taking deep breaths while deeply irritated that he was forced to do so, Trevor explained the situation to Sam.

"And they're still there now?" Sam's dark eyes were wide, his expression urging Trevor to tell as much of the story as he possibly could.

"Yes, yes," Trevor said, "And we have to go. We've got to break them out."

"Trevor, we can't do any such thing! Can you imagine the trouble we would be in? We'd be arrested ourselves."

"What else can we do?" Trevor responded, staring imploringly at Sam, "I want to go home!"

"Home?" Sam wondered, stepping back, "You mean Connolly Mills?"

"What? Yes, Connolly Mil—" Trevor trailed off, his face falling as he realized how close he had just been to giving away the secret of the time travellers. He wished the remark away in his mind, but Sam could not seem to forget it so easily.

"Was Grace going to bring you back?" he asked earnestly.

"There's no time to talk about it now!" Trevor said adamantly, "We've got to go!"

"Alright, alright," Sam said, "We'll stop at the boarding house and bring them something to eat. I'm sure they're hungry."

"Yeah. What'll we do after?"

"We'll go to the stationhouse and tell them what we know. It's all we can do right now."

"I don't think we should—"

"Trust me, Trevor. Everything will be alright."

■■

"Here," Trevor said, taking up his discarded books from Mrs. Brown's top step and handing them to Sam, "Take these."

"What are you doing?"

"I'm going to break inside. Just hold those."

Trevor crouched down and peered at the lock, trying to discern what would best be used to gain entrance into Mrs. Brown's boarding house.

"Trevor—"

"Shh, I'm working on it!"

"But, Trevor, I think—"

"Shh!"

Trevor ran his fingers over the lock and over the frame of the door, then reached into his pocket for the bobby pin and math compass he had always kept with him for just such occasions. As he was fishing in his pockets, Sam reached forward and turned the doorknob, pushing open the door with an air of self-satisfaction. Trevor glanced up at him, thoroughly annoyed. Sam let a grin spread across his face.

"I was trying to tell you, I thought it was open."

Trevor only sighed, and ducked past Sam through the doorway. "Come on," he said, "Let's get this over with already and get back to the station."

Chuckling, Sam followed Trevor into the house and glanced around. Past the spotless front room, the chambers of the house were all in various states of disorder. The kitchen had been left a mess; a pile of peeled potatoes lying on the table attracting bugs, cupboards standing wide open.

"Here," said Trevor, tossing a half finished loaf of bread to Sam, who caught it gracelessly, "Help me get some food out."

Sam's heart was all aflutter as he scavenged Mrs. Brown's cupboards. Needless to say, he wasn't accustomed to stealing food from people, even if it was to give back to them. It was a funny feeling of wrongdoing mixed with righteousness; excitement mixed with fear.

Once the pair had gathered what seemed to them enough food for their jailed friends, they made for the front door again, only for Trevor to pause halfway through the hall.

"Hang on," he said, and Sam turned around to face him, "I just need to check something. Wait here."

Trevor handed Sam the load he was carrying in his arms and rushed off, taking the stairs to the second floor two at a time. He reached the landing and paused, taking in his surroundings. Memories of the hours he had spent helping Grace to repair the time machine flooded back to him in a torrent that he was helpless to stop. He had to know. He couldn't wait a moment longer to see whether she had finished it without him. Slowly, he strode towards Grace's bedroom door and opened it, his palm pressed against the wood as he held the knob with his other hand.

"It's around here somewhere," he whispered to himself, stepping gingerly into the room. He scanned the space on all sides, taking in the sight of the neatly made beds and the tightly closed wardrobe. Before long, his eyes passed over a tall room divider which was placed— seemingly uselessly—by the wall. Trevor skipped over to it, holding his breath, and pulled it aside just a fraction.

Sure enough, behind it he beheld the time machine, finished. He slipped behind the divider and stood before his vessel home. It looked different, to be sure, as much of the wood had been replaced and it was no longer collapsible. Trevor had secured much of the new wood himself, nicking it from the mill where Sam worked. Grace didn't know where it came from, and he was never, ever going to tell her. It would be of no use anyway. Now that the machine was finally finished, Trevor could go home. He could leave. He could send himself right into the future and avoid the whole mess that was unfolding before him. Trevor opened the door and stepped inside. The number panel was fixed in place, though it was visibly warped. As far as Trevor could tell, it was finished and ready for use. The time travellers had probably been waiting to send him home when they were taken away.

"I could go," Trevor muttered, his voice barely audible, even to his own ears, "And I would be one less problem for them to deal with. I could get outta here. I could go back to Connolly Mills, where I should be right now. In the future." Trevor swore under his breath, frustration ringing in his voice, and sighed deeply. "But I can't," he said, "I can't leave them. I came here to bring Matthew home, and I bet he wants to leave now more than ever. Maybe now he'll finally get that he shouldn't be here. I have to at least get him out before I leave and ask one last time if he'll come. I can't go yet. No matter how much I want to get out of this stupid place and go home, I can't. I can't..."

Trevor sank to his knees and fell back, leaning against the corner of the machine. He cradled his head in his hands, tormented by his own loyalty to his friend. Regardless of the scope of his desire to return to where he belonged, he would never be able to live with himself if he abandoned Matthew. Not after what had happened with his sister... He sat there for a time unknown—it could have been thirty seconds just as easily as it could have been five minutes. He was a stranger to the world, lost in his own uncertainty.

"Trevor?"

Trevor lifted his head, a terrible sensation of panic gripping his heart. There before him stood Sam, a bemused expression on his dark face.

"Trevor, what is this thing?"

CHAPTER TWENTY-SIX

Time Out

Trevor was frozen to the spot, unable to speak or move. He barely even breathed. What could he say? Would Sam figure out who he was? Who the others were? Did he already know?

"Trevor," Sam repeated, speaking slowly and deliberately, "What is this? Is it some sort of machine?" Trevor's heart missed a beat at the word *machine*. This was it. This was the end. Sam knew. He knew that Sam knew. He could feel it. His conversation with Sam about time travel flitted back into his mind.

"It's nothing," Trevor managed at last, "Nothing at all. It's for... It's for... It's nothing."

"Who does it belong to?"

"Grace. I don't know what she uses it for."

"Don't lie to me, Trevor."

"I'm not."

"You are."

"How can you tell?"

"You're nervous. You're almost shaking."

Trevor winced, angry that his own irritating anxiety had given him away. Never before had he felt so helpless; at least not since the last time he had seen his little sister.

"I'm cold," Trevor countered, bringing his knees closer to his chest to demonstrate his point, "It's freezing in here."

"But what is it?" Sam wondered, stepping past Trevor into the time machine and looking left and right. Trevor, in a panic, leapt to his feet, throwing himself in front of the panel of numbered buttons so that Sam could not see them.

"I told you I don't know, Sam!" Trevor protested, "Now, come on, we have to get to the police station, I bet they're starving down there."

With those words, Trevor pushed past Sam, striding out of the room as confidently as he could. Sam, after a moment of silence spent glancing between Trevor and the machine, followed him out, shaking his head.

Out on the street once more, their arms full of various foodstuffs, Sam and Trevor began to make their way to the police station. Once he had gone a few strides, Trevor realized that Sam was no longer with him. He turned around, heart pounding in his chest, to see Sam a couple paces behind him, struggling to get past a covered wagon that had slipped into his path. Smiling, he met Trevor on the street corner and they continued on their way, Trevor not speaking a single word.

They arrived at the station without incident, and Trevor led Sam wordlessly around the side of the building, kneeling before the window where he had seen Matthew just a short time earlier.

"Matthew!" Trevor hissed, ignoring Sam, who was hovering over his shoulder, "Matthew!"

The interior of the cells were cast in shadow, making their inhabitants difficult to see. Suddenly, from below, there came a creaking sound as Matthew hopped onto the cot once more, pressing his face into the bars at the window. Trevor edged back.

"Trevor!" he exclaimed in a whisper, "I'm so glad you came back! And Sam! It's good to see you!"

"We brought some food," Trevor said, urgency in his voice as he pushed half a loaf of bread through the bars, "Here."

"Thank you so much! Wait just a second."

Matthew leapt from the cot and knelt down next to Mr. Fitzgerald, shaking the man's shoulder to wake him. "Hey," he said, "Hey, wake up! Trevor and Sam are here. They're going to help us get out of here. And they've got food!"

"W-what?" Mr. Fitzgerald yawned, stretching his arms wide, "What's going on?"

"Trevor and Sam are here to help us," Matthew reiterated, "Hurry up, they're at the window!" Matthew pulled his father to his feet and tugged him towards the barred window.

"Trevor! Sam!" Mr. Fitzgerald exclaimed, as though surprised to have found them in the exact location that Matthew had described, "How good it is to see you!" His voice had been loud enough for all the other inmates to hear, and each time traveller, as well as Mrs. Brown, Alvin, and Alice, got as close to the window as they could from inside their cells, clinging desperately to the bars. After a moment of initial shock, mixed with hunger and weariness, they all began to speak at once, greeting their visitors and commenting on their presence to one another. Trevor waited to speak, soon growing impatient.

"Alright, alright, already!" he said, throwing his arms in the air, "Everybody shut up! Listen, we've got food here if you're hungry or anything, and we're here to help you."

"Trevor," Matthew whispered through the corner of his mouth, still clutching the half loaf of bread in his fingers, "You're not seriously still thinking about breaking us out of here, are you?"

"I dunno yet," Trevor replied, "But I am gonna get you outta here, one way or another."

Matthew bit his lip, not wanting to say any more, lest he only convince Trevor that breaking them all out of the police station was the only way to save them.

"We're going to speak with the officers," Sam broke in, "And tell them the truth of what happened."

Grace, concerned for Sam, thrust her head through the bars of her cell and stared up at him, worry plain in her eyes.

"Don't do that, Sam, please, for your own good," she remonstrated, "They won't believe you. They certainly didn't believe any of us."

"Listen, if you ask me," Evan said, his voice resuming its habitual nonchalance, "I think the only—"

"Nobody did ask you," interrupted Trevor, "And you're all looking at this the wrong way! These people have no power over you! They can't make you do or say anything that you don't want to!"

"Actually," Evan said, reclaiming control of the conversation, "They can."

"And they have," Alice muttered miserably, "They already have."

Trevor stared at Alice in confusion, and was about to question her statement when Evan cut in again.

"And like I was saying before I was so rudely interrupted," he cast a cutting glance at Trevor, "I think the only person who can truly help us now is Rachel. *She* has to tell them the truth. From what I heard, she hasn't been doing a very good job of it."

Matthew's stomach lurched, a heavy, sinking feeling of responsibility for his friend's actions twisting up his insides. Mr. Fitzgerald saw this in his face and laid a comforting hand on his shoulder.

"Evan's right," Mr. Fitzgerald admitted, "Rachel needs to tell the truth before any of us—including the pair of you—will be believed." Evan's face took on a look of smug satisfaction.

"Please, Trevor," Matthew implored, knowing that Trevor had no ears for his elders, "You have to find Rachel and convince her to help us. It's the only way."

"It's not the *only* way," Trevor countered.

"But it is the safest," Grace's voice carried across the cells, "And the best."

Trevor looked down at Matthew, and then across the hall at Alice, and back across at Alvin. "I'm doing this for you," he said, letting his eyes rest once more upon the face of his friend, "And if it doesn't work out, you owe me."

"Understood," nodded Matthew, his countenance filled with gratitude, "Understood."

"Okay. I'll see you later," Trevor stood, so that only his shoes were visible, and Sam followed suit. "Let's go, Sam."

"I'll meet you inside," Sam insisted, backing slowly away, "I've thought of something that may help."

"What?"

"You'll see when I return," Sam promised, turning, "I won't be long!"

"Hey, wait!" Trevor called after him, fear settling in his chest once more, "Sam, wait! Would ya stop? Wait up! Come back! I need you..."

■■■

Laura traced her finger along the equator of the globe on Detective Urwin's desk, reading the names of all the countries along which it passed. Eddie sat near her in the Detective's chair, doodling in a pad that one of the constables had given him. The pair had been detained in the police stationhouse for some time, having been placed in the care of Acting Detective Urwin until their family was either set free or sent to trial. Laura had taken it all in stride, allowing her curiosity to override her fear. She had explored every inch of the office, as well as most of the stationhouse. The only place she had yet to go was the basement, where the holding cells were. Urwin had strictly forbidden her from going there. He had the vague notion that Laura and Eddie would soon be of value with regards to the case at hand, and so was guarding them from the destructive influence of the accused.

Laura soon grew bored with the globe and moved on to the typewriter on the Detective's desk. It looked well used; well loved, even. She tapped the keys at random, producing a jumble of meaningless letters on the white page behind the ribbon. The, she spelled out her name. And her father`s name. And Matthew's. Then Eddie's, Mr. Riddell's, and everyone else's she could until the carriage reached the end and the little bell rang out, piercing through the silence. Then she pushed it back and started again.

Laura thought that the typewriter's clicks and clacks and rings were like a little song; a song for all of the people whose names she had painstakingly typed out. If she had been a better typist and more confident writer, Laura might have started to write out the story of the time travellers. A song meant nothing without a story to go along with it, and no story, Laura thought, was more worth telling than theirs.

"Eddie," Laura said, not taking her eyes away from the typewriter keys before her.

"Yes?"

"When do you think that they'll let us see everyone again?"

Eddie looked up from his drawing, his lips pursed. "I don't know," he replied, "Soon, I hope."

"How soon?"

"I don't know Laura!" Eddie's voice was raised, and his fingers tightened around his pencil and notepad, "Why do you always ask such silly questions?"

"I didn't think it was silly."

Laura and Eddie looked up simultaneously at the newcomer, their expressions filled with fear and concern. Detective Urwin knelt down next to them.

"Listen," he said, "Your family... your folks... we believe they may have done something they shouldn't have, and we wish to keep you safe from harm. We don't wish for anything so terrible to happen to you. Do you understand?"

Eddie stared down at his lap, his fists still clenched, refusing to speak. Laura stopped typing and looked the detective in the eyes, her countenance filled with confusion.

"What did they do?"

"We believe that they kidnapped Miss Rachel Reid, and locked her away in the cellar. There is also suspicion— do you know what that means?" Laura nodded. "There is also suspicion that they may have been involved with a murder—the murder of Rachel's mother, Elizabeth—in Connolly Mills."

"That's not true!" Laura exclaimed, her mouth and eyes wide with indignation, "That's not true at all!"

The Detective was startled by the conviction present in the little girl's voice; she truly believed what she said. He remained silent for a moment, then, looking deep into Laura's wide blue eyes, spoke.

"I promise," he vowed, "That if what you say is true, I will not let your family be imprisoned."

"Pinkie swear?"

"What?"

Laura drew back, realizing that she had said something that the man did not understand. Whether it was because the term had not yet been invented, or simply because he was a grown man who had forgotten childish rituals, Laura would never know.

■■

Rachel shook. Her grandfather stood over her, his form and countenance imposing. They were standing together in the Chief Constable's office, while Chief Constable Bentley looked them over. Clay had not let Rachel out of his own sight since he found her. When the officers had questioned her, he had been there, seated next to her, just close enough that he could whisper threats in her ear without the officers noticing. She had said everything he had wanted her to, so great was her fear of the old man. She had claimed to have been kidnapped, locked in the cellar, and supported all of Clay's false claims against her dear friends. She sobbed as she poured out the lies, knowing that she was securing the fates of the people who had been so kind to her. Her tears did nothing to make the officers suspect Clay's abuse, they only served to convince them that she had been rightly and thoroughly traumatised by her alleged kidnappers.

"I trust," Clay began, stretching forward his free hand, the other holding a firm grip on Rachel's shoulder, "That this is enough to secure their conviction?"

Bentley leaned forward, inspecting the bills held in Clay's hand while he twirled a cigar between his fingers. He sniffed at them for effect, though in truth the smell of the money meant nothing to him, and could provide no information as to whether they were real or counterfeit. He leaned back again and lit his cigar, clouds of foul smelling smoke filling the air around his head. Rachel had to stifle a cough.

"I'd say it might," Bentley replied at last, the cigar rising and falling in his mouth as he spoke, "As long as you can both be trusted to keep the matter quiet."

"You have my word," Clay replied, reaching out to shake the officer's hand, "And *my* full trust."

"Of course, of course," Bentley replied absently, "Not to worry." The pair shook hands, and Clay pressed the bills into Bentley's clammy palm. Rachel looked on in awe and astonishment. She wanted so badly to say something, anything, to anyone, but she dared not, for her own safety.

"Come along, Rachel," Clay said, evidently wishing to leave before the Chief Constable changed his mind, "We've other business to attend to."

"I'll post constables outside your lodgings tonight," Bentley called after them as they made to leave, "In the day, too, if you'd like."

Clay glanced down at Rachel for a split second, and then turned back to Bentley, his eyes flashing. "I think that would be wise," he agreed, and with those words took up Rachel's hand and steered her from the room. As they passed the threshold, Rachel brushed against Detective Urwin, who was making his way into the Chief Constable's office. Before Clay had dragged her out of sight, the Detective caught her eye, reading a silent plea within her gaze. Urwin shuddered as he turned in to the office and spied the Chief Constable stowing a wad of bills in his desk.

Rachel and Clay continued on their way at a brisk pace, through the stationhouse, down the front steps, and into the street. It was evening, after dark, but the city was still bustling. Clay did not slow down for a moment; dodging wagons and pedestrians, and taking shortcuts through alleys, all while dragging Rachel behind him. More than once, she brushed up against a passerby, who glared at her angrily. She wanted to apologize, but she dared not so much as open her mouth for fear of Clay's reaction. Rachel simply hung her head and followed her grandfather, lips pressed tightly shut.

At long last, they arrived at their destination. It was a tall, wide building, close to the St. Edward's market, though not as close as Mrs. Brown's boarding house. It too was a white house, though the trim was red as opposed to green. Clay pounded up the steps, and Rachel scurried along behind him. Without knocking, the man flung open the door and dragged his granddaughter inside. The interior of the house was dark, all the lamps having been put out. Clay slammed the door behind him and pushed Rachel ahead, urging her to walk into the darkness towards his room. Rachel's eyes strained as they tried to adjust to the lack of lighting, and she stumbled over numerous pieces of furniture as she made her slow journey down the hall and up two flights of stairs. Suddenly, a light appeared, and a young lady, perhaps no more than a year or two older than Rachel, stepped into the hall, the candlestick she held illuminating her delicate features. She was a fellow boarder, a parlour maid for a wealthy family in King's Park. She had been boarding in the same house for over two years.

"Mr. Kennedy!" she exclaimed in a harsh whisper, "It's past curfew! What were you doing out so late? And who's this?" The girl glowered at Rachel.

"That's no business of yours, and she's my granddaughter," Clay replied, shoving Rachel onward. She stumbled in the darkness. Once more, the young lady's voice filled the silence.

"Mr. Kennedy, I daresay it is my business! If Mrs. Thompson were to find out about your being so late, she'd certainly throw you out!"

"That's why she's not going to hear a word about it," Clay responded icily, "Is she?" He stepped forward menacingly, towering over the little parlour maid. She did not cower before him, as he had expected, but merely shot Rachel a pitying glance, glared up at the old man, and blew out the candle with a flourish. When she was gone, Clay gripped Rachel by the shoulders and steered her into his room, then stopped in the doorway to light a lamp. Once it was lit, he turned and shut the door behind him, the hinges creaking loudly as it swung to.

The interior of the room was really quite pleasant. It had a burgundy colour scheme, with brownish red bed sheets, curtains, and wallpaper. A fireplace with a wide chimney stood against the wall, though there was neither fire nor even wood in it. The room was impeccably neat, and it was evident that Clay did not spend much time in it, as all his things were still packed away in his carpet bag and the wardrobe was empty. Rachel, from where she stood next to the bed, stared blankly at her grandfather, trying to conceal her fear. Clay cleared his throat and stared back at her.

"Are you feeling very well?" the man asked, his tone becoming softer than it had been just moments ago, "You seem pale."

Rachel's face immediately coloured. It felt foreign to hear her grandfather speak in such a soft and gentle voice. She almost wanted to cry. It was as though he had returned after years away, like the true Clay had been hiding beneath the surface all the time and was only now beginning to make an appearance. Rachel hoped it would not be brief.

"I'm fine," she answered, though not as honestly as she would have liked, "Just fine."

"Good, good," Clay muttered, suddenly distracted, "Now, make yourself comfortable and get some rest. You're not to leave this room until I say it is safe. Do I make myself clear?"

Rachel had to stifle a sigh. There he was again, the same old man who had taken the place of her once loving grandfather. There was her warden.

"Yes, sir," she answered, her voice passive, "I understand."

Rachel proceeded to follow his instructions to the best of her abilities, and soon drifted into a fitful sleep upon an armchair across from Clay's bed, which he had pushed in front of the door to prevent her from leaving.

She awoke around midnight, the moonlight sneaking through the window, casting silvery shafts over her chair. She could hear Clay snoring lightly, and could see the rise and fall of his chest under the blankets on his bed. She stared behind him at the door, wondering whether it would be wise to sneak out and return to the police station to tell the truth. But then, even if she managed to sneak past without waking Clay, what good would it truly do? The officers were being paid to accuse her friends, and she had no money to attempt to override Clay's requests. Rachel knew that her only chance was to get help from the outside. She thought of Sam and Trevor, whom she knew hadn't been at the boarding house when the others were apprehended. Could they still be out there somewhere, or had they been caught as well? Rachel silently resolved to find out in the morning as soon as her grandfather left, and fell slowly back to sleep.

■■

Trevor returned to Sam's home that night with a heavy heart. He hadn't found Rachel, and he hadn't the faintest notion of where she might be. After Sam had run off, Trevor had marched into the stationhouse alone and demanded to be allowed to see Rachel. As he had foreseen, they refused, and so he had resorted to sneaking around, avoiding officers as best he could in order to get even a glimpse of poor Rachel. However, it wasn't long before Inspector Tillman had found him skulking about and had him thrown out. And so, until the sky began to grow dark and the street lamps were lit, Trevor had wandered the avenues and alleyways of Norton, looking for Rachel.

Finally, when he could no longer see well enough to recognize her or anyone else, Trevor made his way back to Oakton. Sam was not home, so Trevor sat at the kitchen table and waited for him to return. He wanted desperately to stay awake until Sam came back, but his eyelids soon grew heavy and his head drooped over the table. By the time that the morning light began to stream through the windows, Trevor was fast asleep, his head buried in his arms. Just as the bells of Norton were about to strike ten, Trevor was awoken by a tickling sensation around his right ear. Groaning, he lifted his head, and found himself face to face with a small grey mouse. Startled, he leapt back, knocking his chair on its side.

"Aw, gross!" he mumbled, rubbing his ear with his sleeve. He was about to scold the mouse, who had since disappeared, when he heard the bells begin to chime. Patiently, he counted the rings, his stomach sinking with each new strike. He was losing precious time. Looking around, he saw that Sam still had not returned home. Trevor began to wonder whether Sam had found Rachel himself, and, with this newfound glimmer of hope, he made his way back to the police stationhouse to ask Matthew and the others. When he arrived, he found Matthew waiting at the window, his fists clenched around the bars and his eyes hopeful.

"Did you find her?" he asked as Trevor knelt in front of the tiny window. Trevor shook his head.

"No," Trevor replied, "Hasn't Sam been here? I was hoping he'd have found her." Matthew's brow furrowed.

"The last I saw Sam was yesterday, with you," he said, "Did you two split up to find Rachel?"

Trevor was beginning to feel exasperated. "He ran off yesterday as we were leaving and I haven't seen him since."

"Maybe he found Rachel," Matthew proposed, his face bright with optimism, "Maybe he's bringing her back here right now."

"Here's hoping," Trevor answered, crossing his fingers so Matthew could see, "But, in case he didn't find her, I'm going to keep looking."

"Right," Matthew agreed, bobbing his head, "Keep looking."

Trevor rolled his eyes, tired of Matthew's blind dependence upon him, and left. He checked furtively around the stationhouse once more, but Rachel was still nowhere to be seen. Venturing out into the streets again, Trevor tried desperately to place himself in Rachel's shoes; to think how she might think and go where she might go. His first thought was Mrs. Brown's boarding house, and though he knew she wouldn't be there, he figured there might be a clue as to her whereabouts among her things. His mind made up, Trevor marched onward, towards Mrs.

Brown's. He had just gone past Thompson's Butchery when something hit him in the side of the head. It hadn't hurt, and when Trevor inspected the ground around him for what had been the projectile, he discovered a crumpled sheet of paper lying near his feet.

"What the—?" Trevor bent over and picked it up, unfurling it carefully. He stared at the beautiful handwriting, his eyes narrowing.

"Look up," he read aloud, and followed the instructions. The empty blue sky looked back down at him, and Trevor frowned.

"Up here!" came a voice from his left, and Trevor's head snapped towards the sound. He found himself squinting up at the façade of a tall and imposing building. It had three floors, and was painted white with red trim. Trevor placed a hand over his eyes to shield them from the sun, which was just peeking over the roofline. In the centre window of the third floor, a familiar figure was leaning out over the street.

"Rachel!" Trevor called up, his face breaking into a wide smile, "Rachel! What are you doing up there?"

Rachel's heart skipped a beat. Frantically waving her arms and placing a finger repeatedly to her lips, she attempted to silence Trevor's shouts. Catching the hint, Trevor placed a hand over his mouth to signify his understanding. Rachel held up a hand and disappeared back through the window. Trevor stood patiently below the window, glancing furtively up and down the street. A few minutes later, another ball of paper came sailing down from Rachel's window. Trevor read it quickly and turned his face back up to the window, only to find it closed and Rachel gone.

CHAPTER TWENTY-SEVEN

Escaping Time

*M*y grandfather is in the market, and I am glad to have caught you as you passed beneath the window. As you may know, I was forced to lie to the police and incriminate Matthew and his family, along with Alice, Mrs. Brown, and Alvin. This is why I feel I must return to the police and make things right, but I can't leave now. The police are corrupt, and there are constables around the house at all hours. I shall explain everything in due course, but I must escape tonight, under cover of darkness. There is a window in this room. Bring a rope and climb up to the roof at midnight, and lower the rope down to the window so that I may climb up. When I am ready, I shall tug the rope twice. Do not doubt yourself, Trevor. Please, do this to save Matthew and the others. We are their only hope.*

Rachel

Trevor must have read the note about a hundred times. He had it memorized by the time he finally made it back to the Thompson boarding house at a quarter to midnight. He could see the constables at both entrances to the house, peering every which way to be sure that no one tried to kidnap Rachel again. Trevor swallowed. He was there to do precisely the thing that the police were guarding against. He had taken a rope from Mrs. Brown's cellar, and had it coiled around his shoulder as he approached the boarding house.

"This is it," he muttered to himself, "You can do this. Just... just do it." Taking a deep breath, Trevor stepped forward and quickly ducked into the shadows next to the porch, where the streetlamps could not shine. A constable strode past him, stopping before the front steps to converse with a comrade who had come from the other side of the house.

Moments later, two new constables had arrived to take the place of the previous shift. Trevor saw his chance and took it, darting out of the shadows and around the west side of the house, then to the back. The building had been made in the same fashion as the one on top of which he had found Matthew's letter, with two large balconies; one for each additional floor. There were stairs leading up to the top balcony, and Trevor took these as carefully and quietly as he could. Each step was a gamble, as a loud enough creak would be heard all the way around the front of the house, and it wouldn't be long before one of the new constables made his way around the back and saw him. After what seemed like an eternity, Trevor made it to the uppermost balcony. Looking cautiously down, he could just make out the figure of a constable, who had arrived to guard the open staircase. Trevor took another deep breath and proceeded to hoist himself onto the roof.

Looking down on the police from above had triggered many unhappy memories of flights from the Connolly Mills police force back home. Trevor's heart raced as he was momentarily transported back to his time on the streets. He remembered the rush of adrenaline he felt when he had gotten out of the clutches of the law as a runaway. People had looked for him for a while, but it wasn't long before they had given up. He wasn't important to them. There was no consequence to his disappearance. They knew that he had run away, as opposed to being kidnapped or killed. They knew he was out there, but they didn't care. No one had ever cared.

Trevor shook himself. Now was not the time to be reliving such painful memories! He had a job to do, in order to save the few people in the world who did seem to care about him—at least a little. Now on the roof, Trevor dropped to his belly and squirmed across the flat roof towards the chimney, which stood silhouetted against the pale moon. At last, his outstretched fingers met the rough brick of the chimney, and Trevor relaxed. He was almost there. He glanced up. There were no other chimney stacks protruding from the flat roof, and this fact left no doubt that the one Trevor had located was most certainly the one which led to Rachel's room.

In front of the window, Rachel began to worry. The logs that Clay had lit in the fireplace some hours earlier were slow to burn, and the flames, instead of subsiding, only grew larger and hotter as time passed. Rachel watched the sparks fly and the ashes crumble, biting her lip. She looked over her shoulder, finding Clay still fast asleep in his bed. She had piled some pillows and blankets beneath one large quilt on her chair, hoping that when Clay awoke in the morning, the ruse might give her a few extra moments of freedom. She shook herself. In the light of the fire, Rachel glanced at the clock on the mantel. There was less than five minutes until midnight. What if Trevor didn't know which window was hers from the roof? Her last chance of escape would be lost. No, she decided, shaking her head, Trevor would not let that happen. Rachel glanced up at the clock again. Two minutes until midnight. She stared intently through the window; watching, waiting. At exactly one minute prior to midnight, Trevor's rope slowly crept into view.

Shakily, Rachel slid open the window as high as it would go, stooping low and cautiously poking her head through the window. It was pitch dark outside, and the walls were nearly invisible. Rachel grasped the rope before her and gave it two sharp tugs. Above, Trevor braced himself, tightening his end of the rope around his waist.

"Here we go," he muttered from between gritted teeth, and began to pull on the rope as hard as he could. Holding her breath, Rachel held on tight to the rope, leaning out of the window over the abyss below. The going was slow, Rachel inching herself slowly out the window with the help of Trevor and his rope.

Before too long, Rachel began to feel some progress being made. At last, her feet were out of the window, making tiny steps up the wall. On the roof, Trevor grunted with exertion, pulling the rope with all his might. He strained to step backwards, the rope digging into his waist and chafing his hands. When Rachel was nearly halfway up the outside wall, she looked down for the first time. She saw nothing but darkness. Looking up, she saw darkness as well. No matter how hard she strained her eyes, no light reached them. She felt suddenly trapped; she was moving so slowly that it felt as though she wasn't moving at all. Her breathing became rapid and shallow, and she struggled to remain quiet. Rachel clung to the rope, unmoving.

"Rachel?" Trevor called down in a stage whisper, "What's going on? Why'd you stop?"

Rachel started, remembering the problem at hand, and looked up. "Sorry," she said, staring up into the darkness. Rachel began her climb once more with renewed vigour, eager to escape the endless darkness. Her breathing became rapid. What if she were to fall? There would be no way that she could survive. She began to tense, and suddenly felt weak. The invisible distance between her and the ground seemed to grow. "Trevor, I can't do it…"

Clay's eyes snapped open at the sound of her voice. He blinked twice, sitting up and rubbing his eyes. "Rachel?" he said, his voice hoarse, "Rachel?"

Rachel held her breath, both hands clinging tightly to the rope.

Clay staggered out of bed and lumbered across the room. Rachel listened intently, and, remembering that the end of the rope would still be visible out the window, yanked the line up and coiled it around her hand.

"It's chilly," Clay muttered, just loud enough that Rachel could hear. He walked over to the window and tried to pull it shut. Rachel could just see his hands, and nearly his face, but could not move for fear of him hearing.

"Why won't it close?" Clay's voice floated from the window, "Come on, close!" Frustrated, Clay began to tug on the window with all his might. At last, it closed with a thump, and Rachel's fear of being seen dissipated. She continued her climb, desperate to make it to the top before her arms gave out and she plunged to her death on the cobbles below. At last, she was able to reach up and grasp the edge of the roof. Releasing the rope, she hung on to the roof's edge and hoisted herself over the side.

Trevor, relieved of his heavy burden, dropped the rope and scampered back to the roof's edge, holding out a hand to help Rachel up. She took it gratefully and the pair dropped to their knees on the roof, hiding themselves from the gazes of the police officers below.

"Thank you," Rachel whispered, "I wasn't sure you would come."

"I had to," Trevor replied, "They need you to tell the truth about your grandfather."

"I'm just so glad I finally got out," she said, "I was beginning to doubt that I could ever make it up the wall."

"Well," Trevor sighed, "The worst is still to come, you know."

Rachel nodded. "I know," she said, "I know."

"Let's get out of here, then," Trevor insisted, "I'm starting to feel antsy."

"How do we get down?"

"Follow me," answered Trevor, and, taking her hand, led her, crawling, to the edge of the roof. It had begun to rain, and the thin sprinkling of drops soon became sheets of water as the sky opened up.

"I can't see a thing anymore" Rachel complained as Trevor helped her onto the uppermost balcony, "Even less than I could before."

"Good," Trevor said, and pointed towards the ground, "Neither can they. Come on."

The escape continued without a hitch. Rachel and Trevor reached the ground and left the Thompson property unseen by the constables who guarded the house. Trevor led Rachel through alleys and shortcuts, navigating the maze of Norton by night as though he were a native of the city.

Finally, they arrived in Oakton, soaked to the bones and shivering uncontrollably.

"Where are we going?" Rachel asked, following on Trevor's heels as they ran.

"You'll see," Trevor replied, "We're almost there." After turning one last corner, Trevor stopped in front of a building rendered nearly invisible by the pouring rain. "In here," he said, ushering Rachel through the door. The pair went through and Trevor shut the door behind them.

"We're safe here," Trevor said, his voice deadpan.

"What is this place?"

"It's Sam's place."

"Sam lives here?"

"Yeah."

Rachel looked around, running her finger along the back of a chair. She took in every aspect of the meagre rooms that she could in the darkness, and frowned. She wanted better for Sam, but decided not to mention the state of his home to Trevor. After all, didn't he already know?

"Where's Sam?"

"I dunno. He disappeared a while ago. I thought he had found you, but I guess he didn't."

"Oh."

The pair paused as silence fell over them. They both looked at the ground. After a few moments, Rachel was the first to speak.

"I'm sorry I lied," she said, head still hanging, "I simply couldn't tell the truth—not in front of my grandfather. You understand, don't you?"

"Sure," nodded Trevor, "I get it." He looked up at her. "You'll fix it all tomorrow morning, though, right? Tell the police the real story, I mean."

"I don't know how much good it will do," Rachel sighed, "But I'll certainly try."

"That's right," said Trevor, patting his pockets, "Your note said something about the police being..." Trevor pulled a crumpled sheet of paper from the pocket of his trousers and opened it. "Corrupt," he finished, and stared at Rachel, "Corrupt how?"

Rachel took a seat at her leisure and explained the entire situation about the bribe and the Chief Constable to Trevor. When she finished, Trevor could only nod.

"I understand," he said, "I know how police are." He paused, sighing. "They'll always be that way."

"It isn't all of them, I'm sure," Rachel insisted, "Never all."

"No, no, of course not," Trevor replied absently. Suddenly growing tired of their depressing surroundings, the dark and gloom only reminding him of Sam's absence, Trevor stood.

"Are you tired?" he asked, peering down at Rachel.

"Yes," she answered, "But I don't believe I could sleep."

"Cool," was Trevor's response, causing Rachel to wrinkle her nose in confusion, "Do you wanna go back to Mrs. Brown's? It's stopped raining, and I can't stand it here anymore."

"That's awfully close to my grandfather's boarding house."

"I know, but they wouldn't find you. We'll leave early in the morning for the police station, before your grandfather even knows you're missing."

Rachel shrugged, startled by Trevor's insistence. "Alright," she ceded, "If it would make you happy."

■■

Acting Detective Urwin had remained in his office until long after all the day constables and other officers had gone home for the night. He had no special obligation to fulfill; no papers to file, no evidence over which to pore. He had simply remained after hours, seated at his desk, deep in thought. Laura and Eddie had remained with him, and were curled up on the floor, sleeping soundly. He gazed at them fondly. They behaved so well and were so well mannered that it was impossible for Urwin to believe that they had been raised by criminals. Laura had told him all about what Clay Kennedy had done in Darcy Lake as a result of his belief that her family had killed his daughter. Each and every word which escaped Laura's lips was filled with the sincerity and fervour of truth. Eddie, however, had hardly said a word to him. The boy was so quiet; so wary. His piercing blue eyes seemed to see right through all those he cast his gaze upon.

The clock struck one, waking the Detective from his reveries. He glanced up at it indifferently, and then lowered his head once more. He had been plagued by doubts since the very beginning of the investigation, and his misgivings had been magnified tenfold when the Chief Constable had begun taking bribes from Clay Kennedy. Though he was only Acting Detective, and thus not used to the more intellectual work that the job required, Urwin could see that the evidence was all pointing to one simple fact: the innocence of those who were even now detained below the stationhouse for the kidnapping of Rachel Reid.

Urwin sighed and propped his elbows up on the table. He had to do something, but what? The Chief Constable would never agree to let them go; not with all the money that Mr. Kennedy was showering on him to convict them. He thought of confronting Inspector Tillman with his concerns, but dismissed the idea almost as soon as he had conjured it up. The Inspector too much enjoyed playing with the minds of these suspects, and put too much stock in the results of his art. Where Urwin saw a forced and false confession, Tillman saw success. The Detective shook his head.

Emily Collins was due to arrive tomorrow, and he knew that her visit would not end well for either of the parties involved. She was certain to place the blame on Laura and Eddie's family, though she could offer no solid evidence. Urwin opened up a notepad on the desk and flipped through the pages until he found the one which contained a constable's account of his meeting with Emily Collins in Connolly Mills. It was fairly brief, describing her limited knowledge of the situation and her belief that Mrs. Brown's boarders, who had been staying in a hotel in Connolly Mills at the time, had killed Elizabeth Kennedy with a strange bottle of pills. On the bottom of the page was scribbled the word *sane*, with a question mark following. The constable had clearly been questioning the mental faculties of the accusatory woman.

Urwin shut the notepad and leaned back in his chair, letting out another sigh. It didn't matter if the woman was sane or insane. The Chief Constable would hang on her every word, and the Inspector would be able to convince all those involved that she was indeed a reasonable and intelligent woman. Her testimony, combined with that of

Rachel Reid, would surely be enough to keep Laura and Eddie's family behind bars for the rest of their natural lives. Urwin shuddered. He knew that Rachel had lied; the constable who had brought her in had told him of her vehement protests. And yet, no one would believe that Rachel had altered her story because of the influence of her grandfather. No one would believe that she had made it all up because she was afraid of getting hurt. Urwin not only believed; he knew. He could see it in her eyes and feel it in his gut. There was not an ounce of guilt in the souls of those detained downstairs.

Detective Urwin stood abruptly and slammed his clenched fists down on his desk. "I won't let it happen!" he cried, then quieted, "I won't..." He glanced down, beholding Laura and Eddie. They sat huddled together on the floor, staring up at him with wide, frightened eyes. Feeling his anger subside and be replaced with pity, Urwin skirted around his desk and knelt beside them.

"I'm sorry I frightened you," he said earnestly, "But I wish you to know that I believe that your parents, and the rest of your family, are innocent. I cannot believe that they committed this crime."

Laura and Eddie visibly relaxed. "You mean it?" Laura wondered.

"I do, I truly do. I mean it. I know that they didn't do it. There is so much evidence to support their innocence; I can't ignore it any longer."

"Will you let them out then?"

Urwin faltered. "I can't simply..." He paused, staring into the anxious little pairs of eyes before him. He swallowed, then nodded. "Yes," he said, "Yes, I'll let them out."

It was foolish; reckless even, but he had to try. He would most certainly lose his job, and perhaps be arrested himself, but he could not continue to work in this stationhouse knowing that he had sent innocent people to the noose. He just couldn't.

CHAPTER TWENTY-EIGHT

Only a Matter of Time

Detective Urwin, lantern in hand, plodded down the steps to the holding cells, Laura and Eddie close on his heels. The light was dim, so it did not wake any of the inmates by its mere presence. Two guards stood at the bottom of the steps, watching the inmates attentively.

"Go upstairs, please, Gentlemen, and put on your coats. You have the night off." Urwin looked at each of the guards in turn.

Looking at one another, the guards' faces broke into smiles, and they doffed their helmets to the Detective. They were not ones to question a night off, much like the other constables whom the Detective had dismissed from upstairs.

"Here," said Urwin, handing the lamp to Eddie, once they had gone, "Hold that steady, if you would."

Eddie obeyed, holding the lamp up so that the Detective could recognize the faces of those in the cells. Urwin did not wish to wake any of the uninvolved inmates unnecessarily, for if they saw the others being let out, there would surely be uproar. He spied Alvin leaning against the bars, his arm lying across his abdomen, sound asleep. The Detective summoned Laura with a wave of his finger, and she quickly scampered from her place behind Eddie to crouch beside Urwin.

"Will you wake him for me, Laura?" he asked, motioning towards the dozing Alvin "I think it may be best if he first sees a familiar face. Do it quietly now, lest you wake anyone else."

Nodding, Laura crawled across the floor towards Alvin and passed her hand through the bars to touch his. As he was in a strange place, it did not take much to wake him, and upon her first touch, his eyelids fluttered and opened. He appeared confused for a few moments, but his eyes soon adjusted to the light, and he caught sight of Laura's smiling face.

"Laura!" he exclaimed in a whisper, "How are you? What are you doing here?"

"We're letting everybody out!" she told him enthusiastically, "We're going home!"

"What do you mean, Laura? We can't simply leave, the cells are locked!"

The Detective moved into the light and met Alvin's eyes. "I have the key," he said, "But now is not the time for questions! You must wake the others who are here because of Clay Kennedy, but don't wake anyone else! Hurry, now!"

Still in the daze produced by sleep, Alvin scrambled to obey, carefully waking the others and instructing them to be quiet. As he did so, Laura woke the women on the other side of the hall. Before long, the time travellers, along with Alvin, Alice, and Mrs. Brown, were all awake and filing silently out of the cells and up the rickety stairs. Detective Urwin was the last up, as he had had to remain behind in order to lock the cells behind them. Just as the Detective was about to lock the last cell, Alvin spied Sidney Beagle, curled up in the corner against the bars, snoring peacefully.

"May I have a moment, please," Alvin asked the Detective, "Before you lock this cell."

Detective Urwin gave him a curious sideways glance, but shrugged and let the boy pass. He was about to continue up the stairs when he paused.

"Here," he said, tossing Alvin the keys, "Lock up when you're ready."

Alvin nodded and looked down at the dozing Sidney Beagle. He had some unfinished business with the man...

Matthew was still in a state of grogginess by the time he reached the top of the stairs, and had to concentrate immensely in order to properly register his surroundings. The random thoughts and pictures brought on by sleep continued to float through his mind, but he dismissed them as best he could in favour of the reality that now faced him. Alvin was just coming up the stairs, tossing the cell keys back to the Detective. Matthew wondered what sort of revenge had been exacted against Sidney Beagle, but he dared not ask, for he sensed that it was something that Alvin needed to deal with alone.

Matthew smiled as he watched Mr. Fitzgerald and Mr. Riddell be reunited with their respective children, tears in their eyes. He glanced around, looking to make sure that everyone was finally free. Grace and Sandra, he noticed, were doing the same, standing side by side and counting heads. Evan looked as though he had just risen from the dead, and John did not appear much better. Mrs. Brown was still wary, standing away from the others; Matthew looked upon her with pity. Alvin and Alice were a sorry sight indeed, blood staining their clothes and their eyes red-rimmed.

Urwin watched the situation unfold, giving the newly liberated group a chance to regain their bearings. Once he was satisfied, he dragged a chair out of his office and stood upon it, raising his hands for silence. The first to notice, Grace stepped forward.

"Let me begin by saying that I know you are innocent," Urwin said, raising his voice to be heard above the low drone of conversation, "But I also know that no matter what I believe, or what the truth may be, you would still be convicted of the kidnapping of Rachel Reid, and perhaps even the murder of Elizabeth Kennedy."

There were nods of assent throughout the group. Urwin cleared his throat and began to speak once more.

"You must all leave the city tonight," he insisted, "The Chief Constable will be led to believe that you escaped in the night. I implore you to take your leave of Norton at once, and travel as far away as possible."

"What made you change your mind?" Sandra's voice rang out, voicing the thoughts of all present.

"It was Laura and Eddie, really," he answered earnestly, "They helped me to see your innocence. Mr. Kennedy's bribes also placed suspicion in my mind."

"Mr. Kennedy's bribes?" Evan stood up straighter and took an angry step forward, "Is that what's been going on here? You've all been taking bribes from Clay Kennedy to convict us?"

"Yes," Urwin agreed, his tone calm, "Yes, we were. That's why I felt I must set you free. Now go, and hurry, before I have a change of heart!"

■■

Through the night the former prisoners had flown, avoiding the busy streets. They ducked down alleys and side roads, navigating the maze of Norton as best they could in the dark of night. At last, the weary wanderers arrived in the rear of Mrs. Brown's boarding house and entered through the back door. Once inside, they pulled all the curtains closed and used only the smallest amount of light necessary to see one another.

"Would you go and be sure that the front door is locked, Matthew?" Grace asked, handing Matthew a lamp.

"Sure," he answered, seizing the dim light and making his way across the house. He stumbled against furniture in the darkness, biting his lip with each noise he made. As he tripped nearer to the front room, a low murmur of conversation became apparent. Matthew knew that he recognized the voices, but in his drowsy state, could not tell from where. He crept closer, trying his best to hide his light. His heart beat so wildly in his chest that he was sure it could be heard throughout the whole house. He peered around the doorframe and saw the front door swing shut. Two figures were chatting; coming closer and closer to Matthew. He dared raise his lamp, casting a golden yellow light upon the faces of Trevor and Rachel.

"You!" Matthew exclaimed, his eyes wide with relief, "It was you! What are you doing here? And Rachel! You found her!"

"Yeah, I found her," Trevor answered, as if the fact was common knowledge, "And what do you mean what am I doing here? What are you doing here? Last I saw you, you were locked up!"

"It's a long story," came Matthew's reply. He looked at Rachel, noticing for the first time the soot that streaked her face and clothes. "What happened to you?"

"It's a long story," Rachel smiled, "Where is everyone?"

"This way." Matthew led the pair to the parlour, where the former detainees were gathered. Each long story was exchanged until all present had a working understanding of all that had happened in the past day.

"Detective Urwin is right," Grace decided, "We have to leave the city tonight." The others all nodded in agreement, save for Mrs. Brown. A sudden feeling of regret settled in Grace's heart, as she knew that the actions of the time travellers had ended up costing this innocent woman her home, her reputation, and her trust. Her life would never be the same.

"Mrs. Brown," Grace began, looking upon their hostess with deep seated remorse in her eyes, "I am so, so sorry. I never meant for this to happen. If you wish to stay and inform the police that we've left Norton, then please do so. But... please, please don't tell them about the Detective. He was only trying to help us. I truly am sorry for how much we have cost you."

The others in the room held their breaths, waiting for Mrs. Brown's fiery temper to flare. Her face coloured in the dim light, and she let out a deep sigh.

"If you would permit it," she said, "I would like to be allowed to accompany you. As much as this house, and this city, mean to me, you have all come to mean more." Laura crawled up into her lap and hugged her, and Eddie smiled at her from across the room. Tears threatened to spill from Mrs. Brown's eyes. "You're the nearest thing to family I have."

"Mrs. Brown can come with us, can't she?" Laura pleaded, looking to her father, who in turn looked to Grace. Grace opened her mouth to speak, but was interrupted by Evan.

"Could I see some people upstairs please? Everybody but Alice, Alvin, Rachel, and Mrs. Brown." He looked at each of those mentioned in turn. "It's nothing personal, we just need a minute." He cocked his head to the side meaningfully, and the time travellers followed him up the stairs, much to Grace's chagrin. He led them into Grace's room and stood by the door, waiting to shut it once they had all entered in. He did so, and then began to speak.

"Alright, listen," Evan began, "I know you're all thinking it, especially you, Trevor. We need to go back to the future and regroup, like we did before." He nodded at Grace, who scowled. "We can figure out what to do, come back a few days from now, and leave from Connolly Mills to settle someplace new."

The room fell silent. Of course, the thought of going back to the future had crossed all their minds, and for a few, Trevor included, had stayed there for quite a time. But was it truly their best and safest option? Even Trevor had his misgivings about Evan's plan, glancing up at the divider, behind which he knew the finished time machine stood. Matthew was the first to speak.

"We can't!" he cried, "What about the others? They're involved in this too! We can't just leave them alone! What if they get caught?"

"If we stay with them, we'll all get caught!" Evan countered.

"Better we all go down than leave them with the results of our mistake!"

"*Our* mistake? We did nothing wrong!"

"Neither did they! I can't leave them! I can't leave Rachel to be caught by her grandfather again! I can't let Alvin and Alice suffer any more! I can't leave Mrs. Brown without a family! If you all want to go, then fine, go ahead! I'm staying." Matthew's voice had become low and tremulous by the end of his tirade, and he stared at the floor.

"I agree with Matthew," Mr. Riddell's deep voice cut in, "I can't leave them all alone here."

"For goodness sake, you talk like we were leaving them to die!" Evan shouted, "They're practically all adults! They can take care of themselves!"

"Evan, we destroyed the time machine for a reason, the last time we returned," Grace broke in, "So that we would no longer be able to run from our problems, back to the future. I can't go back on that. I agree with Matthew These are our problems, and we must face them, and be sure that the other people implicated in them aren't hurt because we ran away!"

Matthew sat in silence while those around him began to buzz with conversation. The vast majority were in agreement with Matthew and Grace, though they could all see both sides. Frustrated and overtired, Evan turned to them all once more.

"It's the only way! Don't you all get it? It wouldn't be forever! The time machine's even finished, I mean... I mean..." He paused, then, with a dramatic flair that only he possessed, tore away the screen that stood in front of the time machine. "Look at it!" he implored them, "How would we transport it? It doesn't collapse anymore! The only way to get it out of here is to... What are you all looking at me like that for?" Evan turned to the side and nearly fainted dead away. As though by some absurd magic trick, the time machine was gone. The screen lay on the floor before an empty space. There was no trace left of their vessel of escape. Trevor, wide eyed and open mouthed, cursed. All eyes turned to him.

"Trevor," Grace asked, trembling, "Where is the time machine?"

Trevor staggered back, feeling for the wall behind him. When he reached it, he sank to floor, looking and feeling quite empty inside. He buried his face his hands, unable to take the accusing stares of the time travellers.

"Sam," he muttered, "Sam, Sam, Sam! Why? Why'd you do it? Oh, Sam..." He continued to mutter, tears escaping his eyes. Aside from Matthew, no one had ever seen him show so much emotion.

"What about Sam?" Sandra wondered, kneeling in her motherly way in front of Trevor.

"We were here a while ago," he explained, still not removing his hands from his face, "He saw the time machine. I… I tried to keep him away, and I never told him what it was, but he must have figured it out, or sent himself away by accident or something…"

"You brought him up here?" Grace asked, her tone accusing.

"No!" Trevor looked up, shaking his head, "No! He followed me! I tried to hide it, really I did! I'm sorry…"

Sandra bit her lip, looking between Trevor and Grace. Grace appeared angry at first, but her expression soon dissolved into weariness and regret, something that was, to Sandra, even more troubling.

"There's nothing we can do about it now but travel to Connolly Mills and see if the portal has reappeared there. Then, we can go looking for Sam."

The time travellers were silent, all of them too tired to panic. Evan sank to the floor, wishing he had something to drink. Matthew's heart pounded furiously. Sam's trip, they all knew, could prove disastrous.

"When do we leave?"

Matthew spun round on his heels, his chest threatening to explode. More awake now, he recognized the voice that had spoken almost instantly. He felt sick when he saw Rachel standing in the doorway, flanked on either side by Alvin and Alice. Even Mrs. Brown was there.

Thinking quickly, Grace sprang forward. "What did you hear?" she asked, frantically searching their faces, "What did you hear?"

Rachel shook her head. "Every word," she said, her voice laced with sorrow for the new knowledge she had obtained, "We could hear the shouting from downstairs and came up to see what was wrong. Perhaps we shouldn't have."

Matthew placed his hands on his forehead and breathed deeply, attempting to calm his nerves. Mr. Fitzgerald placed a shaky hand on his shoulder, feeling nearly as ill as he was. Grace, who had succeeded in holding herself together thus far, burst into tears.

The wagon clattered along the dirt road under the vast, dark sky. The clouds that had been present had now deserted their posts, and the stars formed tiny pinpricks of light in the velvet blanket of the sky. The moon was only a tiny sliver. The time travellers, along with Mrs. Brown, Alvin, Alice, and Rachel, were on their way to Connolly Mills, taking only back roads so as not to be caught by anyone who might recognize them.

They had left Mrs. Brown's by two in the morning, each one of them climbing into her wagon with their arms full of food and things with which to cook it. If they ate sparingly, they would have enough food to last them the five day trip to Connolly Mills.

Mr. Fitzgerald was driving the wagon, and Matthew sat beside him, his eyelids drooping. All the others were in the bed of the wagon, and Grace was explaining to Rachel, Alvin, Alice, and Mrs. Brown their entire time travelling journey, from the moment she had first finished building it, through Matthew's unexpected arrival, all the way to Sam's disturbing departure. It was clear that the natives of the early twentieth century were having difficulty understanding and accepting the story, but the more Grace told them, the more everything seemed to fit together, like finding the last pieces of a puzzle that they didn't know were missing. Matthew listened intently; he enjoyed hearing Grace tell of their adventures, particularly the part where he had arrived in their lives for the first time.

However, as the story went on, and Grace's voice grew monotonous, Matthew could not help feeling drowsy. He wanted to stay awake and see Rachel's reaction to the part of the story where Sandra had attempted to save her mother's life, but he simply could not fend off sleep any longer. He drifted slowly off into sleep, curled up on the bench beside his adoptive father. His mind wandered, and he found himself dreaming of their arrival in Connolly Mills. By then, he hoped, the others would understand and believe that their friends had truly travelled back from the future to seek a better life. Then, there would be no more secrets. Everything would be out in the open, and they could speak with one another freely. Matthew smiled in his sleep. It was only a matter of time.

THE END